THE CHRONICLE OF TIME SERIES

Dalen Pax and the Beads of Fire

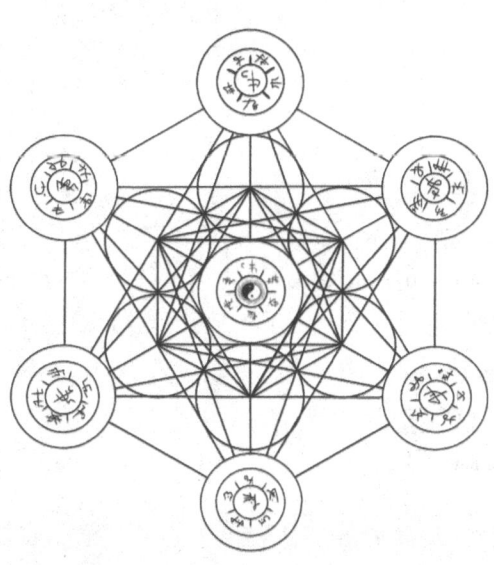

DEDICATED TO

MY WIFE RHIANNON -

IF IT WEREN'T FOR YOU, THIS WOULD NEVER HAVE HAPPENED.

I LOVE YOU WITH ALL THAT I AM.

Dalen Pax and the Beads of Fire Dyslexic Edition

Text©2022 Will Grey (Simon)
Cover Art©2022 David Noceti

The Way of Grey Publishing

merlynsforge42@gmail.com

First Edition

ISBN
Hardcover: 978-1-64372-991-6
Softcover: 978-1-64372-992-3

Dalen Pax
and the
Beads of Fire

BY WILL GREY

ILLUSTRATIONS BY

DAVID NOCETI

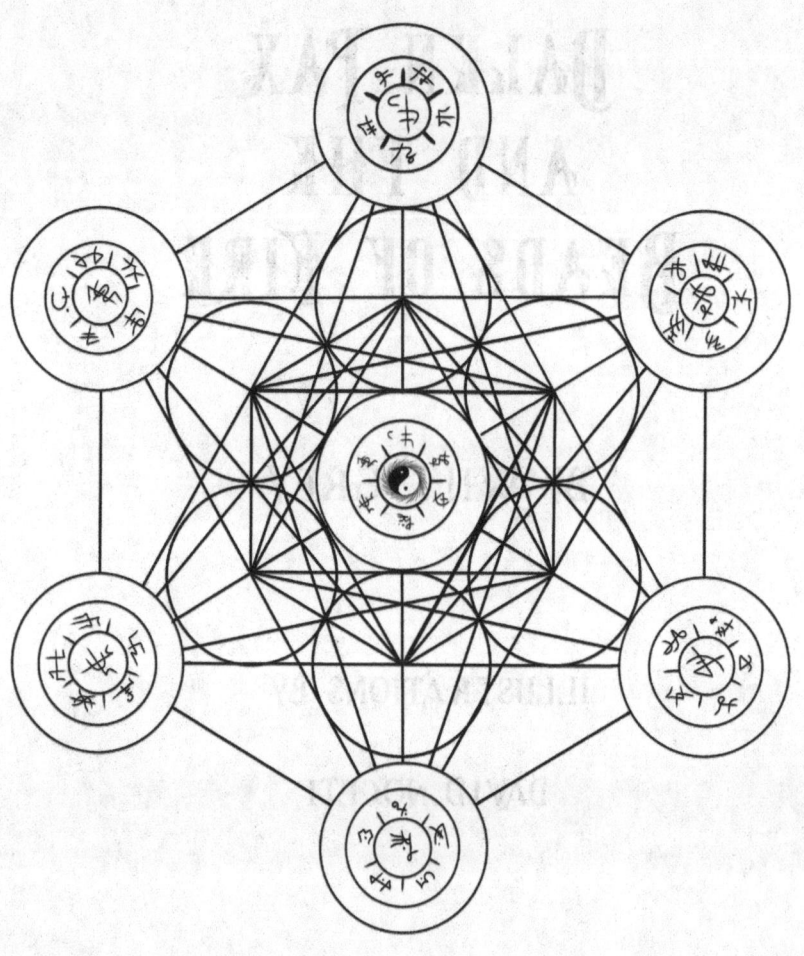

TABLE OF CONTENTS

0

A STORYTELLER
OF VENGER

There are some stories that should never fade or be forgotten. Some stories that hold within them truth in some form. These stories are told again and again through generations. If the story is strong and connects people to that truth, then it will survive the passage of time and drift from story to legend, and from legend to myth.

I am Will of Grey, a Bard of the Grey Continuum. Grey Bards are an interesting sort. We are empathic performers who are also telepathic. What that means is that as I perform, I telepathically send images into your mind, allowing you to think that you are wherever the story is taking place, while also transmitting the actual feelings of the event, both in perception and emotion. So, when I tell tales of the Dragon Wars, you are there as far as the mind can tell, and my ghost stories are truly scary.

The true talents of a Grey Bard are not just limited to entertainment but also extend to healing. My ability to create worlds in your mind that are real can flow more than one way, and while in performance, I can enter worlds that are co-created by your mind. There, I can help with moving through issues like post-traumatic events and childhood terrors or help retrieve lost or blocked memories. I can even create the monsters under your bed so they can be faced once and for all.

My purpose within the Grey Continuum is specifically to narrate and tell the story of this world; in doing so, I help create the myths and legends that drive and inspire people. As a Grey Bard, I am given the opportunity to learn and tell the stories of the lives of some of the most amazing beings that have ever lived. My specialty is the lives of those who grace the Kingdom of Venger, and Venger itself is one of the most magical places you will ever experience.

Within the outer ring of Venger City, there is a tavern that can be found at a fork in the road, and more than a few patrons will tell you that Dorn's can only be found at the fork in the road of your own journey. In truth, people at such a juncture often have the most amazing stories to tell, which is why I can frequently be found there. It may seem like a normal tavern, but it was created during a time of great need, and it can warp not only space but time. Because of this, people have lived whole lifetimes in Dorn's private rooms in a matter of hours. It was at Dorn's where Dalen Pax met me for the first time, and I had the honor to be with him the moment he made one of his most important choices — one that guided him through the rest of his life. It also helped him become the amazing being who worked to shape our world. I now have the honor of telling his story; however, if you are going to understand the choice he made, I will have to take you back to an earlier choice, which is where my story begins. Worlds away from Venger. When Dalen Pax first started making a choice.

1

A FIGHT THAT
WAS DESTINED TO
HAPPEN

It wasn't easy being Toad. At this particular moment,
he has gotten cornered in the hallway with nowhere to go as a
multitude of students poured from the classrooms, leaving him no
room to escape. Now, Dalen Pax saw only two real options in front
of him. He could stand there and let Ben Watts and the other
boys from his senior class laugh at him and call him Toad while all
of the other students of Martin Van Buren High cheered them on.
To make things worse, though, he had to watch Kim Collard, the
girl he'd had a secret crush on all year, laugh along with everyone
else in the hall as the guys who were loved and worshiped by all
mocked and humiliated him. The other option was to stand up for

himself and take a beating in front of the girl he was into, and everyone else, who no doubt would continue to cheer them on. In the end, he chose the path of least resistance. He stood there and took it. He laughed with everyone and even complimented them on this new round of verbal assault, but inside his heart broke, and he gave up on any dream of asking Kim out to anything ever. Or anyone else, for that matter. There was no hope.

Still, Dalen wasn't completely alone. He had a few friends in the crowd, and they were doing their best to keep Ben and his goons from working together as a team to fight Dalen. However, it is a fight that may very well be in Dalen's future. Little did any of them know then that fate is a stubborn aspect of the universe and would not be swayed so easily.

The hallway leading toward the classrooms was filling up too fast for Dalen to make any kind of escape. To Dalen's left were the bathrooms, but trying to get away from the crowd by hiding in there would only lock him in a tighter space with Ben and his friends — four of the biggest guys in the school — where there would be no one watching. He had gotten a swirly before and swore he wouldn't make that mistake again. To his right was the gym. There would be no safety there for Toad, only more of Ben's friends and allies. Behind him was a wall with a giant poster for the 'Arabian Nights' Senior Formal that was coming up that Friday night. His only hope was to get things to calm down.

Dalen tried to reason with Ben. He thought that maybe he could try to persuade him out of violence. He had attempted this before, but the mind of an eighteen-year-old arrogant bully is

11

often full of entitlement, so reason and empathy were seldom to be found. "Why do you keep messing with me, Ben?" Dalen forced himself to speak without his voice giving away all of his frustration and anger.

Ben smirked as if the answer was obvious: "Because you're weird, Toad."

Dalen waited for his knee-jerk reaction to strike that smug little smirk off Ben's smug little face to pass before he responded. "Okay. What is it that I am doing that's weird? Tell me what I am doing, and I will stop doing it."

Ben leaned in as if to tell him quietly but intentionally spoke loudly enough to be heard by all. "You're doing it right now. This. This is why you're weird."

Ben missed how these words hit Dalen. He didn't see in Dalen's eyes that he had been pushed too far and was trying to convince himself that he didn't care what happened next. His friends were busy trying to keep the others from joining. Travis was staring down Biff while his twin brother Adam was trying to keep the other two goons from what they called a free-range beating. They were both bigger than Adam, but he stood his ground without fear and did what he could to keep them calm. Becky had run to get a teacher, so it was only David who saw the rage in Dalen's eyes, and it was left to him to respond before Dalen did.

"Dalen!" The gaze of all present flashed to David. He knew he was only going to get a single chance to tell Dalen one thing — something that he would understand but the others would not. The tension was beginning to build as the swarm of the students began to chant, "FIGHT! FIGHT!"

"Forget the physical challenge, Dalen! That's what he wants. Flip it and hit him with Diplomacy," David suggested.

"The time for diplomacy is over!" Ben's voice was full of mockery and ego. "I'm gonna kick your ass!" The threat was odd in a way: Ben was beautiful with bronze skin and sun-touched blond hair, and somehow it was like being threatened by a Ken doll.

"Wow, Ben, you must be pretty impressed with yourself." Ben's attention shifted quickly back to his prey, as Dalen smiled and acted as if the threat had not been spoken. "I mean, damn, it must be a true challenge to face Toad. It took, what, four of you?" The laughter died down, and small comments could be heard going through the crowd. "I know, being a foster kid makes me scary to you, or is it because I have two different colored eyes?"

"I'm not scared of you." Defensive fury seethed from Ben's words.

"Sure. That's why you needed the Brute Squad to face me."

"I don't need them. I'll beat you myself!"

Dalen didn't give him the chance; his voice swelled to the point he was almost shouting. "...And, oh, what a great triumph it will be! Ben of House Watts versus the weakest loser in school! Your victory is almost assured."

This time when the kids in the halls laughed, it wasn't at Dalen, and Ben knew it. "You're gonna pay for this."

"Yes," Dalen continued, "Yes! Threaten me, for I am Toad! Beat me up! Five bucks says you don't even break a sweat." Again, laughter filled the halls. Dalen began hitting up people in the crowd to see who would take the bet. He reached into his pocket and pulled out a five-dollar bill and began to wave it around. "Oh, come on now . . . it's Toad! You think I even stand any chance?! Come on! This is Ben Watts who's threatening me. He's undefeated this year both in football and wrestling. He's rich and has everything. He is beautiful. He does well in school and all of you love him. That's right! Each one of you was ready and cheering him on to take Toad down a peg. You know... because I am so weird!" The laughter stumbled to a stop altogether. "Come on! What's wrong? Just a minute ago you wanted my blood. What happened?" He grabbed a random person from the crowd. "Come on! Fight! Fight! Fight!" He stood there motionless and stared at all of them. "No? Well, how about you, Benny Boy?" He shrugged as he swung his gaze around to his assailant. "Don't you want to show everyone how amazing and strong you are by beating up the kid who already has it worse than anyone here?" Dalen slowly raised one hand and pointed at Ben accusingly. "You! You want to prove how big of a man you are? Hmm? You want to show everyone here just how amazing you are? Show them why they worship you? Find the weakest kid. The kid that no one wanted, not even his parents. The weird one. The freak. Yeah, that will show your real strength. Let's take down Toad!"

Dalen paused, sizing up his opponent. David had been right. Ben never saw this coming, and Dalen could see it in his eyes. Ben knew that if he swung now, he would lose all face with the others present. Dalen had already won. The halls were laughing at Ben now. Past Ben, Dalen could see Becky coming around the corner with Mr. Sanders, who was one of the English teachers at the school; he only had to stall for another thirty seconds or so.

"It's worse than that, Ben. You've had time to think about it. This is no longer a crime of passion. If you swing now, it's with intent. First-degree assault." Dalen had no idea if that was a real thing, but he had Ben on the ropes, and it was time to drive it home. "You will be arrested. You'll miss graduation. You'll ruin your life and prove to everyone that the only person you can beat up is Toad. So, go ahead. Hit me!" Dalen slowly pivoted. "That goes for all of you." He pointed at one of the goons directly, "I'm looking at you, Biff. This is over." Dalen continued, facing the others in the hallway. "You prove nothing by attacking me. I already understand that none of you can stand that I exist. But if anyone wants to prove they are so tough that they can beat up the social reject, the foster kid with no one, the weird one... Here is your chance." He spun back on Ben and whispered, "This is how I beat you. Never forget it."

At that moment, Ben lost all sense of decorum. He realized that he'd been beaten. Not only had he been beaten, he'd been beaten by Toad. Rage filled him, and before he could make a rational decision, he roared with anger, launching himself at Dalen with everything he had.

Unfortunately for him, Mr. Sanders got to him first and, just like that, it was over. Mr. Sanders was a big guy. His actual height was 6'1", but he wore it like it was 7'5". He was slender and fit and moved with the fluidity of a dancer. He was also immaculately tidy, but anyone who knew him at all knew that was because of his time in the military.

Through the years, rumors about him became legend. It was true that he was once in the military and, of course, everyone knew that he taught foreign kids to speak English on blackboards riddled with bullet holes. There were even whispers among the kids at school that he once forced a student into a locker and locked him in, yet no charges had been made. You would never expect it from him, though, as his smile was inviting and, behind his John Lennon-style glasses, his eyes were often described as warm. Most of the kids liked him, and no one would dare go against him. No doubt these qualities were why Becky went and got him. He pulled Ben off of Dalen with ease, another teacher arrived, and Dalen and Ben were both taken into the office and separated.

Dalen sat in the principal's office for what seemed like an eternity. This was his first time in this room since coming to this school, so as he waited, he looked at the different things in the room, hoping to get an idea of who Principal Denver was. He glanced at the picture on his desk. Mrs. Denver, no doubt. She seemed to be nothing out of the ordinary, but she also looked happy because she was smiling broadly and it didn't seem forced. Dalen remembered the day he'd had his picture taken with a new foster family. It was one of the most ironic moments in his life: being yelled at in public to smile for the photo by a foster parent only two days in so they could show their friends what a happy family they were. Dalen had gotten good at making and recognizing fake smiles, but Principal Denver's wife seemed to be smiling for real. That was a plus, and to Dalen, it suggested that there was a good chance he was a decent enough guy.

There were a few awards for excellence in his field: a very proudly displayed degree in child psychology and another in administration. No doubt these were some of the accolades that helped him get the job of principal in the first place. Dalen then started to look around the office for mementos from the kids: thank you letters perhaps, or even a badly made clay something that only could be liked by someone who cared for what he did and the kids who made it. In every principal's office in every school that Dalen had been forced to go to, there was always something there that showed that the principal and the student body got along. Dalen checked all the familiar places but didn't find anything that connected Mr. Denver to the students, which concerned Dalen. Either the kids didn't like him, or he didn't like them enough to display their gifts.

For some reason, this made Dalen mad. He didn't know why, but old anger rose in him. He started to sweat. Even as he tried to brush it off, it built with strength. He tried to laugh off, telling himself that it was just nerves or the adrenaline from before, but no matter what he did, his temper continued to swell, the heat of the anger blossoming, filling him. In the next moment, he felt like he was being watched. When he spun around, he thought he saw an old man there for a moment, smiling at him with cold black eyes in a way that froze Dalen's heart. As Dalen instinctively stepped back, he

17

bumped into one of the chairs behind him. Momentarily, his attention shifted to it as he stumbled, and when he glanced back to get a better look at the man, there was no one there. His anger drained, and his heart began to beat again.

Dalen stood frozen, staring at the bookshelf where "nothing" was still standing. His eyes searched for hiding places but there was nowhere to go. He was sure that he had seen someone, but now there was nothing. Whatever it was, the aggression had gone with it. The instinct of fight or flight buzzed in his system when the door swung open with a sudden jolt, and Principal Denver and Mr. Sanders entered the room, making him jump as a small yip escaped Dalen's lips.

Mr. Sanders spoke first, and though Dalen hadn't done anything directly to instigate the fight in the hallway, his teacher turned to Dalen with frustration. "Yeah. I would be jumpy, too. What exactly do you think you were doing, goading him like that?"

"Setting a precedent," Dalen was upset still but had his wits about him.

Mr. Sanders smiled and changed his approach, while Principal Denver simply seemed confused. "You're smarter than you let on, Dalen. I'll be expecting more from you in my class from now on."

"I don't understand." Principal Denver was a good facilitator for what the school needed, but it had been a long while since he understood how the students themselves worked.

18

"We are in school," Dalen began, "so let's break this down like a word problem." Dalen was walking a thin line between explaining the situation and talking down to the principal, so he did his best to be straightforward and not rude. "If I fought Ben and won, he would get his guys together away from school and give me a much worse beating. That's not a good option, so I start this problem from the stance that, if it turns into a fight, I cannot win." Dalen paused long enough to let that sink in. "If I fight and lose ... well, not only would Ben prove his dominance, but it would forever establish that picking on me and calling me Toad is acceptable. I would continue to be laughed at by pretty much the entire student body, which is what I already face every day, and so the wheels on the 'business as usual' machine would keep on turning forever. So, I also start this problem from the position that, if there is a fight, I cannot lose. Are you following me so far?"

Principal Denver nodded. It was obvious that the principal was already lost on how to solve the problem himself, and Dalen continued. "Thus, if the starting point of my problem is that if a fight breaks out, I can neither win nor lose, I must choose whatever is behind 'Door Number Three' — an option suggested by one of the only people below the age of twenty who actually calls me by my name. My friend David suggested I use a skill we use in the Role-Playing Game that we play on the weekends. He suggested that, instead of taking one of those unacceptable options involving my imminent doom, I should switch from a physical altercation to a social one by using a skill that I was stronger in than my opponent: Diplomacy."

The principal simply stared at the kid who was obviously

thinking beyond what he believed was possible for a seventeen-year-old mind, and this was undoubtedly the reason for the principal's look of bewilderment. "How did diplomacy save you?" Principal Denver's tone was inquisitive with a hint of anticipation.

Mr. Sanders answered, fully grasping the situation: "He stalled until someone could get there. He used his social position, which is honestly so low it borders on professional outcast," Mr. Sanders glanced apologetically at Dalen before continuing, "but he set a new precedent. Anyone who attacks him now is admitting that they can only attack the weak. He took them from heroes to bullies. And then, just like that . . ."

"Just like that. . . What?" Principal Denver still couldn't comprehend what had happened but was on the edge of his seat.

"And just like that, I won every fight after this. As long as I don't push it in their faces, I should be left alone from now on. They lost too much, and what little they have left will be lost if they attack me now." Dalen took a breath in slowly and let it out, "I am no longer worth it." Dalen grinned victoriously as he sat back down in the chair with his arms folded and waited for Principal Denver to catch up.

"How did you come up with this?" Principal Denver was somewhat in shock as he looked Dalen up and down. Now that he was paying attention to Dalen, he started to feel that there was something different about this student. In most aspects, the kid seemed normal. He didn't have an extra arm or anything. The only different thing about Dalen that he could see was his eyes. Both of them being different colors was extraordinary, but it was hard to look away from the violet one for some reason. Principal Denver realized he was staring and shifted his gaze to observe Dalen as a whole. Dalen had coffee-colored skin and dark, almost black hair. Principal Denver couldn't place his nationality; he could have been Middle Eastern, Mexican, or Italian. "In all of my years of training, schooling, and being a principal, I have never heard of something like this."

Dalen could have tried to explain that when you live a life of continued harassment, you spend hours coming up with plans of what you could have done and even more hours wishing you were brave enough to try half of them. But that is the thing about wishes: just wishing is not enough. You must be brave enough to leap when the opportunity arises because it is not going to wait for you. He could try to explain that every night before he slept, he prepared speeches for days like today. It was his way to not feel helpless in a world that didn't seem to care. He thought that he could explain that, in your mind, you can stand and say your piece. You can scream it in their little faces, and they will just stand there and take it. In your dreams, you talk out every detail because maybe, one day, you will be brave enough to take that leap. Instead, he just chuckled and shrugged. "I have no idea. I think it only worked because no one saw it coming, and I am pretty sure that now it has been seen, whoever tries it next will be hard-pressed to get it to hold."

He was sent back to class and for the rest of the day everyone just kind of ignored him, which in some ways was a relief. But when a few kids who had also suffered at the hands of Ben and his goons approached him during the afternoon break to congratulate him for standing up to Ben, Dalen couldn't help the feeling of pride that filled his chest.

After school, Dalen and his friends walked to Adam and Travis's house. With everything that happened that day, they knew that while in the halls of Martin Van Buren High School Dalen would be safe; however, away from the safety of teachers and a hundred watching eyes, there was the possibility of real retaliation, so they decided to hang out and do homework together.

Life was hard enough just being a foster kid. Although he had been placed in many houses, he had no memory of his original home. He was put into the system early on when he was found abandoned as an infant. He had no idea who his real family was or if any even existed. He got moved around a lot, and he learned to rely on himself more than anyone else. He'd had a couple of bad placements when he was young but was lucky in the respect that he didn't actually remember them, aside from memories of being scared and alone. Most placements weren't bad, but he had never felt like anyone ever cared about him until Ms. Warren.

Ms. Warren was a truly goodhearted woman, but she hadn't stood for one moment of his standard new house attitude. It was the same kind of thing he did every time he was placed with a new family: he'd act out and break a few rules to see who and what he was dealing with. It was nothing that would directly be harmful, like setting fire to something, but something small, like talking back or sneaking downstairs for a midnight snack.

Ms. Warren sat him down and had a talk with him that no one else had ever had with him before. She explained that she was once a foster kid herself, and she honestly knew what it was like. She explained that once she was old enough, she decided to create a home for kids like her — one that would be different from the experiences that she had gone through herself. She wouldn't go into it, but she understood that some things stay with you forever. She said that all she wanted was the opportunity to prove that this could be a good place for him, but he had to give it a fair chance.

That was nine months ago. During that time, Dalen had grown to love Ms. Warren. Her home was a safe place where he could let go and relax. He hadn't relaxed in years because he was always ready for his world to crash. Things like friends were a waste of time until he came to stay here.

His first friend was David. David was the same age as Dalen, and Ms. Warren bunked them in the same room together. David was his guide not only to Ms. Warren's house, but he also helped him navigate school. It was David who first warned him about Ben and his three thugs. He warned, "Chris is the big one, Jim is the dumb one, and Biff is the big, dumb one."

Dalen felt that there were two things about David that were special. He was average in height and build with a very usual color of brown hair, but David had a rare condition called heterochromia that made his eyes two different colors. His right eye was as blue as a sapphire and the other was violet. What made it special for Dalen and made him friends with David instantly was that Dalen had the exact same condition. Because they had the same condition with the same color eyes, they often joked that they were long-lost brothers who found each other in foster care, but Dalen's favorite thing about David was that he always spoke in a way that Dalen understood, almost as if they were on the same frequency.

David introduced him to the only other people in the world that Dalen had come to trust: Adam, Travis, and Becky.

Adam had been going to school with most of the kids at Van Buren since he was in kindergarten, so most people knew him and had gotten bored with making fun of his fiery red hair by third grade; over the years, he had become one of the faceless masses, and he seemed to prefer it that way. David and Adam had been friends ever since David made a roleplaying game reference and Adam responded with a proper response. Their shared joy for gaming was their bond, and they quickly had become friends.

Travis was Adam's twin brother. He didn't have their mother's fiery red hair but instead had his father's sandy blond. Beyond that, they looked almost identical. When Adam introduced David to his brother, Travis welcomed him in without question. Travis never read a book by its cover and didn't care about David's different colored eyes or if he was a foster kid; he was only interested in whether David would be a good player in their RPG or, even better, a good Storyteller for their game.

David proved he was up for the challenge, and now he ran the game on the weekends. Every Saturday since, David was at their house, and once Dalen came into the picture, David brought him along.

The last member of their group was Becky, who was not only an amazing gymnast and the only girl that any of them knew who could even comprehend what it meant to fail a saving throw, but she was also probably the best gamer any of them had ever seen. Every time they got stuck in an adventure, it was Becky who figured out how to save the day.

Becky's grandparents had moved to town from Japan when her grandfather had been sent to oversee the security for an electronics company he'd been working for. When he retired, he felt like this was his home and chose to stay. His son was nearly twelve when they moved and was still very traditional, but Becky had only known living here and was different from the rest of her family, and so she had made it her personal goal to be something other than what was expected of her. Many people said she was pretty, but that kind of thing didn't concern her and, because she refused to bend to the will and fashion sense of the other girls in her class, she was an outcast. She said that being popular was a curse that not only forced you to give up on who you truly are, but you also had to bend your will to a bunch of teenagers.

Dalen now had something that he'd never believed was going to happen yet had always wished for: he had found his family. He found the only people in this world who made him feel wanted and accepted, and he cared for them.

They did their homework at Adam and Travis's house and then decided to go catch a movie before they split ways for the evening. Becky and David called to get permission, but when David called Ms. Warren, she wanted to talk to Dalen directly.

"I got a call from the principal today." Her voice sounded concerned. Dalen talked with her and let her know he was fine. He explained that no one got hurt and that he was safe with friends when she suggested he come home. Eventually, he convinced her to let him stay out, but she warned him to be careful: "I have this feeling in my heart." Ms. Warren was famous for her 'feelings.' In the months that Dalen had lived there, he had never seen one of them be wrong. A few folks from the neighborhood would even come around and talk to Ms. Warren to see if she had a 'feeling' about whatever it was they were curious about, and she was infallibly correct when she did. "I just want you to be careful. Also, come home right after the movie — dinner should be ready." She paused just long enough to think of one more reminder. "And don't fill up on junk and popcorn. You'll be having dinner with the family, no matter how full you are." He chuckled and said okay about twenty times before she'd let him hang up. It was how she showed him she cared. Her feeling gave Dalen enough pause to pay attention to the points she made, but he was with friends and was honestly done worrying about Ben Watts.

After the movie was over, they waited outside for their folks to pick most of them up. They talked and laughed and quoted lines from the movie they had just seen until Adam and Travis were picked up by their mom, and then Becky's dad showed up shortly after. David and Dalen only lived three blocks away, and they didn't want Ms. Warren to have to leave the house for them, so they'd decided earlier that they were going to walk back together.

The edges of summer had brought longer days, and the sun was just setting as they started home. Shadows were being

26

stretched over the pavement, and golden hues of light began to pour from the spaces between buildings like beams of warmth pushing against the shadows as they crawled across the ground. It danced in the branches of the trees that lined the road.

Dalen laughed to himself, "For once, one of Ms. Warren's feelings was wrong." This had been a great evening. Maybe all of them had thrown this way out of proportion. Fear can do that to you. It can bend the truth and create monsters that aren't there.

"I lost my wallet," David muttered, checking all of his pockets. "I must have dropped it when I bought snacks."

They were almost back to the house, but there was some light left. Dalen said, "Don't worry, we'll just run back and get it." As they ran, they requoted all of their favorite lines from the movie. They pretended to be the characters and, for a few short blocks, Dalen got to be a seventeen-year-old boy for the last time.

It was dusk as they made it back to the theater, and David went inside to ask if anyone had found his wallet. Dalen sat on the bench and watched people go by. It was one of his favorite hobbies. He found that people will show you who they truly are if they don't know that someone is watching. He watched Mrs. Campbell sneak a nip from a small flask hidden in her purse. He watched two boys a couple of years older than Dalen walk out of the theater and, as they walked side by side, they allowed their hands to touch. They both looked at each other for a moment and smiled, but then let go. As they walked by, they were looking at their shoes, but they continued to glance up at each other and, when they did it at the same time, they smiled again. Dalen wanted to say something — tell them how sweet that was — but he knew the rules of this game. If he said anything, all he would do is embarrass both of them, and he'd also have to admit that he was watching.

Dalen noticed a street magician performing on the corner. Despite having no real audience, he was doing magic anyway, and Dalen glanced around to see if anyone was watching the performance. As he did so, almost everyone on the street turned a corner or walked into a building at the same time. Dalen barely noted the odd coincidence as he allowed his eyes to drift to the only other people he could see: down the street and moving in their direction was Ben Watts and his three goons.

Immediately, Dalen could tell that Ben was angry, but Dalen couldn't quite make out what he was saying. Whatever it was, Dalen could tell he was really going off about it.

Ben wasn't looking in Dalen's direction, but he chose to duck down behind the bench he was on just in case. Dalen could almost make out what was being said as the quartet came upon the street performer doing magic tricks on the corner.

Dalen held his breath and hoped beyond hope that what he feared was about to happen was wrong. He hoped that maybe Ben liked magic and this was going to be the thing that calmed him down, but all of those dreams were smashed with reality as he watched Ben shove the street magician.

"This is my fault," Dalen said out loud. Again, he had two choices in front of him. He could run for help in the theater and hide where it was safe; maybe he could get someone in there to help in time, although he suspected that Ben had no intention of taking his time after getting caught earlier in the day because he'd been stalled. This innocent street performer was going to get the beating that Dalen had dodged today. Dalen took a deep breath as he understood what the other choice was: he could step in now, alone, and walk into the beating that belonged to him in the first place.

Dalen was still hemming and hawing over this problem when he realized he was already halfway across the street. "Hey! Ben!" he shouted. "You better stop before he makes you disappear completely." It was not Dalen's best, but it did its job, and Ben and his friends turned their attention to Dalen. "Besides, I know I'm the one you want."

Ben's eyes flashed with hate, "You!" Ben shoved the magician down to the ground and strode menacingly toward Dalen. "You are the reason I am suspended. You are the reason my parents are talking about sending me to the military."

Amazed at himself for not running, Dalen grew angry at the accusation. "Don't give me that." The distance between the two was now closed and Dalen found himself eye-to-eye with Ben. His system surged with adrenaline, and he thought to himself that they would never expect him to assert himself. "You did this to yourself."

Ben was now yelling in Dalen's face, "I didn't do anything!"

Dalen's anger rushed through his veins, and he decided he was going to let Ben know exactly what he thought of him, regardless of what might happen. "Every day you make my life a living hell," Dalen said defiantly. "You were the one who started calling me Toad. You were the one who hit me. Tripped me in the hallways. You're the reason I spend every day in fear — and it isn't just me you do this to!" Now Dalen was yelling, too. Tears ran down his face as his emotional dams fell apart. "The only thing I did was finally stop you from being the monster you are!"

Ben stood there, stunned for a moment, trying to process. Dalen knew where this was going and that it was far too late to take anything back.

"A monster, am I? I didn't touch you today, yet I got in trouble. We all did." The four boys looked at each other and smiled with dark intent. "I say, if you got to do the time, you may as well do the crime." Jim chuckled maniacally, and Biff ground his fist into his other hand.

Dalen did his best against the four of them, but with odds like that, it wasn't much. Flashes of pain made it hard to concentrate, and he lost consciousness for a moment. When he awoke, two of them were holding him up by his arms while Ben's fists crashed into Dalen's face again and again. Before he blacked out again, he saw that Chris was trying to get Ben to stop.

It was Chris's voice that got Dalen's attention, "I don't want to do this! He's had enough already!" Chris was pleading with them to stop. Dalen tried to look, but his eyes shot stabbing pain through him when he tried. He wanted to scream in pain or for help, but his throat was on fire, and as he tried to speak, he only coughed up blood.

"You are here and a part of this!" Ben's voice was

threatening. "You don't have a choice anymore. You are either with us or you're next!" Chris's voice cracked as he apologized, and another sharp blow landed, this time on Dalen's stomach. "Yeah!" Ben cried out, "Kick him again!"

After that, all went black.

Dalen woke to the feeling of being dragged along the ground. Someone had him under his arms. In a panic, he flailed, only to find that both of his arms were broken at the elbow. He cried in pain and was set down. Dalen got his right eye to open just enough to see that it was the street magician.

"I can't believe you did that." He was out of breath and straining to speak, "I had to get you out of there. There's no time to call an ambulance." The magician had dragged Dalen down the side street to an alley and from there into an empty carport. "Normally I don't do this and, if this was a different situation, I would have called for help and left you to your fate, but this   is different."

Dalen was in shock, and his face was in near-blinding pain. Fear flooded him, and Dalen realized that this might be the end. "Don't hurt me." Dalen's words only came out as a slurred whisper, and even that shot fire through his throat.

"Hurt you? I would never hurt you. Don't move and try not to speak." He set Dalen down and came around to his right side as he lay on his back, staring at the light in the carport. The light was one of the long fluorescent glass tubes that are always dim yet make you squint when you look at them. "Okay. As far as I can tell, they shattered both your knees and broke your pelvis — you probably don't feel that because I'm pretty sure they broke your back when they put you through the window like that." The magician scanned Dalen's body and his eyes rested on his face. He flinched a little and continued, "You have glass in your left eye about the size of a Post-It note, and your right orbital socket has been broken." Dalen took a stuttering breath as nausea crashed over him. "They dislodged something in your throat. I think you're not only bleeding out but have internal bleeding, as well. Frankly, you are not going to live the six minutes needed for help to arrive." Dalen began to cry, despite the pain it caused. "It's going to be alright," the magician soothed, making shushing noises and stroking his forehead.

Dalen wasn't ready to die. "Help. Please . . ." was all he could force out before he was racked by a coughing fit that left his lips stained with blood.

"I can heal you, but I need your permission," the magician said. "Here is your choice. We don't have time for me to explain, but I can use real magic. With your permission, I can heal you." He stopped long enough to help Dalen through his cough, and then he started feeling his chest. "Your mind will panic. It will be scary for you, but you have to promise not to freak out when I do it." He smiled gently at Dalen. "The other option is that I sit right here with you and hold your hand, and I promise that you will not die alone. It's the least I can do for you. That was an amazing thing you did for me. No doubt the universe was watching you in that moment, and you are not alone. You're the bravest damn kid I've ever seen, and I will not let you die alone. I would rather save you, though. So, tell me quickly, as you only have moments left." He placed one hand over Dalen's forehead and the other over his heart. "I can save you. Do you wish it?"

Dalen tried to speak, scream, whisper but his throat was collapsing, and he could no longer breathe. The world was growing dark at the edges. Dalen got his head to nod and, at the moment he did, he watched as the magician's hands began to glow. Then it was as though his own body started glowing from the inside. At first, it happened in his wrists. Dalen watched the light move through his veins as if his blood were made of light itself, the luminescence splashing into all of his capillaries and then seeping into his skin. It spread quickly and, as it grew brighter, his body began to harmonize. All of the pieces that were broken started to burn, the pain was instant, and Dalen's body went stiff.

"Yes, I know. It hurts. All of your severed nerves are alive and on fire right now. It's the little things about life that they don't tell you." The magician smiled with sad eyes. "Like that healing from anything hurts. I am just forcing your body to do it all at once."

The street magician had been right. Dalen's brain tried to reject the reality that magic was real, but it was happening to him and there was no way to ignore it. His mind couldn't accept it either, and panic set in. Dalen's body was not yet healed, and every moment he tried to struggle was excruciating. He looked back into the eyes of the magician. He met Dalen's gaze and smiled, and it reminded him of what he thought he saw in the principal's office earlier. It frightened him.

"This is where you are going to pass out. Again, thank you." The last thing that Dalen saw was the magician's eyes, looking at him with kindness. There was something else about them, too, but the burning engulfed his whole body then, and the light blinded him from seeing anything else.

2

IN SEARCH OF
A MAGICIAN

Dalen woke up the next morning in his bed. He had no idea
how he got there, but what was more amazing to him at that moment
was the fact that he was perfectly fine. Dalen sat up and checked
himself for injuries and wondered to himself if it had all been
a dream.

David popped his head in and looked to see if Dalen had
gotten up yet. When he saw him, David shook his head and then
turned to yell down the hall, "Yeah, he's awake . . . finally." He
turned back towards Dalen and said, "You got six minutes before
it's time to go to school. Your breakfast is going to be cold soon,
and you know Ms. Warren's rules on eating at the table half-
dressed. You better hurry up, man."

Still half asleep and not sure of anything, Dalen asked, "What happened last night?"

David came into the room a little further. He cocked his head to the side a bit and replied, "What do you mean?"

Dalen's mind was trying to convince him that none of it happened. His mind desperately wanted to believe that none of it was real, but if none of it were real and it was just a dream, then why did he not remember how he got home? "Last night, after the movie."

"Oh. Yeah." David smiled and said, "Everyone got home fine. It's all good. I don't think anything is going to happen."

Dalen couldn't tell where his memory ended and the dream began, or if it was even a dream at all. "No, after you forgot your wallet and we went back for it?"

David seemed confused. "What do you mean? I got it right here." He patted his back right pocket.

"So, you found it then?"

David walked over to Dalen's closet and pulled out a pair of pants and a shirt for him and threw them on the bed. "Never lost it. You okay?"

Dalen was now just as confused as David. "It must have been a dream." It was the closest answer that his mind could make of it.

36

"Must be. Now you have five minutes, and you better hurry." David crossed to the door, but as he walked out, he called back, "Or I am eating your sausage."

"Alright, alright, I'm coming." That's how it was between them. Dalen and David were close like brothers and, where Dalen loved the benefits of having a brother, he knew that it came with a comradery that might end with no sausage for Dalen.

By the time Dalen made it to breakfast with two minutes to spare and minus one sausage courtesy of David, he was all but sure that whatever had happened last night must not have actually occurred. So what if he couldn't remember the rest of the night? He had been under a lot of stress, and with that crazy dream, his brain must have just mixed it up and dumped the memory of it from short-term memory while he slept. He told himself that brains were funny that way, and he put the whole event out of his mind.

The day progressed without much of a hitch. Ben and his friends were not at school that day. Dalen guessed they were suspended because of yesterday, yet something was hanging in the air that Dalen couldn't quite put his finger on.

Twice he had a feeling of being watched. Once was on his way to school, and the other was in the quad during a passing period between second and third, but he could never find where it was coming from. It was an odd sensation that felt almost as if it were coming from everywhere, and it didn't feel friendly. It reminded him of being in Denver's office the day before, but he eventually convinced himself it was just his nerves from the last twenty-four hours. By lunch, he had completely forgotten it.

The day progressed as it usually did, and Dalen found himself walking with his friends after school toward Adam and Travis's house to hang out and do homework when their conversation was cut short by Ben Watts, who was sitting on Adam's front porch, waiting for them.

Adam pushed past Dalen and the others and stood in front of everyone, with David close behind. "You don't have your friends this time, punk! This time you are the one outnumbered. If you want Dalen — yeah, his name is Dalen — you are going to have to face us all!"

Unexpectedly, Ben exploded into tears. The tones of his voice were a mixture of frustration and stress and, more than anything, fear. "I don't want to fight!" He fell to his knees and began to sob.

It took everyone by surprise. No one had ever seen Ben like this. Adam dropped his fists and looked back at the rest, questioningly. Everyone was stunned except for David, who was surprised but not ready to cease his aggression. "Without your friends here, I wouldn't want to fight us either."

Ben looked up and, with a helpless expression on his tear-streaked face, started to say things that made no sense to anyone. "I tried to bring them, but they don't remember, and they just got angry because they had no idea what I was talking about. I did bring them once, but a fight broke out and nothing went right, so I thought it would be better to come alone." Sobs shook him again, but within a few breaths, he composed himself enough to keep speaking. "So I came here by myself, hoping it would be different,

38

but when Adam said what he just said, I yelled back, and then he swung, and then you all beat me up." He began to sob again.

"What are you talking about?" David asked incredulously, though he seemed to be the only one who could do anything other than stare as the one guy they all feared and hated crawled on all fours, crying almost uncontrollably. "We have done no such thing."

"You have. You did." Ben's words were impossible, but he spoke them with truth, and none of them could imagine why he would try to make something like this up. They wondered if somehow yesterday he popped and lost his mind. "I have done this again and again, and it never works." Frustration radiated from his words as he pleaded, "I... beg... you. Please, let this go differently this time. I know I don't deserve it, but please let this end."

"What do you want?" Dalen asked.

"I just want to say I am sorry. Please!" Ben took a breath and quieted down. "Please let me do this."

Ben's pleading felt genuine to Dalen, even as he looked around to see if this was some sort of ambush. He checked trees and hedges for Ben's goons but didn't see anyone, so he turned back to Ben and said to the others, "Let him speak."

"Nine nights ago," Ben paused and looked around at them and then chuckled to himself, "Last night, my friends and I hurt you really bad." Again, Ben began to cry as he spoke, "I don't know what happened." Ben was terrified and desperate — Dalen could see it in his eyes. "I was angry because you got me in trouble and made me look stupid, but that night when I snuck out to hang with my friends, I started getting madder and madder." He tried to catch his breath for a moment and then continued, "I have never been that mad. Ever." Ben's eyes widened as he played it back in his mind. "Then, when we saw you, it became something that was happening *to* us." Ben paused for a moment. His eyes weren't looking at what was around him; he was lost in his memories. "I didn't mean to hurt you like that. I have no idea what happened." Ben snapped back to reality and looked at Dalen as though he was speaking directly into Dalen's being. "Please!" he begged. "Please, you have to forgive me. I don't know what happened!"

"What are you talking about, Ben?" Becky's voice was kind and caring. She knelt next to him and put her hand on his back. At first, he flinched, but when he realized that he was not being attacked, his last vestige of strength gave way and he collapsed into her. "Look, Dalen is fine. He is right here. You didn't hurt him," she soothed, even as she looked up at the others, pleading silently for help. When she saw that Dalen looked as pale as Ben, she knew something more was going on. "Do you know what he is talking about?"

"Yeah, I do, but it was a dream. I thought it was a dream." Dalen's memory started to pull itself free of the box that Dalen had stuffed it into all day.

Ben got up from his knees and moved toward Dalen. "You remember?" Before anyone could react, Ben flung himself at Dalen. As one, his friends lunged forward to pull Ben back, but a quick hand gesture from Dalen let them know that not only was he okay, but that Ben was, in fact, embracing him. "You know what I am talking about?"

"Yeah. I remember. I was hoping it was a dream, but I remember." Dalen didn't know what to do. He was lost and confused, and he no longer knew what was real and what was a dream.

Ben erupted once more, but this time his tears were of relief. "I am so sorry. I don't know what happened. We went insane. I don't know what happened. I am so sorry!" Ben repeated himself over and over, pleading with Dalen for forgiveness.

Dalen had dreamed of a moment like this, with Ben losing his mind as he tried desperately to apologize, but this did not bring Dalen the joy he'd imagined it would. At that moment, he did not see the bully who'd made his life miserable; he only saw a scared kid, and he knew what that was like.

"Ben, I want you to do the one thing you have never done. I want you to really listen to what I am about to say." He pushed him back far enough that he could look Ben in the eyes. "I forgive you." As Ben closed his eyes, tears began to fall again, but Dalen gently placed a hand on either side of Ben's head to get his attention, and when Ben opened his eyes again, he continued. "Today is a new day. It is over. But it is up to you what happens from here. If you go back to the way it was, it will never be over." Dalen felt his heart let go of his anger toward Ben. "I free you of this, I let this go, and we are good. I forgive you." Ben thanked him and just cried for a minute as his stress drained from him.

"This," David said quietly from behind Dalen, "is why you and I are friends."

"Agreed," Becky seconded, wiping tears from her own eyes.

"The greatest way to defeat an enemy is to make him your friend." Travis was visibly impressed, and together he and his brother chimed in, "Epic."

When Ben had regained his composure, they brought him inside to get a drink of water to calm his nerves. They glanced at each other in disbelief as they led Ben down to the basement that had become their unofficial clubhouse. As they descended the stairs, there was a homemade wooden sign that said 'Argue not with Dragons, for thou art crunchy and go well with Brie.' At the bottom of the stairs, cardboard lined the walls and had been painted gray with black lines to make it look like the walls of a castle from a fourth-grade play. Walking in, the cardboard facade continued throughout the room.

A large table took up the center of the room and six chairs surrounded it. An oversized antique wooden chair held the prime position at the head of the table and faced the door. It had been painted so that the back of the chair was split down the middle, with black on the left side and white on the right. The arms of the chair had been done in reverse: the white side on the right had a black armrest and the opposite was on the other side. There were three seats to its right and two on its left.

Facing the table from the entrance, two seats on the right and the two on the left were adorned with personalized decorations and little knick-knacks of different sorts. Each placement had a set of dice, a small hand-painted figure no more than two or three inches tall, and a plaque that had each of their names engraved on them.

Notes and papers of all kinds were strewn across the table. Hand-drawn maps with doodles of dragons and chests of treasure were scribbled on different locations, depicting the monsters and treasures they had found. Behind the main chair were two suits of armor made of tin that stood as guardians of the clubhouse. Discarded holiday lights stretched across the entirety of the ceiling in lines of color. At the moment, only the blue lights were on, but they could be changed from a knob that was on a small table to the left of the black and white chair.

This was their lair, their safe place from the world. This was where they came to game and to be free to be themselves, and now they'd brought Ben to this sacred place, not as a foe, but as a kid in need of help. They were perhaps the only people who might believe him — a bunch of gamers who allowed themselves to believe in the impossible.

They sat him down at the table in the seat that they reserved for new players, directly to the right of the large wooden chair, and began to ask questions about what had happened. Ben's story seemed almost impossible. He swore that he couldn't believe how insane it got, as if he were possessed or something, and again he apologized. He said that, from his point of view, he'd been reliving the day after he and his friends had attacked Dalen over and over again. Every morning, he woke in his bed as if from a hellish nightmare in which he had to repeat the day, but each time he was helpless to do anything about it. At the end of the day, he would fall asleep and, when he woke, it would be today again. So far, he'd lived this day nine times.

He had spent hours begging and praying to whatever was listening to have him wake up just one day before. He swore again and again that if he could just go back a little further, he would do it differently. His friends had no idea what he was talking about because they weren't what he called 'looping.' To them, it was the first time, every time. He spent the first two days skipping school and trying to find which hospital Dalen was in and, when Ben couldn't find him, he'd assumed the worst. He turned himself in on the fourth day, yet he woke the next day in his bed, and it was still today. He believed he was being punished by God for what he did, endlessly reliving the day after the beating with no way of stopping or fixing it.

On day six, he spotted Dalen coming out of the school. He convinced his friends to come with him even though they didn't want to, and he tried to talk to Dalen, but it blew up and a fight broke out. He tried it twice with the same results. On the eighth day, he tried to meet them at the clubhouse without his friends but got a severe beating because of tempers and foolish words. He had all but given up. It was only then that he knew he had to stop being the guy who'd gotten him into this situation in the first place. He'd prayed over and over for another chance, and he kept blowing it because of his ego, so this time when he woke up, he swore he would do it

44

differently. He'd let his guard down and try to do this right.

All of them had questions regarding his impossible tale, but it was Dalen's question that held the most weight at that moment: "Ben. Do you remember the magician?"

"Yes," Ben replied as his eyes got big. He looked a little surprised as if he'd somehow forgotten this detail and being asked about the magician directly had pulled the forgotten memory from the ether of his mind. "The street magician. It was when I first saw him — my anger started building into a rage. I was going to attack him, but you stepped in to stop me."

"He was the one who saved me." Dalen's gaze moved from one friend to another. "I know this sounds crazy, but afterward, the magician saved me. He used real magic and healed me. I know what it sounds like, but I swear to you: he used *real* magic. In the end, something happened that I'm still trying to understand. Last night, David lost his wallet, and we went back to get it. While I was waiting outside, I saw Ben start to mess with a street magician. I tried to help, but..." Dalen's words trailed off for a moment, remembering in fragments the brutal attack. "After the beating, the magician dragged me someplace out of sight and used real magic to heal me."

Over the months that Dalen and David had shared a room, they'd become close. Even their friends said they were like brothers. David was skeptical of Ben, but he wanted to believe Dalen. David believed in chance. He never worked with the impossible. To David, impossible was a blanket term used to describe something you couldn't believe in, whether or not it actually could be real. Because

45

David believed anything could be real, he allowed for the possibility of the impossible. "But I didn't lose my wallet last night. I dropped it, and someone handed it back to me, but it was never lost. I think what you're saying is that you remember time differently. That's why you asked me what happened this morning, correct?" David's voice was quiet, but his words reached out to everyone in the room. David had been the storyteller for their games for some time.

Each of them had grown to trust in his wisdom and to pay attention when he spoke. None of them could believe what was being said, but all of them felt that the two boys weren't lying. Their minds raced to answer the impossible. Their minds tried to tell them that, somehow, they must have shared a dream, or maybe this was an elaborate hoax, but no matter how many times they tried to use logic to make it go away, there were no answers in it. Ben's story was almost impossible to believe, but they believed in Dalen and knew that he wouldn't lie about something like this.

"So, maybe this magician caused a time loop." As always, Becky was the first to let go of confining concepts like what could or couldn't happen and started working on the problem. "Is it possible that instead of healing you directly, he made it so you never went back to find David's wallet at all?"

"As I said, I did drop the wallet earlier, but this stranger picked it up and handed it to me." David's excitement was palpable. In a rush of words, he described the person who had given him back his wallet, and it matched the street magician well enough that both Dalen and Ben agreed it was the same guy.

Becky was getting excited, too. Her mind looked at the problem from points of view that were specifically out of the box. "So, he changed time to prevent the damage. Pretty ingenious actually. But, because he changed it, only the two who were most affected by the time change still remember it, and somehow Ben is caught in a loop."

"So, all you have to do is go find him, and maybe he can fix this," Adam was almost giddy now.

"Yeah!" For the first time, Ben seemed hopeful. "Let's go find this guy and make him fix this!" Everyone stared at him like he was crazy. Ben looked around at them, and then he realized what he had said. "I mean, ask him nicely and please and thank you."

David stood and asked everyone to take their seats and, once they were seated, he cleared his throat and spoke with the same voice that he used anytime he was beginning a new quest. "Today, you face the greatest challenge to date."

"What's going on?" Being new, Ben didn't understand.

David simply replied with "Pregame speech. Got to get psyched. Now hush." He cleared his throat and began again, "Today, you face the greatest challenge to date. I have watched from this chair as you took on the three-headed Rat King. I have seen you save the City of Night from certain doom. I have watched as you earned the right to wield the Blade of Honor." They smiled and nodded to each other in acknowledgment. "I have even seen you face a Shadow Fiend and hoards of the undead, but none of these adventures compare with what lies before you now. This one is real."

47

Adam pounded the table and stood from his chair with a victorious and resounding "Yes!"

"This one has real danger and real consequences," David continued as Travis joined his brother and stood up. "This is what you have trained for." Dalen stood. "Somewhere, out in the city, there is a real magician, and he is our only hope." Becky stood with them, and all looked to Ben.

Ben stared back at them wide-eyed. "This is insane."

David continued as if Ben hadn't spoken. "And now, in this moment, we are given a true gift. Our greatest enemy in the world comes to us, not as a foe, but as an ally. Ben, you are meant to be here. Of this, I have no doubt."

"No, really. Are you all insane?" Ben looked worried.

Again, it was David who made things clear. "No, we're sane, but we have learned as a team that it is better to go in pumped and ready instead of scared out of our living minds because ... Great Caesar's Ghost! Magic is *real* ... And the only thing that we have to hold onto is the strength that we find in ourselves. So, you have two real choices in front of you: you can sit there in fear, or you can join us in arms to do this thing."

David waited for Ben to make his choice and, once he stood up and declared he was in, David picked up the twenty-sided die that was in front of him and cast it onto the table. It bounced and came to a stop with the twenty facing up. David smiled and declared, "I call this quest is in play. Now..." he smiled at them devilishly, "Go get me that Wizard!"

They cheered and roared. They threw their fists in the air and made their best battle cries. Even Ben joined in. They flew up the stairs and out of the house still yelping and hooting as they made their exodus. Chores would have to wait, and homework didn't even occur to them.

They decided the best chance of finding the magician was to split up. Each of them had their phone with them, so it would be easy to stay in contact. They were going to scatter and check any place that they could think of where any kind of street performer might work. Ben and David had both seen the magician, but only Dalen had gotten a good look at him, so it was decided that if any of them found a magician performing, they were going to take a picture of them and send it to Dalen. He would then text them back if that was the guy. The plan was that, once they found him, they would wait to approach him until everyone else could arrive.

The first few hours were exciting. They scoured the parks and checked the malls, but each time they found a magician, it wasn't the right one. The hour leading to sundown slowed their pace, and they began to lose hope. They checked everywhere they could think of and even did a second run on all the parks, hoping that maybe they had just missed him.

Darkness was falling and most of the team had been called home. Even David had gone ahead with news that Dalen would be following shortly. He said he'd explain to Ms. Warren that Ben and Dalen had met up after school, that Ben had given a 'very nice apology,' and that Dalen was talking things out with him. Dalen knew that Ms. Warren would love to hear that they were talking it out, but he knew he was on borrowed time. This is how Dalen found himself sitting on the same bench outside of the theater that he'd sat on the night before, staring at an empty street corner, sitting with the guy who had almost killed him.

"So, Ben... What are you going to do tomorrow?"

"You mean if tomorrow is tomorrow?"

"Yeah. If we can find this guy and he can fix this, what are you going to do tomorrow?"

Ben snorted, "That's an easy one. Sleep. I'm tired."

"Yeah, okay, fair, but then what?"

"You really want to know?"

Dalen thought about it for a moment. "Yeah."

He smiled. "I'm going to kill Toad."

Dalen didn't even try to hide his shock as he exclaimed, "Have you learned nothing?"

"Slow down, Turbo — I've learned plenty," Ben's voice was calm, and his smile was sincere. "I mean, I am going to kill the name. I'm going to tell everyone that I was wrong and that you're an okay dude. I'm going to kill Toad." His smile got bigger. "And I'm going to get Dalen a date for the dance."

Dalen laughed, "Then you are more magical than the guy

we're looking for."

"Seriously, I've had some time to think about it. I think I can do it." He took a moment to consider it again. "No. I know I can do it." Dalen smiled and relaxed. They both sat there, looking at the stars as they twinkled into existence in the evening sky. "Who do you like? Seriously, I'll see if I can put in a good word for you."

Dalen was dumbfounded by this and didn't know what to say. He could only stutter a bit, and then he laughed it off with a quick, "Yeah, right, as anyone will ever want to go out with Toad."

"Agreed," Ben said with a nod, "but remember, I'm going to kill that guy. Dalen has just as much of a chance as anyone else."

Just then the street magician came around the corner and into sight. They both ran as they went to catch him. They were halfway across the street when Dalen nervously said, "Kim Collard."

Ben stopped in his tracks, a look of admiration smeared across his face. "Kim? She's cute and the smartest cheerleader I have ever met. Beautiful and fun, which is my favorite combination. Good call. Way to swing for the fences, man."

"Yeah, she is amazing, but there is no way." The memory of her laughing with the rest of the kids the day before filled Dalen's mind.

"Woah, there, I didn't say it was impossible." Ben quickly glanced to make sure the street magician was still in sight and that no cars were coming since they were standing in the middle of the road. "She just broke up with Jake the other day, and I am pretty sure that no one has asked her yet, so she was just planning on going with some of the other girls."

"How do you know all this?" Dalen asked, keeping an eye on the magician as well.

"I know you think I am just a big dumb jock, but being popular is more work than you can imagine. If you are good at it, you have to know just about everything that is going on with everybody, and besides football, this is what I am good at."

Dalen nodded, "I never thought about it like that, but it makes sense. It's amazing what you can learn about someone if you just take the time to get to know them."

The conversation had slowed them down and, when they looked up again, they barely glimpsed the magician as he turned the corner a block ahead. They ran to catch him but, as they made it to the corner, they only had a second to see him turn down another alley. He was merely walking, and they thought that it shouldn't be hard to catch him but, turn after turn, they didn't seem to be making much ground.

And then it seemed they had lost him. They stopped running and tried to catch their breath. From behind them, the magician stepped out from nowhere into the overhead street light that bathed the alley in a dingy yellow haze. "Well, look who found me, and together no less ... "

52

Both Ben and Dalen jumped a little, surprised, as the magician had truly stepped out of nowhere. The alley they were in was narrow and sandwiched between two buildings. In this section, it was just the back of an apartment building and a convenience store, and neither of them had a door nearby, just two bare gray brick walls. It was as if he had just stepped into the alley through a solid wall.

"I am so glad to see you again, my friend, but I see you have with you the very boy who beat you to death. Yet, here you stand with him as if he is your friend. Is everything alright?" He sounded concerned for Dalen's wellbeing and paid almost no regard to Ben at all. "My friend, do you require my assistance once again?"

"It is good to see you," Dalen was trying to be as friendly as possible. "I thought that you were a dream. When I awoke in my bed, I didn't know what to think."

The magician closed his eyes and said something under his breath that neither Ben nor Dalen could make out. He took a deep breath in and then looked at Dalen with a smile. The alleyway grew warmer. The light became softer and felt welcoming. "You were meant to wake without knowledge. It is easier on the mind for it to think it was all but a dream. I was trying to be kind." With that, the magician bowed deeply to Dalen.

"And I thank you. I am in your debt, but I need to ask of you another favor." Dalen did his best to be cordial; this was all new to him and he had no idea if, in the end, the magician would take kindly to him asking for help — if there was even something to be done — but he had to try. "Ben has been stuck in a time loop for nine days, and we need your help to get him free of it."

"Why does it matter what happens to him? He tried to kill you. No! Worse than that: he did kill you! If it weren't for me, you would have surely died." His tone was completely uncaring for Ben in any way. "Why should you care about any harm that comes to him? He would see you die slowly in the streets, alone."

"But something happened to me. I'm not like that, and I have learned so much." Ben's voice cracked at first but found its strength quickly, "I was wrong. I see that. I have spent the last nine days thinking about how I got here, and I know that I was wrong. That is why I am here, with him." Ben's voice rang with truth as his words poured from his heart, but any hope he had was dashed by the magician's words.

"What do I care about your measly nine days? Come back to me in nine years, once the lesson has had time to settle. You think you know suffering? Wait until you must live this day a thousand times, ten thousand... then you will know what it means to suffer."

"No, please don't – " Ben dropped to his knees and began to plead, "I beg you, please, no. I have learned my lesson."

Time froze, and only Dalen and the magician seemed unaffected by it. The magician strolled up to Dalen with a terrifying smile and asked a simple question: "Do you want me to continue this?"

54

The question was straightforward, but it hit Dalen like wet sand, surrounding and slowing him, its thick weight all around him. This was a real question. Did Dalen want Ben to suffer?

The question played out in his mind for a moment. The power was his to make this choice. He could see it, again and again: Ben would try and fail. He could spend years here, having to realize daily that he was wrong. He would have the time to really think about all that he had done, not just to Dalen, but to all the kids who faced his wrath. What about their justice? What about the payment for all their suffering? Did he have the right to deprive them of justice?

Dalen felt a sense of rage rise within him. He thought about all the pain Ben had placed upon so many others without a thought to what they felt. The rage rose, yet in its chaos, he remembered how the day had gone and how Ben had changed. Was he the same guy as when all of this started? This was the question that filled Dalen's mind. Had Ben changed, or was he just trying to get out of the trouble he was in?

Dalen's gaze fell on Ben. Frozen in time, he didn't seem scary at all. As if Dalen was not really there in the moment but able to view it from afar, his mind raced with the infinite possibilities of what the question truly meant. All of them seemed real. All of them were possible. How could he answer for sure when any of them could be true?

Dalen Pax saw only two real options in front of him: should he take a leap of faith and believe in Ben, or should he sentence his enemy to suffering?

His anger swelled, and again his mind was flooded with all the reasons to leave this monster here. He could be lying. Maybe he didn't mean any of it. How could Dalen be so fooled? The magician brought his attention back to where he was and what he was doing. "What do you think, Dalen? Should we leave him in this time loop forever?" The magician's voice was solid and sincere, and it felt like he meant to leave Ben here like this.

"No. Please don't." Dalen was scared now. The words that David had said ran through his mind: "real consequences." There was no escaping it. Ben's future was on the line and in Dalen's hands. "All I want is for him to be removed from the time loop he is in and for him to be allowed his freedom from this. He has earned it."

"You want me to make it as if the time loop had never happened at all?" The magician continued to smile at Dalen as if he were asking him what flavor of ice cream he would like, but Dalen felt that the question held much more weight.

Dalen's mind cleared and for a moment he remembered that sometimes the wording is important. He rebuilt the question in better terms. "I want him to break free of the time loop from here so that he remembers all that has happened. If the time loop never happens, he will still be the arrogant punk he always was. It is only now, after experiencing the loop, that he has learned his lesson."

The magician suddenly moved with speed and fluidity, floating to him effortlessly. In the blink of an eye, he was almost on top of Dalen. "He was going to kill you, and now, after an afternoon, you trust him!? What makes you feel he has changed? He is afraid. He is acting on instinct. He will do anything and say anything to get out of his peril."

"Agreed, but it doesn't mean that it is not true." Dalen had found his rhythm and was ready to prove his point. "He'd do anything to get out of this, for lack of a better term, personal hell, yes?"

"Indeed," the magician smiled as if Dalen was only proving his point.

"Then, if he is willing to do anything, it is possible that the thing he is willing to do is to honestly change. That is a possibility, right?"

The magician saw where Dalen was going with this, and though he disagreed, it was too late to be effective. "Yes, in all the millions of possibilities that could happen, that is one of the choices he could make."

"Is it possible that he could have found it in nine days or less?"

Both already knew the answer before it was spoken. They played out the conversation as if it were a chess game; both of them were thinking four and five moves ahead, and both of them knew that it was checkmate in two.

"Yes. He could have learned his lesson by then," the magician almost sounded disappointed.

"Then I ask you, great magician, please help my friend, for he has paid his dues and is ready to start a new way. Please let him remember. The time he spent did him good, and I would hate to lose all the progress we have made."

The magician smiled, but as he did, a sense of danger fell upon Dalen. "If that is what you wish."

"It is." Even as Dalen spoke the words, he felt that he'd made a mistake, that somehow he'd given away something that he shouldn't have, but the dice had been rolled and nothing could be done but face the price that came with making wishes.

With a flash of light that seemed to originate from everywhere all at once, Ben was gone.

"What happened?" Dalen asked, shocked. "Where did he go?"

"Don't worry. When your friend wakes up, it will be tomorrow, and he will go on from here as whoever he is at this moment." The magician moved in the flash of light. He was no longer in Dalen's face. Instead, he was a few feet away and his clothes had changed. He had been wearing a worn and faded tuxedo that looked like he'd been living in it for a while. Now he was dressed in linen robes that were dyed black. They flowed with the air as he moved, but they weren't entangling. They looked light and comfortable, and they reminded Dalen of a gi that a martial artist would wear. On his left side, he wore a cloth over his shoulder that draped down to his knee in the front and back. It was mostly black but edged in red along both sides. Running down the length of the cloth like a spine was beautifully embroidered fire that seemed to magically come to life and move as if it were a real fire, and this was held at his waist by a sash of black silk. His face, which seemed somehow familiar, was clean and the hair of his goatee had been manicured. The lines in his face suggested that he may be older than he looked at first glance, but Dalen would have guessed he was in his thirties. He held up two fingers. The ring on his middle finger was made of gold and had a single set ruby, about the size of a bottle cap. "That's two you owe me."

"Yes, thank you. Is there anything I can do to repay you?" Dalen felt the weight of that sentence after he spoke, but he knew that it was far too late to do anything about it.

The magician smiled, and with a silvery tongue he said, "First off, I wish to say 'bravo.' You handled yourself well there. For a moment, I thought you were going to leave poor Ben in his chaos forever."

The bottom fell out of Dalen's world. "You didn't want to punish him? I thought that you did." Dalen was confused. He swore that just moments ago the magician wanted it and was even pushing for it. "I don't understand."

"It was a test."

"A test?"

"Yes, and you passed." The magician smiled as if he had just remembered a funny joke. "I was never going to leave him like that." He thought about what he had just said, and then after a moment he closed his eyes and nodded with certainty. "I just wanted to know what type of upstanding man you really are."

"I thought I proved that last night," Dalen said with a joking tone, but he also meant it.

"Oh, that. That was instinct," the magician pointed out. "If you had the time to think or had known what was coming, you wouldn't have done it." He was right. Dalen knew in his heart that, had he known how badly they were going to hurt him, there would've been a moment of doubt. "I had to see what you would do when you had the time to think about it, and you did fantastically."

Dalen was elated. He sang video game victory themes in his head for a moment as a silent victory, but as he thought it, it played from everywhere. It surprised Dalen and the magician both, and he looked at Dalen as if slightly in shock. He glanced around the alley, and then back at Dalen. He cracked a grin and began to laugh. Dalen had been embarrassed for a moment, but as the magician laughed, it broke the tension, and Dalen laughed too.

"Careful. Thoughts are very real here." The magician took a pose and deeply bowed. "You owe me nothing. It is the least I can do for the man who saved my life. I wouldn't dream of you owing me a thing." He paused for a moment, just long enough for Dalen to start to believe that this might end tonight, and all was well. "But ... If you believe that you owe me something for saving your life and then helping your friend from being left to his fate, and I mean only if you really feel that you should help, there is one thing you can help me with, but I wouldn't want to put you out or anything."

Dalen's insides screamed for him to run, but he ignored it and stayed where he was. They begged for him to be quiet, but he spoke and, as his words fell from his mouth, he knew that he was

60

getting in way further than he ever intended to. "It's no problem. What can I do for you?"

The magician smiled and, with calm tones as if he were asking the simplest of favors from Dalen, he said, "There is an artifact. I want you to retrieve it and bring it to me."

Dalen was waiting for the other shoe to fall. "Sure. Where can I find this artifact?"

The other shoe came with a thump that struck Dalen to his core.

"I need you to retrieve it from The Museum of History that is located here in town." He requested it as if he were asking Dalen to reach over and pick up something from off the ground.

"Simple really, and it shouldn't take you more than a few minutes."

"That is not simple at all," Dalen said, not trying to hide his distress. "I can't break into a museum." Things had changed quickly. Dalen wanted to help, and he did owe this guy his life. 'This guy?!' he thought to himself, as he realized he didn't even know his name. "Why would you think that this is simple? Who are you?"

"Are you asking me my name?"

"To start with."

"I have so many names that many have given me and my kind over the years." His tone never changed — indeed, he spoke as

though he were having a pleasant conversation with a close friend —
but that was no real answer.

"Alright, if that's how you want to do this, then I am going
to go. Look, you are amazing, and I do owe you a lot for saving
my life, and afterward, I asked you for another favor that you also
did, and I thank you for that as well. I am not trying to be rude or
disrespectful. I can't tell you how thankful I am, but if you want
me to repay you by committing crimes, I'm not sure how I feel about
that. If I get caught, I will lose the only safe place I've ever had in
my entire life, and you won't even tell me who you are. I'm going to
have to give it a hard pass."

The magician seemed frustrated and irritated. "Pass?
Really, and for what? So, you don't have to break any rules because
you might get in trouble? I reordered time for you. Twice! You don't
think I had to break some rules for that? You think I can't get
in trouble? Don't you remember how nervous I was? How I had to
hide you in that carport so no one would see? But I did it. I did it
because it was the right thing to do." He put both of his hands on
Dalen's shoulders. "That is all I am asking of you."

"I didn't ask you to." In his heart, Dalen knew that wasn't
the point and, in truth, the magician had asked him before he'd done
anything both times.

The magician scolded him, but he never raised his voice.
He kept it calm and cool as he replied, "Yes, you did, Dalen Pax,
and you asked me directly to break time not two minutes ago." The
magician waited for that to sink in before changing gears. "Look,
Dalen, it doesn't matter. You want to know who I am. I will tell

you. I am the man whose life you saved. I am the one who saved yours. I am the friend who heard your plea and again came to your rescue. I'm the one who was proud of you when you chose to let Ben go. I'm your friend, and yes, I am that very same friend who is now asking you for help in my time of need, as I have done for you a couple of times." The magician paused again as if he were trying to remember additional things he had done and then nodded. "If you agree, I will be the one who will help you through your task with magic. I will be the one who'll be opening doors and blinding cameras. I will be the one that makes sure that the guards will not be able to perceive you. I'm the one who wants you to succeed and bring the artifact to me. I am the one who'll suffer the most if you are captured or fail. If you want to know what I can be, I can be a friend. I can be a mentor and, if you wish, I can be your teacher in the ways of the magic arts." He squeezed Dalen's shoulders once, and then let go and began to walk away. When he was almost to where the light turned to shadows, he turned back around and said one more thing: "Best of all, I am the one who, if you get what I need, will grant you one more wish. Anything you want. Does that answer your question?"

Dalen hung his head. "Damn. You almost had me convinced." He began to walk out of the alley in the direction he had come.

"Mathias."

Dalen turned back around, and the magician was standing directly in front of him with his hands outstretched.

"I'm sorry. Old habits die hard. You can call me Mathias. The apprentice and right hand of the Genie DeSalvo. Sorcerer of the Physical Planes and Seeker of the Beads of Fire." He shook Dalen's hand and then bowed deeply. "At your service."

"Nice to meet you, Mr. Mathias."

"Please, there may be many years between you and me, but I think we are to a point where you can call me just Mathias. So, you'll do it?" Mathias looked hopeful, like a six-year-old asking for a cookie.

"I don't know." Dalen was still unsure about all of it. "This is a lot to take in, but I have time to think it over, right?"

Mathias looked concerned again. "Unfortunately, tomorrow the Beads of Fire will be moving on to their next destination. They are part of a collection that is on tour right now. This may be my only shot." He paused for a breath and then added, "You are the only one I can trust to do this. It takes a special kind of person to do what you did for me. It comes from the heart, and your heart is strong. Plus, you have recently been touched by magic, and the resonance it left behind will allow you to retrieve it. It's why I waited until your friends left before I let you find me. Please, Dalen, you are my only hope."

"I don't know. This is too much, too fast." Dalen felt the pressure of his offer to help. "I want to help you. I do, but this is crazy."

"Okay. I understand." With a wave of his hand, the lights

changed back to normal, and Dalen felt like he was in the right world again. Mathias was once again in his battered tuxedo and scraggly beard. "Think quickly. If you agree to help, come back here and call my name out loud. I will hear you. We don't have much time, but I have faith in you, Dalen, and I know you will do the right thing."

Dalen thanked him and ran off toward home. As he did, the last thing that Mathias said to him repeated in his head: "the right thing." The conflict over what was the right thing to do began to make the term blur. It began to have no meaning, so he did his best to set it aside.

3

PREPARING
FOR THE JOURNEY

Dalen's first move was to get home as quickly as he could.
It was later than he had intended, and he was well past being late.
Dalen wanted to talk to his friends and share everything that had
just happened, but he knew that he'd have to talk with David and
the rest after Ms. Warren gave her "There are rules and curfews for
a reason speech."

Dalen sent a text to David that he had found the magician.
He said he was on his way home and to get the team together.
Dalen knew it was going to be hard to explain to everyone but that
his friends would be there for him no matter what.

Things went as Dalen predicted. Ms. Warren's speech on why there were rules was short but to the point. As he walked in, she started by hitting him with a rolled-up magazine. Not hard, or in a way that Dalen felt he was truly being attacked; in truth, it had the same intensity and danger as a pillow fight. Dalen ducked and smiled. He began to explain but was stopped by a few wild swings.

"You scared me close to death! Is that what you want? Hmm? For me to die of fright and worry?" She pointed the magazine at the table, indicating that Dalen should take a seat.

Dalen went and sat down where a cup of hot tea was waiting for him. Ever since Dalen could remember, it had been his favorite. "I would never want you to die."

Ms. Warren's demeanor softened in a breath, and she smiled at him with warmth in her eyes. "Of course not, dear. But don't interrupt while I am giving my speech, sweety, or I'll get lost and have to start over." She gave him a wink. "Now, where was I? Oh, yes ... angry face." Her demeanor changed again; this time, it took on a tone that suggested frustration and stress. "Send me to my early grave from fright and worry." She walked into the kitchen and pushed a button on the microwave. It made a beep and the whole thing began to hum. "You could have been killed. You could have been snatched up by who knows. Anyone! To do ..." At this point, she began to ham it up, "terrible things. Terrible!" She dramatically threw herself from the counter to the chair, theatrically swooning with her left wrist dashed across her eyes. With a stuttering half-whispered breath, she continued, "Just thinking of what could have happened makes me lightheaded." The microwave finished with a loud ding. She clutched her heart, stood up, and staggered. "That was my heart. Did you hear it?" She opened the microwave and produced his dinner. "Did you hear the Bing of My Despair?"

Dalen, who had been trying to keep a straight face, snorted. He was so glad that he wasn't taking a sip of the mint tea that was in front of him. Warren would have made him clean up the mess. "Your Bing of Despair?"

"Yes. My heart went …" and with three times the volume and four octaves higher, she cried out, "BING!" She broke character and they both laughed, but she quickly recovered. "That is why we have to have rules. That is why we have curfews. It's not because I want to keep you here." She walked over with his plate. "It's because if something happened to you, I would surely die. My heart would go bing." As she set his plate down, she dropped the act and hugged him. "Okay?"

Dalen tried to tap out of the massive hug. "Okay, okay."

Ms. Warren held on to him tight. "And don't you forget it." She let him up for air. "Now, tell me. You were out with the guy who always wants to pick on you and beat you up. How did it go?" She sincerely wanted to know. That was one of the greatest things about Ms. Warren: she cared about Dalen as if he were her own.

"Better than I hoped. I think. I guess we won't know until tomorrow." Realizing how hungry he was, Dalen attacked his food with gusto, which gave Ms. Warren time to respond.

"That is true. Change doesn't always happen overnight. It may take him a couple of tries. Remember to be patient." One of the few beautiful things in Dalen's life was the heart of Ms. Warren.

"I will. I promise." He finished his dinner and put his plate and cup in the dishwasher. He came back long enough to hug her and say, "I am going to go to my room. I have a couple of things that I want to do before bed." She hugged him back and wished him a good night.

By the time Dalen got to his room, David had the video chat room already opened and everyone was waiting for him to join. He brought the group up on his phone, flopped down on the bed flat on his back, and held his phone in front of him.

The lights had been turned off, so the room was dark. The only thing that could be seen in the darkness of the room was David and Dalen's faces, glowing in the shadows.

As Dalen looked at his screen, he saw the excitement in their expressions. He read the same question on each of them, so Dalen answered it while they were still silent and before they tried to ask all at once. "Magic ... is very real!"

All of them exploded into whoops and cheers and reveled in the moment. They were old enough to know that, in everyday life, the concept of magic was not really accepted and was even frowned upon. Most of them had already given up on the idea of ever seeing any for real, but they were also young enough that they believed it could exist nonetheless.

He explained in detail everything he could remember about what had happened. When he was done, he presented his quandary: "I owe him twice. He has done nothing but help me. Hell! He even saved my life and helped me make friends with my greatest enemy. The answer seems so simple. He deserves my help, but I would have to steal an artifact from a museum to do what he wants. How can that be right?"

Silence filled the darkness for a few moments. They were genuinely thinking about the answer. They had previously devised a system so that everyone didn't try to talk all at the same time; in it, when a person wished to speak, they would put up their hand. The first person to do so would hold up one finger, the second person would hold up two, and so on. They called this method "Rolling Initiative."

As each person finished, everyone would lower their number by one. They did this for two reasons. The first was basic etiquette: "Number one gets to speak. If you have a different number, wait your turn." The rule was useful for keeping arguments only to discussions. The second reason worked hand-in-hand with the first; once a person spoke their piece and someone else started, if the first wanted to comment on what the second said, they had to re-enter rotation — this gave each person time to think about what they were going to say and to hear the other people out before responding. Since conversations often went many rounds, they found it best to keep diminishing the number as they went so no one was trying to hold up nine or even sixteen fingers. Dalen waited until all four of them had fingers up. Adam held up one, while his brother Travis held up three. Becky was between them, and David chose to speak last.

"This is what you've been training for, my man. You always play the Sorcerer and the Thief. It's like this situation was built for you. You get a chance to do something we've only dreamed of, including you. This is a once-in-a-lifetime opportunity — no, once in a hundred lives! If you don't go and live your dreams when you have the chance, you'll look back on this moment every day of your life and ask, 'What if?' If it were my choice, I'd get off this chat and run to wherever you are supposed to go and hope that it's not too late. The adventure has tapped your shoulder — don't tell me you aren't going to answer the call." Adam took a deep breath and then added, "Okay, that said, you're my friend and I don't want to see you hurt, so be careful. Just because I say 'follow the adventure,' doesn't mean go out all half-cocked, and get yourself dead or something, but yeah. These are the moments we live for!" It was Adam's catchphrase, and he used it often as a battle cry or for a moment of inspiration.

They all cheered and clapped. Becky waited until things had calmed down to change her number to a one and begin. "You have to go alone?"

"Seemed that way." Since Dalen was the one who initially asked the question, he was allowed to respond and answer questions from the others.

"Any way around that?" she followed.

"I don't think so, plus he mentioned he waited until all of you were gone before he let us meet with him, so I think that's a hard pass for him."

Becky took his answers in and waited until she processed them before she continued, "I agree with Adam in some respects. This is a once-in-a-lifetime chance, but don't be dumb about it. Ask questions. Don't take 'Don't worry about it' as an answer. Tell him that you'll help but only if you can understand what is going to happen inside and out. Pretend you are me because you aren't going to have me to back you. Not any of us. All you will have is some guy that, at the moment, seems friendly and can do magic. Ask yourself, 'Would I fall for this in game?' I mean, be at least as smart as your character." Just before she put her hand down to signal Travis, she added, "And come home. Priority one is for you to come back to us."

"I promise to do my absolute best to come back. Believe me, it's my first priority, too."

Travis waited for a moment. Travis had always been like a big brother to them. They looked up to him and respected his opinions and advice, and for the first time, Dalen felt the full weight of his words. Travis paused for another breath, afraid to give the wrong advice. "One of us has to be the voice of reason, and while I agree with Becky, I need to also add this. This is stupid."

"Okay, I'm listening," Dalen could tell that Travis wasn't just shooting the idea down — he wasn't the kind of guy to just leave it at that.

"This isn't just stupid, it's crazy stupid. Let's look at this from the point of view that legends and myths are real.

Magic is real — okay, why not? Since we don't know otherwise, we have to assume that if some of it is real, it is all real until proven otherwise."

"Okay, that tracks. Keep going."

"If what you said is right, he keeps putting things in the terms of owing wishes, and before helping you in the alley, he asked you if you wished for his help. Four beings come to mind that directly use wishes as currency. The first three are fairies, genies, and leprechauns. Both fairies and leprechauns are fey, and a genie is something completely different. The fey can be unpredictable. If he is a fairy, you have a good chance that the wish he is offering will work out as you hope, but if you disrespect him or anger him, he could choose to twist it and put something like a sleeping curse on you for a hundred years. So, tricky at best. If it's a leprechaun, you are two wishes in and may already be double cursed, and you are shooting for three."

"I didn't see any pot of gold."

"Do not go looking for it," Travis stated solemnly. "Either way, there's no back door. At this point, you're two wishes deep and your only wish might be that you got so lucky as a sleeping curse.

"Genie might be your best bet, but you can't go by what you see in the movies. Everything I know about them suggests that they're immensely powerful and have the ability to fill in all the blanks you leave out of your wish."

"Are they good or bad?"

"Neither." Travis didn't seem to like his answer and switched it to, "Both. They are considered neutral, but, right now, it would be your best hope. You saved his life, and for that he is offering you the customary three wishes. If that's the case, all you have to do is help get him what he wants, and you get a real, honest wish."

"What about the fourth?" asked Dalen.

"That's the scary one. Evil. Pure, straight-up Evil."

"What do you mean?"

"Many religions and beliefs have this concept of true evil incarnate. For simple terms, it is the devil. Evil will tempt you with your greatest wish. This is as much a possibility as any of the other three." Travis pondered for a moment, "Now this is where my reality check kicks in. Maybe he is just a sicko who likes little boys, and he has been drugging you with a hallucinogen that can be transferred by touch and acts fast. You have to remember that there are some messed-up people out there. All of what you said could be very not real, and he has Ben somewhere and is doing unbelievably bad things. You don't know. This is why I say this is crazy stupid. You don't know this guy, and we can't know if you actually saw what you think you saw at this point. Don't get me wrong, I am not saying you didn't see it — I am just saying that there might be another answer other than magic."

His point weighed heavily on all of them. None of them had even considered other possibilities. All of them were so eager to see what could be and were not focused enough on what probably was.

"So, almost any way you look at this, it's really bad for you. We don't know who or what he is, even if all he said is true so far. I don't think you should go." The others gasped a little with shock. "I can't believe I am saying this, and if you choose to go, I will back you all the way, but as much as you might regret not doing this if you don't, I'd regret it my whole life if I didn't say something and you went and disappeared or died. I'm just trying to be a real friend."

Dalen wiped tears from his eyes. "Travis, thank you. No matter what I choose, I heard you, and this is not on you." Dalen took a moment and looked across the room to David. David looked back at him and sheepishly grinned and shrugged his shoulders. Dalen smirked at his friend and then looked back to his screen. "Alright, David. What do I do?"

"So far we have heard some really good points, and as a part of my response I wish to comment on what has been said." David took a deep breath and let it out slowly; he then took another deep breath and began: "First off, I am in complete agreement with Becky. You need to be careful, and you need to be smart. That said, I wish to resonate with Adam. When looking back on one's life, most people regret what they did not do compared to those choices they did. I agree that most feel that way. The ones who go the other way are usually based on the idea that some action they took ruined their lives. I must also echo Travis and remind you that this could all be a hallucination in your mind. I need to remind you that, in all actuality, a pervy stranger who likes to drug little boys is a more 'realistic' explanation than that magic is real, and it is also not the most dangerous thing we've considered tonight." David let his heart pound in his chest for a moment or two, allowing time for that thought to sink in.

"Dalen, before you are two options. The first crossroad question that you need to answer is whether or not magic is real. The truth is your heart knew its answer as I asked the question. Now, whatever answer that is, that is your truth. Now that you know what that truth is, you must make every decision from here based on that truth. So, what is it? Is magic real?"

Everyone held their breath in anticipation of his answer. "I know in my heart that what I saw was real. Real enough to act on it." As a collective, they breathed.

"Then standing before you are two choices, brother." Dalen had been watching his screen and didn't notice David move until he was sitting right next to him. "Do you trust him, or do you ghost him?"

"I don't know if I trust him, but I *believe* him. He has done nothing but help me, and the only problems I have are that he's dodgy about who he is and he wants me to rob a museum."

"Why do you feel he is being dodgy?" David asked.

"I love it when they do this," Becky noted with glee, but Adam shushed Becky to let them continue.

Dalen responded to David's question: "I don't know."

"Guess. Use logic."

"He is trying to avoid telling me his real name."

"Why would he do that?"

"I don't know."

David nodded. "Have you ever heard of anything that would suggest a good reason for this?"

Dalen thought for a moment. "Maybe it has something to do with all of those legends you hear about spirits and things in the magic world — that you are only able to control it if you know its real name?"

"Okay, maybe he is protecting himself. Superman doesn't walk around telling people that he is severely weakened by kryptonite. Fair point, any other reasons?"

"Hang on, I am still on the last one. That's a really good point." David gave him a minute to consider that and when Dalen was ready, he continued. "Okay, umm, he doesn't want me to know who or what he is because if I knew I may not help him. Like he is evil in the flesh or something."

"Did you get any feeling from him that he was evil?"

"When he was using magic, I felt fear."

"Fear because he was evil?"

"No... I didn't feel fear because he was evil; it was because it was so much. Powerful. It blew through me in ways I had never experienced."

"At any time during that did you feel the presence
of evil?"

Dalen thought about it for a moment, replaying the events
in his mind. "Not that I could tell. There were moments it was
scary, but I don't think he is innately evil."

"Do you trust your answer? Does it ring true when you
say it?"

"Yes. I don't believe he is evil."

"Then you have a non-evil, magic individual who can grant
you two wishes. This individual will grant you one more if you are
willing to steal. He will grant you magical help and he wants you to
win because it means he wins, but to do so, you must be willing to
become a thief. Now, here is your big question. The one that only
you can answer."

Everyone sat in silence, not knowing what was going to
come next, but whatever the question was, they were on pins and
needles to find out not only what the question was, but how Dalen
would answer.

Dalen turned to look at his friend directly. "Hit me."

"Is it worth it?" Silence wafted through the room like a fog
rolling in. It held in the air for what seemed to be forever. "Because
if it is, you need to go." David always had a way about him like
this: never telling someone what they should do or even giving a
direction to take, yet at the same time, he got the other person to
understand what they had to decide for themselves. It's what made

him a great Game Master.

Dalen made his choice and began getting ready to go.

As he did so, each of his friends in turn wished him luck and suggested things to take with him on his quest. He changed his clothes to a pair of black sweats and a hoodie, put a pair of sunglasses in his front pocket, and began to pack quickly and as efficiently as he could. He gathered together all they could think of that would fit in his backpack: an extra pair of clothes, a flashlight, a pocket knife, a piece of chalk, a small hand mirror, a laser pointer, two snap and shake glow sticks, a ball of string, a small magnifying glass, a book of matches, four small rubber balls that had a very powerful bounce, two bobby pins, a lighter, an external battery and charging cable, a pair of black leather gloves, one chocolate bar, enough jerky for two days, and a full canteen of water.

In addition to all of that, he made sure he had the small silver figure that he always kept with him. He didn't remember how long he'd had it or where it came from, but he couldn't remember a time when he didn't have it. It was his good luck charm. Becky had said to remember to think like his character. He hoped that having it with him, like a totem, would help him remember.

Dalen crawled out his window onto the roof where there was an attached ladder built as an emergency exit in case of a fire. The rule was not to touch it unless in an emergency, but the rule was also not to sneak out of the house in the shadow of night to meet up with a man who can do real magic so you could pull a heist on a museum either, so down Dalen went.

The first few hundred yards were going to be the hard part of his exodus. Ms. Warren was still downstairs and might see him as he crossed the yard, and there was also a good chance of stirring up one of the neighbor's dogs. If they started to bark, it was likely he'd be seen. Dalen took his time making sure there was no one at the windows before he crawled out the window and onto the ladder. He had not gotten more than ten feet off his property when one of the neighbor's dogs noticed him. The dog knew him and would often run up to the gate to get pet, but the problem is that it often barked with excitement as well. Dalen pulled two strips of jerky from his pack and tossed them gently at the incoming mutt.

"There you go, buddy, now eat that and stay quiet." The dog was more than happy to chew on the meaty goodness for a bit, and Dalen slipped into the night.

Once he was far enough away not to be seen, Dalen pulled out his phone. His friends were still on the chat with him, and he thought that along the way they could cover the questions that they felt needed to be asked. Since Dalen was going, their attention switched to what was coming next. If Dalen was going to do this, he wanted to be clear about what he was going to do, why he was doing it, and who he was doing it for.

Travis was doing his best to be the resident Lore Master — to think of every relevant thing he could remember about the myths and legends that he knew. "Alright, this is something. More often than not, in all of the stuff I've read, it's the humans   who lie."

Dalen stopped in his tracks for a moment and then continued, "What do you mean, it's the humans who lie?"

"In most of the tales and myths on this kind of thing, most magical creatures either can't or don't lie. People do. If he is just a guy with magic, he might lie to you, but if it's a fairy or a genie, there is a good chance that what is said is true."

"A good chance?" Dalen was concerned about the chances of it not being true.

Travis grew solemn for a moment, "One of the only truths I know about any of this is that there is a difference between a myth and the truth that the myth was built on."

It was David who responded, "That's a good point. Myths, legends, and probably even religions are based directly on the point of view of the people who experienced it, which then change as they try to explain it — or the perception of how they understood it — to others. By the time it's written down, you are dealing with secondhand perception and no longer fact."

"Understood," acknowledged Dalen. "I'll keep both in mind."

As he ran to the alley, they stayed with him and gave him the last bits of advice they could think of. They planned to just stay in chat with him while he had his adventure, but the moment he stepped into the alleyway, the connection was lost.

For whatever reason, it had been decided that Dalen had to do this part alone.

4

A SMALL FAVOR
FOR A FRIEND

Just as Dalen made it back to the alley where he was supposed to meet with Mathias, static sizzled through the video call and it went dead. The air crackled around him, and a faint hint of ozone filled the air as if lightning had just struck nearby.

"Mathias! I am here," Dalen called out. Glancing at the unresponsive device in his hand, he then muttered, "What happened to my phone?"

"Technology and magic don't mix well." Mathias was standing next to Dalen, and it took Dalen a little by surprise because it seemed he had appeared out of nowhere. The fire in the banner he wore over his left shoulder was dancing with light and it cast light and shadows everywhere in the alley. "I am so glad to see that you chose to return. I had faith that you would do the right thing."

"Yeah. The right thing. I wanted to ask you a few questions before I agree to go through with this."

Mathias bowed deeply, "Of course, you do. Only a fool would attempt something like this and have no questions, and I imagine that you are no fool."

"Yeah, well ... I'm not," Dalen realized even as he said it that his response was more of a knee-jerk reaction and, as he did, all of the ideas that he and his friends had come up with on the way over drained from his mind. He needed to think. Becky's words came back to him, and he remembered that he needed to have his wits about him. It was an effort to do so, as if his mind didn't want to function, but her words continued to ring in his mind. He thought to himself, "How would my character handle this?" He reached into his pants pocket and touched the small figure of his character and, to Dalen's surprise, it helped him focus. His mind now clear, he remembered what he was going to ask. "Obviously, I came because I intend to help, but first, I have questions."

"I am proud of you. You must be something special. Most people, when they stand in a magic field strong enough to scramble technology, have their minds follow suit. Yet here you stand, still able to reason." Mathias's smile was hard to read. Part respect, but somehow it also felt dangerous.

"Wait. You expected me to be in a haze when I agreed to all of this? That sounds pretty sketchy." Dalen was proud of himself for catching that one, but Mathias didn't even skip a beat in his response, and that put Dalen's mind at ease.

"Not a bit of it. Once you have been touched by magic, you begin to attune yourself to it. Beyond that, though, I have begun to suspect that you are more than what you seem, young Dalen, and where I expected you to be able to think and respond, I am impressed with how much clarity you have. You are truly exceptional, and I am impressed." Mathias walked over and put his hand on Dalen's shoulder. "If it weren't for you, I would not be alive today. My very existence is due to your bravery and sacrifice. When this is all done, if your wish is to learn magic and to be as powerful as me, it would be an honor to give that to you."

Dalen's mind raced with the possibilities. He hadn't thought about the idea of taking power. He had planned on wishing for enough money so that Ms. Warren would never have to worry about the bills that had been building up, but if he had magic, then he could create everything that they would ever need. Not just in monetary terms, but he could create anything that he wanted, and no one would ever harm him or anyone he cared about ever again.

With another squeeze of the figure in his hand, he pulled his mind back to where he was and what he was doing. "That sounds amazing, but first I have to get this thing for you. This umm... What did you call it?"

"The Beads of Fire," Mathias said its name like it was supposed to mean something, and Dalen guessed that it did because, although Dalen had never heard of it, there was a part of him that immediately wanted it.

84

"Right. What is that?" This had been the question that everybody had on his way here. What was this item that was worth a wish and, even more importantly, what did he want with it?

"It is a mystical artifact from another time and another world. If they knew what they had, they would not be putting it on display. They would hide it. They would protect it ... which is what I want to do. The people who own it think it is protected, but they have no idea what to protect it from. Tonight, I am going to show you how easy it is for someone like yourself to just walk in and take it. It is not safe in the general public. Without question, some wouldn't hesitate to kill a hundred bystanders in that building if they arrived in the middle of the day to claim it, and they absolutely would not care if it meant the deaths of three security guards at night. Meanwhile, promoters of the display are putting up flyers and ads in newspapers and on television. Truly, it just depends on when those people find out where it is. No doubt, I am not the only one looking for it."

Dalen stared at Mathias with wide eyes. "That's concerning."

"It's more than concerning." Mathias continued, "If they get their hands on it, who knows what will happen?"

That brought Dalen to his next question. "Why? What does it do?" This was specifically the way Dalen wanted to ask this question because, besides the obvious question, it would answer a few other questions all at once, such as "why do you want it?" and "what are you going to do with it?"

"The Beads of Fire can transform the wearer. This transformation also amplifies the magic ability that is already inside. Once activated, great power is granted to them, far beyond what they had previously been able to wield. It was originally created to grant someone like yourself the ability to connect to a much more powerful and magical world; however, in the hands of evil men who are already magical, it creates something terrifying."

Creatures of myth and legend filled Dalen's mind and, with them, visions of terrifying monsters roaming the shadows and killing anything that moved. Again, Dalen squeezed the figure in his hand; it helped bring clarity and the world began to focus with him. "What are you going to do with it?"

"Nothing like those villains, I assure you." Mathias put his hand over his heart. "I wish to protect the Beads of Fire and keep them out of the hands of others who wish to cause harm to this world or any of the other worlds that the Beads of Fire are connected to. I give you my word of honor that that is the truth."

"Then why don't you go in and get it?" This was another of the questions on his list.

"That is an excellent question, and I was hoping you would ask. It is protected with an imaginative spell. Anyone who is as connected to magic as I am makes the Beads of Fire a possible danger, so it can only be claimed by someone who isn't fully attuned. Then that person must choose to give it to someone of the magic kind. It's a safeguard for the corporeal world."

"The corporeal world?" Dalen asked inquisitively.

"The physical world. What you call the real world. This one, specifically. The safeguard was put into place in hopes that the Beads of Fire could be entrusted to a mage such as myself by being granted the use of them, yet evil would not be able to get their hands on it."

"Then it is safe, right?" Dalen was mainly just hoping at this point.

"No. In the middle of any random day, numerous evil things could walk in, kill half of those there, and then threaten the other half unless someone hands them the beads. Once they have them, they can still kill everyone anyway. That is why I want to sneak in at night. There are only three guards down there, and my magic will allow you to walk right past them without them noticing you. I don't want them hurt; they are just doing their jobs, and they have no idea what they are guarding." Mathias smiled, and he leaned in as if to tell Dalen a secret. "You won't be seen on the cameras either. I don't want anyone to get hurt. Especially you. You are still the guy who gave his life to save mine, and I want to see you win in the end. I know that this must seem like a lot. I am sure there is a part of you that's scared. I remember being in your shoes. I was just a kid about your age when magic found its way into my life. I was scared and nervous. I didn't know for sure if I could trust the mage who helped me."

"What was he like?" asked Dalen, trying to pry any information he could out of Mathias.

"He was a lot like me actually. I had helped him when he was in trouble and, as a reward, he started me on my path. It's what made me offer to start you on yours. You remind me of me when I was your age. The point is that, at one point, I had to trust him enough to take that first step. What do I have to do to earn your trust, Dalen?"

"You can tell me what you are actually going to do with The Beads of Fire." Dalen expected him to again reiterate his whole protection speech. Instead, Mathias leaned in so that he and Dalen were looking eye to eye. The shadows of night intensified the hollows of exhaustion under the mage's eyes, and Dalen was struck suddenly, not only by the loneliness that was reflected in them, but that one eye was blue and the other violet.

Dalen took a step back without thinking. "Your eyes? They are the same as mine."

Mathias nodded, smiling. "Indeed! I was wondering when you would notice. It is a sign in this world of having an affinity for magic. Not so common, are they?" Dalen shook his head, even as a grin spread across his face. "You asked what I am going to do with the Beads, Dalen, and I need you to trust me." Mathias took a deep breath. "Okay," he began solemnly. "Somewhere in my training, I was being taught by something that you would recognize as a genie."

"An actual genie?"

"Let me be clear about this. The concepts that you hold in your mind of what a genie is are based on modern stories that took the idea from a much older set of stories, and those were connected to a specific religion. Those concepts are a part of people's understandings, perceptions, and beliefs. You asked me for the truth.

I have great respect for all religions of this world, and I would never disrespect those ways of faith by trying to say that I was referring to their corporeal understandings of a perception of an incorporeal being or entity."

Mathias stopped for a moment with a look on his face that suggested he was reviewing what he had just said. At some point, he agreed with himself and continued, "In simpler terms, yes, a real genie, but you may want to set aside what you think you know about them — all of it is based on what those people thousands of years ago experienced with the same kind of being I am talking about."

"Okay. I'm still amazed that you have met a real genie." Dalen squeezed his hand around the little figure in his pocket and tried to get his head back in the game. "Okay. Go on."

"My training with the Genie DeSalvo is why my magic is based on wishes. It's because it's genie magic. As I have explained, I am the right hand of the Genie DeSalvo and he has taught me much, but during my training, I lost a chance to work with a free jinn, who are not held to the common rules of a genie. With those beads, I can contact the jinn and finish my training."

Dalen could sense the honesty in his words. Mathias was mysterious more often than not, but at that moment, Dalen knew that Mathias had just laid the truth onto the table, and he decided to trust him.

"Okay, I'm in. Tell me what I have to do." Dalen switched gears now that he had decided to go through with it and was now focused on victory. "Here's a question: what do the beads look like?"

"They are a string of prayer beads made from sacred red fire opals — the rarest in all the worlds. They glint with any amount of light and reflect what looks like fire, which is how they gained their name. Indeed, each bead looks like a drop of living fire. Every eighth stone, there is a piece of black obsidian. This repeats in a pattern with the total being seven sets of seven fire opals, separated by seven pieces of obsidian.

"All you have to do is walk in through the front door. Head through the center of the museum and turn into the western wing. It is the crown jewel of the tour, so there will be banners and posters that will lead you directly to it. You will then lift the case, remove the Beads of Fire, put them in your pocket, and walk right out the way you came."

Dalen cocked his head to the side inquisitively. "It's going to be that easy?"

Mathias smiled, "I really can't get it across to you how useless those guards and cameras are to magic." He chuckled slightly to himself and then continued, "After that, you are going to bring them here and hand them to me."

"Okay," Dalen shrugged. "When I hand them to you, do I have to say something, like an incantation or something?"

"Yes, but the words are not important. You can say, 'Mathias, I grant you the Beads of Fire. May they help you find your path and allow you to finish your training' or you can just say, 'Here you go.' What matters is the Field of Intent."

It was Dalen's turn to laugh, "You make it all sound like instructions on how to make tea."

"Not a bit of it," Mathias scoffed. "Making and pouring proper tea is much harder than this, but I do see a problem."

Here it was. The other shoe, so to speak. Dalen had been waiting for a problem. He imagined something like he had to sell his soul, or give up his unborn children, or some other ghastly sacrifice that was now going to sour the whole thing. Contracts in blood, that kind of thing. "What problem?"

"You are going to have to start believing in the plan." Mathias looked through him to his core. "Believe in me and, above all else, you need to believe in yourself." Dalen was dumbfounded. This was not the direction he thought this was going to take. "I mean, come on, old chap! Where is that guy who walked into the fight last night? That guy knew his worth."

Almost offended, Dalen found his words, "I know my worth."

"If that is true, my friend, then why is it you are afraid? Why do you question how easy this will be?" To Dalen, Mathias felt like a teacher or coach, and before he could answer, Mathias continued. As he spoke, Mathias's enthusiasm swelled. "It's because you aren't sure if you are good enough to do it. Well, let me tell you something, Dalen Pax: You are. You are strong enough and brave enough. Do you feel me?" Dalen did. "I said, do you feel me?!"

"Yeah."

"What?"

This time, Dalen matched Mathias's tone, "Yes."

Mathias smiled. "Now say it again."

"Yes!"

"Now this time feel it. Who's got this?"

"I do."

"Now this time make it grow. Who's a badass?"

"I AM!"

"Who is going to be a sorcerer thief and hit a museum for a magic item on his first heist, like a badass?"

"I AM!"

"Who is powerful?" Together, they began to rise in energy and tone.

"I AM!"

"And who can stop you?!"

"NO ONE!"

"WHY?!"

"BECAUSE I AM UNSTOPPABLE!"

Mathias began a low sound and, as he changed the pitch, he crescendoed into a powerful scream. Dalen joined in, well into the beginning. Neither of them pulled back from it and gave their heart to the moment. When they stopped, they stood there, both out of breath, and looked at each other. Mathias seemed to be so familiar to him, but he couldn't place why.

"You're ready now, right?"

"More than ready."

"Not worried about whether it will be hard?"

Dalen thought about it and smiled, "No."

"This, my dear friend, is the beginning of understanding magic. You are only as powerful as you allow yourself to be. Your skills and your abilities and even your power are based on this concept. You first have to believe."

Dalen shrugged. "Well, you made a believer out of me. Let's do this."

"Wonderful." Mathias clapped his hands together in approval. "Meet me at the museum. When you leave here, take a moment and reconnect with your friends. I don't mean to block them, but your phone will work once you leave here. Talk with them. Let them know what's going on and then meet me at the park. Take the path that leads to the museum. I will meet you right where the park stops and the museum starts. We will go from there. Also, explain to them that while you are in the museum you won't be able to be in contact with them. The magic field that will hide you from the cameras will make your phone useless."

Dalen sheepishly grinned. "You knew about them, eh?"

"Indeed, I did. In the future, you should be extremely selective in who you share your secrets with."

"You don't have to worry," Dalen assured him. "I trust them completely."

"I know," replied Mathias. "If I'd considered them a real threat, I would've erased their memories of the event." It was spoken with such easy nonchalance that it bothered Dalen and made him question if there was a chance Mathias still would.

With that thought still in the back of his mind, Dalen stepped out of the alleyway and back onto the main street. As he did, his phone came back to life. It didn't turn back on like it had been turned off — it simply reactivated, and there were his friends' faces looking back at him.

"Sorry that took so long, folks, but I am back, and I am alright," Dalen said as he smiled and waved.

"What are you talking about?" Even though it was Becky who asked, there was a look of confusion on all their faces. "Your picture blinked out for only a second."

"Really?" Dalen glanced at the clock on his phone that confirmed that, from the outside world, no time had passed. "That blink was a lot longer for me." A flurry of responses all came at once and all conveyed the same sense of confusion. "I stepped into the alley and met with Mathias. He answered all of our questions, I agreed to do this, we had a little pep talk to get me going, and as I stepped back out of the alley, BOOM! I was dropped off at the same time I left." Again, they all spoke at once, this time with excitement. "I am now on my way to the Victory Museum of History, where Mathias will meet me, and I will start this quest."

Travis was the first to hold up a finger and begin to speak; as he did, the rest began to put up fingers.

"Are you alright?"

"I am better than that. I am stoked to do this." Victory Museum of History was located in the middle of Victory Park, the largest park in the whole town and a good ten-minute walk at a hurried pace, so Dalen started moving in that direction.

Adam was the next to respond. "This is so awesome! Are you going to stay online while you are doing the heist?"

"Sorry, my man. That is going to be a big no-can-do," Dalen shook his head and sighed, "but for two exceptionally good reasons." As Dalen continued, he made his way across town. It was late so there weren't a lot of people out, but Dalen still had to be careful as he crossed the larger streets, heading toward the park. "The first one has to do with how magic and tech don't mix. It's part of the reason why I lost you when I went into the alley. From what was explained to me, the magic Mathias is going to use to get me past the guards and unseen by cameras is going to make using my phone impossible." The group, as a whole, nodded in understanding but were still disappointed. "The second reason is

95

simple." Dalen leaned into the phone and made a face: "If you are going to commit a crime, do not broadcast it."

They all laughed at the truth of Dalen's words. The logic was sound and hard to argue.

"What can you tell us about your conversation?" As always, Becky was thinking about the next three moves, and the best way to plan the future was to understand the present.

"It was amazing!" Dalen jumped into the air and turned all the way around before he landed. "Mathias explained a lot to me. I'll try to sum it up but not miss anything." He spent the entire time it took to get to the park sharing everything that had happened. By the time he made it there, they were caught up and on board. There was concern about Mathias's comment about wiping their memories, but it seemed not to be an issue, so they chose to laugh it off nervously and continue. As he reached the edge of the park, they knew it was time to end the conversation. He promised to make contact again when it was over. They'd decided together that since Mathias's magic worked like a genie, each, in turn, would give him their wishes for good luck.

Adam went first because he was too excited to wait. "Dalen, my wish for you is that you have an amazing adventure. I wish that you grasp the reins of this adventure and truly run with it. Oh, and I wish that next time we all get to go as well."

Travis was next. He closed his eyes and made his wish: "Dalen, my wish for you is simple: I wish that you remain safe tonight and that you're not caught or get in trouble ... or end up cursed."

"That was an awesome wish, Travis!" Becky was like that: she believed in aggressive kindness, especially to those who had earned her respect. Travis had never treated her differently because she was a girl. He'd never been surprised by her skills in gaming due to her being a girl, nor had he ever used the phrase "for a girl" — like, you are pretty good at this, *for a girl*. Because he simply saw her as a person, she'd grown to care for Travis and was closer to him than anyone else. "My wish for you is in conjunction with that. I wish that you stay focused and be the brilliant adventurer we know that you are. Pay attention. Don't rush in. Use all the skills that we've been developing for the last year together." There was a long pause and David was about to start when she blurted out a quick, "And next time, we all get to go." There was another round of "Yeah!"

David waited until the cheering went down and then spoke from the heart: "Dalen, I've known you the longest out of everyone here. We share a room and a home. There are so many things that I could wish for, but for me this choice is simple. Dalen, my wish for you is that, no matter what happens, you live the next few minutes well."

Dalen thanked them and again promised to talk to them in a little while. He said his farewells and then turned off his phone. He was ready. He was packed physically and mentally prepared, and with the wishes of his friends in his heart, he was ready to go. He pulled up his hood, readjusted his pack, and headed off into the shadowy darkness of Victory Park.

He should've been worried about getting mugged or worse, but the rush he was already on was compounded by his friends and their over-enthusiastic sense of adventure. He felt like a character in one of David's stories. He crouched slightly so that he could move fluidly from his hips and knees. As he moved, he tried to stay out of the moonlight that was jutting through the branches like silver beams of light. "I must stay in the shadows," he whispered to himself. "I am a sorcerer thief on my way to a heist. I must not be seen."

He snuck past a couple on a date unseen by pressing himself up against a tree and standing motionless in the shadow of its leaves and branches, his head turned away to hide his face. He didn't move until they passed and, once they did, he felt assured that he was ready for whatever was to come.

Mathias was waiting for him near the end of the path where the park ends and the cement area that surrounds the museum began. It was circular with streetlamps about every twenty feet that illuminated the entire circle's outer edge. There were more streetlamps around the building as well, making the entire area visible even at night. Dalen crouched near some bushes for a few minutes, watching. Eventually, he saw a guard carrying a flashlight. Dalen waited for the guard to walk along the side of the building he was on and clear the corner before moving. It didn't seem to Dalen that Mathias was looking in his direction and was more focused on the guard, so he decided to sneak up on him. He took his time. Slowly, he moved closer and closer to Mathias. Just about the time that Dalen got close enough for Mathias to whisper and for Dalen to hear, Mathias spoke in hushed tones: "You disappear into shadow, and you can move without sound, but I can sense your presence with something other than my eyes or ears. You did well, but you cannot hide from me." He looked over his shoulder to where Dalen was and smiled. "Yet."

Dalen chuckled, "Fair." He walked over to stand next to Mathias. "Just practicing. You know, getting ready? I had to try."

"And you did quite well. If it weren't that I have magically known where you were since the beginning, I would've been incredibly surprised."

"Thanks," Dalen shrugged. "Okay. What do I need to do?" By this time, he was eager to begin.

"I am going to put a spell on you that will make it so that no one can perceive you." Mathias raised an eyebrow and then winked at Dalen. "This means you will not be seen and anything that tries to record you will fail to do so." Mathias changed his approach for a moment and tried to be specifically instructive. "This does not mean that you are truly invisible, and do not remove the Beads of Fire while they are directly being looked at by others. Others may not notice you, but because the Beads are as powerful as they are, they will be noticed if they are moved while someone is directly looking at them."

Dalen nodded. "Right. Unnoticed, but not invisible. Get the beads when no one is looking."

"All you have to do is enter the building and go get them. I will open the main door long enough for you to sneak in. When you get to the beads, just lift the glass of the case they are in, retrieve them, and then set the glass back exactly how you found it."

Dalen was still concerned. "Won't there be alarms?"

Mathias rolled his eyes at Dalen. "Yes, but the technology that would sense you and trip the alarms will be affected by the magic field, so they won't function and go off."

"Okay," Dalen sighed, relieved that magic was going to be doing a lot of the heavy lifting in this caper.

"Now pay attention because this is important." Dalen nodded. "This magic field is not going to be able to take the power of The Beads of Fire. If you activate them, the spell will fail. That means you will be able to be seen, and all of the alarms could go off."

"Right. Don't activate the powerful magic object." Dalen clapped his hands a couple of times and nodded, "Good note."

Mathias shook his hand vigorously. "I can't thank you enough. I have waited twenty-two years for this moment. I hope one day you will know how much this means to me. I am sure you will. Are you ready?"

Dalen bowed as he had seen Mathias bow. "You are very welcome. You've already done so much for me. It is an honor to do this for you."

"Do you wish for me to be able to get you in, and while you are in there, do you wish not to be noticed by the guards or cameras?" asked Mathias.

"Yes, sir, I do," replied Dalen.

And with that, Mathias reached out his hands toward Dalen but stopped short of touching him by several inches. Dalen watched in wonderment as the veins in Mathias's hands began to glow as if his blood were made of light. It spread to his hands and then, much like bubbles in a pot that begins to boil, small dots of light erupted from his skin and floated over to Dalen's body. The light quickened and, within a few seconds, light was pouring from Mathias's hand and saturating Dalen. The light dimmed and then faded from sight, but Dalen could still feel it as if it were an electrical current.

"You're ready." He pointed to the front door of the museum, "Now go."

Dalen raced across the open courtyard to the museum. As he reached the front door, he heard the satisfying click of the locking mechanism's release. With a fluid motion, he swung open the door and slipped inside. Dalen paused just long enough to give a two-fingered salute toward Mathias and then headed into the museum.

5

THE HEIST

It was late and most of the lights had been turned off for the evening. Dalen had been to the museum before, but it was a different place in the dark. There were a few lights in the hallways and main exhibit rooms for security purposes but, overall, the museum was filled with shadows. Dalen crept along the side of the entrance hall, clinging to the walls where he could until the hallway opened up into the visitor center. It was dark and spacious, but there was a glass roof and moonlight filled the center of the room, leaving the edges wrapped in darkness. Wafting like ghosts in those shadows, large banners hung from the ceiling to showcase the exhibit, *Treasures of the Desert*, which had been on tour for the last week.

Dalen made his way to the large information desk in the center of the room and took one of the pamphlets that were normally passed out to those who visited. Dalen wasn't sure when the next guard was going to come by and check on this room, and the pamphlet itself was only a couple of pages that unfolded into a map of the museum that pointed out where things were, so he decided to get out of sight for the time being while he got his bearings. He hid underneath the counter and started to read. It had a bunch of information about the tour and a thank you message from the curator, and then it described the exhibit.

About a year ago in the Arabian Desert, archaeologists discovered what they believed at first to be an unknown tomb. There had been no writing or glyphs on it, so the authorities had no idea whose tomb it was. The mystery grew from there because the tomb had been filled with many treasures, but none of them seemed to be connected to a specific culture or time; in fact, the treasures were not discernibly associated with any known culture or era. As a result, the find was now exhibited as the relics of an unknown civilization.

The next part showed a picture of the dig site, which was labeled *The Vault*. The chamber itself had no doors or tunnels into it. They'd had to break through the ceiling and rappel in to access it. It was as if someone had just bricked it off with no intention of ever retrieving the treasure within. When the archaeologists got inside and saw all of the treasure, they assumed it was a tomb, but they never found a sarcophagus or anything that suggested a burial. They hypothesized that there had to be another chamber that had not yet been found or possibly it wasn't a tomb at all, but if that was the case it only brought more questions. Why were these treasures buried in the middle of the desert? Who did they belong to, and where did they come from? The last page was dedicated to acknowledging everyone who gave donations to make this exhibit possible. Dalen fully unfolded the pamphlet and went over the map. Once he decided the path he'd take, he crept up from his hiding place, making his way towards his goal.

Dalen's path led him past the security office, and he cautiously peered around the door. Mathias had said that there were three guards. One was doing laps outside and, as Dalen looked in the office, he saw another who was sitting in a chair and watching a set of monitors, but Dalen could see in the reflection of his glasses that he was actually watching television.

Dalen smiled, "Only one more to locate." He wanted to keep track of the guards, despite Mathias's assurances. He could hear Becky in his head: "Just because you are invisible, it doesn't mean you slack on keeping track of the guards." He continued down the hall but kept his senses sharp.

Just before he got to the exhibit room, the other guard came strolling around the corner. Dalen pressed himself against a large window in the hall and held his breath.

The heavyset guard was humming some old tune that Dalen didn't recognize, holding out his flashlight while slowly swinging it left and right. He had an unkempt mustache and a small smudge of mustard on his uniform halfway down his shirt. He paused for a moment in front of Dalen before turning slowly, cocking his head with a look of suspicion. Dalen was sure he was caught as the guard moved directly toward him.

The guard stopped less than a foot from Dalen. However, he wasn't looking at him but rather slightly above him. The guard caught a glimpse of his paunchy, middle-aged reflection in the window and was now patting his chin with the back of his hand and stretching out his neck, trying to make his double chin vanish.

"Hello, ladies. I'm Roy," Roy burped a little but kept going like it didn't happen. He licked his pinky and index fingers and put them together at the center of his mustache; then, using his fingers as a brush, he attempted to straighten it. He grabbed his belt and then took what was clearly his attempt at a dashing pose. "Do any of you ladies need Roy to protect you?" With that, he flexed both of his arms but, in doing so, nearly blinded himself with the flashlight in his right hand, and he stepped back, rubbing his eyes.

Dalen was so appalled by what he'd just seen, he just stood there, waiting for his left eye to stop twitching in disgust. That was probably the grossest thing he had ever observed, and Roy's belly was so close to Dalen that he could smell the mustard. Going from the fear of being caught to witnessing "The Ladies Man" Roy was a little much, but this encounter did have one positive outcome: Even now, Roy was oblivious to Dalen's presence. This allowed Dalen to finally breathe.

Dalen reached into his hoodie's pocket and retrieved the small silver figure, shifting it from his right hand to the last two fingers of his left, which was also holding the map with his first three fingers. Like in the alleyway, his fear drained away and his mind cleared.

"You seriously don't notice I'm here, do you?" Immediately Dalen clapped his free hand over his mouth, but Roy just blinked back at his own reflection, oblivious to Dalen's presence. Dalen smiled and took a step forward. "I get it," he laughed out loud, amused by it all. "You can't see me because you are too busy looking at yourself in the reflection. It's like how I can't hear Ms. Warren when I'm on my phone." Roy continued to strike manly poses, attempting to look dashing. "My man, if you are going to win the ladies, you might want to lose a few," as he said it, he patted Roy's stomach.

Roy leaped back and frantically brushed at the spot on his abdomen as if he thought a spider was on him. Dalen jumped back as well. He pressed himself against the wall and hoped he didn't just break the spell. Roy lit up the floor around his feet with the flashlight and began to search around for whatever he thought had landed on him.

"That was too close," Dalen whispered to himself. "That was just straight-up stupid." Dalen laid his face in the palm of his right hand. "Rookie move, Dalen. Becky would not be amused."

He waited for Roy to finish his search and continue his circuit, but Roy just continued to stare at the floor, searching. "Okay," Dalen puzzled, trying to figure out how the spell was functioning. "So, because you can't acknowledge me, you are stuck concentrating on the floor until I move. I didn't think you'd be able to notice me. Is it because you can't see me or hear me, but you can feel me?" He began to move slowly around Roy, who was hopelessly lost in the woodgrain of a certain floorboard. Dalen's eyes glanced

106

at the map to make sure he was going the right way. He plotted his course, checked the signs that were at the corner of the T-section that Roy had just popped out from, and then glanced back at the map to verify. He had gotten his focus back and started feeling like his character from David's stories again. He glanced back at the silver figure he was still holding. "If this was one of David's games, it would be based on some sort of odd logic that makes perfect sense — like, you felt it because I chose to touch you." Dalen pondered that for a moment and then frowned. "But if that were true, why didn't you hear me when I directly talked to you? Let's see... You smell of mustard, Roy." At that, Roy stood up straight, turned around, and flashed the light right at Dalen.

Dalen stood as still as he could while Roy sniffed the air as if a new pungent smell had teased his nose and he was trying to detect it again. As he sniffed, the light from the flashlight fell off of Dalen and began to slowly creep toward Roy. The light inched its way up his legs to his abdomen until it rested on the stain. "That's where it's coming from," Roy scoffed and let his air out at once in frustration and started heading back toward the security office. "Perfect! They are going to smell it too, and once they see it, they'll know I was eating on rounds again. I hope I don't get in trouble like last time."

"That is interesting ..." Dalen was still talking to himself out loud, "He heard me, sort of. Almost subconsciously. I'm going to have to be way more careful." Pointing a finger at himself, Dalen scolded, "Bad. Bad Dalen. Stop poking the bear to see if the bear will notice." He turned down the proper corridor and tried to refocus on the task at hand.

Dalen followed the map until he came to the Southern Gallery. It was a large room with ceilings much higher than in the hallway, rising twenty-five feet or more. In the center was a beautiful stained-glass ceiling depicting a phoenix rising from the flames. The moon must have been directly overhead, or perhaps there were artificial lights, because above the stained-glass phoenix light as bright as daylight was pouring through it and casting its image onto the floor.

Displayed around the room were cases and pedestals, each with its own beautiful object of unknown origin. It was hard not to look and even harder to look away. Each one cried out in Dalen's mind to be looked at and pondered. He stopped at a glass case; inside was what looked to be a carved dagger made of sapphire with an ivory handle. The plaque on the case stated that neither the blade's tang, which ran the entire length of the dagger, nor the handle had tool marks of any kind. As he stared at it, he swore for a moment that he could feel it in his hand. He refocused and pulled his mind away with effort. This was not the treasure he was here for, and he hadn't yet finished what he had come to do.

On the pedestal to his right was a glass case that housed a gold coin roughly thirty millimeters in size. The plaque that was connected to the glass that encased it said that the coin was the only object found that had any writing on it, but there was not enough of the lettering to begin the process of deciphering it. What caught Dalen's attention was that the plaque referred to it as "The Dragon Coin," so named because where the face of a president or a king would normally be stamped, there was the face of a dragon. As before, Dalen felt as though he held it in his hand and a longing to take it swelled within him.

Dalen stepped back and took a breath. He stopped for a moment, putting the map in his pants pocket and sliding the silver figure into his glove so he still could feel it in his hand. "Okay, I have to remember what I am doing here." He focused on not looking at the items directly but only glancing at each thing peripherally so that he could find what he had come for.

Dalen made his way through the cases quickly but carefully. He passed one so large it encased what seemed to be a silver coach of some kind, but it had no rigging for wheels. To Dalen, it looked like it was a boat designed to be pulled by some aquatic animal.

Some cases were small and only held a single object on a stand, such as the one with the coin. Another of like size held a brooch that was made of three concentric circles of different metals, and another a single teacup with no handle. In one, there was a simple white marble, and in another, there was a beautifully etched crystal ball with strange symbols all over it. In the center of all of it was the prize of Dalen's quest.

Once he saw the Beads of Fire, Dalen couldn't take his eyes off them. They were more beautiful than Mathias had described. Each bead looked as if someone had taken a bit of fire and rolled it up in their hands like dough or molten glass into a bead twice the size of a pea. Each bead generated a faint glow of its own, and the case shone like a lantern. The line that held the beads together looked as if it was made of woven gold thread. As Dalen drew closer, he could see the detail of the beads. Each one was a gem of some kind that had been masterfully cut to have thousands of facets. It was impossible to hold still enough for it not to glint in some way. The very act of breathing was enough to change the eye's perspective; thus, the sparkle continued to dance and move as if it were alive, no matter how he looked at it.

Dalen felt odd, almost queasy, and his mind filled with fog until there was nothing. It seemed to last only a second, and then everything refocused.

After snapping back to what was going on around him, the first thought that Dalen had was to ask himself how long he had been staring at the beads. He blinked a couple of times and looked around, befuddled. 'What had grabbed my attention?' he asked himself. 'Had there been a sound?'

Entering the room were multiple individuals. Most of them were clad in navy blue jumpsuits with the museum's logo on their backs in white. Two armed individuals were in security uniforms that were different from the standard security of the museum. The two women who came in with them wore clothes that suggested they worked here in a more executive manner.

As a second surprise, and only after his brain had identified the possible danger, did he look around the room and realize it was dawn. Dalen could see out the window on the eastern side of the room that, past the courtyard, the sun had crept over the trees and was now pouring light into the room. Dalen stood there, stunned, unable to process the time loss. Several hours had gone by. As one of the women began talking, his mind was driven back from the depths of his thought and to what was going on in the present.

"Over the next week, Charlie, I am handing this project to you." Just looking at her, it was clear that she was the boss at the museum. The way the jacket and vest accentuated her form without restricting her suggested that it was tailored to her. The matching skirt was slightly longer than the knee and allowed her to move freely. The boots she wore covered everything the skirt did not. "The movers are here to remove the artifacts now and ship them off to their next stop on their tour, but next Monday we will be opening the South American exhibit here and it will be your responsibility to make sure that happens."

"Yes, ma'am." Charlie was obviously excited. She was a young woman with chestnut hair that was conservatively pulled back to keep it out of her face. Her dress was modest and simple.

"You have worked your way through hundreds of applicants to be able to do this post-grad work and, at 23, you are the youngest person to take on this responsibility. I expect great things from you, but the question is, do you think you can handle it?"

"Yes, ma'am," Charlie nodded. "I absolutely can do this. You can count on me."

"Oh, good. I can't afford to have people working under me who have no belief in themselves. Now, prove us both right." With that, she smiled, gave Charlie a wink, turned on her heel, and left.

Charlie looked around for a moment, her expression shifting from feeling exhilarated to overwhelmed and panicked, and then back to exhilarated. "Okay, guys, how long are you going to need to secure everything and get it ready to be shipped?"

"All the small pieces we can remove quickly, probably within three hours or so. The big coach thing will be removed last, once everything else is out of the way, and just because of the size it may take an hour by itself. You should have the room by noon."

"How are you going to move it all? I ask because I have a huge South American statue I have to put in here, and I have no idea how to get it down the hallway, let alone through the doors," Charlie was obviously embarrassed to ask but had no real idea how to solve the problems ahead of her for this exhibit.

The mover that had been speaking smiled and went over to the center of the room. Dalen had to move out of his way as he passed. He went over to the corner of the huge Persian rug that was centered in the room and lifted a corner that revealed some sort of metal plate underneath it. "The center of the room is an elevator. It goes directly down into storage. The north, east, and west wings are set up the same way, as is the visitor center. They built it that way for security reasons. That way they never have to move anything through the halls."

Charlie ran up and hugged him. "Thank you, thank you, thank you! I didn't know how I was going to do this." He didn't know what to do, so he just stood there with his arms out from his body, looking around the room for assistance. When she pulled her head out of his chest, he realized that she had been crying for a moment and had left two wet spots on his uniform. "I am so sorry!" Charlie tried to wipe it dry but realized that she was now just petting him. She pulled back in embarrassment and tried to change the subject. "I figured it was a test, right? See if I could handle the task. I figured there had to be a way, but I didn't know what it was, and I was sure I was going to fail." Her eyes again welled with tears, and she buried her face into the mover once more.

He finally gave in and hugged her back, patting her back as he tried to calm her. "Yeah, she likes trying to break the new ones." He took her by the shoulders and separated her from him while still looking her in the eyes. "That's how she figures out which ones to keep. If you don't break over a hard assignment, then she knows she can keep giving you the kind of work you want. We all face these challenges. Do you think I got to a place where I am trusted to touch and move priceless pieces of history, just because I'm good at lifting stuff?" Charlie stopped crying and began to listen. "It doesn't matter if it's hard — it matters who you are when things get hard. You know what you have to do; now seize your dreams." Then he let her go. He smiled but gently pushed Charlie back a bit.

She smiled and nodded, "Thank you." She took a personal moment and regathered her thoughts. She apologized for covering him in tears before addressing the others, "Alright guys, I'll get out of your way and come back after lunch." She left with new strength.

Dalen felt that strength, too. The mover hadn't been talking to Dalen — he didn't even know he was there — but he had inspired him nonetheless. This guy was right. Dalen waited for him to turn back toward him so he could see his name. Woven onto his uniform was a white patch with the name 'Carl' embroidered in the same navy blue color as his jumpsuit.

"Carl, you're right." Dalen got as close to him as he could without touching him directly. "I hope that you can hear this subconsciously. You are awesome. I don't know about the rest of your life, but you handled that like a champ, and I want you to know that someone saw it. You are a good man." Carl stopped for a moment. He looked back at the door that Charlie had just walked through. He took a deep breath in and smiled as he let it out. He only paused for a moment, and then he went back to his work. Dalen backed away from him a bit and started to create a plan. "Unfortunately, Carl, you gave me encouragement and an answer as to how I am going to get out of here, so I am going to be robbing the museum now."

The plan was simple. They were going to remove everything and take them downstairs. Once they were there, the contents would be removed from their cases and put into some sort of security container for moving them to their next location. Dalen would ride the elevator down into the secure storage as they removed everything. Once he was down there, he would wait until they opened the display case. As they did, he would take the beads without touching anyone. The spell was still working, so the moment he reached to take them, Dalen would have to find a way to distract everyone so that they would look away. The plan was foolproof, and Dalen prayed he was not the fool who would prove himself foolish to think so.

The first load was all the pedestals and light cases in the room. They were brought to the center of the room and placed on the elevator. When it was full, they pulled up the sides of the rug all around to ensure it did not get caught on anything. When

114

they were ready, one of the officers near the door opened a panel alongside the wall and activated the elevator. While all of this was going on, Dalen did his best to not get caught up in staring at any of the artifacts. He couldn't afford to get lost in them again. He noticed that nobody else seemed to have the same problem he had.

When the elevator got to the bottom of the floor, Dalen got off quickly and tried to maneuver himself so as to avoid bumping into anybody. As they unloaded everything, Dalen saw that there were more guards down here and a large big rig that was attached to a trailer with no markings.

A man with thick glasses and a white lab coat was going over a checklist with someone who was clearly the head of security. The man in the lab coat scanned each piece as it was brought to him with a small handheld device and compared it to the tablet that the head security officer held to confirm the item. Once it was confirmed by the security officer, the guy in the lab coat would then use a key to unlock the case. One of the security members would next remove the item from its display case and put it into a security box with a keypad. That box was then loaded into a crate and put on the truck. It was being done in steps with six people at a time. As one security member would take an item away, another would step up with a display case to be scanned. Any time that a case was open, there were three to four sets of eyes on it. Magic or not, this was going to be tricky.

Dalen huddled in the shadows about twenty feet away from the security team and tried to devise a plan. He had started to sweat, so he took off his gloves and wiped his brow. "How am I going to do this?" Even though the spell was up, Dalen was nervous and hiding. Whispering to himself felt safer than talking out loud. "This just keeps getting harder. Even with magic, I don't know if I can do this. Yesterday, I was Toad. I'm just a kid who is in way over his head." Speaking the words out loud made them real, even if they were whispered, and Dalen broke. He brought his knees into his chest and held them. Tears rolled down his cheeks as he imagined his life from here. After he failed, he was going to be seen and then promptly arrested. Being a foster kid meant that even if they didn't get him on anything other than trespassing and failing to steal something, they'd probably put him back in the system, and he'd be removed from Ms. Warren's house. Either way, he'd lose her and all of his friends. He'd destroyed everything he cared about.

Dalen decided that it would be much better to just turn himself in. The museum was still closed, and he was dressed all in black. There was no chance that he could say he was just lost and get away with it, but just trespassing was better than getting caught trying to steal, so he got up, wiped his eyes, and prepared to turn himself in. He bent over to retrieve his gloves and heard a clinking sound of metal on concrete, like a coin being dropped on the ground. When Dalen glanced at his feet to see what had made the sound, he found his silver figure looking up at him. It had slipped out of his glove when he picked them up. Dalen could feel it staring at him disapprovingly.

"Yeah, I know." This was an old habit from when Dalen was young. When he had nobody, he still had his silver friend, and he'd talk with him like a sounding board, working stuff out from time to time. "Pity Party of one, check please!" Dalen stared back at it. He knew that it wasn't real and that, in truth, he was just talking to himself, but it helped him think. "I'm just scared because this didn't go the way I expected it to." Dalen allowed his mind to fill in the conversation. "You're right. It's hard, but I can do it. This is that moment that Becky was talking about. This is where I need to use my head. This is where I have to think like my character." He picked up the silver figurine. "What's that? My character has always been me? Right." Dalen smiled as it dawned on him. "It has always been me. I don't have to try to be something I am not. I'm trying to be something I always have been." Dalen put his gloves back on with conviction and slid the figurine back into his left glove.

"I can do this!"

Dalen started walking toward where they were checking in the pieces. He had to time it exactly right. When he got close enough, the magic field was probably going to mess with the scanner and tablet. If he waited for the Beads to be put in a security box, the field may very well lock down the box permanently; he had to get it before then, so the best time to act was going to be the moment they opened the case.

The Beads of Fire were two objects back in line to be checked in. Dalen swung off his backpack and opened one of the small pockets on the side. He took out the four bouncy balls, closed up the pocket, put his backpack back on, and waited for his moment.

"Ah, yes. The crown jewels of the collection," sighed the guy in the lab coat and thick glasses. "The Beads of Fire. They are truly magnificent, aren't they, Emmerson?"

"They are shiny rocks, Mr. Jericho, nothing more," Emmerson's tone didn't waver from his flatline monotone that suggested he neither cared about the object nor the conversation being had.

"Then you have rocks in your head if you can look at them and say that," Mr. Jericho's frustration at Emmerson's lack of enthusiasm as he scanned the display case seemed to be almost personal.

Emmerson found the scan on his tablet and marked it off as he spoke, "Look, I don't care about rocks. I don't care if they sparkle. Diamonds are compressed carbon. Before they sparkled, they were coal. At least coal has a purpose. I understand that most people think different," he paused just for a moment as Mr. Jericho unlocked and opened the display case, "but my security team gets multi-million-dollar jobs because we are trained to think this way."

"What the heck is that?!" exclaimed one of the guards who'd been holding the case for the Beads of Fire as four small, bright green bouncy balls seemed to appear out of nowhere as they hit the floor and careened high into the air. It was a curious thing. No one was sure where they had come from. As they bounced again, they scattered in four different directions, causing a few of the guards to go investigate.

"That was odd," Mr. Jericho just watched the balls bounce off with a puzzled look on his face. After a moment, he shook his head and looked back at the empty case. "Where were we? This case is number 63121."

Emmerson checked his tablet but the screen was blank. Emmerson tapped it twice to wake it up and the screen came back to life. "Yes, I have it here marked as received. What's the next item?" They had continued with their work through two more items when a security guard returned with the four balls.

"I retrieved all four of them, sir." She held them out for him to inspect.

Emmerson looked at her with professional disregard.

"Report."

"There are four standard bouncy balls. They seem to be mundane and not a threat. Three of them were simple to retrieve but the fourth was the reason it took me so long. Sir."

Emmerson reached into one of the many pockets on his vest and pulled out a voice recorder. "Note to self: remind the team not to bring playthings into the workplace. Fire whoever did." He turned off the recorder. "Are these yours?"

"No, sir. I like my job too much to do anything so foolish. Sir." She responded in the same tone that he had used in speaking to her.

"Good. You may go back to it," he stated in dismissal.

Dalen sat behind some boxes on the far side of the elevator, trying to slow down his breathing and heart, which was pounding in his chest. He sat there for what seemed like forever, but once his adrenaline stopped pumping through his brain and slowed to the point that he could think, he looked over at his right hand and began to laugh to himself. The Beads of Fire were glowing in the palm of his hand, and he could feel the warmth through his glove.

He waited there until they finished unloading the elevator, as he planned to ride it back up for his escape. He was just about to get into position when he heard one of the security members mention that he saw a light in Dalen's direction. Dalen remembered Mathias's warning that the magic was strong enough to overcome his spell. Dalen knew that he was going to have to hide the light or possibly get caught, so he coiled it around his right wrist and pulled his sleeve over them to douse out the light. He decided to get up and into position. As he did, the two security guards who were getting on the elevator saw him.

"Who are you?" They were alarmed and started to shout. "Hey, we got someone!" They both reached for their guns and trained them on Dalen. From behind them, Dalen could see the others looking over and moving in his direction.

Dalen already knew what had happened. Wrapping the beads around his wrist had somehow activated them, and the spell that was keeping everyone from noticing him had been negated. He thought to himself that he had done so well, only to trip now at the finish line.

Dalen froze, not knowing what to do. He knew he was caught and there was nothing to be done. He put his hands in the air, knowing what would be next.

Then the strangest thing happened.

Time seemed to slow from Dalen's point of view. The guards had started to direct him to get on the ground, but Dalen could no longer understand their words. Dalen sensed what they wanted, but it was no longer direct input from his eyes and ears. It was more like an impression of an idea, much like trying to read in a dream: Dalen understood what they were saying but didn't hear the words. The men and women of the security force had sprung into action and were making their way to him, but their movements seemed to slow to a crawl. Behind them, Mr. Jericho and Emmerson were both calling out orders, but time had slowed so that Dalen couldn't even make out what they were saying anymore.

Time finally stopped completely, and Dalen began to ask himself questions like, "How did this happen?" and "Am I going to be trapped this way?" He knew that it was the Beads of Fire that must have stopped time, but he had no idea how it happened and whether or not he could ever get time to start again. He thought about taking off the Beads of Fire, but he was concerned that if he did, he might be trapped like this forever, and if time started moving again, he was still about to be arrested. Panic was starting to creep in as Dalen caught something out of the corner of his eye. Time had stopped, but he was not the only thing still moving.

6

THE JINN

Dalen could do nothing to conceal his terror as he stared at what looked to be a woman with red skin. The sheer material that scantily covered it suggested a harem girl of some sort, and it glowed much like the embers of a dying campfire. Its hair was brilliant and looked as if it were made of pure fire. Stones that resembled the Beads of Fire ran down its body, radiating light. There was one in its hair at the top of its head, and Dalen could see one in the center of its forehead. One was on its throat; another was over its heart. A stone was nestled over its solar plexus, and yet another rested lower over its abdomen.

"Hi there," it quipped as it looked around, taking in the security officers who were frozen in place. "Looks like you could use my help."

Dalen was stunned and stood frozen with his mouth open. Whatever it was, it cocked its head to the side and waved at him, with one flaming eyebrow raised in amusement.

Dalen finally managed to croak out, "Who are you? What are you?"

"Silly boy." It shook its head and smiled at him and, when it did, its smile somehow warmed Dalen's heart. "I'm the jinn that is connected to the beads you are wearing."

This was far beyond what he had expected or planned, and fear gripped him while all of the potential scenarios of how bad this could go raced through his mind, which screamed at him to run, but all he could do was stare at the jinn as it approached him. Dalen tried to focus, but his mind was desperately trying to remember what Travis had said about jinn. Besides, he wondered if he could even run from something that powerful. He envisioned an almost cartoon scenario where every way he tried to run or even look, the jinn was standing there, waving at him or batting its eyes at him playfully.

"Dalen, I am going to need you to focus on this moment, and yes, if you tried to run, I would be there." Its voice was soothing, but the idea that the jinn could read his mind terrified him even more. The jinn was not standing; instead, it was hovering about a foot and a half off the ground. It glided right next to him and stroked his hair. "You see, I am not here physically. The Beads of Fire are allowing your mind to make a connection to me and, as long as you wear them, I am also connected to you, so I can hear and see your thoughts as if they were small realities that you   are living."

Still gripped in fear, Dalen continued to stare, slack-jawed, and did his best not to pee himself. The jinn was linked to him, and it couldn't just hear but also see his thoughts. All he could muster was a terrified, "What?"

"Dalen. This will not do." The jinn placed its left hand on the stone in the nape of its neck and, with its right hand, it moved from stroking Dalen's hair to placing its index finger in the center of Dalen's forehead. "Relax," the jinn commanded.

As the jinn let go, the fog of panic dissipated, and Dalen's mind cleared. He was still wary of the situation, and he was conscious of the possible danger, but now it was on the same emotional scale as being aware of gravity.

"Thank you. This is so much better," Dalen acknowledged, and the jinn smiled and gave an exaggerated bow. "What did you do?"

"I temporarily relieved you of an instinctual anomaly." It gave a more modest bow, yet it conveyed a greater sense of sincerity.

"Amazing." Dalen felt calm, but not lethargic.

"You're welcome. Enjoy it while you can — it's only temporary."

"Wait, only temporary?" Now that fear was out of the way, the thinking part of Dalen's mind was curious.

"Yes. Your entire system will be fighting it. Your mind

wants to work the way it is used to, whether or not it is good for you. Besides, I would never change anything permanently without you wishing for me to do so. I don't mess with free will."

"You don't? Why not?" Dalen was pleased to see that the jinn was willing to answer questions.

"Oh, Dalen," the jinn smirked, observing the guards that were pointing their firearms at them. Languidly, it bent lower, looking down the barrel of one of their guns. "Your free will is one of those real inalienable rights that has been gifted to you by all that created all. Even the gods don't mess with free will."

Dalen could now remember all that his friends had told him that night. He pressed his left palm against his leg so he could feel the silver figurine. He had made a few mistakes tonight, but now he was here. It was time to make Becky proud.

"Okay. Fair enough. What about these guys? Is not freezing them into place messing with their free will?"

The jinn stood up with a shocked look on its face, one hand over its heart, "I would never." It then smiled warmly at Dalen. "Their free will and sense of time have not been altered in any way. You, on the other hand, chose to wear the Beads of Fire of your own volition, which allows its wearer to see the moments between the moments." Dalen had barely formed the next question when the jinn began to answer him. "What does that mean? Well ... corporeal minds can only perceive so much information at a time — little slivers of time, much like frames in a film. On average, a corporeal mind perceives this corporeal reality at about twenty-five to fifty of these frames a second." It paused for a moment to make sure that Dalen was keeping up. "So, if a corporeal brain perceives reality at such a rate, how many frames per second are happening in truth?"

Dalen realized it was a rhetorical question, but he was curious and so he took a guess: "A hundred?"

The jinn's eyes and hair grew in brightness. "Thousands upon thousands." It leaned up against one of the guards and crossed its arms. "They are still moving, you know? Just at a much slower frame rate than us right now."

Dalen was amazed by this revelation. He took a moment to let that sink in while the jinn explored the room. Dalen cleared his thoughts and decided to start this conversation over from the beginning, "I am sorry. You caught me off guard, Ma'am, and I was terribly rude." He laughed nervously, "Gripped in fear and all. It's a pleasure to meet you."

The jinn acted as if it had tasted something delicious as it relished Dalen's greeting. "Pleasantries! Oh, how I have missed pleasantries. More often than not, when my kind has the opportunity to speak to someone from this corporeal world, it is always, demand this, wish that. So rarely am I afforded the courtesy of pleasantries! I almost do not want to ruin the moment, but I should tell you," the jinn stated while looking down at itself with a grin, "I am not a *ma'am*'"

"I am terribly sorry — I did not mean to offend!" Heat rushed to his cheeks, yet Dalen was not sure what to call it if not *ma'am*.

The jinn traversed the distance between them almost instantly and was once again floating in front of Dalen in all its glory. "My friend, I identify as jinn, and I am not a corporeal being. I do not have a physical form. What you are seeing is the closest thing your mind can perceive to what is truly happening. When you picture a ball in your mind, there is no physical ball that is being seen with your eyes. Your corporeal eyes are just an organ that translates light into electrical impulses. The picture of what you see is an image being drawn in your mind one frame at a time.

"Now pay attention because this is where it gets fun. As an incorporeal being, I do not have an actual form. If I did, I would imagine it to be close to a maelstrom of light and smoke that can shift from being smaller than an insect to larger than your sun. Your mind can't process that I'm talking to you in this room, so it has to create something from its known experiences — really, it is much like when you dream. At this time, this is the closest thing your mind can conceive to what I truly am." It looked at itself admiringly, "Which brings me back to my point: this is not what I am. This is what you imagine me to be." The jinn stroked its arm and, as it did, Dalen saw that it also had stones like the others in its palms. It ran its fingers through its hair and squealed just a little. "I do say, well done, Dalen, but as you can see," smirking, the jinn floated back to the ground and struck a sensual pose "...this is not the body of a *ma'am*."

"Again, I meant no offense. I know *ma'am* can be based on age, but that is not what I meant. I didn't mean to imply that you are old."

"Clearly, you aren't getting this incorporeal thing, are you, Dalen? Age, like time, does not affect me, just like you are not affected by the direction *left*. I am not the age this image seems."

Dalen knew that he was missing a part of this equation that would make it make sense. "How old are you?"

"Dalen, I am not affected by 'time,'" the jinn repeated, making quotation marks with its fingers. "Officially, from your perception, I have only existed since you activated the Beads of Fire, so I guess you could say that I am about three minutes old."

"Did you exist before I activated the Beads?"

"Yes and no. I have existed throughout time as a constant. Asking me if I existed before I existed is still dealing with time. If you are going to grasp this, you have to let go of corporeal thinking."

"Okay, I can do this." Dalen took a moment to gather himself and pressed his hands together so he could feel the silver figure in his glove. "So, since you exist outside of time, you are not directly affected by it, so you have no age. You are older than the universe yet have only existed in this form for about three or four minutes now."

"Now we're cooking." The jinn smiled and pointed to its form, "And what about this?"

"You aren't real in the sense of physically being in this

room," Dalen scrunched up his face, thinking extremely hard. "Are you even female?"

"Male and female are corporeal constructs, but I do admit I like this form." The jinn looked off to the side at a space where Dalen perceived nothing, "For now, let's just stick with *her*, eh? This whole, 'the jinn' this and 'the jinn' that has grown tiresome, and I am not fond of being referred to as 'it,' if you don't mind?"

Dalen glanced back to where she had been looking but didn't see anything. "Who are you talking to?"

She looked back at him and smiled broadly, a twinkle lighting her already bright eyes, "That one may be too big to grasp for now but ask me again sometime."

That response felt true to Dalen — both that this may not be the time to ask about everything, but also that when he was ready, Dalen felt that she would explain. "I can respect that, and I trust your judgment. Okay, so what's your name?"

"You really need to wrap your mind around this incorporeal thing, Dalen. My name is this," she put one finger on the stone on her throat and her other hand on the stone on her forehead. As she did, she made a sound with her mind. Dalen's mind opened wider than he ever imagined it could, and he perceived the vastness of space and time made bare before him. Throughout all of it was a force made up of light and thought. As Dalen looked at it, he could feel enormous power radiating from it. At first, he thought that he was outside of it but, as he looked all around, he could see that he too was engulfed in this cosmic energy flow of power that filled the universe with light. The amount, the force, the size of it was overwhelming.

Dalen was then pulled to its center. There, in the middle of it all, was a sense of perfect calm. The energy pulsed and stormed all around, but even as it pushed and pulled, this place of peace was unaffected. The energy passed through, the peace and control of this perfect place untouched within the chaotic maelstrom of universal flow.

Dalen's mind closed back to something that could be recognized as normal. The jinn smiled and tousled his hair. "Spoken communication is a corporeal thing. Lisa. Steven. Those, like every other word in every language, are just agreed-upon grunts that you use to communicate. If you ever reach a true understanding of what it means to be a jinn, I will tell you my name."

Dalen had no choice but to let tears fall from his eyes. What he had experienced was bigger than his physical body. "What the hell was that? I mean... What?" Whatever he had just experienced was intensely real to him. He was once again in the basement of the museum, but his entire system was no longer sure if this place was real; wherever he just was, was very real as well, and Dalen's mind was having a difficult time separating them, much like waking up too fast from a vivid dream. It was abstract, but he understood it completely. This was nothing like what he expected but so much better than he could have ever hoped. He wanted to know more. He wanted to understand what was happening around him, to him. "I wish I truly knew what it meant to be a jinn."

She smiled and hugged him, her embrace warm and caring.

"Dalen. Oh, sweet Dalen. That's what I was hoping to hear." She closed her eyes and took a deep breath in. "As you wish."

Dalen was shocked yet excited, and he hugged her tighter. "I get wishes?"

She squeezed him back and then pulled back far enough so that she could talk to him face-to-face. "Pleasantries, my dear Dalen, go a long way."

"I only get three, right?" Chances were good that he may only get one, Dalen thought to himself, but it couldn't hurt to ask about more.

"I see you know the legends," she smiled and turned to face the chaos of the guards and guns that were still creeping along at a speed that Dalen could not perceive. "This must be some time after the new Mayan Calendar. The room that I kept all my personal belongings in wasn't to be uncovered until then." She moved past the armed guards and looked at one of the items in a case. As she floated further down the hall, Dalen could see that she had stones in the arches of her feet as well.

"I am trying to understand," Dalen said, following her. "Why does an incorporeal being have a room full of corporeal things?"

She turned with a gasp and gave him a hurt look, "What? Am I not allowed to have nice things?"

"No," he blurted, then paused for a moment before stumbling on. "I mean, yes, of course, you can have nice things.

I meant... No, that's not what I meant." He couldn't tell if she was teasing him or not. "I meant, 'What use do you have for such things?'"

"I know, sweety — I am playing. Try to remember that we are friends now, and I am on your side." She smiled at him to ease his concern, "You don't need to be afraid of me just because I am an all-powerful jinn."

"I'm so sorry. I don't mean to be rude," Dalen stammered as fear began to fill his mind once more. He didn't want to disappoint everyone, but he felt like, somehow, he was failing.

"Can I ask you something?" Her tone was kind, and Dalen nodded. "If you had to drive nails into a board, would you use an apple to do it?"

It was one of the oddest questions that anyone had ever asked him, and it caught him off guard. He scoffed and replied, "Of course not."

She cocked her head to the side and asked, "Why not?"

Dalen thought that the answer was obvious. "Because the apple is too soft — it would only drive the nail into the apple. It is completely the wrong tool for the job."

"Right." She crossed her arms and dropped her hip to one side. "Then why do you keep relying on fear? It's the wrong tool for the job."

Dalen opened his mouth to say something but shut it again.

He knew he didn't have any kind of argument to counter her logic.

"And he listens. This keeps getting better and better." She paused for a moment and pointed directly to Dalen's left hand: "You know that silver figurine in your glove?"

Dalen reflexively clenched his hand around it, as he responded, "Yeah. What about it?"

She reached in the direction of the security boxes and, when she brought her hand forward, she was holding the gold dragon coin. "Trade you."

Dalen answered without thinking, "No, thank you."

She almost looked surprised. "Oh, come on. Yours is made of silver, and this is made of gold."

Dalen clenched his hand tighter. "It doesn't matter what it's made of; I'd rather not trade."

She floated toward him and held the coin up for him to look at more closely. "It's a magic coin," she added enticingly, though Dalen simply shrugged noncommittally in response. "It is a promissory note that guarantees a conversation with the Golden Dragon of the East, the wisest being on any corporeal plane," she explained further.

Dalen thought about that for a moment. Thoughts like "dragons exist" and "I could get to talk with one" clouded his mind for a moment, but Dalen felt the small silver figure in his hand and, in his heart, he knew the answer. "That is an amazing offer, but I am going to have to decline. This little thing means more to me than any magic object you can offer. The value of it is priceless."

She smiled at him and waved her hand, and the coin was gone. "Does that answer your question about why I have these things?" She winked at him and headed over to the rest of the boxes. "So, I am sure you understand why I will be taking all of this back."

Dalen nodded. He trailed behind her while she made her way back to Mr. Jericho and Emmerson. "Won't they notice that everything is gone?"

The jinn winked at Dalen. She took off the thick-rimmed glasses that Mr. Jericho was wearing, cleaned them on Dalen's hoodie, and put them back on his face. Dalen following close behind, she moved over to a garage door next to the truck they were loading. She extended her arm and then gently moved him out of the way as the door swung open.

Time once again moved in the room as it usually did. The security guards moved as one toward the elevator while two of them called out that they had lost the target. Moments later, five men, masked and hooded, rushed into the room through the open door. Each man was heavily armed. The guards didn't even notice the thieves that had just entered.

"Oh, I think that they are going to notice later on, but they will be looking for these guys, not you," she chuckled as she floated out the door.

"What about those men? Your things? What are you going to do?"

"Those men are a part of your wish. They are no more corporeal than I am, but they will be a rational explanation for why everything is gone."

"That seems like a long roundabout way to cover your tracks," Dalen mused, confused as they moved from the back of the delivery area toward the park while they spoke.

"If I had just made the items disappear, there would have been a lot of questions and investigations, but more importantly, every person in that room would then have to come to terms with it. Their minds would wrestle with it for days. A few of them could even become ill because of it."

"They would become ill? Is that a side effect of being around magic?"

She shook her head. "No. It is one of the side effects of messing with someone's free will. If you convince a devout follower of a religion to doubt their faith, they go through what many call a 'crisis of faith.' Do you follow?" Dalen nodded his head. "If you make someone doubt their reality, it can have the same kind of effect on their mind, body, and soul. It's one of the many reasons I do not mess with free will. You let certain people see magic, it can break their whole world's foundation; they crumble."

Dalen was overwhelmed with all of this information. He'd walked to the trees at the edge of the park before he spoke again,

"Alright, so their minds can completely accept a bunch of guys breaking in and robbing the place."

"Exactly. Sure, some of them will have a few bad nights and some nightmares, but they will be okay. So much better than having their mind crumble into insanity." She stopped and turned to look at him, "There's just one more thing you have to deal with."

Dalen raised an eyebrow at her. He was kidding but, with a very suspicious tone, he asked, "Okay, what do I have to do?"

"In a moment, the individual who sent you into the museum to begin with will be upon you, and he is going to want you to give him the Beads of Fire and, in effect, me along with them. You're going to have to decide what you're going to do about that." She pointed to Dalen's left and, when he looked over to where she was pointing, he could see that Mathias was making his way over to Dalen through the trees. "I am right here if you wish for me to handle this."

Dalen looked back at the jinn. He had just met her, and she was the most amazing being he had ever met. He wasn't ready to say goodbye. *Besides*, Dalen thought to himself, *I have to keep her around long enough to meet David and everybody else.* "Do you know this guy?" he asked her.

"Yes. I met him another life ago. He will do what is needed to get the beads, I have no doubt. Remember, though, he cannot take them; you have to give them to him willingly."

"He has been a friend. He saved my life. He said if I give

136

him the beads, he will grant me a wish," Dalen was conflicted, but she knew him and might be able to give him insight on what to do.

"The only person that he can grant wishes to is himself. You meeting him was no accident. He needs someone to get him the beads. You think he is doing you favors, but all he is doing is putting pressure on you so that you'll decide to give them to him willingly." She sighed and added, "To keep things in balance and allow you to make a fair choice, he has even offered a reward too good to pass up. I tell you now that if it fulfills his own wish, he will give it to you, but at the price of everything else."

Dalen didn't like the sound of that at all, and all of his worries and concerns flared up. "What do you mean? Everything else?"

There was no time to answer because, even as Dalen asked the question, Mathias called out to him. "There you are!" The concern in his tone was genuine. "Why didn't you come out right away? I lost you for hours! Were you trapped somewhere? I was so worried. It didn't happen like this before."

Dalen tried to stall because he was still unsure of what he wanted to do. "What didn't happen like this before?"

Mathias rushed up to him and hugged him, "That doesn't matter right now. The only thing that matters is that you are alright." Mathias began to pat Dalen down. "You are alright, aren't you?"

Dalen released himself from Mathias's grip and stepped

back a bit. "Yeah. Yeah. Yeah, I'm fine. Thanks for checking."

"I saw those thieves come around to the back and then I could sense you again, so I thought I should check. Did you get the Beads of Fire?"

Dalen took another step back. "Yes, I got them, and thanks for telling me if I looked at them directly, they might lock me into staring at them for hours."

Mathias matched Dalen's step backward with a forward one of his own. "Is that what happened? I promise you that I had no idea that would happen."

"That's true, by the way," the jinn added. "He was not expecting that at all at this time."

Dalen stepped back again. "It's alright. I made it out in one piece."

Once more, Mathias matched his movements. "Then can you please give me the beads?" Dalen took a few steps back, but Mathias continued to follow him, his anger rising. "Why are you backing away from me? I thought we had a deal. You aren't backing out of our deal, are you?"

Dalen put his hand out in a stopping motion, "Whoa there, friend, I just need a minute to think is all."

"What's there to think about?" His voice swelled with fury, "You give me the beads and I give you a wish, and we walk our separate ways." Mathias moved toward him aggressively. "You are ruining everything! It's not supposed to be this way! I have waited all night! You were supposed to give me what I want, and you get what you want. I don't want to hurt you, but I am going to make you give me those beads." Something dark flared in Mathias's eyes, and fear poured into Dalen.

Even as Dalen called for the jinn to help, she appeared next to him and asked, "Do you wish for me to handle this?"

"I wish it."

"You wish what?" Dalen could see it in Mathias's eyes: Mathias knew he had activated the Beads of Fire. "No. Tell me you didn't." But it was too late.

Dalen lost all control of his body. Something entered his mind and pushed him aside. It was violent and terrified Dalen to his core. He had been rendered helpless. All he could do was stand back in his own mind while something or someone took control of his body. It surged with raw power, and he felt himself float off the ground. He screamed in his head as loud as he could but was only met with the deafening sound of silence echoing back at him.

Mathias fell to his knees. "Please, I beg you!" Tears poured from his eyes and his words choked as he spoke. "Please. Don't leave me again. I have come back for you. You can't imagine what I have been through to get here."

The jinn's words came from Dalen's body as he hovered over the foliage. "I am going to train him instead. What you seek will not bring back those you have lost. You can't bring them back. Do you really want him to do it your way? There is still a chance for him. He can still save his loved ones."

Mathias clenched his fist in rage and shook it at Dalen. "But what about me?!"

"I'm sorry, old friend. It is too late for you. You are already as lost as those you wish to recover. It's over. Dalen has a chance to make right what you have done."

"He doesn't know what I know. I can fix this. I know I can. Please, just let me fix things." Dalen could feel Mathias's pain as if it were his own. Whatever happened, it had left him broken and alone.

Dalen's feet touched the ground, and he watched himself walk over to Mathias and help him up. "You never grasped the whole incorporeal 'not a part of time' thing, did you?"

Mathias looked up and met the jinn's gaze.

The jinn spoke through Dalen with compassion, "It is too late. The chance that you could help them does not exist anymore." Dalen's body reached out and held Mathias's face in his hands. "And the next time you shift through time or space, neither will you, my old friend." Mathias's eyes widened when he realized the truth of it. "I send you much love. Goodbye."

When Dalen's body let go of him, Mathias knelt in stillness for a moment. Then resolve mixed with defiant rage overtook him, and he screamed at both of them, "I'm not done yet! I will make him give them to me. I will have them again! You'll see!" He stood and turned his back on them but looked back and, with a quietly determined voice, he said, "You'll both see." He ran off through the wooded park muttering to himself how it would never be over.

When he was gone from sight, the jinn separated herself from Dalen, and his mind became free. He was once again in charge of his own body.

"What the hell was that?" Dalen was filled with exhaustion, as if he had run ten miles. He could barely stand. He allowed himself to crumple to the ground and just lay there for a moment.

"You wished for me to handle it. I don't have a corporeal body. How else was I going to talk to him, if not through you?" She knelt beside him. "I had to possess your body for a short while. Don't worry. Your strength will return in a bit."

Dalen was shocked by her response. "You possessed me? Like a demon?"

"Yes. Just like a demon except, unlike a demon, I waited until you wished for it."

Dalen was neither happy about what happened nor at how easy it was for her to agree that it was like demonic possession. "Are you a demon?"

She wrinkled her nose as if the idea were disgusting to her. "No. I am a jinn. There is a difference." Dalen still needed a moment to catch his breath, so he asked her to continue. "Alright, I am going to use some truly basic, blanket terms to try to explain this." She cleared her throat, "Create a sliding scale in your mind. This scale is a representation of 'beings that are from the divine realm.' On the far end on one side, you have a positive extreme. In this extreme positive position, you might call the beings angels. On the other side, you have the negative extreme; there, you would call those beings demons. Jinn are neutral. We exist exactly in the middle of that scale. A neutral demon or angel, if you will. Yet, in truth, I am neither and both. To try to compare me to either would be like if I asked you if a staircase went up or down."

That took a moment to congeal into an understanding of what the jinn was explaining. "Okay. I can work with that. Could you not possess me anymore? It was ... traumatic." He lay motionless for a moment, looking up at the trees.

Her face swung into view as she bent over him. "That is only because you weren't ready or used to it. Besides, no-can-do. That's how this works. If I am going to manifest a wish you make, I have to do it through you. You are my avatar in this corporeal world. We are a team. You make the wish; I make it happen."

That was not the answer that Dalen was hoping for. "Is there any way around that?"

"Sure," she smiled slyly at him and raised a single eyebrow. "Stop making wishes."

7

THE PLANS
MADE TOMORROW

After Dalen finished his call and left the chat to enter the museum, David and the others had stayed online and talked. During the first hour, they joked and laughed about all the possible thrills and spills Dalen might be facing. During the second hour, they eagerly awaited the moment he returned to the chat, or left a message, or something. During the third hour, they allowed themselves to start to worry. Worry turned into fear and, once that happened, their imaginations played in the shadows of all the horrible things that could have gone wrong.

They agreed to meet at Adam and Travis's house at first light, and each of them signed off one by one, but each of them kept their phones with them, just in case he tried to reach anyone. None of them slept. Their minds were filled with the nightmares of doubt.

When dawn broke, they each got ready as if they were going to school and then made excuses to their families for why they needed to meet up before class. Surprisingly, the first one to arrive was Ben. When Becky arrived at the house, he was standing outside, waiting. He had his shoulders scrunched and his hands in his coat pockets. The poor kid looked like he had been out there for a while.

"Good morning," he greeted her, shivering with cold. "This was the only place I knew I could go, so I got here as soon as I could, but I didn't want to wake anybody up." He looked a little like he was going to explode with excitement and was trying   not to.

Becky was famous for her ability to read a situation and come up with the answers that everyone else missed. Often her friends believed it was due to her stunning intellect, which was indeed impressive, but what made this ability so strong was that she had always been empathic. She could read a room or someone's face as easily as she could read a book. In truth, her abilities were a melding of the two. Her empathic ability allowed her to see that Ben was excited and that he was trying to keep calm. She could tell that he wanted to jump up and down and scream, but it was her intellect that allowed her to put the pieces together and to infer why he was so excited.

She smiled, "It's tomorrow."

Ben threw his fists in the air so hard his body followed them off the ground with a jump. "It's tomorrow!" He quickly cupped both hands over his mouth and tried to muffle his laughter. He squatted down, took his hands away, and very excitedly scream-whispered, "It's tomorrow!"

"You made it!" Becky enthused. Ben rose victoriously, and Becky hugged him tightly. Even as his triumph turned into tears of relief, Becky held him, reassuringly. "You are going to be okay now."

It would be some time later before Ben would look back on this moment and realize that this was when he first understood what friendship truly meant. This was also the first time, outside of his family, he had felt love for anyone other than himself.

After a long moment, he let her go and, with a sniff and a wipe of his sleeve across his eyes, he pulled himself together. "Thank you. I needed someone to understand."

Her smile was kind and welcoming. She turned and put one arm around him again and started leading him toward the house. "That's what friends are for. Now come in and get warm. A lot has happened since we saw you last, and we need to catch you up."

Ben caught the concern in her voice. "Is everything okay?"

"Come in and get warm first." She got him to the back door that led toward the basement.

"I'll take that as a no." Ben didn't push the matter further.

Adam and Travis had already gotten coffee for the few who drank it and prepared hot cocoa for the rest. At the table was also juice and breakfast for everyone. David asked for hot water because he always brought tea from Ms. Warren's house. They each got some breakfast, mugs and juice glasses were clinked together in a toast, and all sat down at the table to eat.

"Are we not going to wait for Dalen?" Ben asked as he started to catch on to the problem at hand.

David stood up and tried to field the question: "Dalen is missing. I will tell you what we know." David was kind enough to give Ben a moment to take in the distressing information.

"Missing? What happened?" Ben was obviously alarmed, and there was genuine concern in his voice. "The last time I saw him, we were both with that street magician. He was threatening to leave me in the time loop for years. Then, all of a sudden, I awoke and it was tomorrow."

Adam put his finger up and then asked, "Tomorrow?"

"Yeah, tomorrow. You know, today." Adam and Travis both looked puzzled at Ben's answer. They were aware that he had been in a loop but had not thought about the implications for Ben, who was now getting flustered. Dalen was missing, and now he had to try to explain why today was tomorrow, so he simply pointed over to Becky. "Ask her, she gets it."

Everyone looked over to Becky in hopes of an explanation. She was surprised at first that she had to explain it, but then again, their minds were on other problems.

"He looped the same day for over a week. The idea of it

being tomorrow was something he begged for ... prayed for, but after days of it being the same day, again and again, tomorrow became a dream, not a reality. Also, if you remember his version of those nine days, it was not a good day to relive. He thought that he had killed Dalen and had to live with that pain. Plus, he honestly believed it was never going to end ... always today, with no chance of tomorrow. This morning, Ben woke up and it was tomorrow."

As each one of them began to understand, they also saw Ben in a new way. They held true to the kind of friend they always hoped that they'd be when the cards were on the table. They all took a moment and welcomed Ben into this new day. Ben had never experienced this kind of understanding with the friends he had known before. He wanted to take the time to say thank you to each of them separately, but there were pressing matters and he needed to be caught up. He said thank you collectively and then asked David to continue.

"Okay, let me tell you what happened after that." David grabbed his tea and took his position at the front of the table before continuing. "Alright. The name the street magician gave Dalen is Mathias. He was reluctant to do so at first, but Dalen insisted on getting a name. In many stories, legends, and belief systems, it has been suggested that knowing something's name is a way to protect yourself against it or sometimes control it. We are fairly sure this is why Mathias was reluctant to give a name at first, and there is a good chance that Mathias is not his real name.

"Mathias also gave Dalen the option to leave you in your loop for a lot longer, but Dalen had your back. The choice was his to make, and Dalen pleaded with Mathias to let you go, specifically with your memory intact because he believed it would be a travesty for things to go back to the way they were before and you hated us ... and so today you woke up, back in a normal timeline. Again, welcome to tomorrow." Everyone at the table made some sign of congratulations and took a sip of their beverage. "Then Mathias asked for Dalen's help. We held a council meeting about it. You would have been invited, but the way that Dalen explained it, you went from the alleyway to waking up this morning. We had no idea what would happen if we tried to get ahold of you before then, but know that now that you're in the same time stream as us, you will be a part of what is happening from here. We weren't kidding yesterday: we are all glad you are here."

There was another round of agreement and raised mugs and glasses.

Ben smiled and raised his glass of juice, but then regained his focus on the situation at hand. "What did Mathias want him to do?"

"Mathias asked him to break into the museum that is in the park."

"Why?"

"Mathias needed an artifact that was there, and he needed Dalen to retrieve it," David answered.

"Okay, cool. How did that go?" Ben was starting to lean in on the table as he listened.

"Collectively, we don't know." The feel of the room grew colder as David's words hung in the air. "We were with him in video chat until he reached the park, but it seems that magic and tech are like oil and water, so we said goodbye and expected to hear from him an hour or two later. That was..."

"Seven hours, forty-four minutes ago," Travis interrupted. He had been keeping track since Dalen went silent.

Ben stood up. His face was twisted with frustration, "Why aren't any of you doing anything to find him?"

It was Adam who responded and with the same intensity that Ben had brought to the conversation. "First of all, I would like to remind you that we have been Dalen's friends for some time, and I guarantee that even with what you have been through, everyone at this table cares at least as much about Dalen and his safety as you. Second, I would suggest to you that, instead of getting mad and running out into the streets randomly, which will only help us find him if we are extremely lucky, you consider the idea that we are here to make a coherent plan so that we can find him efficiently. This *is* us doing something."

Ben stopped. He took a moment to gather his thoughts. It had become a habit to respond aggressively when someone talked to him like that. "Don't." He took a breath. "Don't be that guy. Being an asshat is what got you locked into a time loop," Ben mumbled quietly to himself. When he sat back down, he was still agitated but much calmer. "What is the plan?"

David picked up and rolled his twenty-sided die that was nearby. He looked at it for a moment and then looked to the group and smiled, "Willpower Save ... pass."

Another round of agreement and mugs. It was the oddest thing that Ben had ever experienced. None of them were mad. They just let it go when he did and even complimented him.

"Thanks, guys," Ben said, still trying to believe what he just saw. "This is hard for me. I have been doing it one way for a long time, and even though I know the way that I was doing it was wrong, I'm not practiced in doing it any other way."

Again, it was Adam who responded to Ben, "I'm just as guilty as you. We're all going to have to change our perspectives." Adam looked Ben right in the eyes. "I'm not mad at you. I was barking at the old Ben. It wasn't fair. I am stressed about Dalen, too. I'm sorry." There was respect in Adam's voice, and his apology was sincere.

Ben nodded to Adam, "Accepted." He then turned his attention back to David, "So, what's the plan?"

David paused. Just for a moment. Just long enough to look to the far side of the room and then back at them. "The plan is a mixture of excitement and relief. I guess that, after that, Dalen is going to explain what's been going on to us."

"How is he going to do that?" asked Travis.

David smiled, "It should be pretty simple. He just walked into the room."

They all turned to see Dalen at the foot of the stairs, just standing there, alive and well. "Hi, guys." They were still staring in shock, which gave Dalen enough time to hold up his phone and add, "Damn thing still won't work. Too much magic interference, but I knew I would find you all here."

David pointed at Dalen and called out to everyone, "Carpe Dalen!" And seize him, they did.

Dalen was happy to be back with his friends. It had been a crazy night and he was tired. He knew that things weren't over and, as much as he was relieved to be back there with them, he knew that danger was surely on the way, if not already there. There was a lot to explain.

Dalen glanced over to his left. The jinn was standing there, smiling and being very patient. She slowly took in the room while all his friends rushed him in their relief. "Take in these moments. After watching all of time, I know this to be true," she assured him. "You will never find a more beautiful treasure than moments like these." Dalen was engulfed by the lot of them. All of them poured out their excitement that he was alright. Once they confirmed that he was okay, their questions and excitement began to move toward what had happened.

"Alright, everyone," David said. "Give him some air. Let him grab some breakfast. He's going to need his strength to explain everything." They all laughed and let go of Dalen and headed back to their seats.

At first, Becky clung to him, and finally Travis coaxed her

151

to let him go though she had tears in her eyes. Travis knew she didn't handle loss well, but he reminded her that Dalen was fine and got her smiling again by the time everyone else was in their seats, waiting to find out what had happened.

Travis set Dalen up with a plate of eggs and toast, and David made him a cup of tea to warm him up. Dalen sat down, ate his food quickly, and slowly sipped on his tea while he began to tell them of his adventure.

He caught them up through the park, talking with Mathias, and even his misadventures with Roy — and he was right: Becky was completely disappointed in Dalen's rookie move with him. He moved on to how he had lost time and the arrival of the security team to move the exhibit.

"So I told myself, this was my moment, right?" Everyone was entranced and hung on his every word. "I took the four bouncy balls and, just as Mr. Jericho opened the case, I threw them between him, Emmerson, and the security guard that was going to take the beads. Everyone watched them bounce and, at that moment, no one was specifically looking at the Beads of Fire. Right then, I grabbed them. The guard that was going to take the Beads of Fire was so distracted, she went off to chase all of them down. Mr. Jericho had an empty case. Emmerson's tablet had it marked as received, and no security officer was waiting to receive them. Their minds just accepted it and moved on."

Everyone erupted. They threw their hands in the air, whooping and cheering.

Adam banged his fists on the table like a drum roll for a moment. "That is what I'm talking about, my man! These are the moments that we live for! That is some Grade A, choice cut adventure!"

Dalen waited for the revelry to quiet down, and then he leaned in close like he was going to tell them a secret. He smiled devilishly at them and held them in anticipation. "But wait! There's more."

"There's more?!" David saw the opening and decided not to leave him hanging. "Do tell."

"Even though they didn't notice me, they could see the light from the damn beads. I was concerned it was so magical that they would be able to catch me because they 'd see them, so I wrapped them around my wrist to hide them with my sleeve and to keep them safe." He thrust out his arm and pulled back the sleeve to reveal the Beads of Fire.

The room gasped in unison except for Adam, who sprayed a mouthful of coffee over himself and his section of the table.

The Beads of Fire were now awake. Their luminance had tripled, and the golden line that ran through them was alive as if it was made of light and had multiple pulses of light slowly traveling the length of it. The room was silent for a few moments, and one by one they began to take Initiative and hold up fingers.

Travis was holding the first position. He looked concerned. "You still have it? I thought that you were supposed to give it to Mathias."

Dalen nodded, "That was the plan, but the plan has changed greatly."

Travis's response was quick, "Why? What happened?"

"The jinn that is connected to the Beads of Fire convinced me that he was not to be trusted." Another fresh gasp was had by all, and Adam once again was relieved of his sip.

Adam wiped his face, and then broke rank with the question that was on everyone's minds: "You have a genie?!" His voice was a mix of shock, excitement, and fear. Dalen was about to continue, but Adam's question was somewhat rhetorical. "Way to bury the lead!"

Becky also broke rank. Her excitement was past standard regulations. "Can you summon them? Can we meet them?"

Dalen looked over to the jinn to get her response to the question. She shrugged her shoulders. "I'm incorporeal. If you want me to be able to interact with them, the fastest way to achieve that is to allow me to interact with the physical world."

Dalen pulled his sleeve back over the beads. As he did, he noticed that everyone took a reflexive exhalation as if they collectively had been holding their breath. "She isn't what you are expecting."

Travis's thirst for knowledge of the truth about real magic had already overridden any sort of warning in Dalen's voice. "The jinn is a 'she'?"

"Sort of." Most had questions about what that meant. "The jinn doesn't have a physical corporeal body, so officially she is neither. I can see her because I am now connected to her through the beads, and when I picture her in my mind's eye, I see her as a female. She said she likes how I see her and for now I should refer to her as 'she.'"

Travis had his eyes closed, trying to picture what Dalen was saying. While he was listening, he had his pointer finger out and was moving it around, almost as if he was trying to solve a complex equation; with his other hand, he was writing in a notebook he'd started the night before last when he began trying to break down what Dalen was up against. Travis finished writing at the same time he finished the first part of his equation. "But she's not ..." Travis looked at what he wrote to confirm his guess "... because she isn't anything, since she isn't corporeal."

"Correct," repeated Dalen.

The equation came to its conclusion, and Travis just nodded at that and finished his notes. "So, you can see her right now? She is in the room?" Instinctually, everybody looked around the room. Only David looked in the right direction.

Dalen was impressed with that and asked, "Can you see her as well?"

"You keep glancing over to that part of the room; I made an educated guess." David looked back to Dalen and stated, "Tell us the part you're skipping."

Dalen and David locked eyes for a moment. Dalen could tell that David knew something was up. He wouldn't have missed the warning in Dalen's tone like Travis did, and he was certainly already piecing most of it together.

Dalen sighed, "It's not that I am skipping it. More like still trying to figure out how to explain it, so it doesn't come out wrong."

Becky responded with worry in her eyes and apprehension in her question, "Why would it come out wrong?" It was a fair question, but it carried other questions with it that hopefully didn't have to be asked directly.

Dalen was growing agitated because he wasn't sure how to explain it. He reached for his silver figurine and, once it was in hand, he began to think clearly.

"Because I don't have the proper words to explain it without using terms that you will probably jump to conclusions about. I know I have."

David chimed in with, "That's rather presumptuous, don't you think?"

"Fine," David's tone pushed Dalen too far, and he blurted it out without thinking. "You think you are so cool that you won't jump to conclusions? Okay. There is an easy way for her to talk with you. I can let her take over my body and run me like a puppet."

Travis's face didn't change at all from the quizzical concentration of trying to solve the problem. He looked back at his

156

notes for a moment and then asked, "Because she doesn't have a body of her own?"

Everyone including the jinn stopped and stared at Travis, marveling at his locked focus. Ben leaned in close across the table and, in a hushed tone, said, "Bro. Dalen is saying that she can puppet him."

"Yeah..." Travis looked up from writing in his notebook and blinked at him.

"You know ..." Ben tried his best to pantomime stepping into his own body and then did a little dance, "like possession."

That was the word Dalen was trying to avoid. Becky stood up and declared that she wasn't going to get involved with anything demonic. The word *demonic* set everyone afire with fear, and panic flared.

Dalen looked at David with sadness and resignation. "Told you."

David hadn't moved. While the others were panicking, he sat there with a kind look on his face. "I'm right here, and I am not panicking."

Dalen looked over to the jinn who was still waiting patiently. He pulled back his sleeve, and with a heavy heart, he said, "I wish for you to be able to talk to them."

She simply nodded and added, "As you wish."

The beads at first filled the room with light and sharp shadows, but as Dalen made his wish, the lights pulled inward and began to fill Dalen with the light instead. Dalen seemed almost as if he were feeding on it. He opened his eyes, and they looked like a pair of stones from the Beads of Fire. He stood up from his chair and, even though he did not speak with any force, his voice was louder than all of them together. He asked them to be quiet, and the surprise of it alone got them to resettle and refocus.

Dalen was ready for it this time. He was aware of what was going to happen and was prepared for it. The transition was smoother. There was still an awkward feel to it, and Dalen felt disjointed from his system, but he was okay. *See? This is a lot easier the second time, now that you aren't fighting it.* The thought happened in Dalen's mind, and it was one that he knew for a fact was not his own. It was the jinn and, somehow, she was talking to him on the inside while talking to them on the outside. *Just relax and stay calm,* she told him. *You are doing great.*

Travis was the first to ask a question, "So, you're the jinn?"

"Yes, that would be me, and to save us all time, the next answers to your questions are as follows. Dalen is perfectly fine. He can speak if he so chooses, but it will be difficult for me to carry out his wish if he does, so he will be quiet during this conversation, and afterward, you can make sure he is all that I say he is. For now, I am going to keep this short. Each of you will be afforded one question for now, and I will answer it to the best of your abilities to comprehend, but after that, I am going to return Dalen to you. He is just learning how to do this properly, and it will be taxing on him for now. I don't wish to push him too hard too fast. Can we all agree that this is what is best for Dalen, and even if you have a bunch of questions, for now, what matters is his health, mentally, emotionally, and physically? Can we agree to these terms?"

They all accepted the jinn's terms and agreed.

Becky seemed to need to ask her question first, so the group decided she'd be the first to go. "Are you demonically possessing Dalen right now?"

The jinn chuckled, "To do anything demonically, I would first have to be a demon. I am no more demonic than you are. I am a jinn. In some cultures, being a jinn would be considered a neutral demon, but not by the cultural understanding that drives your question. Many cultures — and religions, for that matter — have different concepts of what that word means, and from culture to culture that definition changes, so allow me to introduce myself under different terms. My indigenous plane of existence is one that you would recognize as Divine in nature and does not manifest itself at such a slow vibration of reality that it solidifies into something you would recognize as corporeal. My natural state of existence is that of neutrality, and I am neither fully good nor bad, which is also true about everyone sitting at this table."

Ben was the next to ask. "Is Dalen okay? I mean, is being taken over like that painful?"

Dalen thought it was awesome that Ben was looking out for him.

"Dalen appreciates that you are worried for him."

"He can hear me?" Ben smiled and waved.

"Of course, he can," the jinn replied. "He has complete awareness of what is going on, and if he wished me out, I would leave. He still is uneasy with this process. It is a little scary, but then again, your amusement rides are built to be scary, and people go on those on purpose all the time."

Travis had been thinking for a while, but now it was his turn to ask a question and he had no intention of wasting it. "Are you trapped in the Beads of Fire? I mean, are you enslaved to them and must do as the wearer demands?"

"What a glorious question!" The look on Dalen's face was one of amusement. "You are thinking of the old tales of the genie. I am not enslaved to anything. At one point in what you consider to be ancient times, there were a few who had found the mystical knowledge needed to enslave a jinn to an object. It was much like certain spirits might connect to or, as you might say, haunt a place or object, but it's a blasphemous art and, fortunately for the whole world, the knowledge of it was lost when those who used it incurred the wrath of the jinn. Indeed, a wish can be either a blessing or a curse depending on the mood of the jinn enacting it. An imprisoned jinn was referred to as a genie. I am a free jinn," she nodded once with pride in her freedom. "The beads don't tie me to the owner. It ties the owner to me."

"Which leads me to my question," Adam had been patient, but the jinn had brought it up, and Adam was the kind of guy who took the leap. "Is it possible for us to have a wish, in a way that is not disrespectful to you or what you are doing, because I would love to have a wish ... but if it incurs the wrath of the jinn, then I'll pass."

The jinn laughed, "Well said." The jinn looked around and saw all the hopeful faces. She knew how this was going to go: the same way it always did. "Ah, yes. The question of wishes. I can, at a later date, discuss this in great detail, and you can debate me all you wish, but for now, the answer is no. I will not grant you any wishes. I already have to teach Dalen to understand the nature of magic, as just one step of a wish he has already made. And, for the time being, I will not be able to grant someone else wishes as long as I am still fulfilling that one."

All were a little heartbroken at that. Even Dalen was sad because he didn't want to imagine this journey without his friends, but then David raised his hand slowly and waited for the jinn to acknowledge him.

"After Dalen learns magic from you, can he grant us wishes?" Everyone's hope was rekindled, and all their eyes turned to the jinn.

"Another fantastic question. The answer is yes." They couldn't help but cheer. The jinn began to look at each one of them, going around the room and finishing on David. As the jinn looked through Dalen's eyes at David, Dalen noticed that there was something more than just him. Dalen couldn't put his finger on what he was seeing, but it almost seemed like a heatwave was between him and David. Dalen was unsure if it was just a trick of the light, but he noticed that it was only David who had it. He wanted to ponder it more, but the jinn started talking and it pulled his attention to what was happening. "I am about to leave with Dalen. When he is done with his training, I will bring him back to you and only twelve of your hours will have passed. I will return him to you this very evening and, when he returns, he will be strong enough to grant each of you a wish. Get yourselves prepared."

Fatigue swept through Dalen. He tried to focus on David's face but when he tried to do so through the eyes of the jinn, the world wavered for a moment, and the distance between David and the wall behind him stretched out longer than it should.

Dalen became dizzy. Voice trembling, Dalen pleaded weakly, "Whoa there. Things are getting weird in here. I think I am going to need you to get out please." Yet, by the time he could finish saying it, she was already out, as if she could feel his stress and responded before he'd had a chance to voice his need.

Dalen's blood pressure dropped out and all the blood rushed from his face. His vision blurred and the world grew dark for a moment. Dalen was sure that he was going to pass out. He could hear his friends somewhere in the shadows telling him to stay with them, but they were fading quickly. The only thing Dalen could see was the jinn. She touched her palms together and the large gems in her palms began to glow.

"I didn't mean to drain you so hard." She placed her right hand over her heart so that the gem in her palm touched the one in the center of her chest. Her left hand she placed over the gem in the center of her forehead. Both of the gems began to glow, and as they did, every fourth and sixth bead in the sets of seven in the Beads of Fire began to radiate light as well. "It will get easier. You have my word."

The color came back into Dalen's face and his vision cleared. All his friends were around him, either asking him if he was okay or shaking him slightly as if to wake him from a nap.

"I'm alright." What he truly needed was for everyone to give him a little space and some air. "Just give me a moment and some space."

"Are you hurt?" Becky's voice was riddled with concern, "We thought we lost you there for a moment."

Dalen had to think about it. Was he hurt? He took a second and looked around. He swallowed and blinked. He seemed to be in complete control of himself, and better than that, whatever the jinn had done to re-energize him not only worked, but he now felt refreshed and ready to take on the world.

He laughed, "It's going to take a lot more than divine possession by a mythical, incorporeal being to take me down." He reached up and placed his hand on Becky's cheek, giving her the softest of pats and looking her in the eyes. "I am okay. I promise."

There was a sweet moment with all of them as they took a breath of relief that Dalen was okay. Then it was Adam who decided that the moment had passed.

"I would like to say," Adam looked around to his friends with excitement in his eyes, "that was the most amazing thing I have ever experienced in my entire life." He was getting more and more excited with every word he spoke, "These are the moments we live for! I mean, we just talked to a genie!"

Travis was quick to correct his younger brother, "A jinn, not a genie."

Adam threw his hands in the air dramatically, "What's the difference?"

Travis was hoping someone would ask him that. "After our talk last night and Dalen went to do his thing, I stayed up and poured through everything I could find on the web about the things we thought Mathias could be. Jinn were one of them."

The jinn seemed highly fascinated with what Travis was saying. "This should be good. I love it when folk try to label me." She sat cross-legged directly in front of him, resting her elbows on her knees and her chin in her hands.

"I started with the stories about genii," Travis continued. "All the old slave in a lamp stuff." Everyone nodded to express that they followed. "You know how in the story, the genie is a slave and the only way he can be free has to do with the master wishing him free, right? Well, I started looking into that. Why were they enslaved, and what were they before and after their enslavement?" He paused for a moment and started thumbing through his notebook. "Okay, with the research that I have done, what I can find is that those stories are based on something older. Something called the jinn."

Adam was interested in what his brother was saying but was too excited to wait for the drama of all of it. "Again, what's the difference?"

Travis glanced over to Adam. "What I found was something much older. There are references to them in the early Islamic faith. The Quran talks about them as immensely powerful spirits that are similar to angels and demons. I mean, we are talking about that level of direct connection to whatever is out there. If you take those references as records of experiences with real beings, then you are talking about something way more powerful than we thought."

Adam was finally able to read his brother's face through his own excitement and, for the first time, he considered that this could also be dangerous. "How much more powerful are you talking?"

"Don't you see?" Travis was almost disappointed in his brother. "A genie in all of its power is a jinn that has been crammed into a prison and forced into slave labor. It's hobbled from the very beginning. We are talking about a free jinn."

"That's a bad thing?" asked Adam.

The jinn turned back to Dalen with a small cup in her hand and said, "I like Sir Adam. He has a very pure heart." She smiled like she knew something, but before Dalen could ask her about it, she took a sip from her cup and turned back to listen to them talk about her.

Travis paused and glanced around the room as if he were looking to see if he could locate the jinn. Dalen thought this was amusing because she was a foot from him, sitting at his feet.

"No. Not directly. Being a genie would have given us some sort of protection. You know, whoever has the lamp is safe from the genie's wrath — that kind of thing. With a free jinn, none of us are safe, especially the guy with the object connected to the jinn." Travis squirmed a little in his seat as he tried to find the right words. "In a way, that thing is haunted."

"Haunted?" This time it was Ben who needed clarification.

Travis thought for a moment, trying to come up with an example. "You know those stories of a doll that they keep locked away in a case because it's dangerous?"

"Yeah," Ben nodded slowly with a little concern. "Everyone knows that doll. They made movies about it, right?"

"Yeah," continued Travis, "that would be the one." His expression changed to that of foreboding concern. "They lock it up because it is an object that is directly connected to a powerful spirit, and where the object goes, the spirit follows. Those beads are like that doll, but instead of a dark and evil spirit, it is connected to a free jinn, with no rules."

The jinn flopped onto her back with an exaggerated sigh. "He was so close."

Dalen didn't want to disturb the conversation, so he decided to try something. He looked at the jinn and tried to think as hard as he could for her to explain.

She rolled over onto her stomach and slowly swung her feet

166

back and forth. "Dalen, I am incredibly proud of you for figuring out that you can do that, but sweety, don't push so hard. You are going to pop something. I can hear you just fine." She smiled playfully and raised an eyebrow, "What I mean is that your friend Travis here actually did his homework, and I would say he was rather accurate about the little he did say. But ..." She paused long enough to get to her feet and to float slightly off the ground. "His conclusions are a little off."

Example? Dalen thought to the jinn, who just continued to speak out loud.

"For what little you know about the subject, haunting the beads is a close understanding. But he has it backward. I am not attached to them; whoever is wearing them is attached to me. I can't go wherever they go. I can't 'go' anywhere — I am incorporeal. I'm not being dragged around by those things."

You're not? Dalen thought.

"No," she laughingly scoffed at the idea. "While you are wearing the beads, you can perceive me, but that doesn't mean that I am drawn to the location that you're at. What it means is that your perception is being brought to a high enough understanding that you can perceive me in your mind."

"Dalen!" Dalen's attention snapped back into the room to see who was calling him. It was Travis, who was waiting for a response. "I said, are you able to take them off?"

Dalen hadn't even considered taking them off since the

initial moments after putting them on. He looked over to the jinn, who just smiled at him. "I have no interest in slaves, but you made a wish, and until it is fulfilled, the beads stay with you."

Dalen translated everything the jinn had said, from Travis's thoughts on the situation to the point that Dalen was not trapped by them but that, as long as there was a wish happening, he should not take them off. He even told Adam that the jinn specifically liked him.

That was it. Adam could no longer contain his enthusiasm: "A jinn likes me? These are the moments we live for!" His revelry was contagious, and for a few moments, they set aside the concern and worry and celebrated. It was greatly needed by all. Each of them had spent the last few hours dreaming of the possibilities. They had always wanted to believe in such things. After Mathias, they reached into their faith and hearts to the core of their being, where their inner child still believed in magic, and brought it forth; now they were having a conversation with a real jinn, and tonight, when their friend returned from his training, they were going to set out and have their own magical adventure.

They were finally brought back to the moment when Adam and Travis's mom opened the basement door and hollered down to them, "Good morning, everyone!" Everyone called back to her their good mornings. She was awesome and considered a second mom to all of them. "You guys just missed the bus. I'm late for work, or I would drive you. You're going to be fine walking today?" They all responded that walking was fine, and they all wished her a fantastic day. "You, too. Bye. Love you!" Then she was gone.

When they brought their attention away from the door, Ben had his finger up to say something. "Okay, here are my thoughts. First off, I have got to say that I should have done this a long time ago. You guys are cool." They all said 'thank you' or 'here-here.' "It's Friday and tonight is the dance. I think we should all meet up there. First off, I made a promise to this guy right here that I would personally find him a date to it, and I want to make good on that promise. Also, our parents won't think twice about where we are and what we're doing if we are supposed to be at the dance, right? So, the plan should be we go to school and try to act as normally as anyone can after what just happened. I'll talk to Kim..."

"Kim? Which Kim are you talking about?" Adam's attention was piqued.

"Kim Collard. As I was saying..."

"Kim Collard?" asked Travis. "She's in my homeroom. Shooting for the stars there, D."

"Kim?" You could hear the disappointment in Becky's voice. "Really? Besides being unbelievably pretty, why would you want to go to the dance with her?" All the boys just stared at her with an occasional blink, completely baffled by the question. She rolled her eyes, shook her head, and remembered who she was talking to. "Boys," she muttered.

"Look. I am telling you all what to do, and you aren't listening," This time it was Ben's turn to stare at a bunch of blank faces. "Sorry. Wow! Old Ben just jumped right out of my mouth there for a min." Disappointed in himself, he stared at the table for a moment as he worked to regain his composure. "I'm sorry. Look. I'm used to being the guy that comes up with the plan and, because of this, I have gotten good at it, but I am trying not to be that guy. I was him for years, and I have only been me for a few days. I didn't mean to be rude like that."

His guilt was written all over his face, but it was Becky who could truly see that he was facing an inner struggle and that it truly was a battle.

"It's okay," she reassured him as she went over and hugged him. "What matters is that you are giving us your best. If you give us your best every time, it won't matter if you fail.

David had his twenty-sided die in his hand, and he tossed it onto the table, "That's how we roll."

With that, the tension broke. They laughed and groaned at his pun, and then they turned their attention back to Ben.

"Go ahead," David encouraged him. "I believe you had Initiative."

Ben smiled and gave a short bow. "Okay. I'll go talk to Kim." Adam's finger shot in the air. "And I'll see if she has a friend." Adam smiled and put his hand down. Ben looked over at the others, eyebrow raised questioningly. All three of them were happy going together as a group of friends. "We will meet up after school and plan from there. Sound good?" Everyone agreed. "Sweet. Let's do this."

Dalen thought that it would be wise to also warn them

about Mathias. He explained to them what happened outside of the museum at the edge of the park. His threats seemed genuine and, if they saw him, they should keep their distance. Everyone was getting their things as Dalen explained, and they promised to keep an eye out for him.

"Wait!" David had just one last reminder. "Tonight, if things go well, you will be able to ask for a single wish. Take some time to think about what you want. Like tattoos, they are permanent." They all decided to listen to the wisdom in that, grabbed their belongings, and got ready to go.

Adam stopped Dalen just before he made it to the door. "Is she still here?"

Dalen smiled, "Never left."

"Where is she right now?" With a little help from Dalen and the jinn, Adam positioned himself directly in front of her. "Madam, I'm Adam."

The jinn asked Dalen if he would speak for her to Adam. Dalen agreed.

"It's a palindrome. You're very clever. Your sense of adventure will constantly get you into trouble, but it is your heart that will continue to save the day. Never change. Your kind of spirit is in small supply. They will need that heart of yours, and your bravery." Both boys were in tears by the end. They hugged and pounded the other's back with their fists in camaraderie as they did.

Adam sniffed and cleared his throat. "Now get the hell out

of here and learn magic so that you can get your butt back to the dance and start granting us some wishes." They both laughed at how insane that sentence was.

Everyone left and headed for school, save Dalen. He looked back to where the jinn was to see if she was ready to go. She was looking at something on the table, so he went to see what she was looking at.

It was the die that David had rolled a few moments earlier. "That is a twenty-sided die," Dalen explained. "It is used for the games we play. It has numbers from one to twenty. It's used to randomize certain aspects of the game with the higher number suggesting a stronger random occurrence. Right now, the twenty is up, suggesting the highest possible outcome."

She smirked at the concept. "It's an icosahedron, and where we are going it can do a lot more than that." She reached down and picked it up, examining it for a moment. "I think I will keep this. It might come in handy one day." She rolled it onto the gem that was in the center of her hand, and the icosahedron phased into it. "Ready?"

"I was born ready." Dalen put on his sunglasses that were still in his hoodie.

She snorted and then tried to stifle her laughter. "Indeed, you were, Dalen. Indeed, you were."

8

THE GREAT SEAL
OF VENGER

Dalen and the jinn appeared on the top of a hillside next to a beautiful white tree that stood proudly by itself on the crest of a valley, which was shaped much like half of a bowl, or maybe an amphitheater. At the bottom of the valley, right on the edge of the sea, was a large city that, from that distance, appeared to be separated into three concentric circles. In the center circle, a beautiful castle rose above the rest of the city.

The colors seemed almost too perfect to be real. The sky was a beautiful sapphire blue with only a smattering of white clouds that provided depth and dimension. The grass was a vibrant emerald with patches of wildflowers. Beyond the city, the sea shimmered in the morning sun, creating a peaceful, picturesque scene.

"Where are we?" Dalen had never seen anything so beautiful and majestic.

"May I present to you the capital city of the Kingdom of Venger?"

"Venger? Cool name. What can you tell me about this place?" Dalen was extremely excited. Moments ago, they had been somewhere else, a place that somehow began to fade from his thoughts, like a dream fading from the mind once it was awakened. It wasn't as if he had forgotten where he had been, but rather it no longer was a real place, and his focus was on the world he was now in.

"Venger is a peaceful kingdom ruled by His Majesty King Gavin, who is considered to be one of the wisest beings in this world, and Her Majesty Queen Hope. You will never find a more sincerely kind and caring ruler if you searched for a thousand years. She is known as the Heart of Venger. Their daughter's name is Joanna, who is a few years younger than you, but she has been trained since she was little in her role as Crown Princess and someday Queen. She is the best part of both of her parents and, even at such a young age, she is revered and respected by both her own people and those from other kingdoms, such as the elves, who share a border with Venger to the southeast of here."

"I'm sorry. You said what now?" Dalen heard the jinn, but his mind was still trying to accept certain realities. "Did you say elves? As in an elf?"

"Dalen. I brought you to this world because, unlike the

174

world we were just in, magic still thrives here. Any remnants of magical folks, such as elves and fey, left that world or went into hiding a long time ago, but here they are commonplace."

"What happened to make them all leave?" Dalen asked.

"Humans," she huffed with disappointment. "Where you just came from, humans decided that their entitlement knew no bounds. They encroached on the lands of all. They hunted down and killed the magical and sacred animals they could find, and they waged war on anything different from them, believing that they were superior to all things. They believed it was their right to not just rule but own their entire world." She stopped for a moment. The light from her hair and stones faded slightly as her tone grew sad, "Many tried to protect the land, but humans were relentless. Hundreds of species were killed, sometimes out of a perceived threat and sometimes just for sport. But it was nothing compared to the devastation that fell upon everyone — including humans and the world itself — once they discovered magic." She stopped for a moment, trying to decide something. She looked out over the valley toward the castle. "We need to be clear about magic," she said while staring directly at the city. "I am not talking tricks on a stage. That magic is harmless and is about sleight of hand. I am talking about the other kind of magic. Sleight of body, mind, and soul. It is a different thing and should have separation."

She looked back to Dalen and continued, "It was magic that almost destroyed the entire world. Instead of seeing a force and flow of the universe, they only saw it as a weapon and the power it could grant them. In the end, those of us who remained

175

decided that it was best to hide and remove all magic from the world, to save and preserve what was still left."

"A lot of them are still like that," Dalen admitted, almost embarrassed to be connected to humans. "Why teach me magic then?"

The jinn had been lost in thought, and Dalen's question seemed to bring her attention back to this moment. She smiled at him and, as she did, all of her light brightened once more. "Two reasons. The first is simple. You wished it. The second one has to do with something completely different. I think you are already magical in your own way. Besides, how can anyone earn trust if they are not given the opportunity to do so?"

Dalen took that in. "I can't think of a good reason to argue that logic." He looked out over the valley toward the castle. "So, where do we go from here?"

She raised an eyebrow. "A tavern."

"A tavern? What's there?" Dalen asked skeptically, eager to start his adventure.

"A drink."

"A drink?" He thought of all the amazing magical potions from the games he had been playing with his friends. He imagined all the possibilities that it could be. "What will it do?"

The jinn laughed. "It will quench your thirst."

Dalen was confused by this. "But I am not thirsty."

"You will be, by the time that we get there. Venger is much larger than you imagine, and we are further from it than you think. It is ten miles from the front gate to this tree. It is the closest anyone can teleport to the city directly without one of the magical pins that the elite guards and royal family wear."

They set off together, talking about what was to be expected when they arrived. "You will find all kinds of beings in Venger," the jinn explained. "I would suggest that you take this time to prepare yourself for such things. I will warn you if you need to be wary of something or someone. I mention this now because it is considered rude to stare or gawk at people in the streets. This place may very well be one of the most magical places in this world; because of that, you will see many things, creatures, and people that by their very nature are magical. To them, this is normal, and there will be consequences for treating them like freaks." Dalen understood and nodded. "That doesn't mean you can't be amazed. This is an amazing, magical city. Just remember that magic folks are still people."

The conversation continued as they walked through the valley toward the magic city. The jinn tried her best to prepare him for the different rules and laws that needed to be known.

They cut across the valley and connected to a road that was paved with cobblestone. Four large ruts had been worn into the stones as hundreds of years' worth of carts and wagons had traversed this road to gain access to the capital city. They followed the road north until they were about to reach the city.

"We are about to pass through a standard security check.

177

With the Beads of Fire active and the guards' abilities, they will be aware of more than most. They will have questions, no doubt. I would like to suggest that you allow me to speak through you." The Fire Jinn shrugged, adding, "It will make things go a lot easier, and we have things to do."

"Okay, but let's not take too long. It's exhausting." Dalen opened his mind to her, and the both of them walked up to the two guards that were posted outside of the city walls.

Dalen first noticed that both guards held spears, but both were also armed with swords on their backs and daggers on their belts. They were wearing long tabards that had been separated into quadrants consisting of offset red and black. Both were clad in metal armor that protected their shins and forearms, and Dalen could see by their bulk that they were also wearing a chest plate of armor under their tabards. They also wore steel bands on the middle finger of their right hands and gold studs in their left ears.

"Good day to you, traveler," the guard's tone was friendly but still held a sense of authority. "What brings you to the beautiful capital city of Venger?"

The Fire Jinn let him know that he could answer as easily as she could, so Dalen said, "I have traveled far, and I have heard that Venger City is a magical place that I should see."

Both of the guards flashed each other a look and a smile. "You heard correctly." They looked at Dalen curiously. "If you don't mind me asking ... Angelic?"

The Fire Jinn fielded their question, "I can see how you would think so, but I am neither angelic nor celestial." She took a long formal bow. "I am jinn."

Both of them widened their eyes a little, and both gave a respectful bow in return. "By Gavin's Beard, you are..." The guard didn't finish his thought; he just put his hand over his mouth in surprise.

"We are truly honored," added the second. "It's been a long time." Then he leaned in close and spoke with hush tones, "Why have you arrived today? Should we be concerned?"

The Fire Jinn spoke for Dalen, "This is my first time in your fair city. I am on a quest to understand the nature of magic. I am headed to Dorn's."

Both of the guards glanced at each other and then back to Dalen. "Well, that is as good a place as any to learn the true nature of magic." They shook his hand and then added, "We wish you luck on your quest." They gave a small bow again and wished them a fantastic time in the city.

Once they passed the guards and made it to the front gate, the Fire Jinn let go of Dalen and floated again next to him. "I don't mean to sound unappreciative, but that seemed an easy security checkpoint to pass," Dalen noted quietly once they passed the guards.

The Fire Jinn reached out with her empty hand and, from the stone in her palm, a burst of fire and light appeared and then dissipated just as quickly. She was now holding a small teacup that looked to be made of molten steel. "Each of them was wearing a golden stud in their left ear. Did you notice?" Dalen nodded. "They allow the wearer to perceive Truth. There are very few people who can see me without the Beads of Fire. They are either extremely powerful beings themselves or they have extremely powerful magic to allow them to see the truth. It is practically impossible to lie to Vengerian Guards, so they were able to see me and knew what I said was true — that I posed no threat to the kingdom. Besides, the real security is directly in front of you. Do you see Venger City's seal on the ground?"

Dalen looked ahead. Directly in their path at the arch of the front gates — and large enough to not be avoided — was the Great Seal of Venger. As he first looked at it, he felt a powerful sense that he had seen this before, perhaps in a dream. It was inlaid in the stone as a large circle and was made with the most beautiful craftsmanship that Dalen had ever seen. Shining brilliantly in the sunlight, the seal itself was three concentric circles, and on either side of them were a dragon and a unicorn, both reared up on their hind legs and holding the circles.

Dalen looked at the seal and did his best to take it all in. "It's beautiful."

"Oh, yes," she replied. "It is very beautiful and very powerful."

They stopped walking just before Dalen was to cross over it. He looked down at the seal. "Powerful? What do you mean?"

"Before you is the Great Seal of Venger. The Dragon is a symbol of True Power. The Dragon is recognized as a being of raw power — this is not only because of their sheer size but also because they are powerfully intelligent and wise with centuries of knowledge. Their very species is so powerful that even the hatchlings can use magic.

The Fire Jinn continued, "The Unicorn is a representation of the Purity of Magic. Often thought to be connected to goodness and light, it is said that they can only be found by the purest of souls. It is also recognized as a symbol for those who have ascended to find the greatest version of themselves." She glanced at Dalen before moving on.

"The three rings are a representation of the three Spheres of Reality: Body, Mind, and Soul. The outer ring is a symbol of the Body. As you move inward, you discover the Mind and, as you move past the Mind, you find the Soul. The seal itself is therefore a representation of the unity of Body, Mind, and Soul — and it is guarded and held by Pure Power that has been brought to the greatest version of itself. The city itself is built on this design, with the outer ring being the homes and the basic lives of the citizens of Venger. The middle ring is where you find the schools of learning and the master crafters who create the most splendid of magic items and devices. Finally, in the center, the Soul of Venger is represented by the castle and the royal family, who rule this kingdom with great power and the wisdom and kindness of their greatest selves."

"Every second I am here, I love this place more and more." Dalen was still curious about how this was a security device, and so he asked, "How does this work?"

She put her hands on her hips. As she did, she gave off an extra bit of fire and light. "Those who mean the city, its people, or the royal family harm cannot cross over this seal."

Dalen looked down again in wonderment. "No way." His mind tried to imagine what kind of magic would be needed to create such a spell.

She gestured for him to try and cross it. "Why don't you give it a shot?"

Dalen felt strangely nervous. "Is it safe?"

She folded her arms and cocked her head to one side. "Do you mean to cause Venger or her people any harm?"

"No," Dalen scoffed at the idea.

She laughed, "Then yeah, it's safe." Dalen looked down at the seal and then back to her, still hesitant. "This is the main southern gate, Dalen. A hundred people walk over this thing every day," she noted with a smirk.

Dalen suddenly felt a little silly about the whole thing. He walked across it but still hurried. As he crossed the center of it, he felt a presence all around him and it questioned his heart.

"Can you feel her?" The jinn put out her arms and slowly turned. Her hair floated as if it were weightless.

It pressed in close to the very essence of his being. "Yes."

Dalen wanted to run, but the presence surrounded him. "She is everywhere. Who is she?"

"Dalen Pax," the jinn bowed deeply, "may I introduce you to Venger City?"

"Wait! You mean the actual city ... is *alive*?!" Dalen had understood what she had meant, but his mind could not accept what it was being told.

The jinn's gossamer clothing and veils suddenly ignited into flame, and all of the stones on her body and the Beads of Fire on Dalen radiated as if they were made of molten starlight.

"This is one of those moments where you need to see more than the ancient humans did." Her voice was no longer an external thing but felt more like when she was controlling him, though without the feeling of being crowded or pushed aside. This was something different. He could still see her, and he was still completely in control of himself, but here, in this moment, they were connected, like two drops of water that had bonded together. Her thoughts were as if they were his own. "You can imagine something the shape of you as a being. Can something be shaped like a tiger and still be a being?"

"Of course, it can. I have even seen a few in my life."

"Can something that you haven't seen be a being? Can something shaped like an elf be a being?"

"Yes."

"How about the shape of a troll? The shape of a giant? A dragon?"

"Yes. I follow, no matter the race or species, they are sentient beings."

"How about the shape of a tree?"

That was a question he had never considered. It was a life form. "Yes, it is. The shape does not matter."

"Then why not the shape of a city?"

And there it was. In this state, he could feel her intent. He had to remind himself where he was. The standard rules of reality may not apply. She was right. There was no real reason why a being could not be the shape of the city.

"So, what you are saying is that Venger is a magical city. She is a living being, and she is not only aware of me, but she is the presence that I feel all around me ..." he laughed, knowing the answer before she could confirm it, "because she is literally all around me?"

The deep understanding that came with this new truth turned into an explosion of amazed excitement and joy. "I am so excited, I barely know what to say. This... is... amazing!" Dalen leaped into the air and didn't land until he had spun all the way around. "You are amazing and wonderful. I am sorry I didn't understand. Hello. I am Dalen." He could feel a sense of movement from the presence. It converged on his location.

"She can feel your intent." The jinn continued to float in the air, wreathed in fire. "She likes you. She has offered to say hello and impart to you a gift. Do you wish it?" Dalen nodded. She reached up and put her palm to the gem on her forehead. "As you wish." With that, light streamed from the gem on her head and every sixth gem on the Beads of Fire ignited with her.

His vision suddenly shifted, and he found he was seeing himself from outside his body. Seven silver cords of light streamed from the gems that ran along the center of the jinn's body and attached themselves in the congruent places on his. He understood that he was seeing himself from the point of view of the city somehow. Then Venger's perception moved with blinding speed towards the center of the city. It flew through streets and marketplaces, past shops and gates. As it approached a garden with five statues in a circle, it dropped down underneath layers of streets and tunnels and moved to the center of the city, to the heart of what lies beneath.

Dalen stood before a large crystal that was twenty feet in height and so broad that it would take three or four people to reach around it. It was magically suspended in mid-air and spun slowly. A glowing light grew inside that radiated outward, and Dalen could sense motherly love and protection from it. The light refracted through the innumerable facets in a way that could not be described without the use of words such as *magnificent* and *breathtaking*.

"You are the most beautiful thing I have ever seen," Dalen didn't say it aloud but spoke it from the center of his being, and Dalen knew that she understood and believed him.

Directly below the crystal were four blades, each representing one of the four Natural Elements. Earth, Air, Fire, and Water were placed in a stone that was suspended above a pool of water. Each blade had a slot in the stone, and each one was placed in their slot as if the blades of the weapons were keys in a lock. In the center was a sword that was placed much like the four that were around it, but this blade was made of pure light.

"The Eye of the Dragon within the Horn of the Unicorn," Dalen whispered in awe, knowing it by sight even though he had never heard of it until this moment.

"You brought this into existence," Venger's voice resonated from everywhere, but Dalen felt that the origin was the light from within the crystal. Dalen looked into the jewel and, when he did, he saw the image of a beautiful woman with dark skin standing within the crystal. She wore an ornate red and blue dress made of velvet and satin, and her long hair cascaded down her shoulders.

"I don't understand." Dalen had never seen it until this moment, and he had no idea how to create it; he was sure there must be a mistake. "I have not created anything."

Venger engulfed him in joy and a sense of thanks. "Today is not the first time I have met you."

From the center of the crystal, the light built up in its intensity, and then it all released at once in a pulse that literally knocked Dalen off his feet as he stumbled back and fell to a sitting position at the center of the Great Seal of Venger. He could still feel the light lingering with him. It was warm and soothing as it moved through his body. The light and heat finally coalesced on his right arm. When Dalen looked, he found there was now a marking of the three concentric circles made of light, like a glowing tattoo.

"Can you imagine dealing with all of that if you were here to cause harm to her or her people?" The jinn was walking again, and her fire had diminished so it once again seemed as though she was wearing gossamer clothes. She walked over to Dalen and offered a hand to him.

Dalen took her hand and she pulled him up. "Oh... That would be so bad for them," he mused at the idea of angering an entire city; he was sure that she had been very gentle with his mind, and it was still overwhelming. Then a new thought streaked through Dalen's mind. "Wait! What?" He looked at this hand and then at the jinn. "How did you just pull me up if you don't have a form?"

"Magic." She wiggled her fingers at him as if she were pretending to cast a spell. Dalen had hoped for more of an answer. "First rule of magic: 'It is only as real as you have faith in it and yourself.' The more time we spend together, the more real I will become to you. The more real I am to you, the more we can directly affect each other." She smiled, "It's a good thing." Dalen reached out to touch her arm, but his hand moved through her. "You're trying too hard. You're thinking about it too much. When I pulled you up, you didn't think — you responded partly on faith."

Dalen was confused. "On faith? And what do you mean when you said that I was thinking about it too much?"

"On faith. You assumed that I was real and reached out

to take my hand without proof, but you believed it would be there."
The jinn took a moment to let that sink in. "So, try again, but this
time don't focus on the point that you think that you can't do it."

"You want me to stop thinking about doing something while
I am doing it?"

"Yeah."

"And you want me to not only just stop thinking
that I can't, but you want me to stop *believing* that I can't.
That's impossible."

She walked right up to him, so close that Dalen could
see that her irises were wreaths of burning fire. He swallowed
hard. She grinned devilishly and stared into him. Her movement was
quick and the only thing on Dalen's mind was the feel of her lips
on his forehead. She pulled him in so close that her body pressed
against his. Then, just as quick as the embrace had started, it
was over, and she was walking away down the street toward an
intersection. "Seems to me, Dalen Pax, that you were built to do
impossible things."

"You kissed me?"

She turned around to see Dalen still standing there,
stunned. "I know that was a big moment for you, but Dalen, it would
never work out between us like that. It's not that you aren't an
awesome kid, because you are."

Dalen reached into his pocket and took a second to focus
on his figurine. He started to refocus. When his mind cleared, he

nodded. "No, I get it."

"Do you?" She took a few steps closer. "Remember when I told you that the anomaly would naturally resurface?" Dalen said he did. "You were spouting off some crazy ideas to yourself that you couldn't do things — that some things were impossible. You just needed to see that it is completely possible to take an action without thinking about it the way you were. That it was possible to set aside your prejudiced beliefs about Reality and Magic and take an action that your rational mind cannot believe can be done. A leap of faith. This is the 'Impossible Step.' And it is the fundamental building block of all magic. Rule One. 'It is only as real as you have faith in it and yourself.' Fair enough?"

It was. The jinn had the same ability that David had to explain things to Dalen in a way that made complete sense to him. At that moment, Dalen was not thinking about whether or not he could or could not. He was just perfectly in the moment. Mind, Body, and Soul. And that was the fundamental state one must be in to allow magic to flow. It made perfect sense to him. "Fair enough."

"Good!" the jinn exclaimed, and her fires surged a bit as if they were fueled by her joy. "Now that you understand all of that, we can go and meet some friends who are going to help along the way."

"Then let's go," he said as they headed down the street together. A moment later, he added, "You were right."

"I am?"

"I am thirsty now."

She grinned at his attempt at humor. "Well, we are going to a place that doesn't actually exist. You have to know where it is or stumble upon it due to fate. It is run by an immortal being that — rumor has it — literally created this entire world.

"You mean like a god?" Dalen was no longer paying attention to the streets and was simply letting her guide the way.

"No, nothing like that. Don't be ridiculous." They turned a corner and then another before she spoke, "Think much bigger. The gods come to his place for advice." Dalen's mind had seen too much in the last hour to be surprised by much, but that seemed to do it.

"What's bigger than a god?" At this point, Dalen was lost.

The jinn stopped walking outside what looked to be a tavern of some sort, yet it was located exactly in the center of a fork in the middle of the road. "I guess we will have to find out, won't we?"

She gestured for Dalen to go in. From outside, it was a quaint little tavern, and its foundation was made of large, flat river stones and mortar, with the rest of it made of wood. There was a large window in the front, but no matter how hard Dalen tried to look in, there was always a reflection or a glare from the sun that made it impossible to see inside. The one thing that Dalen could see was a light that was slowly changing colors and dropping little magical sparkles from the bottom of it that read "Dorn's."

Dalen rubbed his chin. "This is the place? Seems small for

someone more powerful than a god."

The jinn folded her arms. "What were you expecting?"

"I don't know. Gold? Giant marble pillars?" Dalen's voice didn't hide his disappointment.

"Dalen," she wasn't trying to hide hers either, "you know better than to judge anything on its appearance. We just went through this."

Dalen felt dumb and apologized. He even added, "Something all-powerful can live in a place that is shaped like a tavern," just so the jinn knew that he understood.

The jinn gave a sigh of relief. "Good. Keep that in mind while we're here. Now let's go — you're starved." She was right: Dalen was starving. It had been a lifetime since he'd had breakfast with his friends this morning and, after everything that had happened, Dalen was ready to relax.

9

THE CIRCLES
AT DORN'S

Usually, Dorn can be found behind the bar in the evenings, but on this day, one of his favorite bards in the entire world was performing for the lunch crowd, and so he had decided to stay on through the day and listen to her spin her tales of adventure and excitement. Her name was simply Silver. She was named by her fans due to her silvery tongue. She was a Tea Faerie, which are rare. They were known by many sources for their ability to soothe those who had fallen into states of hysteria.

Once, someone stumbled into Dorn's tavern, lost. That was not uncommon because the tavern was given a blessing that allows those who truly need to find it to do so. He was muttering to himself something about how "The squirrels are coming." Dorn could tell that he was reacting to some sort of toxin and went to prepare a potion that would counter it. Even as Dorn got up, Silver fluttered over, sat on the man's shoulder, and started talking to him. By the time Dorn was able to get to the counter for the potion and return, the man's mind was clearing. He was still extremely intoxicated, but he had gotten a grip on it and was able to focus and function.

The man explained that he had eaten at a fancy elven restaurant for the first time to try to impress a girl. They had the waiter make suggestions, which turned out to be a mistake. The server had assumed that they had taken antitoxins before they had arrived, which is customary for humans to do before dining on elven cuisine. They had not and, because of this, their systems were having adverse effects. Silver had asked him his date's name and left Dorn to take care of the man. By the time the potion Dorn had given him had taken effect, Silver had returned with the other unfortunate diner. Immediately after she had found her, Silver had wielded her Tea Faerie magic, using a charm that allowed the human's mind to flow through the chaos. Upon arrival at Dorn's, she was much like her date: highly intoxicated on elven cuisine but holding it together.

Dorn and Silver had become friends after that, and now, when she comes into town, Dorn provides her with food and lodgings, and she tells her tales of magic and adventure. She, like many of the performers who grace Dorn's stage, uses magic in her art. Sometimes it is in the form of elaborately detailed grand illusions that help one visualize the story, and others depend on more subtle aspects that allow the listener to connect better with the performer. Silver used both, and when she performed, she always drew a crowd.

She'd been a long-standing friend of mine as well, and in many ways, I consider her a sister in my trade. I had arrived in town and stopped off at Dorn's to watch one of her performances. That's how I found myself there that late afternoon, as Dalen Pax came through the tavern's door.

Dalen walked in from the day, blinking, eyes adjusting to the new light. As he did, he was first surprised at the size of Dorn's. It's much larger once you step inside — at least twice the size than one would have guessed from looking at it from the outside. To his right was an area sectioned off with a golden cord running along a series of posts that were able to be moved to adjust the size of the enclosed space. The golden cord roped off a good quarter of the tavern's common room. Inside the roped-off area, many individuals sat in chairs, all facing the same direction. Dalen's heart raced with excitement as he saw many races of folk that, until this day, he'd believed were only myth. He tried to manage his excitement as he recognized that not only were a few patrons elven, but there were also two dwarves and some members of a halfling race, who looked overall human but only stood about waist-high to their human equivalent. Dalen's eyes followed the patrons' gaze to a stage, where a faerie small enough Dalen could carry her in the palm of his hand stood on a stool. Whatever the faerie was saying, Dalen could not hear her.

The Fire Jinn pointed out the golden cord and explained that it kept all the magic that was going on with the performance inside the perimeter.

Further back on the right-hand side was a scattering of tables and chairs next to what seemed to be a large buffet area. There were four separate tables lined up in rows and one of the staff was erecting a tent around it.

The left-hand wall was lined with large booths that could easily hold ten people. The seats reached the ceiling, effectively making circular alcoves with large round tables in them. At the back end of that side, Dalen saw a staircase leading upward, which he found interesting considering that from the outside Dorn's only had one story.

In the center of the tavern and along the back wall was a bar lined with stools. As they approached, Dalen noticed that the bartender was listening to whatever was going on inside the golden cord, even though he was way over at the bar. Dalen was excited and wanted to understand everything. "I thought you said you couldn't hear what was going on outside of the cord — why can he hear it?"

"You are paying attention. That's good," the jinn smirked. "He owns the bar. He hears it anyway. I have no idea how he does it."

Dalen remembered what the jinn had said about the guy who owned the place and wanted to make sure. "You mean Dorn? Like 'Dorn's', Dorn?"

"That would be him." She strolled right up to the bar.

"Dalen Pax, I would like you to meet Dorn, owner and operator of everything you see here."

Dorn looked to be in his sixties and had a beard that had long turned gray, much like the hair on the top of his head he'd pulled up into a ponytail, but he also had the back and sides shaved. He wore a red tunic edged in black, and it hung on him loosely. Dalen was not quite sure if he was supposed to bow or drop to a knee; his mind stalled and he began to panic.

Dorn could see it in his eyes: the poor kid had been thrown into the deep end, and the water just got too deep. He said, "It's nice to meet you, Dalen. I know that you want to do this right, but you aren't sure what to do." Dalen nodded and grinned sheepishly. "First off, forget what your other half has told you about me, and for right now I want you to see me as only one thing. You know what that is?" Dalen shook his head. "I am the guy who is about to serve you at his tavern. My daughter is the cook here, and I guarantee that you've never had better. Whatever you like. What will it be?"

Dalen's stomach overruled his head, and a craving came over him. "Anything?"

Dorn smiled at him, "Push me."

"I want a bacon cheeseburger with barbecue sauce and onion rings on the side."

Dalen watched as Dorn wrote down the order and walked over to the open window that allowed him to pass the order to his daughter, Jax. He was even more amazed as Dorn turned around and had Dalen's order in his hand. He walked back over to where Dalen was still standing at the bar and set it down in front of him.

"How did you do that?!" Dalen asked as he sat down at one of the stools. The smell of the food had only heightened his craving.

"Magic," replied Dorn. "The kitchen was built with time magic. Once an order is put up, the rest of the tavern moves at a different speed than the kitchen. That way your order seems to arrive almost instantaneously. What can I get you to drink with that?" Dalen asked for a beverage that Dorn had never heard of before, but he didn't need to. Dorn reached his hand down below the bar and, as he did, the glass materialized in his hand. The bar had been enchanted to produce whatever a patron wanted using their memories. In this case, it was a dark brown liquid that looked almost black. It was effervescent and, by the feel of the glass, meant to be served cold. Dorn gave it to him and decided that he wanted one himself. After taking a drink, he stated, "I may have to add this to the menu."

Dalen took his burger with both hands and dived into it. He chewed twice and paused for a moment. It was the greatest thing he had ever put in his mouth. It was perfect in every way that he had hoped for. Every bite of his meal seemed to be better than the next. A tear welled up and hung from his eye, seemingly defying gravity. He wanted to say how good it was. He wanted to ask how anything could be so good, but every time he opened his mouth to speak, his hands put another bite in the way of his words.

"I got this." The jinn hopped up onto the stool and sat right next to Dalen, who was still eating. She spun herself around, leaned herself back onto the bar, and dramatically laid one of her hands over her eyes. "Oh my god, Dorn! I have never had anything so wonderfully juicy and delicious in my entire life. This is, flat out, the best burger I have ever eaten! Om nom!" The entire time Dalen kept pointing at the jinn, nodding.

Dalen continued to eat, and every bite until the end was glorious. Just as he was finishing, a young boy came by with a tray. "Hi. Can I take that for you?"

Dalen was surprised at how young the boy looked. "Do you work here?"

"My whole life. My father created Dorn's — you could say it's a family business. I'm Aiden. If you need or want anything, just let me know. Whatever you wish for, I can get."

Dalen shook his hand. "Nice to meet you, Aiden. I'll keep that in mind. My name is Dalen Pax."

Aiden looked over to Dorn and commented, "Seems like a good guy." Then he took Dalen's plate and, as he walked off, he said, "I'm sure I'll see you around, Dalen Pax."

Once Aiden left with his tray, the Fire Jinn and Dorn got down to business. "Dalen made a wish, and we're going to require a room for a while."

Dorn knew that the room was needed to complete the wish that Dalen had made but wanted to remind the teen that he needed to be more than just a spectator in its fulfillment. "Dalen," he said, "she wants me to allow you to have access to one of the rooms that I have. This room will allow you to learn what you came here to learn, but this isn't about what she wants. She is trying to be a guide for you, but your direct actions are needed for this. As you can see, many of the enchantments are specifically created to give you what you want. Do you understand?"

Dalen wanted to impress both the jinn and Dorn. He wanted so badly to say that he understood. He reached into his pocket and produced the silver figurine. He thought about what he would do if he was his character.

The Fire Jinn, always present in his thoughts now, knew Dalen was questioning himself and wanted to remind him of his strength and worthiness. "You are, Dalen. Every character that you have ever played came from you. Their strength was given to them by you. Their ingenuity and their bravery were yours. Always have been. Right now, you are trying to become something other than yourself. Stop. Stop trying to be those characters and masks and, instead, for once in your life, be you. It's the most powerful character you've got."

Dorn liked the rare opportunities when he was able to help directly and added, "The real you made those characters. They are but figments of truth. You create everything you perceive in a way, and being you is a necessity if you ever intend to wield true magic. Rule Number One: You're only as powerful as you believe." Then they both let him sit on that for a moment.

It was a big idea for Dalen to take in. He had spent

so much of his life being told over and over that he was neither special nor wanted. He had been teased and bullied. How could he be enough?

The jinn shook her head, "Dalen, do you see what you are doing to yourself?"

He heard his own thoughts and realized that he was doubting himself. This threw him further into despair. This was his big moment. This is where he had to believe in himself, and here he was, blowing it with doubt. Doubts about everything. Doubts about magic and himself, and he had doubts about whether he was good enough for any of this. "Look at yourself!" he yelled at himself in his thoughts. "How can you be good enough when, when you reach the moment you must believe that you are good enough, standing in front of the two most magical beings ever, you just freeze up. You are obviously not ready or good enough."

The jinn's voice cut through the chaos of Dalen's self-deprecating thoughts: "Dalen Pax, you have a choice in front of you. This is the fork in the road that you face. You are in the grips of the anomaly I mentioned to you before. People by their very nature rely on their instinct. One of their instincts that was developed as part of survival is to be wary of things not completely understood. It was originally developed by people so that they would not foolishly wander into unperceived danger. This is all well and good and has served people since the dawn of time. Over the years, people have grown and adapted to an ever-changing environment that was both created by the environment itself and the actions and growth of people. Now, that is generally a good thing, but there have been some anomalies that have changed the very face of how people interact with their instincts.

"At one point, instincts — such as the recognition of tragedy or loss or injustice — were developed in people in the form of mental and emotional signals so that they had a better ability to be aware of and respond to their environment and the actions of those around them. Today, those instincts are called sadness and anger. The anomaly takes form in how these mental and emotional signals are processed. Instead of acting as signals to bring a person's attention to injustice, anger now overrides the logical mind. The consequences, in some, are overwhelming and cause a number of both mental and emotional effects, none of which are beneficial to the person's mind, body, or soul. Very rarely does this overwhelming emotional state, with its lack of clarity, bring a positive resolution to the injustice that triggered the instinctual response. This is also true of sadness. The anomaly has affected the instinctual ability to recognize tragedy or loss and has become a crippling condition that many people 'suffer' from.

"Another instinct that was cultivated by people in the dawn of their time was the ability to recognize possible danger: to be wary of things that are not completely understood. The anomaly has developed into what people now call fear. Specifically, in this case, fear of the unknown. Fear was originally cultivated in people to have two purposes. The first was to allow the person to be aware of possible danger, which kept early humans from many dangers that existed. The other was to prepare the body to be able to react if danger did indeed happen. The most common of the side effects of this was often heightened senses, which allowed one to perceive the danger more easily, with a small burst of adrenaline to allow extra strength if they were to face the danger or extra speed to escape the threat. The anomaly has infected this instinct as well. Many humans either do not understand the heightened state or its purpose, or they are unable to adapt to it. In this case, the person can often get locked in a cycle of heightened awareness. Because of this, a third option other than fight or flight was developed. Until their system can cope with the 'fear' state, they remain somewhat catatonic, where they are aware of the events unfolding around them but are unable to act until they have acclimated to the heightened state. By then, it is often too late to respond.

"This is why all three are considered to have an anomaly: they are survival instincts that often cause harm and cultivate actions that do not truly facilitate survival.

"You can wish me to take over, and I will clear your mind as I have done before to relieve you of this torment. Or you can face it here and now."

Dalen's thoughts were terrifying, overwhelming. "I want it to stop."

"I can only relieve you of it, Dalen," the jinn's voice was the kindest he'd ever felt it. "Only you can stop it."

Dalen's heart wept.

"I need to be very clear about something, Dalen," Dorn explained. Dalen needed to believe in himself and what was happening; Dorn knew that it was key: "The universe does not place hurdles in front of you that you cannot pass. A hurdle, by its very design, is built to be overcome. The universe would not have placed you here if both choices were not possible. How is it free will to make the choice, if there truly isn't a choice to be made?" Dalen looked up from his doubt. "You, being good enough, is now a choice in your hands. What do you choose?"

Dalen looked back to his figurine. Dorn recognized what it was immediately. It was his totem, a magic item that allowed him to focus and empower himself, almost as if the object allowed him to tap into his strength and will. Dalen had had it for so long that it had connected to him and become a part of who he was. It helped him focus his thoughts and emotions. Dorn thought to himself, "The kid is already doing magic and does not realize it."

Dalen focused. "What would I do?" Dalen thought to himself. Every character he ever played with this figurine was him or at least a part of him. He understood what the jinn had said, and he believed her. He was every character and every mask he had ever worn. He was better than the mask of this scared kid. This figure represented who he truly was. The real him. That was the real person inside. It was no longer about him trying to be one of his characters. "What would I do?"

Dalen glanced around and noticed he was no longer in the tavern. The world was black and without depth. The only thing that Dalen could see was a cobblestone road that he stood on. It split going two directions and then finally fell out of the light and back into the darkness of the unknown future. When he looked up to see what was creating the light, the jinn was floating above him. She was ablaze in the most beautiful display of fire that wreathed her whole body.

Dalen looked down and saw Dorn standing at the fork. He simply echoed his own question, "What would the real you do?"

Dalen held the figure tight and forced his mind to clear. He was going to be fine. He was going to get past this. "I am strong enough." The voice of fear in his mind that was still breaking down begged him to stop. He turned and looked down one of the paths and saw a disjointed, dark, broken version of himself.

"Stop!" that dark self cried.

Dalen could feel its pain and fear, and responded softly, "I have to do this."

"No!" it pleaded, "You don't. You can come back here. I'll calm down. I'm just upset because you ask the impossible from me. I can't do this."

Seeing himself like this made Dalen sad. He knew that he had to step away from this fear. "Maybe you can't, but I have to." Dalen turned and started walking down the other path.

His fear dropped to its knees and begged, "Please! You have no idea how bad it can get! We... You and me. We don't even know what danger might exist. Please! Please, don't do this."

Dalen closed his eyes and forced himself to take another step away from it.

"Please! Please, I beg you," it sobbed, collapsing prone on

204

the floor. "I can't go with you. You will be alone."

Dalen forced another step. "No, it will be you who is alone. I am leaving you here."

"Don't leave me! I need you!"

"But I no longer need you!"

"You will fail!"

Dalen turned and with all his being he screamed, "THEN I WILL FAIL!"

Then there was only darkness.

The moment echoed through time. Dalen stood alone in the dark with only the silver figure he held in his hand. It was the only thing that could be seen in the darkness as it lit up with the strength of Dalen's defiance of his fear. His heart was calm and at ease. He smiled and whispered, "But I will never give up again." When Dalen looked back up, he was standing in Dorn's.

Dorn was in tears. "Now, Dalen Pax," he reached below the bar and felt a key appear in his hand and he presented it to Dalen, "Now you are ready to learn magic. This key will grant you access to one of the rooms upstairs, and it is magical by its very nature. Time and space can be changed and molded there. You could spend a hundred years in there and be back out for supper. But inside, you will find exactly what you need."

Silver had ended her performance and flittered over to the bar for her post-performance victory ice cream, which was a tradition of hers. When she and Dorn had first met, she had ordered some and, ever since, she always has some after every performance. "That was amazing!"

Dalen wasn't sure what to make of the tiny faerie, but he was glad that she seemed happy with him. "Wait... Did that just really happen? Did everyone in the bar just see that?" he asked. He had thought that all of that had been in his head and not for the world to see.

"Not a bit of it." She gave a small curtsy, "I am a Tea Faerie. We can see the visions of others."

"Visions?" Dalen hadn't realized what he experienced was a 'vision.' Honestly, he wasn't sure what that was.

"Visions, hallucinations, daydreams — that kind of thing." She took a spoonful of ice cream and had a bite. "Hey Dorn, get this guy some ice cream. He has a victory to celebrate. It's on me." Dorn produced some in a suitable size for him. "I am Silver the Bard, and I would ask if you have ever heard of me, but from your attire, I would say that you aren't from around here."

Her entire manner put Dalen at ease. Dalen thought that he would be nervous the first time talking to a fey. He thought about how Travis would've been nervous, but he would nonetheless have a hundred questions for her. Becky would have already scanned the room and assessed the threat level of everyone in the tavern. Adam would have truly been in the moment and probably have ordered a beer or hit on a waitress or something by now. David would've been the guy holding the key and waiting for Dalen to start his adventure.

"I wish I could say I have, but even though I didn't know of you before this moment, I know that I will never forget you," he said it as truth, and Silver could tell.

She fluttered over and clinked her tiny bowl against his. She smiled. "Few ever do."

It was time. Time to start his own adventure. He took the key from Dorn and thanked him. Then he gave his attention to Silver. He scooped a spoonful of ice cream and lowered it to where she could reach, "Here's to the adventure."

She scooped a faerie-size spoonful out of his, clinked her spoon against it, and said, "May it be better than you dreamed." They both took their bites and enjoyed the moment.

10

ELEMENTAL
UNDERSTANDING

It was time for Dalen to get to work, so he said his thanks again to Silver and Dorn. He and the Fire Jinn then went up the stairs to find the room. The key had the number three engraved in it. They reached the top of the stairs and started counting doors until they found number three. Dalen slid the key into the lock and turned it. The lock turned easily and, once unlocked, the door swung open.

The room was dark except for a beam of light that came from the ceiling. The light itself was bright, but it seemed focused in the middle of the room and kept the outer edges cast in deep shadows. As Dalen's eyes adjusted to the light, he could tell the room was made of white marble. It had the feel of a cathedral, but Dalen could not see anything on the walls that suggested a religion, nor did he see any statues, but the feel of the room   was sacred.

The floor was made of polished black stone that was like walking on a black mirror. In the center of the room was a circle made of a white metal that gave off its own radiant light. Inside the circle was an inlay of pure white quartz that formed Metatron's Cube. The six outer circles were made of gemstones, and the glyphs etched into them glowed with a magical light. The gemstones were massive and made of a single piece of stone, and each was a different color: red, orange, yellow, blue, indigo, and violet. In the center was another gemstone; this one was vibrant green. Each one of the gems had two concentric circles in them made of the same obsidian that covered the floor. In the center of the circles was a glyph, and then five more glyphs that wreathed the first. The center circle was different: it had the six glyphs from the center of the other locations wreathed around a Yin and Yang symbol that was surrounded by what looked to be a vortex pulling everything toward that center point.

"This is your training circle." The jinn's voice became more authoritative, "Go and stand in the center of it."

As Dalen arrived at the center, all of the quartz began to light up. It stretched out like fingers as it reached across the pattern and finally the colored section. The light encircled them and then, as if it were reaching out to itself, it connected each section along the lines that ran between them. Once all of the quartz was lit, small eddies of energy made of colored light built around the corresponding gemstones.

The jinn gestured at the areas of energy. "From here you

will learn to harness the Elements of Reality and Magic." Dalen slowly looked around the room. "Once you can harness them, you will learn to harmonize them and bring them to a place where the six become one." She pointed to the glyph that Dalen was standing on. "Once you can take the six and generate the seventh Element, which is pure Reality itself, you will have learned how to wield Reality. This is the truest form of magic, and with it, anything is possible. As long as you can follow the rules, that is. You have already learned Rule One."

"Me and, in turn, my magic is only as strong as I believe myself to be," Dalen was still flowing strong from his experience in the tavern and was excited to learn it all.

"Alright then," the jinn smiled and her fire brightened, "let us begin."

Before Dalen could use the training circle in the room, he had to first learn what each part of it meant. The jinn had referred to each of the areas as 'Elements,' which confused him because he thought that there were four basic Elements: Fire, Earth, Water, and Air. Somehow, when those are put together, it makes a fifth Element, Ether or Spirit. This circle had seven altogether, and Dalen couldn't determine which was which or even what they were, for that matter.

The Fire Jinn hadn't moved. She stood there watching him. Dalen felt as if she was looking through him into his soul. "She seems to be waiting, but waiting for what?" Dalen thought to himself. The jinn lowered her head slightly but maintained eye contact. From this angle, her look became more predatory, and Dalen felt she was getting tired of waiting.

Dalen decided to try to answer this as if it were a riddle. What did he know? She was waiting for him to say or do something. That was 'X.' In any good riddle, the person who is supposed to figure it out is given enough information to solve it. So, that means that he already had been given the answer. Dalen kept his mind focused the best he could. "What was she waiting for him to do?" he thought to himself. "I need to solve for X."

The second part of the riddle was X, so Dalen decided to focus on the first part. Instead of focusing on the 'what,' Dalen decided to focus on the 'why.' Why was she waiting on him? For some reason, she believed it was his turn to speak or act. She was teaching him — shouldn't she teach? Why was it not her turn to speak and his to listen? Why was it his turn?

Dalen thought for a while, trying to remember everything she had said. Nothing she had said recently gave any answers to what he was looking for, so he began to look back further and further until he stumbled across something that he believed to be the answer.

"You aren't actually here," Dalen's words were confident in his answer.

"So?" The Fire Jinn raised her head back up and folded her arms.

"So, I am the only one actually here, and here may not even exist completely either."

The jinn smiled, "You're two for two."

Her encouragement let him know that he was on the right path, so he continued with this line of thinking. "Since I am the only thing that may very well be real here, it is going to have to be me that makes the choices." His eyes widened as he understood what was before him. He didn't fully believe it until he heard himself say it out loud, "I have to teach myself how to do magic. You are only here to help me when I have questions."

She nodded. "That is correct."

"Is this how you learned it?"

"This is how it is learned."

Dalen looked at the floor. "Everything that I need is right here?"

She smiled, "You would not be given this challenge if it could not be done." She looked up and smirked, "Hurdles by their very design are meant to be overcome."

No longer enveloped with irrational fear, Dalen only saw the challenge. He pictured Adam raising both of his hands in victory. "Alright, then we better get to work." Dalen looked over to the jinn and took a deep bow, "There is obviously more than just the four, because here there are six, and I don't even know if Earth, Air, Fire, and Water are even the Elements for this circle. I need to know what the Elements of Reality and Magic are and how they are different. I wish for you to teach me the Elements of Reality and Magic."

Her fire burned bright as she bowed in return, "As you wish." She put her arms behind her back and began to float, slowly meandering around while she spoke. "Let's start with what you know about Elements of the Nature." Her small cup appeared in her hand, and she began to sip on it while she instructed him.

"I know the basics." Even as Dalen spoke, though, he realized that he didn't know. His information was what he'd learned from stories and movies. "Fire, Earth, Water, Air."

The Fire Jinn stopped him there, "What does that mean?" Dalen felt like he was talking to David. She was putting him through the steps to find answers on his own.

"You know? Fire ..." He gestured at her.

"Yes. I know Fire. What can you tell me about Fire as an Element?" The question seemed simple, but Dalen didn't have an answer. "Then this is a good place to begin. Elements can be perceived in many ways and are, by many folks. To start, let's talk about how each Element differs from one another from a certain point of view." Dalen nodded. "Each Element can be expressed by how it is utilized in change." She waited for him to nod that he understood and continued.

"Fire, for example, is a hot flash change. What was there is burned away, and there is often loss, but what was lost makes way for new things to grow. In the same way, a forest fire will clear all the dead brush and trees away, and new growth will spring from it; in a short time, a new forest will grow.

"Earth can be recognized as the patterns of change and cycles. Summer to autumn, autumn to winter, winter to spring, spring back to summer, and so on. You can see this Element in people's lives. Earth has partly to do with the connection to the physical and the people in it. Often people who get locked into cycles in their lives have something that they are connected to. Until they let go of that connection, using an Earth Elemental action, they will continue to cycle on it.

"Water can change its form but keep its essence. Pour it into a circular cup, the water becomes circular. Pour it into a cube container, and it becomes a cube, yet it's still the same water in either case. Water can change its form so easily that it has been proven that anyone can change its shape merely with thought. You can write something on the container, and the intent you put into writing it will change it. It can become ice or steam, but in either case, it continues to be water.

"Air is a free-flowing sense of the possibility of change. Indeed, air will envelop an area and just move to take the form of whatever the free space around everything is. If you throw a rock through the air, the air will simply move around and with the rock. Minds that can adapt like the Element of Air can be given any idea, any truth, and they will have their thoughts envelop it and fill in all the negative space to be able to move with it and around it."

Dalen's mind spun for a moment as all of that understanding was directly integrated into his thoughts. He could hear the Fire Jinn in his mind now as if her thoughts were his, but once they were in his thoughts, he had to try to understand

214

what he now knew. These new concepts made him think about the examples, helping him comprehend what the Elements meant from this understanding.

The Fire Jinn took another sip from her cup. "Now let's discuss the fifth Element of Nature, the one in the center. What can you tell me about that?"

"It has something to do with spirit or magic, I think, but I've always heard that it's created when you put the other four together."

The Fire Jinn pondered his answer for a moment. "Well, let's look at that, shall we? She put her hand on her chin, closed one eye, and scrunched up her face like she was pondering the idea. "Going from an outward concept inward, to create the thing at the center. You need the four to make the fifth." She smiled and nodded in agreement, but then she switched hands and went back into her pondering face. She thought again for a moment and then said, "But can you imagine it from the center, moving outward?"

"I am not sure what that would look like." It was almost like trying to reverse engineer something, but you haven't learned what the finished product was to begin with. It made Dalen's mind throb.

The Fire Jinn could tell that he was stuck. She was kind and supportive, but she wouldn't let him quit. She just continued her task to help him understand. "Instead of having four that combine to make one, start with only one in the center."

"Alright," Dalen closed his eyes and tried to picture it. He imagined a circle with four points on it: up, down, left, and right. Each one represented one Element. In the center, the fifth. He first pictured the four coming together and forming the fifth. Then he tried what the Fire Jinn had suggested: he started from the center with that Element being the only thing there was, and then he imagined it separating into four parts. "Each Element is a part of a single thing." Dalen took a breath and tried to understand what that meant. "I'm not sure if I am looking at it right, but if I am, that means that the Element in the center is the only thing that is real, and the four Elements around it are parts, or maybe ways of looking at the one thing that is real."

"Yes!" Excitement flowed into her words, "In the same way that a man can be a father, son, friend, and a husband all at the same time. They are merely just aspects of one thing." She smiled at him and coaxed him further, "What is the simplest understanding about Air?"

Dalen tried to be as remedial as he could: "It's a gas?"

"Yes! What about Water?"

"It's mainly a liquid."

"...and Earth?"

"It's solid."

"Okay, what about Fire?"

"It's straight energy, right?" Dalen started to see where

this was going and ran with the thought. "So that means the four main Elements of Nature are the main four states of existence. So, what is the thing that, if you break it down into its facets, would give you the four states of reality? I guess it would be reality itself." As Dalen spoke, it was the first time he had ever thought of the idea, but in the core of his being, he felt that it had always been true. His mind was looking at it from as many angles as it could, trying to find a flaw in his logic. As he did, he stared off at nothing as the images of this understanding filled his mind with awe.

He remembered how each of the Elements worked and tried to have his mind take on each of the Element's ways of change. He knew that he would have to cycle this kind of learning again and again to learn all that was going to be required of him. He allowed his truths to be ready to be burned away so that new truths could take their place, and even though his mind would have to take a new shape, it would still be him, so he opened his mind to take the form that would come. He would envelop it in whatever form it took in an all-encompassing acceptance of what was to come next.

Dalen's mind opened like the iris of a camera and, for a moment, his mind expanded his line of thinking in ways that were surprising to him. They didn't even feel like his own thoughts at that moment, just truth being poured into his mind from something more powerful than he could perceive.

In that moment, he saw the entire Circle of Elements as a whole. One single thing. Reality itself was perceived as different aspects, but in the end, never separate. Existence and Reality were never just one concept. They could be perceived one aspect at a time, but when perceived as a whole, it became Dalen and Dalen became it, and he knew at that moment that it was true for everyone and everything that exists.

In the same sense, he could see that any of the Elements was singular on its own but became the fifth Element of Nature when they came together. Yet, all five Elements were also a single piece of the Elemental Circle.

The first bead on each of the seven sets of the Beads of Fire was glowing fiercely. Dalen looked over to the jinn, and there was a red glow coming from her pelvis, and a line of magical silver cord connected them. He could feel this connection in the base of his body. It sat at the center of his pelvis and made him feel grounded and solid. As he felt the connection, he sensed that they were connected as if they, too, were one in the everything of existence.

The iris of Dalen's mind closed, and he found himself on his hands and knees, trying to catch his breath.

The silver line was no longer tethering them together, and the Fire Jinn was dancing triumphantly while in flight around the room, "You did it!"

"What the hell was that?" Dalen didn't move; he just knelt there, catching his breath.

"That was you opening up one of the Elements of Reality and Magic. Only five more to go before things get really interesting." Dalen needed a minute, so she flew around a bit while

Dalen found his feet again. When he did, she landed and got back to business. She pointed behind him and to his right. The red Element had ignited and was now casting light high into the darkness. Dalen had not realized it until the light from the Element was bright enough to illuminate the room he was in, but the room was larger than he thought. The walls were at least fifty feet high with arches and a glass ceiling. It was hard to make out what was on the ceiling because the focused light in the center of the room made it difficult to see, but Dalen guessed that it was some sort of stained glass, which reminded him of a temple or church.

Gesturing to the Element that was producing the red light, Dalen asked, "Is that the Element of Fire?" He looked back at her because, even as he said it, he knew he was wrong. "No, wait. Is this the Element of all of them together?"

"You're close." She took another sip from her cup. "Try again."

"It's the whole thing. Not just the basic Elements. Those too, but it's the connection to everything, but not just that." Dalen paused and allowed his mind to build the idea. "It's not just that I am connected to everything but, just like the Elements, I am an aspect of the thing as a whole, just as everything and everyone else that exists." Dalen closed his eyes and tried to picture it again. "It felt as if there was a flow to it. I was in that flow and, for a moment, I was one with everything, even you."

She smiled, "This is the Natural Element. It is the representation of the connection that everything existing has with everything else that exists as a complete singularity. This Element is a fundamental part of many faiths and practices that connect directly to Nature, and those whose magic and abilities stem from the knowledge that there is a 'oneness' to everything and that everything that exists is connected to it."

"Like Druids?" It was one of the only Nature-based groups he was sure about.

"Yes, they are but one of many that reach not only across your world but many worlds, because this concept is universal and recognized as a magical truth on all worlds." She took a moment to allow Dalen to grasp what was being explained. When she could sense that he was ready, she continued. "As you mentioned, the connection to the singularity has a flow." She pointed to the circle directly across from the Natural Element. "The next Element of Reality and Magic that you will learn is how to channel that flow, but before you learn this, you must learn how they connect as two parts of a whole and what that whole means." Dalen was thankful for her. Even though he was the one who had to take the steps, she was at least helping him know where to move to.

Another new thought entered his mind and gave him a different way of looking at it. "A place, and a way of moving in it? An Elemental Field, and a tool to act within it." Dalen looked down at where he stood. In the center of it all was a Yin and Yang symbol, and he laughed at himself in his head. "Or at least that is what I see because that is the symbol that my mind allows me to see since it can't understand what I am truly seeing. What is there is the balance of two equal parts." He was sure he was right, but he looked to the jinn for confirmation.

She nodded. "Think of it as a single breath. The exhale is a Field of Intent. It is the field in which you work. The other is the inhale, which brings that field inward to be able to use as a tool. Much like the relationship a vehicle has with the road. Breathe out and you create the field; breathe in and you create the tool that is used for that field."

Dalen looked around. "There are six Elements in the circle. My guess is that the others will do the same. So, there are three Fields and three Tools."

She smiled and pretended to be dumbfounded. "Why three?"

Dalen smiled and sang a tune from a long past childhood: "Because 'Three: it's a magic number.'"

The Fire Jinn laughed as he did, and her light brightened with her laughter and gave off a pulsating effect. When she had caught her breath, she asked him again, "No, seriously, why three — or better than that, what are the three?"

"You think I know this answer?" His tone did not suggest a high level of confidence in himself.

She wrinkled her nose and nodded, "Think back to The Great Seal of Venger."

So, Dalen did. He closed his eyes and pictured it. The Unicorn and Dragon: he remembered those first, and then he recalled that they were reared up and holding something. The symbol that was made of light on his right arm began to radiate heat on his skin.

He thought for a moment to recollect what the jinn had called them. A representation of ... "They are the three Spheres of Reality: Body, Mind, and Soul."

"Very good, Dalen." Dalen could see it in her face: she was truly proud of him and how well he was doing. As he looked at her, he could feel it in his essence. "So, which one are you working with right now?"

That was a good question, and Dalen felt it deserved an equally good answer. He thought about the Natural Element as a whole. It defined the natural state of the physical world. The physical world was corporeal, so that left only one real answer. "It's the Body Sphere."

"That is correct." Dalen pumped his arm but let her continue. "So, if you have learned to connect to the Body Sphere, how would you move within it?"

Dalen thought about the question as literally as he could. What is motion in the physical world? "Kinetics? That's the force of movement in the physical world."

"Your insight is impressive." Again, Dalen gave himself a victory pump. "The second of the Elements that you will learn is called the Kinetic Element. Now, explain movement within the Element that connects you to everything."

The bottom fell out of his victorious attitude. Dalen wasn't sure what she meant, and the question forced his mind into trying to reset. "The connection between all living things is a field of existence happening all at once. It's non-corporeal, yet every physical thing in existence is a part of it." Dalen couldn't comprehend how to move in that field. He understood how to move in the physical world. That was simple — but how to move through the non-corporeal connection just made his brain hurt. Dalen sat down right in the center of the training circle and decided that he was not going to move from that spot until he understood.

He meditated on it for what seemed like forever, attempting to picture physical movement in a non-physical way.

"I suggest that you take a break. You should get something to eat and come back with a fresh mind." As soon as the jinn suggested it, Dalen's body remembered it was hungry and pulled him from whatever thought he was trying to create.

Dalen looked up from where he was still sitting. "Yeah. I think you are right. I am completely stuck on this, and sometimes taking a break and coming back to it can help." Dalen got up and headed toward the door, "How long have I been meditating?"

"From your point of view?" She put her hands on her hips and cocked her head. "About five hours." The look on Dalen's face reflected his surprise. "There are a couple of things you should understand, Dalen. I will take you back to the moment with your friends that we agreed upon, but that doesn't mean that that is how much time you'll have spent learning this. This will take weeks of learning and months of practice. Maybe even years."

Dalen flinched at the idea. "Is there a faster way?"

"This is the fast way." She ruffled his hair with her fingers and gestured for them to leave the room. "Come on. The secrets of the universe will be here after you have eaten, and there is something that I want you to see."

Dalen looked back at the training circle; the idea of months and maybe even years seemed daunting. He was only kind of listening and lazily responded, "Yeah? What's that?"

She turned around at the door and gestured toward it. "I guess you will have to go downstairs to find out." Dalen didn't want to stop working on the solution, but he was hungry and knew when he was beaten, so he reluctantly went downstairs.

11

A BALANCED MEAL

The dinner rush was in full swing as Dalen made his way downstairs. As he looked around, he noticed that a few extra staff members were working the tables and booths. Dalen spotted Aiden and waved to him as he went by. Aiden smiled and waved back as he took some plates through a door that led to the kitchen.

"Good evening, sir." One of the waiters approached Dalen with a smile. He wore a white, loose-fitting, linen shirt with leather pants, and his hair seemed windblown. A tray of drinks was balanced in one hand and three plates of food were in the other. "Follow me and I will seat you at a table." As he glided past Dalen, he gestured with his head for Dalen to follow.

It was a busy night, and many people were shifting in and out of the area where the tables were. Dalen almost had to jog to keep up with the waiter, who was weaving in and out of the way of patrons. One of the customers abruptly slid out from his chair and stood up directly in the waiter's path. In a single motion, the waiter dropped down to his knees, spinning fluidly as he did so. The patron caught the waiter out of his peripheral vision and raised his arms to protect himself from what he was sure was going to be a collision. By dropping to his knee, the waiter lowered the trays enough that the patron did not hit them with his arms. Still in motion, the waiter stepped around the patron while on one knee and stood back up, completing his spin and continuing in the direction he was going without ever losing his pace, and not a single drop was spilled.

Dalen made it to his table and, as he sat down, the waiter asked him if he wanted something to drink. "Water for now," Dalen responded. "That was a pretty fancy move back there."

"Thank you," he smiled with a small bow and a wink. "Remember that when it's time for the tip." He turned his attention to the table next to Dalen's and jutted his hand forward at the level of the table, and the tray with the drinks slid perfectly onto it. He put his hand in the center of the tray and, with a flick of his wrist, spun it. Centrifugal force took over, and all five drinks that were on the tray slid off in different directions from the center of the table, each beverage stopping directly in front of its correct patron. At this point, he picked up the tray and continued on his way.

"How did you do that?" Dalen called out.

In a fluid motion, he turned on his heel, ducked under one of the other servers who was passing by him, and said with another wink, "Practice." He finished his spin and continued on his way. "Lots and lots of practice."

"That's Jed. He is one of Dorn's sons," the jinn informed Dalen as she settled into the seat across from Dalen. "The server who just passed him is his sister, Blaze," the jinn added, pointing out a beautiful girl who looked to be in her early twenties. She had a beautiful, bronzed complexion and fiery red hair. "The other in the back is their brother, Blizzard." Dalen looked toward the other side of the tavern and saw another server who looked exactly like his brother Jed, except that he was albino. "And Jax works in the back as Executive Chef."

"Are they gods too?" Dalen asked.

"*Gods* is the wrong word and it creates the wrong perception." Dalen looked back over to the jinn. Her cup was now filled with something that looked like molten glass, and she was taking little sips of it as they talked. "The clearest description I can give you right now is that they are Elementals."

Dalen pondered that for a moment, and then asked, "Do you mean they can wield an Element or that they are an Elemental aspect of a fifth Element?"

Dalen had thought his question was intelligent, but he wasn't ready for her response. "Both. Each of them can wield one of the four Natural Elements, but they are also very much four aspects of a single whole."

Dalen couldn't take the suspense, "Okay, who is that

'single whole'?" He was expecting her to say Dorn's name, but she surprised him again.

"They are aspects of the union between Dorn and his wife. They are the children of him and their mother."

"Who is that?" Dalen started to look around the room in hopes of seeing her.

The Fire Jinn waited for Dalen to finish looking around the room and to look back at her before she answered: "Venger."

"Venger, the city?" Dalen's mind had no idea how to process that or how it made children.

"Venger, the being that you met at the Great Seal," she read his thoughts through their connection and could tell that he was still lost on the concept. "The city is sentient, and it can create a physical avatar that the sentients can maintain for a short time. The first avatar she ever created was a woman with whom Dorn fell in love and had four children."

"That is amazing!" Dalen's ability to accept this had become stronger now that he understood more about the Natural Element. "Where is she now?"

"Holding a form like that for a long period is taxing on Venger, but she managed to do it while the quadruplets were being carried. Once they were born, she just couldn't hold the form any longer and it was finally let go."

"She died giving birth to them?" Unexplainably, Dalen felt

a sense of loss over this.

"In a way. You met her today. You even carry her blessing with you." Dalen instinctively touched the three rings that were still lit upon his arm. "If needed by Dorn or her children, she recreates the avatar of their mother, but she does not hold the form for months like she did so that her children could be born."

"I just talked to her before I came on shift."

Dalen was caught off guard and let out a small yelp as he turned to face Blizzard. His hair and skin were like porcelain. His eyes, like frosted sapphires, were the only hint of color on his being, and they twinkled brightly. "I always take a minute to say hello to her. Sometimes I feel she is the only one who gets me." He had brought Dalen his water. Just before he set it down, he blew on the glass and Dalen watched it fog over as the liquid became ice cold. "Are you ready to order?"

Dalen just stared at him for a moment. "Thank you. I haven't even looked at the menu yet. Do you have any suggestions?"

"My sister is the greatest chef I have ever heard of. No matter what you order, it is going to be amazing, but if you aren't sure what you want, may I suggest the Traveler's Special?" He pointed to a large blackboard that had 'Today's Special' written on it.

Dalen read that it was a whole roasted chicken, and the sides were two kinds of cheese and some grilled vegetables with a small loaf of bread. Dalen agreed to try it. Blizzard told him it would be right out and moved on from the table.

Dalen looked over to the jinn and asked, "You aren't going to order anything?" Then Dalen remembered that she was not physically there and tried to apologize.

"It's alright. Besides, I'll have some of yours," she smiled and her eyes glinted with fire.

"You are going to possess me so you can eat my dinner?" Dalen was surprised at first, but then assumed she was only playing.

"Absolutely." She smiled at him and took another sip of her drink. "Girl's got to eat."

"You can't ..." Dalen paused and remembered that he was in a public place and talking to himself, so he brought down his volume to hushed tones. "You can't just do that whenever you like. Besides, you are incorporeal — you don't need to eat right?"

The jinn's smile waned from her face and her tone grew serious. "As long as you wear those beads, I can do with you as I please."

Dalen was shocked by this answer. "What about not messing with free will?"

She didn't even skip a beat. "You can take the beads off and be on your own whenever you choose." Dalen looked down at the beads and knew he wasn't ready to do this alone. "Secondly, you are right." She tossed back the rest of her drink like a shot and continued, "But I will flat-out possess you for a bite of   Jax's cooking."

"How can you say that?" Horrified, Dalen did not attempt to hide the feelings in his mind or on his face. "You would be willing to possess me just so you can get a bite of her cooking. How good can it possibly be?"

Jed glided in with Dalen's dinner. "Why don't you try it out for yourself?" Jed slid a plate in front of Dalen and, for the first time that Dalen had seen, he stood still and waited.

Dalen looked over to the Fire Jinn, who just pointed at his plate. "Go ahead."

Dalen pulled a piece of meat from the chicken and bit it in half. It was the greatest thing Dalen had ever tasted. It was succulent and juicy. The herbs and spices that Jax had used were the perfect combination for this dish, and the only thing that Dalen could do was to moan in delicious bliss. Jed smiled and continued on.

Dalen finished off most of his meal without conversation, but towards the end, he slowed down to savor what was left. "Is this like at the counter, where it just magically creates what you wish?"

"No. This is far superior magic than that." She produced another drink and took another sip from it.

"Really? What kind of magic is that?" She was being vague and Dalen felt like he was being set up for something, but he had learned to trust her, so he decided to spring the trap and see what happened next.

"First and foremost, she has practiced for years and years and has perfected her craft through endless hours of tuning her skill until it becomes art."

"Practice a skill until it becomes art. I have heard of this kind of thing," Dalen replied. "Warrior monks who train every day in martial arts to become one with the action they are doing."

The jinn finished her drink and leaned in. "It's not just the warriors. Just in the world you came from, some painters can do this. Some bakers have this ability. It is not just something found in fighting. It can be found in any action you take." She waited for Dalen to digest the thought that was now filling his mind. "Haven't you ever had a moment where everything just came into balance, and whatever you were doing at that moment was perfect? Almost as if you were no longer in control and were just another part of what was happening?"

Dalen thought about it for a moment. "There have been a couple of times when my friends and I were playing our game, and we were up against a really hard challenge, and then it was like we just knew what each other was going to do."

She nodded. "What happened? What did it feel like?"

"It felt like we were in complete synchronization. Kind of like when I don't fight our connection." Dalen thought about it for a moment. "We were perfect. We came up with ideas and tactics that we had never thought of before. Time slowed down, and we had forever to think in the blink of an eye. Without talking, we knew what the others were going to do and responded as one. Even the dice were on our side."

"Those moments are what I am talking about. Jax has learned how to actively be in that state and, while she is there, she cooks and is in perfect harmony with what she is doing, almost as if she and the action she is taking are one." She had another drink in her hand and took a well-deserved victory sip.

"That's it!" Dalen said it way louder than a guy sitting by himself should exclaim.

The jinn smiled at him innocently. "What's it?"

Dalen was excited to the point of giddiness. "That's what you wanted me to see."

The jinn didn't even look up from her glass of liquid fire. "Whatever do you mean?"

"I mean, this is how you take an action while in the state of oneness." He took a sip of his water and then plopped a small red potato into his mouth, enjoying the dance the flavors created for a moment. "I'll tell you what ..."

The jinn looked up to meet his gaze. "Hmm?"

"I have always wanted to learn martial arts. I think it would be a good tool for me to learn this on."

She considered the idea for a moment. "I think that it would be a good route to take. It suits you and, in the end, you will need those skills if you are ever going to be prepared to do battle."

"How so?" Dalen hadn't thought about getting into a battle.

"Often a duel between those wielding magic has many similarities to that of fighters who are trained in martial arts." She laid out both hands, palm up, moving one up while the other went down like she was pretending to be a scale. "The ability to move with the flow of the moment is needed for both kinds of combat. One can even say that they are the same skill, just used somewhat differently."

"Then I wish to train in combat so that I can learn how to actively enter that state of oneness. If you can arrange it, I will willingly sit back and let you have the rest of this dinner."

The jinn smirked and folded her fingers together.

"As you wish."

12

THE FIRST DAY AT
THE TEMPLE OF LIGHT

Dalen awoke the next morning to unfamiliar surroundings. He was lying on a grass mat in a room that was wide enough to perfectly accommodate the length of the mat, which took up a third of the floor. The floors were wooden but had been worn to perfect smoothness by more years of use than Dalen would have liked to guess.

Dalen sat up, and with a wall now in front of him, behind him, and to his right, Dalen looked to his left and saw a sliding door made of paper and wood. When he reached up to scratch his head, he noticed that he was no longer wearing the same clothes he had worn when he went downstairs for dinner.

The clothes were lightweight and hung loosely on his frame.

The cloth was neither dyed nor bleached, and so the color was light tan. Dalen looked himself up and down, trying to understand where he was and how he ended up wearing these new clothes. It was then that Dalen noticed that the Beads of Fire were missing. He searched his robes in an attempt to find them, but the only thing he found was his silver figure in a small leather pouch that hung around his neck. Also in the pouch was a single bead. Although it was the same size, it was different than any in the Beads of Fire and looked as if someone had trapped a storm inside a ball. Dalen put both back in the pouch and pulled the strings tight until it closed. He wanted to find the Beads of Fire. He didn't have time to focus on either the figure or the bead at the moment.

In a panic, Dalen searched the empty room for the beads. The only thing in the room aside from the mat he had awoken on was a large clay pot that, when Dalen checked, he found was empty as well. When he still couldn't find the Beads of Fire, he tried to leave the room. In his haste and without thinking, he tried to push the door open, effectively putting his hand through the paper on the sliding door. By the time he realized that his hand had gone through it, he didn't have enough time to stop the inevitability of him stumbling through the entire thing, landing on the floor in a heap of wood and paper.

Dalen looked up and saw an old monk dressed in attire similar to his own, except his robes were stark white and an impressive gold medallion stood out in contrast against them. He held a cup of tea that was hot enough that wafts of steam rose from it. The monk's slender physique and pointed ears suggested to Dalen that he was an elf in his elder years. The monk stood there, staring at him with wide eyes.

Dalen scrambled to his feet and began to apologize but was interrupted by the monk, who let out a blast of laughter. Dalen was stunned and had no idea what to do as the monk bent over and grabbed his stomach with his free hand. The monk then knelt on the floor and gently sat the cup of tea down. The monk ran out of air, but his body wasn't done convulsing. He knelt there in silence for a moment and finally took a loud, exaggerated inhalation. This only fueled his laughter, and he rolled onto his side and began to snort between fits of laughter. His laughter was infectious, and Dalen began to laugh as well. A couple of monks came in to see what the commotion was about. All the elder monk could do was point at Dalen and giggle. He sat up, still pointing at Dalen three or four times, and then he threw both of his arms in the air and dramatically made crashing sounds as he fell to the ground and into another fit of laughter. The other monks caught on to the situation and laughed as well.

One of them finally approached Dalen and greeted him with a smile and a hug. His face showed the signs of years, but the lines that drew his face spoke of laughter along his eyes and very few worries in his brow. His hair was just long enough to not be shaved and was speckled with silver around the sides of his head. "Hello, I am Brother Faith."

Dalen, relieved by the laughter, smile, and hug but still concerned that he was in trouble, said, "I am so sorry about the door."

"It is alright. It is made of paper and this happens to

newcomers more often than you think. I see you have met Master Joy. You caught him off guard — we haven't had a new initiate plow through a door like that in a while." Faith checked on the fallen monk who was still giggling and snorting. The old monk waved him off, still trying to catch his breath. "He has not made a sound except for laughter in a long time. I don't believe I have ever heard him snort."

Dalen was still concerned about the lost beads, but the fall and the monk had distracted him enough that he was able to maintain himself. "Really? That's fascinating. Why laughter?" Dalen was trying to be polite, but he had not forgotten his main concern. "Have you seen a set of beads that glow like they are on fire?"

Brother Faith walked him past the elf, who was finally regaining his sense of decorum. "He is a fascinating man. The reason he kept laughter was that, when he chose to take a vow of silence, he also chose to not deprive himself of one of the greatest gifts life has to offer. And yes, I know exactly where the Beads of Fire are."

Dalen was relieved to know that they were not lost. "That's wonderful. I will need them back."

"Agreed," said Faith. "If you are ever going to get back to the world you came from and save your friends from the desperate acts of a mad man, you will definitely need them."

Dalen's mind filled with questions. How did this monk know so much about him? Were his friends in danger? Had Mathias done something to them? "You seem to know a lot about me. I feel you have me at a disadvantage, Brother Faith."

238

Brother Faith guided him to an open courtyard. "Welcome to the Temple of the Brotherhood of Light. You are here to continue your training." Dalen marveled at what his eyes were telling him. The temple was built on a stone spire that rose hundreds of feet in the air. The spire itself was in the center of a circular canyon, and the spire rose high enough to be level with the canyon's lip, effectively creating a vast pit around the temple.

This was definitely not Venger.

Dalen had no idea where he was and even less of an idea about how to leave. "It's two hundred feet to the closest edge. How does someone get here?" he asked.

"With a Leap of Faith." Brother Faith turned to the far side of the courtyard and gave a bow. Dalen looked over and saw what he thought was the ghost of another monk sitting on the stone railing that ran along the edge of the drop-off.

Brother Faith signaled for Dalen to follow him as he began to head toward the monk made of smoke. As Dalen approached, he asked out loud, "Are you a ghost?"

The monk chuckled to himself before playfully adding, "Are you?"

Brother Faith stopped Dalen directly in front of the semi-transparent monk. He bowed again and gave Dalen a look that suggested he follow suit. When Dalen did, Brother Faith said, "Dalen Pax, may I introduce the Grand Master of the Brotherhood of Light, Master Truth?"

When Dalen stood back up, he understood what his eyes were trying to tell him: Master Truth was a jinn. He had an overall form of an old man with long hair, mustache, and beard. He seemed to be wearing long robes that hid his lower half, but he was completely made of smoke. Some parts were darker than others, which helped Dalen make out his form, but overall, he was wisps of smoke and looked as if he could be blown away with the slightest of breezes. In seven spots through the center of him and one in each of his limbs were stones that matched the bead that Dalen had found in his pouch earlier.

Dalen patted the pouch around his neck, "My guess is this is why I can see you."

The jinn's form moved as if pushed by air and then bloomed upward to a standing position. "Aren't you the quick one?"

"Do you know the jinn that is connected to the Beads of Fire?" Dalen was hoping to create some common ground.

Master Truth puckered his mouth to one side, "But not that quick."

Dalen realized he had missed something. Possibly all jinn knew each other or perhaps they were related like Dorn's children, each with their own Element. "Okay. So, yeah. She is a friend of mine, and I am looking for the Beads of Fire so that I can contact her again."

The jinn smiled at Dalen. "Do you wish to see her?"

Dalen gave a short bow, "With all due respect to your

question, I believe that wishing things is how I found myself here."

"You are demonstrating that you can be taught. This is a good beginning for your training." The jinn paused for a moment and reached out to his right with his hand. The stone in his palm grew brighter for a moment, and the smoke around it formed a cup, which he then closed his spindly fingers of smoke around as if he were holding it. Master Truth blew on the cup as if it were hot and then chuckled to himself as if that were amusing to him. Just then, smoke began to rise from the cup as if it were filled with a hot liquid. "Master Ki will be your teacher during this trial. You will not be needing the help of your fiery friend at this time."

Dalen bowed again and didn't rise until the jinn finished what he was saying. "I require clarification, please. Are you saying you won't give me back the Beads of Fire until I finish my training?"

"No, dear boy." The wind picked up and lifted him across the courtyard to the other side, where he fluttered down and landed with a slight poof of smoke. He pointed across the way to the other side of the canyon. "Do you see the tree across the span?" Dalen moved to where the jinn was and looked across the chasm to the other side. A beautiful white willow tree was growing at the edge of the cliff. "That tree is the marker from where one must leap to arrive at the temple or leap to in order to leave it. The Beads of Fire will be found on the other side of the leap to that tree." The jinn's form changed so that, instead of looking at the tree, the jinn was looking at Dalen. "The day you can make the leap is the day you can leave. The Beads of Fire are waiting for you. You may have them now," Master Truth closed his eyes and seemed to take a deep breath in, "if you can reach them." The wind picked up and, without another word, the jinn was gone.

Dalen watched the smoke rise and be taken to some other part of the temple. He turned on his heel to find Brother Faith, who had a look of excitement as if he were a child seeing this for the first time. "That ... just happened!"

"What the ..." Dalen was feeding off of Brother Faith's excitement.

"I know! Right? Do you see why I choose to live here? This place —" he ended with a sharp whoop.

"How long have you lived here?"

"Well, let's see ..." Faith tapped his nose a few times with his finger. "I left the army at the end of The Dragon Wars at the age of twenty-seven. I came here to heal from what war had done to me and to find peace again in my heart. I am sixty this year, so that was thirty-three years ago."

Dalen's attention had been pulled back to this moment. "Dragon Wars?"

"Yeah, ten dragons forged an alliance and thought that they could take over the world. The war raged on until every last one of them had perished." Brother Faith's tone grew somber for a moment. "Those were dark times. They almost won." Then Brother Faith shook it off, as a dog would shake off water. He took a deep breath in slowly and as he did, Dalen could feel a change in Brother Faith. Even the environment of the courtyard changed. Brother Faith stood there with his eyes closed, swaying ever so slightly with the wind.

Dalen politely waited for a moment, but after a while his impatience got the better of him. "Are you alright?"

Brother Faith smiled, and a single tear rolled down his cheek. "Just paying respect to an old friend."

"Did they die?" Dalen regretted asking the question even as he spoke it, and so with the same breath he added, "I'm sorry — that was rude of me."

"It's alright. Your heart asked for kind reasons." Brother Faith continued to sway with the breeze, but he took a deep breath in slowly and spoke. "Yao was a soldier in The Dragon Wars. He had enlisted in his homelands, ready to protect it. He wanted to protect his family and his home, but the battles moved and raged across this world, and Yao found himself across oceans to do battle on lands that were not his own. Still, he believed in the cause, for the people he was protecting may not be his family, but they were somebody's family. Maybe there was someone on a faraway shore, praying that there would be someone to protect all that he loved while he was gone. He wanted to believe this, in hopes that someone was standing in his home doing the same thing.

"His division had suffered many losses and was merged with other armies. The individuals that then gave him orders were strangers from other lands, but he knew his duty and carried on.

"There was a particularly bad encounter between his army

and two of the dragons who had also amassed a hoard of dragon-folk, a reptilian species that have some shared bloodlines with dragons and who revere them as gods. Yao and his battalion had been hit with overwhelming numbers; they were beaten and left to bleed to death from their wounds. A young soldier from another battalion found them and carried them one by one to safety while also fighting off dragon-folk who came across them. He saved nine of them, including Yao.

"His name was Mordecai, and he was given many honors for what he'd done that day. He was given a field promotion to captain and given men under him, including the men he saved. While Yao was directly under this man, he learned to trust and respect Mordechai, who was one of the greatest men to fight in that war.

"One day, Mordecai was given an order by his general to obliterate an entire village because they were harboring dragon-folk. Mordecai argued that, whether or not the dragon-folk were there, there were innocent civilians in the village as well. The general, though, was an uncaring man and demanded that Mordecai follow orders or be charged with treason. When Mordecai again refused to kill the innocent, he was immediately arrested. The general decided to make an example of him and was going to kill him right there.

"With the general's elite guard surrounding him, Mordecai was forced to his knees and the general stood before him with Mordecai's own sword raised above his head to strike. It was Yao who interrupted the general and said that if Mordecai was guilty of treason, then so was he because he refused the order as well. In the moment that everyone's attention was on Yao, Mordecai pulled a dagger from the general's belt and killed him. He caught his sword as it fell from the general's hands and, as he touched it, the blade began to glow with a white light.

"It turns out Mordecai was a Holy Knight — a Divine Warrior, who at that moment proved to the Divine that he was worthy to wield its power and was granted new gifts and abilities. Thirty evil men fell to his blade that day, and Yao fought by his side the entire way. There were a few others who took up arms to try and protect the people, but were killed early in the battle. Yao had thought that the battle was won and did not see the last soldier coming up behind him with a spear. Mordecai got to Yao in time to push him out of harm's way but took the spear himself. Yao dispatched his would-be killer and repaid his debt by carrying Mordecai away from the battlefield. Yao patched him up the best he could, but he was not a healer. Yao carried him for two days until he came upon this temple. He had heard stories and myths about the mystic healers of the Brotherhood of Light. He also knew the story that said the only way to get there was with a Leap of Faith from the tree.

"Mordecai had lost a lot of blood and was dying, and Yao knew that the only chance that Mordecai had was for Yao to get him to the temple. So, with a half-dead man on his back, Yao closed his eyes and leaped."

Dalen was engrossed in the story and his excitement got the better of him. "What happened? Did he make the leap?"

"He did. Mordecai survived and now lives in Venger City as

the guardian and protector of Crown Princess Joanna."

"And Yao? What happened to Yao?"

Brother Faith opened his eyes and tears caressed both of his cheeks. "I never left," he smiled and the world seemed a little warmer. "It is how I earned the name Brother Faith. No one had ever made the leap on their first try, let alone while carrying another on his back."

"I thought you said Yao was an old friend," Dalen's implied question was born from real curiosity.

"I am no longer the soldier who was filled with pain and loss. I haven't been Yao since the day I made the leap. I have spent years letting the pain and suffering go and learning to embrace the beauty of this world instead of holding onto the loss and sadness." Brother Faith smiled, "Yet, I remember who I used to be and revere him as an old friend."

"You revere the broken, sad version of you that was in pain?" Dalen's question brought Brother Faith's attention away from his memories.

Without hesitation, Brother Faith said, "Absolutely."

"Why revere the dark broken part?"

"Because he was the one who made the leap." One final tear made its way to his cheeks. "It was the most amazing moment of my life, and possibly the strongest I have ever been." It resonated in Dalen unlike anything Dalen had experienced before, and Dalen knew it was Truth.

Dalen nodded and then took a moment himself to remember who he had been and the moments of strength that he'd had. He glimpsed a truth that the darkest moments of his life were always the moments he truly showed his strength. He then took a moment to remember his friends. They would never believe all that he'd seen. He remembered that if he were ever going to see them or Ms. Warren again, he was going to have to get to work and, even though this was going to be hard, he would have to find   the strength.

"Are you ready?" Brother Faith's voice was calm and collected.

Dalen nodded, "Any advice before we start?"

Brother Faith thought for a moment. "The largest obstacle that we will first face is everything you think you know. It is useless to you now."

"I don't understand," Dalen replied, confused.

"Alright." Brother Faith turned to Dalen and looked him directly in the eyes. It made Dalen feel a little uncomfortable, like he was peering into his soul. "Imagine that you are a student in a classroom. You sit at a desk with a single piece of parchment to write upon to learn this lesson. This parchment is your mind. I, as your teacher, will require you to learn things, and so you will need to write them down on this parchment. Once you have, it has now been learned. Can you follow this concept so far?"

Dalen nodded, answering, "My mind is the paper; when I

247

learn something, I am writing on the page."

Brother Faith nodded. "You look at your parchment, and it is filled with other lessons you've learned, and there's more that already fills the page. There are little drawings on the sides from daydreams. There are also opinions about things like gravity or time that are neither fact nor knowledge." Faith shook his head slowly. "Now you are left with little space to write what must be learned. Do you see the problem?" Dalen nodded. "You want to be able to start with a clean page, so that you not only have enough room to write, but nothing that is written will conflict with what now needs to be known."

"How do I do that?" Dalen asked excitedly.

"Practice. Lots and lots of practice," he laughed at his own joke, which Dalen assumed was much funnier than he understood from Brother Faith's laughter. "Meditation is a good place to start. It is something that will become a part of your everyday life. There will be a rigorous training schedule of theory and physical training that we will end right here at the end of each day."

Dalen looked around at the courtyard. It was made mostly of stone. It looked like it was carved directly from the spire that the Temple of Light was on because it was as seamless as a single piece of stone. There was a circle carved in the center of the courtyard with four circles running along the outer edge and a fifth in the center. Based on what Dalen had learned, he believed it was an Elemental Circle for the Natural Elements. The courtyard stretched to the edge of the spire and dropped off into a straight cliff-face. There was a stone railing or bench that covered most of the drop-off, and Dalen could see the majestic beauty of the canyon. There was a waterfall on the far end to his right, and the water ran along the canyon floor and finally into a cave on Dalen's far left. He loved the view but felt that there was more than that to this courtyard. "Why will it end here every day?"

"Because every day you will finish your training with me. You will come to this courtyard and attempt to leap to the other side." Brother Faith placed his hand on Dalen's back and began to move him toward the ledge. "Your first attempt will be right now."

"Hey! Whoa there!" Dalen leaned back against Brother Faith's hand. "I have had no training in this. I can't do it yet!"

"I was not trained when I made my leap and I was carrying someone, yet I made it. Your parchment is full, Dalen. How can I teach you anything if you have already decided it is impossible?" Faith continued to move Dalen toward the ledge.

Dalen started to push back in earnest. He pressed himself backward against Faith's hand as hard as he could, but the monk moved him as if he had the strength of ten men. "Okay, say you're right," Dalen made a panicked attempt to stall. "My page already says I can't. You have to let me try to learn how to erase it before you make me jump to my death, right?"

Faith scoffed, "You won't die. You are a bird."

"No, I'm not a bird!" Dalen screamed as the edge got closer.

Faith roared with laughter, "Do you see how easy it is to

249

erase an idea?"

Dalen desperately tried to hold on to Brother Faith. "Sure, that's simple because it's not true!"

Faith pushed him right to an open edge of the courtyard, and Dalen's toes hung over the edge. "Neither is it true that you cannot do this."

From the shadows of Dalen's fear, a familiar voice cried out, "You can't do it!"

Brother Faith rolled his eyes at Dalen. "Very well," he said as he wrapped a white canvas belt around Dalen twice and tied it in the front. "This belt will save you when you fall. It will bring you back to this position when you don't make it."

Dalen breathed a giant sigh of relief and reached back to feel the rope that the belt was connected to. To his dismay, there was no rope. "How does this save me?"

Brother Faith pointed at the canyon. "If the belt drops more than thirty feet, it activates and teleports the wearer to the place from where they leapt."

Dalen couldn't help but smile, "Okay, that's awesome!"

Faith smiled . "I know, right? What? You thought I was just going to kill you on your first day?"

All of Dalen's fear and nervous energy erupted into laughter. Faith laughed with him and let him take a step back from the edge. He put an arm around him and patted his shoulder as they quelled their laughter, but then pushed him right back to the edge.

"Hey! Whoa there. Is this thing on right? You know it's going to work?"

"You don't even need the belt. It's a Leap of Faith. Have some. That's why I'm here." He chuckled to himself and shook his head, "Clear your page. It is not a Leap of Faith that involves some holy God thing that you can't even imagine. This is a Leap of Faith in yourself. The only question is whether or not you believe in yourself." Brother Faith let him go and stepped away from him. "Now jump."

Dalen's fear howled from the darkness, "You will never make this jump. That guy was trained as a soldier. He'd been in real danger and there was a life on the line. You are just a seventeen-year-old boy with no experience, and you will never make it." Dalen agreed. He pulled on the belt to make sure it was tight and tried to jump. On his first attempt, fear won, and he moved like he was going to jump but didn't. He tried to make himself jump for what seemed to be forever, first edging closer to the precipice, but then fear would override his choice and, even though he wanted to, Dalen could not make his limbs obey. Dalen took out the silver figure from his pouch. He rubbed it and told himself that he was brave enough to do this, and in what felt like a moment of madness, he closed his eyes, screamed, and stepped off.

Flailing wildly, Dalen plummeted. Thirty feet was further than Dalen was expecting, and as he reappeared on the edge of the courtyard, he was still screaming. He backed away from the edge in terror. "I am NOT doing that again!"

Brother Faith took Dalen by the shoulders and shook him gently. "I am so proud of you!" Brother Faith let him go and leaped in the air. He went up about twenty feet and came down slightly slower than gravity would have dictated. "That was amazing!" His joy was infectious, and it waged war on the mini freak-out session Dalen was in the middle of.

Dalen shouted, "What are you talking about?" His adrenaline was flooding his system, and he couldn't put together a clear understanding of why Brother Faith would be happy with him. "I failed! I told you I knew I wasn't ready!"

Brother Faith hopped up and down and clapped in time with his statement: "And yet you jumped!" Brother Faith stopped and gave Dalen a very respectful bow. "That was some next-level stuff right there. I have seen people take weeks before they have the faith to even leap, and yet on day one, you jumped." With his hand, he pointed two fingers down like a man with legs and then had him jump off an imaginary edge. He whistled lower and lower while the little man dropped. "You, Dalen Pax, are going to do very well here."

Dalen's fear was being crushed by the positive energy that was pulsating through Brother Faith, but Dalen still didn't understand. "But I failed."

Brother Faith stepped to Dalen and looked him in the eye. "The difference between a Master and a Novice is that a Master has failed more times than the Novice has ever tried." Faith put his hand on Dalen's shoulder. "Failure is a part of learning. It should not be seen as a negative. Instead, it should be seen as our greatest teacher."

Dalen understood. He caught his breath, looking over to the edge. "Do you want me to try again?"

Brother Faith patted his hand on Dalen's shoulder. "You have been brave enough for now." He took the belt off Dalen. "For now, allow me to show you around the rest of the temple, and we will try to help you clear your page. Once you have had a chance to do so, we will try again at the end of the day."

"That sounds wonderful." Dalen backed away from the edge. "Master Truth said that I will be taught by Master Ki. Will I get to meet them today?"

Brother Faith nodded. "Master Ki is at the end of the tour."

Dalen had a question that he thought should be asked but wasn't sure how to approach it. Eventually, he decided that being direct was going to be the easiest route. "Brother Faith," Dalen began, "this place has been described as the Brotherhood of Light. Does that mean everyone here is a brother?"

Faith laughed with glee. "Both males and females are welcome here. Why do you ask?"

Dalen shrugged. "I am about to meet the teacher who is going to be training me, and I don't know if they are male or female. I just don't know if I should say Brother or Sister when I come across them. I could see either making sense, depending on how this temple works, and I don't want to be offensive on my first day."

"It doesn't matter for two reasons," replied Faith. "The

first reason is easy: you will refer to Master Ki as 'Master,' and so it matters not, either way."

Dalen laughed. "Fair enough. What is the other reason?"

"The second is that Master Ki is a Water Jinn. Master Ki's form can and will change to what is required at the time, and because of this is neither male nor female."

"The jinn I know has no name. She says physical names are just grunts that we corporeal beings do to communicate. How do you know what to call them?

"Dalen, I wish for you to try to clear your page for this." Brother Faith looked him in the eyes with warmth and peaceful understanding. "Your name here is based on who you choose to be. Even the term Master is only given when the person knows that it has been earned. They would call me Master Faith if I so choose."

"Why do you choose not to be called a Master?"

"From time to time, someone has been able to make the Leap and never land," Brother Faith said with respect flowing from his words.

"I don't understand. How do they never land?"

Faith looked up past the sky and into the heavens. "Sometimes you can make a perfect Leap of Faith, where you become one with everything and, in that moment, you are plucked from this world and land in the Divine Unknown."

The only thing Dalen could get out was, "Wow."

"Wow, indeed." Brother Faith wiped his eyes with his sleeve. "On the day I make that Leap, they can call me Master Faith."

Dalen patted him on the shoulder. "I hope that I am there to see it."

Faith patted the hand that was on his shoulder and smiled. "I hope you are there, too."

Brother Faith continued with his tour. He taught Dalen how to find the kitchen and where to empty his chamber pot. Then he showed Dalen the library and the meditation halls. After that, he met many monks, both male and female, with ages ranging from Master Joy — who was sixteen-hundred-years-old — to one of the newest members, who was orphaned at the age of two and had been living at the temple for about six weeks and had not yet been named.

Eventually, Faith led Dalen to a training room. This room was a large square that was fifty feet across from wall to wall. The floors were polished wood and there was a large mat in the center of the room that was thirty feet square. A grass mat was placed in front of the larger mat on the side that was closest to where Dalen was entering, and there was a large basin of water on the far end. Many large pieces of parchment showed various stances, as well as how to enact certain moves.

"This is where you will study with Master Ki," indicated Faith.

"So, what can you tell me about Master Ki before they get here?"

"Very little, actually," Faith looked at Dalen and smiled. "I only met them this morning and haven't had much time to get to know them ... as a person."

"You only just met?"

"Master Truth requested Master Ki when you arrived. Master Truth has known Ki for a long time, but they had never set foot in the temple until today. When I met them, though, I got a feeling that they are a good person." Faith scooted Dalen toward the door and added, "When you are all done, come find me in the courtyard and we will jump one more time before bed." Brother Faith started to walk away, but he turned around and kept walking backward long enough to say, "Clear that page." Then he finished his turn and continued down the hall.

"I will do my best," Dalen called out.

Just before Brother Faith turned the corner, he added, "Good! Master Ki will expect nothing less." And then he disappeared from sight.

Dalen walked further into the training room. "Hello?" he called out, but there was no response. Since no one seemed to be there yet, Dalen reverted to his old habit and began to study the room that he was in. He slowly meandered around the room, looking at the diagrams that were on the walls. Dalen lost track of time, and by the time he'd prowled around the room and arrived back at the entrance, he started to wonder if perhaps he was in the wrong place.

He began to pay closer attention to his environment and toward the center of the room. His eyes caught a glint of something that was lying on the grass mat in front. When Dalen walked over to it, he noticed that there was a set of prayer beads that were almost identical to the Beads of Fire, with the exception that they looked as if they were made of drops of water.

As Dalen examined them, he counted out the beads and, just like the Beads of Fire, seven sets of seven were separated by seven brilliant sapphires.

Dalen felt dumb. He rolled his eyes at himself and chided, "Becky would be so disappointed." Dalen knelt on the grass mat facing the larger mat and wrapped the Beads around his wrist. When the Water Jinn rose from the basin and formed in the shape of a humanoid with no distinguishing features, crossed its arms, and stared at him, Dalen immediately apologized.

The jinn raised its hand for him to stop and Dalen did. "You have done nothing wrong. You passed your test."

"This was a test?"

The jinn ignored his question. "Clear your mind."

Dalen stopped what he was doing and worked to make all the questions in his mind stop.

"Good. The questions you have are all based on the

conclusions you have already made about what is happening in this moment. Clear them. They do you no good. In fact, they are obviously causing you harm."

Dalen took another breath to calm himself emotionally.

"Good. When you are calm, you will be able to think clearly. Your fear is doing you no good. Let it go. The next step is going to be simple. You have to accept the truth that you do not know what the truth is." The Water Jinn could feel the conflicting thoughts coming from Dalen. "Simple does not mean easy."

Dalen was struggling and, because of that, his frustration was rapidly shifting to anger. That emotion asked the next question, "What's the difference?"

"Running forty miles is simple. It's just one foot in front of the other." The Water Jinn locked eyes with Dalen until it saw recognition and understanding. "Take another breath, Dalen. You are pushing yourself hard, which is good, but you are pushing yourself in the wrong direction." Dalen took another breath and began to calm down. "Good. See, isn't that better?" Dalen nodded. "Alright. This is a simple question. It requires a simple answer, and when I say this, I mean that the answer is simple, but you need to keep it simple in your mind and not begin to fill your entire page with the garbage of what you think the answer means. So, a simple yes or no answer will do. Do you know specifically what the test was?"

"No," Dalen responded and immediately was disappointed in himself for not knowing the answer.

"Stop making it complicated in your mind and heart." The jinn moved like a wave and flowed so it was directly in front of Dalen. "You were not supposed to know of the test. That's why it was a test. Stop feeling bad for not knowing an answer. From what I understand, you are here to learn. If we are going to deal with a constant depression every time you are to be taught anything new, then this is going to take much longer than is necessary." The Water Jinn paused and waited for all of that to filter into Dalen's mind. "Can we agree that you are here because you don't know what you have come to learn; it is expected that you will not have answers to many of the questions asked because learning what you don't know is an integral part of learning?"

"Yes, I agree," Dalen affirmed. "You are right."

The jinn smiled. "Good. Then can we agree that if you do not know something, it is better to openly admit it so that it can be taught, and that filling your mind with garbage is not helping you at all?"

"Agreed."

"Excellent! I will require you to act according to our agreement from here on in." The Water Jinn stood up and, as it did, it took the form of a middle-aged man, who, if they were in the world that Dalen came from, he would say had distinctively Asian features. He appeared to be wearing clothes and had skin and hair. In the same locations as the other jinn, the man in front of Dalen also had stones, but they were like the ones that Dalen had around his wrist.

"You look real," Dalen said with obvious surprise in his voice.

"I am real," the Water Jinn winked at him.

"No, I mean, you look corporeal," Dalen retorted as he reached out and poked him — and was surprised that he had substance.

"What is the nature of water?" Master Ki asked.

"Its form can change outwardly but the essence remains," Dalen caught on as he spoke, so he just continued speaking in the same breath, "which is why Master Truth requested you. Because you can change your form."

"In a way," Master Ki raised an eyebrow. "Why would Master Truth feel that I was required? There are two parts to this answer. Do you know what they are?"

Dalen had no idea why, but this time he didn't fill himself with dread over it. "I have no idea, but please, teach me."

"Better! You have the ability to learn," Master Ki gave Dalen a small bow. "I am going to be honest with you. We have a fiery friend in common. When I found out that the two of you had met and she'd brought you here to Master Truth, I was interested in meeting you. Then when Master Truth asked me to train you, I knew what you were training for and accepted the challenge. I would've only been asked for by Master Truth if you were to be trained in the Martial Art of Magic. Who better to teach you flow than a jinn seen from the perspective of Water?"

Dalen had no option but to agree with that logic. "And the other?"

"You will need someone to train with that you can actually punch and that can punch back." He laughed, "There will be a lot of punching."

"Okay." Dalen took a deep breath, "What are we to do first?"

"Today is already done. Since you passed your test, I would like to teach you what the test was." Dalen nodded for him to continue. "The test was to see what you would do. There was no wrong answer. It was going to just keep going until you understood that if you were to be taught by a jinn, you would have to be able to perceive your teacher. You won the moment you realized you had to put on the Beads of Water to be taught. You also granted yourself a victory by understanding that you are here to learn, thus accepting that there is knowledge that you don't have and that that is nothing to be ashamed of."

"Thank you, Master Ki. I feel a lot better about today." Master Ki gave Dalen a little bow. "What do we learn tomorrow?"

"That will be tomorrow's lesson." Dalen nodded because he saw that one coming. "I will offer you this. Over your training, I will take many forms. All of them will be for a single purpose."

"What is it?" Dalen asked.

"To grant you the wish that you have enacted." He then returned to his shapeless water form. "Goodbye for now, Dalen. I will be waiting for you tomorrow."

Dalen bowed to his teacher and said goodbye. As he did, Master Ki reverted directly back to water and poured himself back into the basin from which it came. Dalen left the room and went in search of the courtyard again. When he found it, Brother Faith was waiting for him, and he asked how training went. Dalen did his best to share his experience, during which Brother Faith kept walking him closer and closer to the edge of the courtyard.

"Can I have the safety belt, please?" Dalen asked.

Faith groaned and rolled his eyes at Dalen again. "I'm telling you that you don't need it."

Dalen put it on anyway and claimed it gave him the courage to jump.

"It gives you the courage to know you can fail."

Dalen took a couple of quick breaths once it was securely on and then jumped. When he appeared back on the ledge, he pointed out, "See, good thing I was wearing it."

"It's alright," assured Faith. "You can jump again tomorrow."

On the first night Dalen was alone, he missed his friends. He thought of them and Ms. Warren. He thought of the Fire Jinn. He was connected to her and, without those Beads, he felt as if something had been cut off. He cried himself to sleep that night, and the next night as well. By the third night, he was so tired from training he forgot to be sad and was simply happy to rest. By the end of the first week, the ones he missed became fuel for his training. By the third week, he stopped counting the days. By the third month, he felt like the temple was his home.

And so it went.

He became close friends with every monk at the Temple of Light, and they grew to see him as one of their own. When he was not training, he was in the library, searching through scrolls and texts, trying to understand and unlock the secrets of the Kinetic Element.

In his second year of training, Master Tome, who was the head of the library, said that Dalen sought after truth as vigorously as Master Truth and petitioned Master Truth for permission for the use of his name. With Master Truth's amused blessing, the brothers began to call Dalen Brother Truth and, within a few months, Brother Truth had almost forgotten he had ever been called anything else.

13

THE LAST DAY AT THE TEMPLE OF LIGHT

Brother Truth awoke. It was early morning and the sun had not yet risen above the horizon. He prepared himself for the day, quietly slid open his paneled door, and made his way to the kitchen where Master Joy was waiting. At his age, he had let go of the common concept of diurnal living and often napped in the day and was up throughout the night.

When he first arrived at this place, Brother Truth couldn't sleep well, and he found himself alone and afraid. One morning, he went to the courtyard that he was shown on his first day to get some air. Master Truth was also there and had gestured for him to come and speak with him. Ever since that day, he would get up early in the morning and meet with the Air Jinn. Master Truth seemed to like the early dawn and watched the sunrise every morning. "There is nothing like the fresh start of a new day," Master Truth would always say.

Somewhere along the way, Brother Truth started to bring tea. Even though the Air Jinn did not drink it, Brother Truth always brought two cups out of respect. Master Truth would reach out as if he were taking it and, as he pulled back his hand, a cup made of smoke would be there as if he had taken it.

Together they would sip their tea and talk while watching the sun rise. Often, they would talk about what Brother Truth had been learning about the Kinetic Element. Master Truth passed on many hints and suggestions, but he rarely gave direct answers. The Air Jinn believed a lesson worked out on its own carried more weight than a truth told by someone else, and he refused to stunt someone's learning by giving them answers. Brother Truth would ask a question and Master Truth would answer it with a question in return. Then Brother Truth would answer that question, which would lead to more questions from the Air Jinn until Brother Truth would see what Master Truth had been circling and eventually he'd answer his original question himself. Master Truth called this their "Moment of Truth."

Since his arrival, Brother Truth and Master Joy had become great friends. They had taught each other their customary greetings initially as a way to share each other's culture. Over time, though, they had decided that this was a greater knowledge than they expected it to be. There was a beautiful understanding of brotherhood between the seventeen-year-old adept and the sixteen-hundred-year-old master. So, as they had done every morning for over two years, they bowed to each other, including the traditional hand gestures of the Royal High Elven Court, and then they would look up from their bows and high five. They called this ritual the Joyous Truth.

On that morning, Brother Truth had finished preparing the tea and was about to head to the courtyard when the old elf stopped him. "What can I do for you, Master Joy?"

Master Joy looked at him with so much love in his eyes. "You have brought me joy from the moment we met, Dalen."

"You spoke?" Master Joy had not spoken in over a thousand years, so hearing him speak came as quite a shock to Brother Truth.

Master Joy laughed, "I did." They both laughed at that for a moment, and then Master Joy said, "This is my last day in this world, and I finally have something worth saying."

Brother Truth was concerned. "Last day? Are you ill?"

Master Joy laughed again, "Age is not an Illness. I'm old, that's all. I have used up the time that has been allotted to me, and I do say, it was probably more than my fair share."

Brother Truth began to feel the loss, and his heart wept. "Can anything be done?"

"Yes, you can listen to and heed the only words this dying man will say before his end."

Brother Truth nodded as tears rolled down his face.

"I have a request."

"All you need do is ask it, and if it is in my power, I will grant it with all that I am, Brother." It was not just words; Brother Truth spoke it as a vow.

"There is only one joy that I have left in this world to achieve before I go." Master Joy placed his hand over Brother Truth's heart, and Master Joy sent his energy, his Ki, through his own body and into Brother Truth's. Everything fell away. The years dissolved into nothing, and the Joyous Truth resonated in both of them. There was no adept. There was no master. There were only two brothers. "I wish to see you fly."

Brother Truth had been learning the techniques of energy movement, also known as Ki and Reiki, as well as other ways to move one's energy with the natural flow of the Kinetic Element, and so he brought up his hand and made the same connection to Master Joy. This amplified everything and, in that moment, they changed from being brothers to being two parts of the same being. "As you wish."

Master Joy broke contact, and their perception became separate again. "When you make it, you will leave this place. Take the time to say your farewells." Master Joy took Truth's hand and squeezed it. "The first moment I saw you, you brought me great joy. May the last time I see you be the same."

• • •

Dawn was approaching the Temple of Light. Its founder and Grand Master was creating moving animals with wisps of smoke in the northern courtyard. Today he had created two kittens, and he had encouraged them to chase off after a wonderful butterfly he created. Brother Truth came out into the courtyard from a side door that led to the kitchen. His eyes were red, and they had the look of tears. The Air Jinn felt the effects of joy and sadness that had been in him, but the sadness was only a memory in the young adept. Only resolve moved him now.

"Good morning," Master Truth said. "I see you wish to change the outcome of your leap today."

"You are just going to let Master Joy die, eh?" Brother Truth was still grappling with the news he had received.

"Master Joy will never truly die." A gust of wind blew the Air Jinn over to where Brother Truth stood and reformed, pointing to his heart. "You can choose to let Joy die, or you can choose to carry Joy with you."

It wasn't fair. Brother Truth wanted to blame someone else or try to change fate, and instead, the Air Jinn put all of the responsibility of keeping Master Joy alive in his heart.

Brother Truth pleaded with the Air Jinn, "Can't you do something?"

Master Truth put his hands on Brother Truth's shoulders. "I am going to do something. I am going to keep the joy that crazy old elf poured into this world alive. I will do his memory proud."

"You knew it was coming, didn't you?"

"You still don't quite grasp the whole 'not connected to time' thing, eh?" the jinn smirked. "I experience every moment as a whole. You move through it like a boat upon the sea. I experience tomorrow at the same moment I experience yesterday, which is no different than experiencing now. The only thing that separates any of it is you. You experience 'Now' as a continuous moving position in time, ever driving forward. My concept of 'Now' is that it is a universal constant. It is only when both of our 'Now' perceptions are in harmony that you can perceive me."

"Then you know what I am going to do."

"I do."

"Will it work?"

The jinn laughed as a gust of wind blew him back so he was near the kittens, who were still playing with the butterfly. "And what? Deprive you of Free Will? I would never harm you in such a manner."

"Oh, come on, Master Truth. You know I am going to try. You aren't affecting my Free Will by telling me if it works." He'd had this conversation with the Air Jinn a few times before, so when Master Truth cocked his head to the side and gave him a look that suggested disbelief that he would say something so silly, Brother Truth added, "I know, I know. It would absolutely change my answer if I knew it failed."

"That is true," the Air Jinn replied, "but that is not all."

269

"There are more reasons?" Brother Truth was frustrated, but after years of training, he chose to take a deep breath. Master Truth patiently waited while Brother Truth found his center. He reminded himself that he was very emotional about what Master Joy had said and that he wasn't thinking clearly. He took another breath and focused his energy and thought on the concept of calming down. As he breathed, he actively allowed his emotions to drain, and he regained focus. "Help me understand, Master Truth."

The Air Jinn had Brother Truth sit down and plopped a smoke kitten in his lap. It batted at the leather pouch around his neck. "Everything you have ever needed has been with you since the day you arrived. Nine hundred and ninety-nine times you have jumped, and nine hundred and ninety-nine times you have fallen. The ability to succeed is found in the understanding of why you have failed."

"I do not know why I have failed." Brother Truth played with the kitten for a moment, hoping the answer would fall in his lap. "I have wanted to succeed every time I have jumped."

Master Truth slowly nodded with understanding. "Wanting it is not enough. You must intend to succeed as well."

"I don't understand."

"That's why you fall."

"What am I not doing?"

The Air Jinn smiled. "Answer that, and you will grant Master Joy the wish to see Truth soar." A soft breeze passed by

270

them both and, when it stopped, Master Truth had faded away.

Brother Truth looked down and saw that the smoke kitten still had its attention on its prey. It was purring and flicking its tail back and forth. It crouched down and sprung up at the bag around Brother Truth's neck and, as the kitten caught the pouch, it puffed into formless smoke and dissipated. Brother Truth opened it up and emptied the contents into his hand.

"Dalen," a voice whispered. It seemed to come from somewhere across the canyon. The small cave underneath the white willow flickered with light as if someone had lit a fire. "Your skills are complete, but your training is not yet over." He hadn't heard her voice in so long he'd almost forgotten what the Fire Jinn sounded like. "Train with Ki and Faith. Find real Truth. Only then will you be ready to take the step needed to make this drastic change."

Brother Truth noticed that in his hand there were two objects: his silver figure and a single stone. For almost three years the stone had looked like a small storm trapped inside a ball, but as he stood there in disbelief, he found himself staring at a stone that looked exactly like one of the Beads of Fire. He only saw it for a moment because it began to fade and lose its glow. As it clouded over, Brother Truth looked to the cave below the willow and saw that the light there was also dwindling.

"Today is my day. I will see you soon." The stone had changed back to its original form, and he watched as it flashed like lightning in a cloud. Brother Truth was confused about this stone. He had never seen it change like that before. Admittedly, he had not paid it much attention over his time here. It had just stayed in the bag with his silver figure and had been almost forgotten.

Before, it had always looked like the stones that were at the locations of Master Truth's Chakra points, feet, and hands. For almost three years now, he had studied chakras and energy movement. During that training, he'd learned that there was a positive polarity and negative polarity of energy flow, much like a magnet or electric flow. A push and a pull. A breath in, and a breath out. Over time, Brother Truth had managed to become very adept at moving his own energy, or 'Ki,' through his body by having one of his hands resonate with a positive flow and the other with the negative. This allowed him to create a current by forming a circuit between the two. He had learned how each chakra point was connected to a different vortex of energy and that one could tune the current through the circuit by raising or lowering the vortices of his chakras to produce different styles of energy. They were a harmony of himself — energy throughout his body that he could focus on for all manner of use and styles.

During his training, he had figured out that the stones in Master Truth were reflections of those points of power. He knew that somehow the stone he had was connected to Master Truth like the Beads of Fire were connected to the Fire Jinn, and that all of the stones were a conduit that allowed the keeper of the stones to see the corresponding jinn. He just wasn't sure what this new piece of the puzzle meant. Was this stone some sort of OmniStone and would change from Element to Element so that one could connect to many jinn? What caused it to change? Was it the jinn? Was it him?

Brother Truth started to put the silver figure back in his

pouch, but before he could get the stone in, he saw a glimpse of movement from his peripheral vision. He'd been so focused on the stone, he'd missed any sound that might have alerted him. Brother Truth looked over just in time to see Master Ki leap with a high-pitched "KA-KA-KA!" from the railing that was along two-thirds of the open courtyard. On the other side of the railing, there was nothing but the sheer precipice below.

Today, Master Ki was a white man with shaggy brown hair and a mustache. Due to his current size and the momentum produced from his leap, gravity, and the 'Ki' he was building and amplifying with the sound he'd made, Brother Truth would normally have used both arms to take the blow that was coming. He would've tried to divert the impact through his body and ground it by taking a stance that would allow his legs to work as a shock.

Normally.

Instead, he pivoted on his right foot and stepped around himself and forward with his left. As the left foot touched the polished stone of the courtyard, Brother Truth shifted his weight to it and crouched down while pushing off with his right, effectively stepping around himself again, and then stood up. This nullified Brother Ki's strike because he'd now overshot his jump. He landed where no one stood with his back to Brother Truth, who was facing him.

Master Ki looked back, impressed. "What was that?"

Brother Truth seemed just as surprised. "I have no idea."

Master Ki made a face, and they both shrugged. Master Ki pushed off from the ground from where he stood and got enough lift to not only clear the distance but to bring his right leg around for a kick to Brother Truth's head.

Brother Truth ducked under it. He reached out toward the ground with his left hand and used it as leverage as he spun around. Again, Master Ki found himself not landing his strike and being positioned with his back to Brother Truth. He swung his elbow around at where he thought Brother Truth's head should be, but Truth had ducked away backward, leaving Master Ki with nothing to hit but open air.

Master Ki stood there for a moment. "Well done. This is the best example of spatial awareness you've ever demonstrated. Normally you would block or deflect, but now you are just flowing. It usually takes you an hour of practice before you focus, and you have never used those moves." Then Master Ki smiled like he knew something secret. "What's different?"

"I am not sure, Master. All I know is that instead of acting to stop you, I am moving with what is already happening, just taking up a space where the blow will not be." Brother Truth's mind had caught something but had not yet figured out what it meant. "I was standing here a moment ago, and the stone I was holding changed." Brother Truth opened his hand and showed Master Ki the stone.

Master Ki nodded, smiling. "Well ..." He stroked an imaginary long beard and, as he did, his form changed to that of a thin, elderly man that resembled what Brother Truth thought Master Truth would look like if he were corporeal.

274

"That would explain a lot."

Master Ki changed forms often. It had been a training tool from the start. Every time Master Ki taught a new discipline, it would be from a completely different teacher. Except for moments like this where the form was specific, Master Ki was never the same person twice. Some days, Master Ki would start the class as a star-folk, who was half Brother Truth's height. This small form would spend hours demonstrating how someone much smaller than Brother Truth's size could defeat him, using his larger size against him. Then they would break for a meal and, when Brother Truth came back to continue his training, he would be met by a giant twice his size, so that he could then practice the day's lessons. Master Ki would also use it as a distraction. This moment was a good example of that. Master Ki's resemblance to Master Truth was making him lose focus. "What would explain what?" Brother Truth replied, trying to grasp what Ki understood.

"That is an Elemental Stone," Ki said, as if that was enough information to explain everything. When he could tell that Brother Truth's mind was about to get it, he jump-started it. "Explain to me what that means." Master Ki grounded his stance and prepared his legs for a quick forward movement. "NOW!" he commanded and, as he did so, he lunged at Brother Truth with a solid punch aimed at his face.

As Brother Truth moved his head to the left to sway to the outside of Ki's strike, he thought about what that could mean. He crouched down and put all of his weight on his left leg and used it as a pivot while he allowed his right leg to spin him counterclockwise and away, allowing him to stand side-by-side with Master Ki. "Since I got here, it has always matched the stones that are part of Master Truth. I assumed it was like the Beads of Fire that allow me to connect to the Fire Jinn or the Beads of Water that allow me to see you." He took a step back as Master Ki tried to strike him from the side. "Why it changed is beyond me at this moment." He dropped to the ground and rolled away from Master Ki, standing back up just as the Water Jinn swung midrange with a kick. "But right now, this Elemental Stone is somehow connecting me to the Element of Air."

"Yeah?" Master Ki tried a leaping kick to clear the distance but only found himself alone, while Brother Truth, who had slid underneath him while he leaped, now stood where Ki had jumped from. "What gives you that opinion?"

Master Ki's form changed to a powerful dark-skinned fighter. This time, Master Ki moved in slowly, guiding him toward the edge by herding him with her movements.

Brother Truth kept moving as Master Ki shifted to keep her distance. "During the first part of my training, the Fire Jinn suggested that each Element can be seen as a form of change. The Element of Air has to do with the ability to move past fluidity and be completely encompassing to whatever happens before you." Brother Truth's heel stepped past the edge and it was only then that he realized how far he'd moved. That's when Master Ki pushed her advance. She threw punch after punch, yet with only the smallest of movements needed, Brother Truth dodged and ducked every swing.

"Good!" Master Ki exclaimed. "You are doing wonderfully!" Brother Truth loosened for a moment to say thank you, and that was what Master Ki was waiting for. Just as Brother Truth's body started to relax, Master Ki pressed the advantage and tried to push him off the edge, but instead of going backward, Brother Truth leaped to his left.

Brother Truth landed with both hands on the stone railing and carried his momentum into a cartwheel, ending with him standing up, balanced on the railing. "That's why I am here, isn't it?" Master Ki leaped onto the railing as well to continue the attack. "I am here to learn to accept a truth." Brother Truth continued to dodge her attacks as they moved along the railing. "To encompass it completely and allow the truth of it to move through me like a stone through the air. No matter how it moves, I move with it."

"So far you are doing great." Master Ki leaped up and tried to hit Brother Truth with a spinning kick. She missed but landed back on the railing and then continued her attack. "What else can you see?" She moved at him with such speed that it no longer seemed natural. Brother Truth now had to respond on instinct. Strike after strike, Ki backed him along the railing to the other side of the courtyard, but Brother Truth was able to move with each new attack.

Suddenly, the world slowed down. Brother Truth leaped from the railing into the air much higher than intended. He came down, doing a backflip in a long sweeping arc, slightly slower than gravity. Brother Truth's attention broke, and time slammed into him. "What the hell was that?"

Master Ki sighed a breath of relief and hopped off the railing. As she did, her form changed to that of a young man about Brother Truth's age, with coffee skin tones and long black hair that was pulled into a ponytail to keep it out of his face. "That was you utilizing the Element of Air in the same way that you have been training to utilize your own energy during your time here at the temple."

Brother Truth looked at the stone that was still in his hand. "So, it is an Air Stone?"

Brother Ki shook his head. "No. It's not. If it were just an Air Stone, it would not have been able to change as you suggested."

Truth opened the small pouch and took out the silver figure. "It only changed when I had them both together." He placed them both in one hand and waited for something to happen.

Master Ki folded his arms and cocked his head. "What are you trying to do?"

Brother Truth concentrated on both of the objects in his hand. "I am hoping it will change again."

"Into what?" Master Ki asked with a chuckle. "You have no Field of Intent. It has to know what you want it to change to."

Brother Truth nodded. "You are right."

"Yes." Master Ki was standing right next to the railing where earlier Brother Truth had set down the tea tray earlier. He bent down and took the second cup. Master Ki gestured to Brother Truth, as he drank. "So, what are you going to do about it?"

Brother Truth walked over to Master Ki and picked up his cup and dropped the stone in. Master Ki raised an eyebrow and leaned back on the railing.

Brother Truth swung his hand over the railing and poured his tea into his hand. The liquid spilled away and left only the silver figure and a large drop of water the size of the stone in his hand. It began to glow with a bright blue light that intensified quickly until a myriad of ripples of light reflected through the liquid and onto Brother Truth's face. He marveled at it for a moment and then realized that he was dangling it over the drop-off and moved back a few steps. When he did, something came into his view that he wasn't prepared for.

Brother Ki was standing in the same place as before but had reverted to its Water Jinn form. It was still leaning back on both elbows and still had the same "I know way more about what is going on than you do" grin on its face.

The stones throughout its body radiated with streams of light that were the same as the drop of water in Brother Truth's hand. The light cascaded through its liquid form in beautiful moving rays that shone throughout the Water Jinn's form and created dancing ripples on any surface that was around it.

Dalen was entranced by the sight of Master Ki in all their glory. "You are beautiful, Master Ki."

Ki shook its head. "You will eventually have to let go of that corporeal thinking of yours." The Water Jinn's teacup filled and Master Ki sipped on it as they spoke. "I am what your mind can perceive. It is your perception of me that changes how you see me. Same as you, Brother Truth."

Brother Truth didn't understand. He felt the initial hit of frustration. He took a breath and tried to refocus. "I don't understand — I have always been me."

Master Ki looked surprised. "Have you?"

"I haven't?"

"Very well." The Water Jinn took another sip. "Who are you?"

"You know who I am." He didn't see it coming. "I am Brother Truth."

The trap had been sprung. Master Ki smiled again at Brother Truth. "Then tell me." Master Ki slowly finished its cup. "Who is Dalen Pax?"

Brother Truth's entire train of thought derailed. He watched it in slow motion as his mind began to grasp what Master Ki was saying. "I am Dalen Pax."

"Then who is Brother Truth?"

Dalen asked himself the same question at the same time the Water Jinn did, and he was hoping that Brother Truth would have an answer. He stared at the drop of water in his hand.

280

Echoes of thoughts and memories danced in Dalen's mind as everything began to fall into place.

"That's why I am here, isn't it?" He looked over at the railing and saw a ghostlike image of himself from just a few moments before. "I am here to learn to accept a truth. To encompass it completely and allow the truth of it to move through me like a stone through the air. No matter how it moves, I move with it." That ghost faded, but it was not the only memory that returned.

He glanced over to see the light in the cave below the willow where he believed the Beads of Fire were. He heard the Fire Jinn's voice move through his mind and thoughts, as new understandings burned their way through his neural net: "Train with Ki and find real Truth. Only then will you be ready to take the step needed to make this drastic change."

"I need to ask you a direct question, Master Ki."

Master Ki stood up straight and smiled. "What do you wish to know?"

Dalen gathered his thoughts and made sure he knew his words. "The reason I am at a temple run by a jinn harmonized to air is because there was a truth that I had to envelop and have its existence determine the shape of my understanding, like the Element of Air. And I am trained to move and flow by a jinn harmonized with water, because the truth that I was enveloping had, in part, to do with changing my form but holding my essence, which is why I am Brother Truth and yet still Dalen Pax. My direct question is this: is this correct?"

"As a whole? No, but you are close."

Dalen nodded, "Please help me see more."

Master Ki gave Brother Truth a small bow. "Jinn are not held to a single Element." The jinn pointed to the set of beads that Brother Truth had been wearing since his arrival. "You are the one harmonized to the specific Element."

Brother Truth could see it. Master Truth's words from the day he arrived floated on a breeze to him: "Master Ki will be your teacher during this trial. You will not be needing the help of your fiery friend."

"That's why I don't have the Beads of Fire. I needed to harmonize myself to this understanding of change. It's not a fast burn. It's a slow change at the speed of understanding."

Master Ki clapped. "Good! Now, what are you going to do with that information?"

Brother Truth didn't think. He didn't wonder if he was right or wrong. He made a choice and acted on it. He reached over and took off the beads from around his wrist and threw them to Master Ki. Brother Truth watched as they were absorbed into its body.

Brother Truth's smile cracked just on one side. He had let the Beads of Water go, but he could still see Master Ki.

"Now, we're talking," Master Ki's chest swelled with pride.

"What's the final step?" Brother Truth asked with conviction.

Master Ki raised both hands and water poured from them, creating four streams that pooled in front of Brother Truth. Much like the Water Jinn, the water began to form humanoid shapes. The four shapes then started to solidify into four individuals.

One was the form of the dark-skinned fighter. Now that Brother Truth had time to look at her, he realized that it looked like a younger version of someone he recognized.

Brother Truth looked at her with confusion. "Ms. Warren?" he questioned.

Master Ki's response was more of a warning, "Don't dismiss Ms. Warren. I know you see her as a mother, but in her day, she was one of the strongest fighters ever seen. Had no choice but to grow up strong and as hard as stone."

The second was the form that looked much like Master Truth.

Master Ki instructed, "This fighter is like the Element of Air and is formless. Any tactic that you use will only work once, and afterward, he will use it against you to his advantage."

The third was the form that Master Ki took the first time they'd met.

"This fighter is the Element of Water and will flow with your attacks," Master Ki said. "He will move in harmony with you and use your force and momentum to his advantage."

The fourth was no surprise. She was a young woman with

fiery red hair. Brother Truth had imagined what his friend the Fire Jinn would have looked like if she were corporeal many times, and he recognized her immediately.

"This fighter is the Element of Fire and will strike with great speed and fury. Her tactics will be aggressive and fierce." The last of Master Ki's water was used to make the fourth combatant, leaving Brother Truth alone with the four opponents.

Together they spoke as one: "We are the Warriors of the Four Elements, and you must conquer us to move forward."

Brother Truth placed the silver figure in his left hand and the Elemental Stone in his right. "Alright. Who's first?"

Fire chuckled, "First?"

With that, all of them took their own stance according to their Elemental Flow, and the fight began. All four surrounded Brother Truth and began to attack him based on whoever he had his back to at the time.

Brother Truth did his best to expect the next strike, but as he dodged it, the next strike came in. He dropped down to one knee, going under the second strike, and pushed off with his other leg, allowing his momentum to be channeled into a forward motion toward Air. Air deftly moved out of the way, but in doing so left him an opening to break out of the circle; once he turned around, Brother Truth was able to get all four of them in front of him again.

Fire charged him with fast attacks directly at his face. He was able to bob and weave to avoid the punches, but her attacks were more for show and as a distraction while Air leaped over both of them to close off any further escape.

Brother Truth was able to swing under Fire's attack and land a blow to her midsection, but as she stumbled back, Water spun around her. He feigned a foot sweep but just as Brother Truth jumped to clear it, Water planted the foot and pushed off the ground with both hands. Water was standing before Truth had landed, and he reached out with both hands to grab Brother Truth, using his momentum to toss him sideways ... directly at Earth.

Brother Truth reoriented himself in mid-air and landed facing Earth. She took a boxer's stance and began to bob back and forth as she threw quick jabs. Her eyes were watching for his patterns and, when she found what she was looking for, she came at him with an avalanche of powerful blows, each stronger than the last. Brother Truth switched stances and used her movement against her as Water had done to him. Instead of trying to stop them, he moved them aside. Once he had her timing, he stepped out of the way of her punch and grabbed her wrist with his outside hand and her elbow with his inside hand, and leaped in the direction she was punching. It pulled her off balance, and she fell to the ground.

Brother Truth knew that the others weren't going to stand around to give him time to rise, so as soon as he hit the ground, he somersaulted backward and rolled to his feet. His hunch was right, and he narrowly missed Fire's attack, who had moved to intercept him where he would have landed.

Water came at him, so Brother Truth tried to leap out of the way. As he did, Air swept his feet and turned him horizontally in the air. Water got to him in mid-flight and hit him hard enough to send him spinning.

Brother Truth landed with a thud and, before he could recover, Fire was straddling him and taking jabs at his face. Truth locked his jaw and reset his mind as the next two hits came in. They were fast but not particularly powerful. He ignored the pain and cleared his mind. He looked around and saw that Earth was moving in from his right and Air from the left. As the next strike came in, he used a block with his free hand so that she narrowly missed his head, and Fire punched the stone floor of the courtyard instead. As she winced in pain, he used the distraction to push her to the right, blocking Earth and moving him left toward Air.

Air was prepared for that and, unlike last time, didn't move out of the way. Instead, he leaped into the air and came down with a heel strike. Dalen grounded himself and allowed his knees to take the impact. As the kick came down, Dalen crossed his forearms in front of him and, like an oak tree, took the impact and caught Air's leg. Oak then turned to Willow as Dalen switched Elements in himself.

"It is said that it is impossible to catch the wind." Brother Truth switched his stance and turned his hips. From there, he had leverage and flung Air at Water, who caught him and shifted his direction so Air could land on his feet. He gave Air and Water a wink and boasted, "It seems I am built to do impossible things."

From behind, two strong arms grabbed Brother Truth, pinning his arms against his body. He struggled against them, but Earth's grip was like stone. Fire strutted up and punched him seven or eight times in his midsection. She took one step back and pivoted on her foot and, with a quick spin, brought her other heel right into the side of Brother Truth's head.

He was dazed and almost fell over when Earth let him go and turned him around to face her. "Do me a favor," Earth said. She helped Brother Truth regain his balance, but he was still reeling from the last kick. "Say, 'Goodnight'." And, in a single punch, Earth dropped him to the floor.

· · ·

Dalen. A voice from inside his mind called out to him. *Dalen, you are alone in the courtyard.* Whispers of past conversations echoed around him. *"I am what your mind can perceive. It is your perception of me that changes how you see me. Same as you, Brother Truth."*

Brother Truth looked up and saw that he was surrounded again on all four sides. They taunted him to get up. His face stung with pain and his eyes were beginning to tear up, but he found his balance and wiped the blood away from his nose.

Dalen. The voice whispered. *It is time for you to understand what is happening.* The voice came from everywhere. Both inside and out. Brother Truth couldn't tell if it was someone speaking directly into his mind or if it was his own thoughts. He opened his hand that held the stone, and a silver light from it poured out from it. It looked like condensed light and Brother Truth could feel the power from it. *See this moment from a different point of view.*

Truth's perspective left his body. He could see himself from above, and then his perspective rose what seemed to be another twenty feet into the air. He could see the four of them moving slowly inward toward Truth, who was now standing still, as though in a trance.

Who are they? asked the voice.

"They are the four fighters who are kicking my butt." Dalen was growing concerned that they were moving closer and closer, and he was not in a position to respond.

Yes, yes. But who are they? The tone in its voice suggested they were trying to guide him to a specific thought.

"They are representations of the Four Elements."

The voice whispered to him, *Look closely.* Dalen looked down at himself. He was standing in the middle of a stone circle carved into the center of the courtyard meant for meditation. At the edge of the circle were four symbols that represented the Natural Elements, and each of the fighters was moving to stand on them.

Dalen. Brother Truth. Who are you?

"I am the Element in the center. The thing that is all." He looked down at his hands again and realized he was back in his body. One was holding the silver figure. The other held the stone. It had turned into a ball of pure energy. "Just like this stone, and I am one with all of it." Dalen clapped his hands together, merging the Elemental Stone with his silver figure. As they touched each other, he felt a great surge move through his body as if every nerve had been activated. It didn't hurt, but it was nearly overwhelming. All of his chakras lit up and he began to float off the ground.

Dalen Pax's life flashed before his eyes. He saw the path of his life and how it brought him to this moment. He recognized every aspect of his life as a part of who he was and the creators of who he became. The timeline shot forward and time seemed to split into many different possibilities of future events; he recognized that these were the moments that he would create as his potential future, and he recognized himself as those future beings, too. Then his perception brought him back to the present.

The Elements had changed, and now each of them looked like Brother Truth but wore different colored clothes that corresponded to their Element.

Dalen. The voice whispered again. *You are alone in the courtyard.*

Brother Truth felt it in his core. Each one was an aspect of himself. It was like he was a prism and, as light passed through him, it was split into different parts of the spectrum, but instead of light, it was existence. As they moved, he could feel them. He understood them. He sensed their actions as they happened and saw them as reflections of himself. Brother Truth relaxed his body yet prepared his mind and, as he did, he felt time begin to slow.

Fire was the first to reach Brother Truth. Initially, Fire struck from behind, but Brother Truth was aware of everything that was happening in the circle. He sensed Fire pivot on their foot to attempt another kick to his head, but this time he was not bound.

This time he was centered, and time was moving at a different rate of speed.

Like Air, he tucked and spun in towards Fire. The kick missed him completely, and Brother Truth was upon Fire while they were still in the motion of kicking. Like Water, he used Fire's momentum against them and was able to spin Fire into the air. Then Brother Truth's stance changed and, with all of his strength, he planted Fire into the stone floor. As they hit, Fire puffed into smoke with small embers of light swirling in it. The smoke became infused into Brother Truth and, as it became a part of him, his hands caught fire.

Brother Truth felt the Element of Fire fuel him. It was powerful and wild. His heart pounded in his chest. He felt his emotions begin to build, and he could tell that he could easily lose control if he wasn't careful. "Well, this is new," he remarked.

The other Elements looked at him with concern. Each of them stopped their advance and took a defensive position. Brother Truth, still fueled by Fire, decided to take the initiative. He knew he had to balance himself out, so he chose to face Water. As soon as he moved, Air and Earth took aggressive stances and moved toward Water and Brother Truth. Brother Truth began his attack with quick punches that gave Water little room to build momentum. Water's defensive position could only move the strikes away, and the Fire in Brother Truth's hands roared as he pulled them through the air to strike. And as each blow was blocked and moved, Water had to make sure they did not get burned. It was a perfect distraction.

Earth came in with a powerful strike, but Dalen sensed it

one move ahead. He changed his punch and practically gave Water his arm. Water saw the open strike and grabbed Brother Truth by his wrist and elbow, beginning to twist his body to gain momentum and leverage for a hip toss, but Brother Truth was expecting it. As Water turned, Brother Truth leaped with him and landed just past him, still facing him. When he landed, he swung his momentum back at Water, who quickly stepped back, directly into Earth's swing.

Water exploded with the hit back into his Element. It completely doused Brother Truth, but as the water landed on him, it soaked into his being. It cooled his thoughts and calmed his heart. He was in balance for the time being and was able to focus clearly.

Earth came in with everything they had. Dalen moved past one of Earth's punches and tried to throw them, but Earth was planted with every strike, and Brother Truth couldn't make them budge. Earth used this failure to regain the advantage and, strike after strike, pushed Brother Truth toward the edge of the courtyard.

Brother Truth could sense it coming and leaped back out of Earth's range. He landed with his heels teetering off the edge. Brother Truth shifted his weight to his toes to recover his balance. Lunging forward, he took a three-point stance with one hand.

"Come on. Hit me with all you got!" Brother Truth scraped the edge with his toes to check his footing. "If you do, you lose."

Earth came at him like a freight train. A breath away from being hit, Truth reached over with his free hand, grabbing the white canvas belt that was always left there to save him when he failed his Leap. As the hit came, Dalen dropped one knee and wrapped both arms around Earth, then shifted his weight and, taking all of Earth's momentum, pulled Earth off the ledge with him.

It was quiet for a moment, and then Brother Truth reappeared at the edge of the courtyard. He tossed the belt to the side and advanced toward Air. "Come here. I wish to talk to you."

As Air cautiously moved toward him, a cloud of dust and sand rose from the edge and enveloped Brother Truth. The cloud infused into his being; Brother Truth's skin looked like stone, and his stride was slower but solid.

Air leaped from fifteen feet away and landed a kick directly into Brother Truth's chest. Truth didn't even try to block it. All he did was plant his feet. As he did, he melded with the stone of the courtyard. Air bounced off him and landed a few feet back.

Again and again, Air attacked Brother Truth, and over and over, he stood unyielding. "I am the mountain," Brother Truth growled. "I will not be moved."

"Fight me!" Air demanded.

"Why?" asked Truth. "You have already been defeated. I am waiting for you to grasp that."

Air stood there for a moment, considering, and Air knew that Brother Truth was right. No matter how hard the wind blows, it always yields to the mountain. "I relent." They bowed before fading into a breeze that swirled around Brother Truth. Brother Truth breathed it in, and with that he was whole. His mind and body centered itself, and he became one with the moment. Time had no meaning, and he marveled as he watched the sun move across the sky.

He was still standing in the middle of the courtyard at sunset when the monks of the Brotherhood of Light gathered to witness this moment. When Brother Truth glanced down at himself, he was wearing new robes that he'd only rarely seen worn by masters during important ceremonies during his time there. He wore a pair of black pants and boots that went to his knee. The undershirt was black as well but only had a sleeve on the left. Over this, he wore a set of white armor that only covered his chest, left shoulder, and arm, as well as his left knee, shin, and ankle. Over that was a sleeveless black gi. A white prayer cloth was draped over his right shoulder, hanging to his knees in the front and back and held in place with a black leather belt. Without being told, Brother Truth knew that this was a representation of the balance that a Brother of Light must hold: on one side a monk, and the other a warrior. On his right wrist, he wore three cords braided together: one black, one white, and one gray, representing the weaving of Destiny, Fate, and Free Will.

As Brother Truth looked over his new apparel, he noticed the silver figure in his hand. After years of being in his pocket and rubbed and held, the silver figure had lost most of its form and all its details, but now all the detail had returned. Brother Truth stared in wonderment as he looked at a silver figurine of himself, dressed exactly the way he was at that moment. The only difference was the addition of a prayer cloth over the figure's left shoulder that hung the same length as the other and was held in place with the belt as well.

The monks clapped and cheered as Brother Truth stood there in bewilderment, still trying to fully process what had just happened.

It was Master Joy who approached him first. "Now you're ready to fly, and I have decided to leap with you." The old elf began to pull Brother Truth toward the place where he was to jump.

"I thought you were dying."

Master Joy laughed until he coughed. "Yeah. So?"

Concerned, Brother Truth asked, "Should you be making this leap right now?"

Master Joy laughed again. "What's the worst that could happen? I die? That's happening anyway."

"Wait, is today your last day because we don't make it and we both plummet to our deaths?" asked Brother Truth.

"You worry too much." With that, Master Joy stepped out onto the edge, "You coming?"

Brother Truth picked up the belt that would teleport him back if he failed and walked out to the edge with Master Joy.

The old elf just laughed at him until another coughing fit forced him to stop. Freckles of crimson were left on his hand where he'd covered his mouth to cough. Brother Truth tried to ask about it, but Master Joy shooed away the prattle.

Brother Truth returned his focus to the leap in front of

him. He was about to ask Master Joy if he was ready to go, but there was something in the back of his mind that he could not ignore. Something was wrong, and he had to figure it out before he leaped. He checked his footing and made sure Master Joy was ready. He reached up to make sure the belt was secured, and then it dawned on him. Brother Truth face-palmed himself and slowly dragged his hand down across his face.

"Of course." There had been something since the first day that had always bothered him about the jumps, but it wasn't until this moment that he realized that he was what had made the leap impossible. He rolled his eyes at himself and removed the belt. "In a true Leap of Faith, you can have no doubt." It had been there the entire time.

"This is where it gets fun," said Brother Faith with the same infectious sense of excitement that he was known for as he approached and stepped over to the edge. "You have to step away from your security and the comfort of 'safe' and choose to step into the unknown." Brother Faith turned to Brother Truth and nudged him with his elbow. "But it is also the moment in which you step into a greater and more powerful world. Sure, there is a chance of failure, but if there was no chance of failure, how can it truly be Free Will when you choose?"

Master Joy patted him on the cheek and turned back toward the edge. Brother Truth looked out at his brothers. His home. So many of them had become like family, and they had come to see him off. Most had gathered in the courtyard, but a few were standing in the doorways and one was even waving earnestly from a different part of the temple. He looked for Master Truth and Master Ki but could not see them anywhere.

Master Joy's voice broke his concentration. "You aren't going to find them out there, Brother." Master Joy reached over and touched Brother Truth's heart, "You take them with you, son."

Brother Truth looked back to the edge. He took a deep bow and spoke to the canyon. "You have been a perfect teacher, but today you have to be defeated. With all my respect ... Thank you."

"Well put," nodded Master Joy. For the last time, they bowed to each other in grand splendor and then gave each other a high five.

Brother Faith turned to Brother Truth. "I am ready to take my place with the masters."

Master Joy laughed until he coughed. "With Truth, Faith, and Joy, how could this leap ever fail?"

It couldn't, and together they leaped.

They launched into the air with great speed and height. Master Joy squealed with laughter. The moment that Brother Truth leaped into the air, his right hand and forearm burst into flames. Even as it burned, Brother Truth watched as the Beads of Fire appeared on his wrist. In the same moment, Master Joy and Brother Faith burst into a pure light that engulfed Brother Truth. He felt weightless as he floated in the light.

Master Joy's voice could be heard all around Brother

Truth. "My wish has been granted, and you have given me the greatest gift. I leave this world in peace."

Then Master Faith's voice echoed in, "Thank you for everything. I have complete faith in you."

14

A QUANTUM VIEW OF REALITY

As he landed, Dalen found himself standing in the middle of his Training Circle. "Yes!" Dalen whooped with elation. "I made it! Oh my god! I made it!" Dalen broke into a victory dance. The spontaneity of that moment brought about another realization: he was seventeen again and dressed in the clothes he'd first arrived in.

The jinn was floating nearby. "Hello, Dalen. Welcome back."

Dalen looked at himself with confusion. "Was it all a dream?"

She laughed and her fire bloomed. "Look at your figurine." Dalen did and saw that it was still in perfect detail. "This entire process may take years. Did you want to meet up with Kim Collard at the dance looking thirty? I promise you that if we did it that way, it would be very confusing to everyone."

"But it did happen?" Dalen needed to be sure.

"Everything happened. Do you remember Dorn's daughter Jax?" Dalen nodded. "When the order comes in, she still has to cook it. She sometimes cooks it fifteen times until she perfects it. But when she puts it in the window to be served, no time has passed."

Dalen was surprised. "I didn't know she cooked it more than once."

"Yeah ... she cooks it over and over sometimes until she has it right. That's not the point. The point is, no matter how long it takes her, she still finishes the order just as it is sent in from the outside point of view."

"How is that possible?"

The Fire Jinn smiled from the side of her mouth. "Magic."

Dalen rolled his eyes at her. "You know what I mean." Even in his exasperation, Dalen was genuinely happy to see her again.

The Fire Jinn smiled. "Changing time is extremely difficult. It also goes against the Natural Law, and I tend to stay away from such things. I have done it, but it is dangerous, and I don't suggest it. But creating a pocket of time where you can have three years of experience in a matter of moments? That I can do."

"Yes, but did it really happen?"

"Yes," she smiled. "If you went there today, they would recognize you and know who you are."

"Thank you," Dalen responded, holding the silver figure up to his heart. "It mattered to me that it was real. How about my abilities?"

"Oh indeed, those are real. Why don't you try it out for yourself and see?" She gestured to the floor.

Dalen took her up on that challenge. He focused his mind and reignited the Natural Element. When it ignited, a vivid red glow shot into the air and a small vortex appeared around the sigil.

Dalen focused again, this time on bringing forth what he had just learned, and all of his chakras opened. A moment later, his clothes transformed on his body, and once again, he was wearing the black and white robes of the Brotherhood of Light. His body moved with precision through the sequence of his katas, he was flowing with the energy, and from within that flow a moment of perfection was created. Time stood still and Dalen Pax and Brother Truth were one.

Once he'd built up enough Ki, he directed it toward the other side of the circle and the Kinetic Element lit up. The jinn was ablaze in beautiful reds and oranges, and Dalen observed that two silver lines connected her first two chakra stones to him in the same locations. At the same time, energy from the Natural Element channeled through him into the Kinetic Element.

The surge passed, but both of the Elemental Glyphs remained active. The Fire Jinn landed and her fire subsided. "Congratulations, Dalen Pax, you have opened the Body Sphere and now understand the first of the three truths of Magic.

. . .

Dalen slept the rest of the day and through the night. His time with the Brotherhood had accustomed him to certain requirements for sleeping, such as a mat on the floor instead of a bed. When asked, Dorn was more than happy to set him up with a small room that would suffice for his needs. As another requirement, he wanted darkness and quiet. The problem was that, even when he closed his eyes, the Fire Jinn was there. It was the Beads of Fire that connected him to her; so as long as he had the beads on, he could see her, whether or not his eyes were closed. Eventually, he took them off to sleep. He promised her he would put them on again later. She nodded in agreement, noting that the difference between that moment and the one he was in was only separated by Dalen's linear thinking, but that moment for Dalen would have to wait until time brought him to it.

The next morning when he woke up at dawn as he had for years, he headed down to the kitchen to make some tea. As he stepped out of his room, he remembered that he was no longer at the temple. Instead of the serenity and peace that he was used to, Dalen heard the sounds of conversation and laughter coming from downstairs.

Dalen made his way downstairs and into the common room in Dorn's tavern. When he reached the bottom floor, he found Dorn in conversation with Christoph, his day manager. He was an immortal and the original King of Venger, who had ruled for an exceptionally long time. Eventually, Christoph had grown tired of ruling and passed his throne to his son. He'd decided to work the day shift at Dorn's because, even for an immortal who had seen it all, Dorn's never got dull. Dorn was currently regaling Christoph with the previous night's festivities.

"We had someone stand in The Circle last night," Dorn commented before taking a bite of something from a small bowl.

"That is fantastic!" Christoph said enthusiastically. "Sorry I missed it. Who went?"

"Elrick Nightshade." Dorn noticed Dalen had come downstairs and waved him over.

"Elrick?" Christoph sounded surprised at the name. "I thought that he left Venger with his son when Jade died." As Dalen approached, he gave Dalen a nod. "Good morning."

Dalen gave the bow that he had learned while at the temple out of habit. "Good morning. I hope I am not disturbing your conversation." He pointed to the bar. "Can that thing make a good cup of tea?"

Christoph smiled. He looked over to Dorn to see if he wanted to answer Dalen, but he just gestured for Christoph to answer. "Of course, it can. That is the whole point of what it does.

But, in the end, it is an illusion. How would you like it if I made you some real tea? I already have a kettle on." He glanced over to Dorn and then back to Dalen. "From what I understand, you have been at the Temple of Light. I spent some time there and have a small supply of the mint tea and the black tea that they often use there."

Dalen was happy to hear this. Dalen already felt homesick for the Temple of Light. It was a part of him now, and he knew he was going to miss all of the family he'd created while he was there. His morning ritual had involved the mint tea, and he was glad that he wouldn't have to give that up yet as well. "Mint. Please."

Dorn offered him a stool and then continued with his story while Christoph prepared Dalen's tea. "So, Elrick comes in ..." Dorn paused for a moment. "He says 'Hi,' by the way."

Christoph smiled. "Hi."

"He comes in and asks for 'something impressive,' and I tell him I have just the thing. You see, I've been saving a bottle or two from his and Jade's wedding. I knew it was risky because it might've also been in bad taste, but it's what came to my mind when he said to impress him."

Christoph set a large tray down in front of Dalen, who noticed that Christoph's right hand and arm were covered in burn scars. Dalen didn't want to be rude, so he forced his eyes to the tray that Christoph had brought. There was a teapot steeped and prepared, and an arrangement of things to add to it, like sugar and honey, cream, and lemon wedges. Dalen asked for a second cup. Christoph brought him an extra and Dalen thanked him, explaining it was tradition.

While this was going on, Dorn continued with his anecdote, "I went down to the wine cellar and over to the star-folk section. There I procured a Blue Bottle One Fifty-Two."

"I still have no idea how you got your hands on imported star-folk wine," Christoph shook his head in disbelief. "And a One Fifty-Two. By their calendar, that would make it ... like what, eight hundred years old?"

Dorn raised an eyebrow. "Eight hundred and thirteen," he specified. "So, I brought him the bottle, and he recognized it instantly. Elrick looked me right in the eyes. 'Thank you, it's perfect,' and then he hugged me. He then leaped onto the counter and walked the length of the bar, took the cup from its place, and hopped down to the Circle of Healing Truth."

The Circle of Healing Truth was a wish that was made during the first year that Dorn's opened. At the time, a friend of theirs was grieving over a loss that they all had felt but had worked through. Her heart was larger than most, and no matter how they tried to help, she couldn't let it go. One day she came to her friends and announced she had decided that it was time to find peace. She had been granted a real wish and she had been holding on to it, hoping to find a way to wish their friend back into existence, but her wish wasn't able to be used to directly counter death. She tried everything from wishing he would be brought back to wishing that he'd never been taken from them in the first place, but no matter how she tried to word it, the wish would not respond, because, in the end, the wish she was making was still to bring him

304

back from oblivion in the core of its Intent. She was hoping to find another solution that would render their friend alive and well.

She had hoarded the wish for a while, but she came to understand that as long as she had the wish, she was convinced that she could save him. Worse, all the time that she was not able to do it, she felt she was somehow failing him. She'd decided that she wanted to use the wish, but she wanted it to do two things. The first was that she wished to be healed from her pain and suffering. The second part she considered more important: she wished that the healing would not erase the memories, but instead transform them into a source of strength and joy. She didn't want to lose the person again — she just wanted his memory to become something beautiful and empowering. She said that's what he would have wanted.

The wish was invoked and what appeared was a piece of chalk. She took it and stood next to the end of the bar. She drew a small circle on the bar with the chalk and, from the pouch she carried on her belt, produced a small cup that used to belong to their friend. She placed it in the circle. She then drew a larger circle on the floor right next to the bar and stood in it. She was guessing what to do and making it up as she went, but often that is how wishes work. You have to be an active participant in the creation of the wish.

The cup was filled with their friend's favorite drink, and she raised the cup and poured her heart out. They all wept together as her pain rippled from her in waves of sadness. They wanted to hug her, but they knew not to break the circle. This was something she had to be able to do alone if she was going to heal herself of this. She dropped to her knees and confessed her love. Dorn and their friends bore her pain as she wept and wept. Then she stood and finished her toast. It was not just to them, but to their friendship and the love she had found and lost, and she called out to them and promised that they would always be loved. That they would always be remembered. And then she took the shot. The wish was fulfilled and the pain was gone. They now wept tears of joy as all of their memories were flooded with the greatest moments of their friend's life. The joy of him filled their hearts, and they knew his memory would stay with them forever.

To this day his memory touches Dorn's soul.

The interesting thing is that the chalk itself had vanished, but the circles had somehow become a permanent part of the bar — and its power was permanent as well. Anyone can stand in the circle, make a toast about what hurts them, haunts them, things that make them sad or angry, and the wish will work for them, too.

"So," Dorn said, "I walked over to Elrick and filled the cup with the wine he and Jade got married with."

"Yeah?" Christoph was enthralled with the story. "What did he say?"

Dorn gestured with his hand, "He raised the cup and said, 'As many of you know, a long while back I was the Headmaster of the Venger School of Skills and Stealth. My wife and I were Vengerian Guardians and Skill Masters for King Gavin himself.'"

"What's a Skill Master?" asked Dalen.

"Take a master thief and trap engineer and combine them with a shadow assassin." Dalen nodded appreciatively, feeling that Christoph's words evoked a fantastic understanding of the profession. "Very useful in a dungeon raid or tomb exploration." Both he and Dalen returned their attention to Dorn, who was still holding up his imaginary cup. "Sorry, Dorn. Go on."

Dorn tipped his imaginary glass and continued. "Elrick said, 'Seventeen years ago, the job took the life of my wife and, with her dying breath, she made me promise to protect our son Eldon from the life that took hers. So, I moved to a city far from here and lived among humans who were not kind to me or my son, but we carved a life away from here. I did my best to keep my old life a secret from him, but I was attacked at my home by three men and was forced to use my skills. My son saw it and questioned how his simple locksmith father was able to deftly protect himself from three men twice his size.' Elrick looked around the room and shrugged sheepishly.

"'The time had finally come to tell him the truth about my old life and about his mother, who, in my opinion, was a greater Skill Master than I was. Once he knew, he understood why he'd never been happy with his life. As our offspring, it was in his blood. He wanted me to teach him, and I told him of the promise I had made. He then did something that reminded me so intensely of his mother it broke my heart. He told me that he was going to become a Skill Master and someday work for the royal family. He told me that he would do it himself, but if I were going to truly honor his mother's last wish, I would have no choice but to teach him everything I knew, so that he would be protected from the life that took hers.'"

Christoph chuckled, "The cheeky little goblin."

"Right?" Dorn had thought that Eldon had been pretty clever himself. He held up his hand and continued with the tale. "Elrick took a moment and a breath as he was recounting what had occurred. He then looked up into the heavens as if he were talking to Jade herself. 'So, I trained him.'

"He said, 'I trained him better and harder than I have ever trained anyone in my life.' Elrick began to cry. 'I know this is not what you wanted, my love, but I swear to you I did what I believed would someday save his life.' The grief and turmoil from his decision had been eating him up every day as he had been training his son. 'He's good, Jade. He's really good. Better than either of us. He has my mind and your skill, and I believe in my heart I did the right thing. I would never want to disappoint you, my love. Please forgive me.' And then he took his shot."

Now Dalen was the one enthralled. He sipped his tea thoughtfully and then asked, "What happened next?"

"It's customary for the house to then buy a shot for everyone who was there," explained Dorn. "Anyone who witnesses the Circle also shares in the pain of the person who stands in the Circle. It is one of the beautiful things about it. When you share your pain, it is truly shared, and — more importantly — it is understood and felt. So, I offer a drink to all who experienced it with them. We celebrated the return of an old friend who found it in his heart to let go of the pain that had been eating him for years. As he let go of the pain, we all felt it and together we were freed from it. It was absolutely beautiful."

"So, it functions in the Natural Element and connects everyone together?" asked Dalen.

"Partly," agreed Dorn. "It affects all three spheres. It connects everyone as a whole, but it then shares the mind and heart of the person who is standing in the Circle through that connection."

"How does it do that?" Dalen was trying to see it. "You mean like empathy?"

Christoph was impressed at how much this kid seemed to grasp. "Yes," he said, "but not just empathy — telepathy as well."

"That sounds amazing!" Dalen's eyes widened. "You mean like real telepathy? Like reading someone's thoughts?"

"Reading or sending thoughts is a powerful ability, and it requires all three spheres to obtain it," Dorn explained. "One of the spheres you have learned, but there is much more to learn before you are able to do so. I suggest you begin focusing on the Mind Sphere, but don't take my word for it. I suggest you ask the jinn you carry with you."

Dalen soon finished his tea, thanked Christoph and Dorn both for the tea and conversation, and headed back upstairs to put on the Beads of Fire. As he left, Dorn called him back, "Remind the jinn that tonight is the full moon."

"Sure thing." Dalen headed back up the stairs and returned to his sleeping quarters. The Beads of Fire had been coiled up and placed next to the head of his mat where he had left them. He gathered them in his hand and wrapped them around his wrist.

The Beads of Fire lit up once again, and the Fire Jinn bloomed with fire into existence. "Good morning."

"Good morning. I am glad to see you again. And I hope that it's ok that I went down and got some tea before I put the Beads of Fire back on."

"There is nothing to forgive." She languidly yawned and stretched. "I hope you are rested and ready to continue your training."

"Yes, I am," said Dalen, "but I have a question for you. I thought about it often while I was at the temple. If you are not imprisoned by the beads and you are a free jinn, then why are you granting me wishes?"

"That is a fantastic question." She gave a look of surprise and placed her hand over her heart, "It seems that spending time with the monks was very agreeable to you."

Dalen folded his arms in front of him. "Thank you. Now, if you could answer the question."

"It has done you well. You are thinking more clearly now. That will be required as you continue to learn." She snapped her fingers and Dalen found himself in the center of his training circle.

"I am asking you nicely and with respect," Dalen bowed to the Fire Jinn and held it. "If you want to be partners in this, then we need to be partners in this." When he stood back up, she was standing directly in front of him, with her fire burning bright.

"Do you remember when we first met, and I talked to you about pleasantries?" Dalen nodded. "There are fewer and fewer people in this world who believe that pleasantries matter — the kind of person who is not like the humans of old, who wish to wipe out or control anything different than themselves. You were abandoned from birth, you have had trials set upon you from an early age, and yet your heart is still good. Someone like that can wield the power that magic possesses and not fall to the darkness of their own hearts. That's why I teach you. Do you remember that in the Natural Elemental Field we are all one?" Dalen nodded again. The jinn put her hand on Dalen's chest. "This heart is one with mine. And I want to see it grow into something, not only powerful but beautiful."

Dalen stood in silence, soaking it all in. "Wow."

"Yeah, wow." She smiled and floated back a little, "The rest of it has to do with possible quantum realities and the potential for them to be the moment that actually comes into existence as it is perceived through the eyes of an observer and thus manifests into reality."

Dalen's mind had gotten lost in the last part, so his mouth was on its own. "You said what now?"

"It has to do with the Mind Sphere. I will explain in detail, but so you can catch up, what I mean is that multiple possible futures can occur and that they are taking place at the same time. Mathias is one of those possible futures that is happening and yet may not happen, depending on what happens in what you consider your present."

Dalen was still wildly confused. "That only helped a little."

"A version of myself that is happening in what you consider the future is witnessing your utter defeat at the hands of Mathias when you return because you were not trained enough." Dalen's eyes widened with fear. "Another part of me is watching you defeat him because you were trained properly." Dalen sighed in relief. "The difference is what I do to help you in what you consider to be 'now.' Time is extremely difficult to change, and even I am only allowed to affect it the same way you do: in the present. Thus, I am only able to have an impact on time while you are perceiving me in any given moment."

"Why can you only do it when I am perceiving you?"

"Because I am in a state that is much like being in superposition, or maybe the idea of being omnipresent would be clearer to you." She shrugged. "Either way, it is your perception of me that pulls me from this state to a specific moment of existence, thus making me 'real.' In that state, I can affect the movement of time, the same as you, with my choices and actions."

"Okay," Dalen nodded. "I think I understood most of that."

The Fire Jinn scrunched up her face like she was thinking

hard. "You are still thinking corporeally. Not being affected by time allows me to be in every possible moment that I experience. I perceive this as a single understanding. *Now*, to me, is every moment that I have even been in. You are experiencing time linearly, and so *now* continues to move along the timeline. You are perceiving me and, as you do, you force me into a state where I am dragged along by time with you. During those moments, I can affect time the same way you do."

"Okay, okay. I understand, but why do you care?"

The jinn looked almost sad, and her fire dimmed, and she moved directly in front of Dalen and confessed, "The man that you know as Mathias is the outcome of a decision that I was a part of. I gave him his powers in the first place, but he was never trained. Because of this, he made mistakes that he can never take back. I don't want that to happen to you."

Both Natural and Kinetic Glyphs lit up together, and Dalen reached out and hugged the jinn. "Thank you. Thank you for everything." She lit up and hugged him back.

"Alright." She let him go and flew over to outside of the circle. "We have work to do."

"Dorn suggested the Mind Sphere," Dalen offered as a choice.

"He would be correct. The Mind Sphere is next. You have learned how to connect to everything and have everything be connected to you. You've learned the movements, the kata. Now you must understand how to train your mind and perception."

It made sense to Dalen. Each Sphere, like the Elements, was an aspect of Magic in a way. If he was going to wield true Magic, he would have to learn to think like a sorcerer. "Fantastic! Oh yeah ... and Dorn wanted me to remind you that tonight is the full moon."

"It's tonight?" She flared with delight. "Are you sure that's what he said?"

"Yeah," responded Dalen, "He asked me to remind you specifically. Why is that important?"

The Fire Jinn smiled at him devilishly. "The Buffet Banquet-Blitz Bonanza During Dorn's Dinner Dash Delirium! He does it every full moon, and it's happening tonight." Dalen's attention was piqued. Gushing with the enthusiasm of a spokesperson on a TV advertisement, she tried to explain what he was about to experience. "The buffet works a lot like how the bar works. Are you familiar with how it works?"

"No. How does it work?"

"The basic principle of it has to do with a minor manifestation but gets way more interesting than that."

She had hooked him on the sales pitch, and Dalen was willingly reeled in. "How could it be more interesting than that?"

She glided back over to him. "I am so glad you asked." She dramatically nudged him with her elbow and then leaned in, as if what she was telling him was very secretive. "It manifests what you wish."

Dalen couldn't tell what the difference was and why that difference mattered. "I don't follow."

"Welcome to your first glimpse into the field of the Quantum Element," she beamed as she pointed to the glyph that was behind him to the left. "This is the field of infinite possibility." She paused for effect. "Imagine for a moment that every possible outcome of the next few moments is all present in a wave of possibility. *All of them.* Every possible way it might work out, and here we are, at that moment. Look around." Dalen glanced about. "This is the possibility that you are perceiving. It is being poured into your understanding at what standardly tops out about fifty frames of perception a second. What that means is that, as you observe the infinite wave of possibility, it no longer is a possibility, but a fact. This makes the wave of endless possibility snap into a singularity of what is known as corporeal reality, and you do this about thirty to forty times a second."

"You mentioned that when we first met and you stopped all the guards." Dalen finally could comprehend what had happened that day.

"If you remember," she corrected, "I did nothing to those men. What I did do was bring you to a state where you were perceiving more of the field. Even though most can see anywhere from twenty-four to fifty frames of reality or so a second, there are thousands of them happening."

"That's right." Dalen thought for a moment. "Like filming something with a high-speed camera, when you play it back, it goes in slow motion. Hey, when I was in the Temple of Light, Brother Ki taught me to slow down time in the Kinetic field — was he effectively teaching me to see more frames?"

The Fire Jinn gave a small clap. "Yes."

"But he was teaching me Body Sphere, and this is Mind Sphere. It seems to me to be the same thing."

"It is the same thing." The jinn beamed proudly at Dalen. "The same way that the Elements of Fire, Earth, Water, and Air are all one thing — simply different understandings of that one thing — these Elements are no different. The only thing that is different between the Body Sphere and the Mind Sphere is how you perceive them and how you utilize them. Beyond that, there is only one Element." The jinn pointed to the green glyph that Dalen stood on in the center of the circle.

Dalen looked down and comprehended what she was saying. The Training Circle itself was beginning to make sense. "And what is that Element?"

"You."

The answer was only a glancing blow. Dalen felt the impact of it, but it didn't stick long enough for true understanding.

"The Element is Reality itself. When you can wield the Element as a whole, you will be able to bend Reality. This is the true nature of Magic." She paused before continuing. "Dalen. You are the Reality Generator. I could have simply handed you magic as it was handed to Mathias. Instilled it in you with no real connection to it. He is as powerful as the wish that created his power, and it will be his downfall."

"Wasn't that a wish that was powered by you? Did you make him weak on purpose?" Dalen asked.

"No. He was empowered by me, but it was instilled by another," explained the Fire Jinn. "He is immensely powerful. More powerful than I made him. He took on a master ... a master who is not kind, nor does he relinquish what he is given. It is his master who named him Mathias, a name that he now uses as his own and in many ways has become. But even with all of that, he is bound to the magic he was given, not learned."

"Are you saying if I learn this, I will be stronger than Mathias?"

"I am saying that if you learn this, the only limit will be you."

"Rule one?"

"Rule one."

"Okay." Dalen took out his silver figure and gave it a squeeze. He remembered how the OmniStone became a drop of water, and then a part of his figure and, in return, him. "Okay. I am the center Element, which is Reality. Does that mean the reality of me?" He knew he wasn't grasping it, so he tried to break it down further. "What was it?" he thought, "How am I the Element? If I

am the main Element, then I am all of the Elements as well, right?"
He looked to the Fire Jinn for guidance. "Each glyph has lit up as I
learned to ignite them in myself."

The Fire Jinn flared up with excitement. "Take one
more step!"

It was right there staring at him, but his mind was getting
in the way. He could hear Becky in the back of his mind reminding
him to "think simple." He stopped for a moment and then tried
again, and all at once it snapped into place. "To ignite the Reality
Field, I must ignite each of the Elements within myself. I am the
creating force of my own magic, and I am the generator of my
own reality."

The jinn's light filled the room in a burst of fire. "Activate
the Body Sphere."

Dalen's training with the monks took over as he centered
himself and found his source. He grounded himself and sent his
energy outward in all directions. He reached out with his being and
connected to the source of all things and found himself at peace. As
he did, the Glyph of the Natural Element ignited. He then collapsed
the field into himself and concentrated all of the energy through his
body and out his hands. As he did this, he pointed both palms in the
direction of the Kinetic Glyph and it lit up. Dalen kept his focus and
held it, but looked over to the jinn for the next step. Her fire flared
in a dazzling red flame that was edged in a brilliant orange. Her
lower chakras were alight, and a magical line connected her to Dalen
from each as the correlating stones on the Beads of Fire began to
glow brightly.

"Now slow it down." She produced a candle and lit it with her finger. "Something for you to concentrate on." She let it go and it floated over until it stopped about ten feet in front of Dalen. "Take in more. Perceive more and let it wind all the way down."

Dalen focused, and as he took his next breath, he let his Ki flow through him. Time began to slow. With each breath, Dalen drew out reality slower and slower until the flame barely moved.

"Now open your mind past that." The jinn's fire cooled rapidly and diminished until her color changed to a rich indigo flame, and the brightest parts emitted lights that were well into the ultraviolet. Time slowed further, and Dalen perceived the gaps between the frames.

"It's too much. Reality is coming in bursts like waves on a shore." Dalen stared into the void, and the void stared back. "There is something here!"

"Calm down, Dalen, it is only you echoing off the universe as you move into superposition." The jinn's words were soothing, and Dalen's fear drained from him.

"Thank you," Dalen remembered when she calmed him down before. He knew he wasn't going to be able to do any work here if he was panicking. He glanced at the jinn again, and now there was a third magical line that came from the top of her head and connected to Dalen in the same place. Instinctively, he glanced at the beads and the corresponding beads were aglow as well.

"Look past the frames with your mind: what is out there?"

Although time had come to an almost complete standstill, Dalen noticed the Fire Jinn's flames continued to flicker at a normal rate. The light she produced was now fully ultraviolet, so the effect was much like a slow strobe light in a black-lit room.

The flicker of the strobe became erratic, making it hard for Dalen to focus. "I can't see anything past the frames."

"That's because you are trying to observe it; as you do, you force it into reality, which is why the frames are off. Use your figure and focus." It took Dalen a few attempts, but he got himself back to a place where the frames were blinking in and out in rhythm. "Fantastic. Now, instead of 'looking,' reach out with your being the same way you would in the Natural Field and connect to it."

Dalen did as she suggested and, as he reached out, he perceived the Fire Jinn in multiple possible places in the room. He felt her in every place and in none of them at the same time.

She knew he could sense it, and so she took turns talking to him from different possible locations where she could be, shifting from sentence to sentence. "Now what can you see?"

"You are everywhere," Dalen thought out loud, knowing that they were connected in the Natural Element and she would hear him.

"Good," replied another possibility of her. "And what of the candle? Where is it?"

The candle, between the frames, was everywhere. He could sense it in every inch of the room and, as a flash of reality happened, it was only in the spot it had been, floating in front of him.

"It is everywhere and nowhere at the same time." Dalen was almost mesmerized by it all.

"Many call this state *superposition*. It is the state that all things are in when they are not specifically being pulled into the singularity known as reality.

"Put out your hand," she commanded, and Dalen did as she asked. "When you are between the frames, can the candle be in your hand?"

"Between the frames, it is everywhere." Dalen started losing his grasp on superposition. It was taxing on him, and his strength was waning. "I can't hold this much longer!"

"After the next flash, I want you to not only picture the candle in your hand — when it goes into superposition and is everywhere, I want you to directly look at the candle in your hand!" The flashes were coming faster and faster as Dalen was losing his hold on the Quantum Elemental state. "Look at it and see it in your hand! Don't look away — only see it in your hand!" The stone on her forehead lit up and a magical line appeared, connecting directly to Dalen's third eye.

The same way that Dalen took in his energy and focused it to ignite the Kinetic field, Dalen felt the candle in all of the places it could be in superposition collapse into a single location in his hand. The flashes bled together and soon there weren't any. The flame on the candle began to move again, rapidly picking up speed until it was burning normally as Dalen lost his control of time.

"Where is that candle, Dalen?" She was back to her normal coloring, but she was now standing in a different location than she was before.

Dalen looked down at the candle. "It's in my hand." He was exhausted, but the candle had manifested from where it was to his hand.

"Well done. You didn't rip a hole in the universe or anything." She smiled and crossed her eyes at him.

"Wait." Dalen had not even thought about what consequences might exist for doing such things. "Is that a thing?"

The Fire Jinn laughed. "Not at this level. I bet you are tired. You held that a lot longer than you think. In that quantum state, time acts differently. Being in superposition is a little like being incorporeal."

"Does that mean I can travel in time?" Dalen's mind began to consider the possibilities.

"That," warned the Fire Jinn, "can rip a hole in the universe. Time travel is serious business and there is always the chance that you can and will destroy an entire timeline of existence... But yeah."

"Right. Time travel is dangerous. Might destroy the timeline. Good to know."

Exhaustion claimed him, and Dalen slept deeply for a while. When he awoke, he was lying on the floor of his room. The Fire Jinn was leaning up against one of the walls. "I said, 'Wake up, Dalen. You don't want to miss it.'"

"Miss what?" Dalen got up and shook off the cloudiness from sleep.

"The Buffet Banquet-Blitz Bonanza During Dorn's Dinner Dash Delirium."

15

DORN'S DINNER DASH DELIRIUM

That night, when Dalen came down the stairs, Dorn's was in full swing. Dorn had hired me as a Grey Bard for a show, and I was already performing. My abilities and talents for immersive entertainment were requested for the night's festivities, but Dorn had also asked me to help someone later that evening who he called an old friend. I had my suspicions, but I didn't know for sure that it was Dalen he'd asked me to help.

That night, Dorn had me doing an hour of standup comedy, and the rest of the night I was going to spin family-friendly tales. In the front row, of course, was my manager, wife, and biggest fan. Our relationship is that of legend. We have always been counterparts to one another and, together, we are unstoppable. She keeps me in reality, and I keep her believing in miracles.

• • •

A line had formed past the stage. All manner of folk and creatures had come that night. The line would take one step, pause for a moment, and then take another step, much like a wedding procession. It was moving quickly, so Dalen got in line and did his best to keep up with the motion of it. He tried to remember that most people could not see the Fire Jinn, so he decided to whisper to her instead of talking out loud. "Okay, exactly what is this Dinner Delirium thing?

"It is amazing." She glanced over to whatever being was directly in front of Dalen, who stood about nine feet tall and had ashy grey skin.

Abruptly, she stopped dead in her tracks and peered out over the tables to a seemingly random spot in the tavern. "You just talked about Grey Bards. Try not to be confusing." Dalen was baffled by the comment and shot the jinn a questioning look. "Sorry." She coughed and cleared her throat. "Do you see this gray gentleman directly in front of you? Why don't you ask him what he thinks of this event?"

"Sometimes you are odder than others," he noted. She smiled and nodded proudly. Dalen turned to the large gray individual. "Excuse me, sir?"

The guy turned around and looked at Dalen. He had two large tusks jutting from his lower jaw and his nose looked strikingly like a dog's. Dalen was surprised and, unfortunately, his face did not hide that well. "You got a problem, little man? What? Never seen no orc-kin before?"

Dalen recovered quickly and was able to respond in a reasonable amount of time, "No, sir, I have not. You are probably the coolest being I have met today!"

The orc-kin grinned and, even though Dalen could read that he was happy, it was still a little scary. "Thank you, little buddy." There was something about the way he spoke that made Dalen think that maybe he was a little slow, but then again, he thought, maybe that is just his way. "My name is Aartinauk Grlaskus in Orc. In your common tongue, it means Snuggle Bunny."

Time slowed to almost nothing. "Careful in your response," the Fire Jinn warned. "His mother, who has died, named him. He wears it like a badge of pride and does not take kindly to it being mocked."

Time caught up, Dalen smiled, and he tried some diplomacy. "I'm guessing Orc names are intended to honor the heart of the orc who wields it."

Snuggle Bunny puffed his chest out proudly. "Yes. But I am only orc-kin. My Mum was orc. She named me."

Dalen liked how this was going, and even the Fire Jinn nodded and gave him a thumbs up. "Do you do your name proud and

326

bring her honor?"

Snuggle Bunny's eyes welled up. "I bring great honor to Mum."

Dalen gave the bow of respect from the brotherhood. "It's a great honor to meet you, Snuggle Bunny."

Snuggle Bunny let out a roar of laughter, "You understand!" He playfully pushed Dalen in the chest so hard that it knocked him over. Snuggle Bunny stopped laughing and looked concerned. "Sorry about that. Snuggle Bunny is strong, and you are little."

Dalen got up laughing, "I'm fine, Snuggle B — you just caught me off guard."

"Why you call Snuggle Bunny, Snuggle B?" Then he spoke very slowly, emphasizing the syllables, "Snuuuug-gle Buuuun-ny."

"I didn't mean to offend," Dalen apologized quickly. "It's just a nickname."

Snuggle Bunny shook his head and looked at Dalen like he was dumb. "Nick not name. Snuuuug-gle Buuuun-ny."

"I wish you understood."

As soon as Dalen spoke, the Fire Jinn moved between them. With one hand, she touched Dalen's throat and pressed the other gently to Snuggle Bunny's forehead. "Try it now," she suggested.

Dalen took a breath and focused on being clear. "I know

your name is Snuggle Bunny. Where I come from, we have a term called a 'nickname'. A nickname is sometimes a fun way to say someone's name that is shorter and easier to say quickly. I felt like you are now a friend, so it was my custom to call you by a nickname, showing you that I saw you as a friend. Snuggle B. The same way you called me Little Buddy."

The jinn let go, and Snuggle Bunny blinked a couple of times, trying to shake free the cobwebs. Then, before Dalen could respond, Snuggle Bunny had him. He picked up Dalen and held him close, rocking slightly back and forth. "Friend! You can call Snuggle Bunny 'Snuggle B,' and Snuggle Bunny will call Little Buddy, Little Buddy." Dalen tapped out for air and Snuggle B set him down. "Little Buddy, what real name?"

"Dalen Pax."

Snuggle Bunny looked up and to the left as if he were thinking really hard. "Daaaalen Pax." He mouthed it a couple more times. "Okay, Little Buddy, what you want?"

By this time, Dalen and Snuggle Bunny had moved halfway through the line. "Tell me about why we are in line."

Snuggle Bunny looked surprised. "You don't know?" He did a little hopping dance. "This is the line for the Buffet Banquet-Blitz Bonanza."

"During Dorn's Dinner Dash Delirium?" Dalen repeated the Fire Jinn's words.

"Yes!" Snuggle Bunny loudly hooted. "So, you know?"

"I only know its name," Dalen laughed. "What is it?"

"The Buffet Banquet-Blitz Bonanza is Snuggle Bunny's happy place!" He gave another hoot. He pointed to a tent that had been erected toward the back where the line eventually ended. "In there is a magic place that is different for every person who goes in." He stopped for a moment and put up a finger, and then recited something that Dalen guessed had been told to him many times in the same tone as he spoke. "Only one person goes in at a time."

Dalen was intrigued. "What do you mean it is different for each person?"

Snuggle Bunny bent down and put his hand up to the side of his mouth as if he were going to tell Dalen a secret, but then failed to whisper and almost shouted in Dalen's face. "It's different for each person who goes in!" He was so incredibly excited. Snuggle Bunny stood back up and pointed out different people who were eating at the tables. First was an elven man enjoying a colorful salad with vegetation Dalen couldn't recognize. "He went in, and that was there." Then he indicated another table where a human woman was sitting in front of a huge pile of crab legs while watching the show. "She went in and that was there."

Dalen was absolutely amazed by the idea. "So, when you go in, it is tailor-made for each customer?"

"Different for everybody," Snuggle Bunny nodded with a sense of satisfaction. "In there is what you want the most."

Dalen nudged the big guy with his elbow. "What's in there

for you?"

Snuggle Bunny's eyes glazed over slightly. "Meat!"

Dalen wasn't honestly surprised at his answer but wanted to keep the conversation going, "Just meat, no salad?"

Snuggle Bunny was swallowing at that exact moment and choked himself with laughter. "Salad?" Snuggle Bunny pretended to throw up a little. "No, Little Buddy." He raised his fist into the air and in a strong voice called out, "Snuggle Bunny does not want salad!" He glanced around and, when he realized he was making a scene, grew embarrassed. The orc-kin slouched over a bit and with a sheepish voice uttered an apologetic "Sorry."

"It's all good, Big Guy — I probably won't get a salad either. I have had a craving for years, and I am sure that is what awaits me. Don't get me wrong, salads are wonderful, and in the last few years, it is mainly all I have eaten. Yay, salad! But if this gives you what you crave, there are only a few things it would be. I can't wait to see." Trying to continue the conversation, Dalen added, "Tell me about yours."

"I like Big Guy. I want Big Guy to be my nickname." He had the same look on his face as if he'd asked for a puppy.

"You got it, Big Guy." Dalen watched as Snuggle Bunny's face went through a myriad of emotions, starting with elation, swinging through hardcore victory, and landing somewhere in tears of happiness and contentment.

"You are my best friend." Dalen could tell that he meant

that, and his heart went out to Snuggle Bunny.

"Hey, Big Guy. You are awesome, and I am glad I am your friend." He looked over at the Fire Jinn and shrugged.

She smiled and shrugged back. "I think you made a friend for life."

"So, tell me," Dalen inquired, trying to get Snuggle Bunny back on track, "what exactly is going to be in the tent?"

That did the job immediately, and Snuggle Bunny grinned. They were now next in line. "Oh, in the orc lands, there are five master meat pits. They are the greatest in the world. Others, such as dwarves, come to the orc lands and ask permission to come in, just so they can go to one of the meat pits." He rubbed his belly and smacked his lips. "In there are all five meat pits. I will get something for you. You get something for me, and we will trade. Sound like a deal, Little Buddy?" He gave Dalen another friendly push.

Dalen braced for the impact of his push this time and didn't fall over. "Sounds like a deal, Big Guy." Then Dalen focused his Ki and pushed him back as hard as he could.

Snuggle Bunny took two steps back and nodded with respect. "You may be tiny, but your heart is orc!" He looked over to Dorn and called out. "Put him on my tab!" Then he laughed and walked into the tent. A waft of the greatest smelling barbecue hit Dalen's senses, and he knew whatever Snuggle Bunny was going to bring him, it was going to be good.

Dalen glanced over to the Fire Jinn and whispered, "How long do I have to wait?"

"Oh, you can go now. As soon as the tent closes, you can enter." She gestured toward the tent.

"I thought that it was one at a time," Dalen reminded her.

"It is," the jinn affirmed, smiling. "You will find that there is no one in there."

Dalen walked in and found himself in a tent that was much bigger on the inside. There were five banquet tables filled with food. In front of him was a table that had a tray with a large dinner plate, a deep bowl, and a glass with a sign directly in front of it that read Mc-Tucky Fried-Taco-King's-Table-Jr.-In the Box.

"Snuggle Bunny was right," acknowledged Dalen. "This is my happy place." Dalen took samples of every fast food place he'd ever eaten. He took a taco from one table and a burger from another, and then sought out his favorite fries. He grabbed a handful of chicken nuggets and found himself in front of a section devoted to pizza. He grabbed a slice of his favorite kind, but as he did, he noticed that the pizza on the table was still whole. "Hey!" he called to the Fire Jinn, who was studying a section of a table that had forty-two different sauces. "Come take a look at this." She approached him, giving Dalen an inquisitive look.

"See how the pizza has all of its slices?" The Fire Jinn nodded. "Watch this!" He pulled another slice from the pie. It was hot and fresh, and cheese pulled into long gooey strings as he took it, but when Dalen looked at the pizza, it was still whole. "See? What's happening?"

The Fire Jinn spoke as if what she was saying was as simple as could be. "The pizza is in a state of superposition while in this room."

Dalen looked at the pizza but couldn't grasp what she meant. "In what way?"

"It is both in a state of you taking a slice and you not taking the slice. The whole tent is, for that matter. That's why only one person at a time can go in. Somewhere in the quantum waves of possibility, Snuggle Bunny is filling a platter with his favorite ribs as we speak. Just not this wave of reality."

"So, he's in here now?" Dalen instinctively looked around.

"In one possible wave of who came into the tent tonight, Snuggle Bunny is in the tent. But you are traveling on a completely different wave of quantum possibility, so there is no point in looking for him, and when either of you leaves the tent, you will return to a shared wave of possibility." She went back over to the sauces that were right next to the nuggets. She reached down to take a nugget and pulled one made of light from the bowl and dipped it into something that looked like lava and ate it. "Oh, and the plateware and cup are ever-fill, so a slice will do. Being able to use the Element of Imagination is the direct action of observing the Quantum Field. As the Observer, you normally create reality continuously. But the magic used here overrides that, frame by frame. The tent itself counts as an Observer, and so do the plates and cups. They aren't sentient in most respects, but they continuously, frame by frame, observe the food in existence. Being able to choose what you observe by controlling the Imagination Element in the Quantum Field is the very foundation of manifestation."

"So, the plate is aware?" Dalen didn't know how to feel about that.

"Not quite," replied the jinn. "The plate is aware that there is food on it, but that is where it stops. It doesn't have feelings or dreams. It's not called Mike, and it doesn't hang out with its plate friends at night in the cupboard. It is only aware of what is in or on it, but once something is there, it will continuously recreate it there, frame by frame."

Dalen looked at his plate. There were six nuggets on it that he'd grabbed. Dalen popped one in his mouth, and it was the most delicious nugget he'd ever had. He moaned with the goodness of it, but stopped short when he glanced at his plate and saw that there were still six nuggets.

"This is awesome!" He planned out the rest of his plate carefully. He grabbed a wing and a breast of fried chicken, along with an accompanying bonus biscuit. He took a burger from three different locations for the Big Guy to try and filled his bowl with mashed potatoes on one side and macaroni and cheese on the other.

"It gets even more awesome than that," the Fire Jinn chortled with delight. "When you are all full, you can leave your plate at your table and get back in line. When you walk back into the tent, you reset to a possible version of you that hasn't eaten yet. So, your fifth trip can be like your first."

Dalen's mouth nearly hit the floor. "Are you saying I can eat again and again, and never actually get full?"

"Not until your last trip," the jinn explained. "If you don't go back in, you won't reset."

"So, eat until I am literally bored with it, and then have a nice light meal and then go about my evening?" Dalen smiled. "This really is my happy place."

Dalen stepped outside and found Snuggle Bunny at a booth with a platter of ribs, cuts of meat, and steaks. He had a single rib that was the length of Dalen's arm that he gave Dalen as soon as Dalen sat down. Dalen set down the trio of burgers and slowly articulated, "Buuuurger," which Snuggle Bunny repeated. He grabbed a nugget off of his plate, leaving six, and handed it to Snuggle Bunny and said, "Chicken nuggets."

The Big Guy ate it and smiled at Dalen. "I love chicken nuggets!" and from time to time would grab one and pop it in his mouth. They sat together and ate, and while they did, Snuggle Bunny explained how he came to be in Venger.

"When Snuggle Bunny was little, other orc didn't want to fight and hunt with Snuggle Bunny. They said Snuggle Bunny too little," remembered the nine-and-a-half-foot wall of meat. "Mum was orc. Dad was orc-kin, and half of his blood was human." The Big Guy raised his hand to about his chin. "Very small." He was holding a steak in his hand and took a bite from it like it was a meat cookie. "Dad died when Snuggle Bunny reached the age of full orc-hood. He was small, but he died defending the village from big monster. He died an orc."

Dalen could see from how the Big Guy repositioned himself that this was a moment of pride for him. "He sounds like he was a good orc."

Snuggle Bunny nodded and took another bite of his meat cookie. "Yes. Dad was good orc. Then three summers after that, Mum and Snuggle Bunny were exploring a new cave for the tribe, but the cave fell down. Snuggle Bunny and Mum were trapped. Snuggle Bunny got free and tried to save Mum." The Big Guy started to cry. "Mum die. Love Mum. Miss Mum." He began to openly weep and then howled. "Mum! Miss Mum."

Dalen didn't care that the Big Guy was making a scene. He just consoled his friend until he calmed down a bit. Once he had, Dalen patted him on his shoulder. "Hey, Big Guy, you're okay. You want a burger?"

The Big Guy smiled through swollen eyes and nodded. By the time he had eaten one of each of the three that Dalen brought him, he was doing a lot better. "Tribe say, both Dad and Mum die for tribe. Tribe, Snuggle Bunny's family now. Other orc now hunt with Snuggle Bunny and other orc fight with Snuggle Bunny." His excitement swelled once more. "Tribe make Snuggle Bunny hunter. No more cave-looker." The Big Guy's eyes widened. "Snuggle Bunny no like caves now. Too small. Snuggle Bunny feels trapped like when Mum died." He mellowed into sadness again and whimpered, "Mum."

The Fire Jinn just smiled at the Big Guy and took a sip from a cup she had once again produced. "This guy's heart is huge, but he is easily distracted."

"Stay with me, Big Guy. So, your tribe began to treat you like one of their own and even made you a hunter. Then what happened?"

It worked, and the Big Guy cheered up. "One night, a pack of razor beasts attacked the village. Tribe was all killed except for Snuggle Bunny and two tribe brothers."

"A razor beast is kind of like a mix between a wolf and a panther but about the size of a car. Bone ridges that are extremely sharp run along its shoulders, hips, and paws. That, plus its teeth and claws, earned them the moniker 'razor beast,'" the Fire Jinn explained to keep Dalen up with the story.

Snuggle Bunny focused his attention on a rib for a moment and then took a swig of an ale he had by his platter. Dalen noticed that the Big Guy seemed to accept the death of his tribe well. He thought about it while Snuggle Bunny went into detail about how they all died in glorious battle. Dalen guessed it was different to die in battle than in a random cave-in, or maybe Snuggle Bunny just loved his mom that much.

"Snuggle Bunny and the last two tribe brothers were tracking the razor beasts that ran, to bring honor to our tribe. Found them attacking a patrol of humans. Four of them. Tribe brothers wanted to wait until fight was over and then attack what was left, but Snuggle Bunny looked at the humans being slaughtered and could not stand by." He held up a rib like a sword. "Snuggle Bunny say, 'You want to honor our tribe? You want to do right thing for family who died?'" He pointed his rib forward and shouted, "'This is your tribe! Save them!'" The Big Guy bit a whole chunk of meat from his rib. "Brothers agree. Snuggle Bunny leaped into fight and killed one before it knew Snuggle Bunny was there. Brothers attacked another." He took a swig of ale. "All of the humans were protecting one, and Snuggle Bunny thought, 'I bet that's the chief.' So, Snuggle Bunny yelled, 'We are here to help,' so he does not think he is being attacked by two enemies." He held up his ale toward Dalen. "Tribe brother Hard Face killed the second but not before the razor beast killed tribe brother Anvil Breaker."

The Fire Jinn gestured with her head toward the Big Guy. "He is honoring the dead, don't leave him hanging."

Dalen took his cup which was filled with a mix of five different flavors of soft drink. It was a combination of his own design that he called "The Kamikaze." He raised it toward his new friend in a toast, but Snuggle Bunny saw it coming and met him a third of the way there with a forceful bump that sent beverage spilling from both.

"Together, Hard Face and Snuggle Bunny faced off against the largest razor beast Snuggle Bunny had ever seen." He grabbed another steak and tore into it. "It clawed and bit and howled in pain. Snuggle Bunny was hurt badly and fell to the ground." He held up his mug again. "Hard Face fell to the razor beast, as well, but died where he lay." Dalen slammed his cup against the orc's and let him finish. "The human chief had killed his own razor beast and made it to the other razor beast before it got to Snuggle Bunny. He stabbed it with a blade Snuggle Bunny could not see. The chief called it the Air Blade of Wisdom." The Big Guy shrugged and finished his steak. "The razor beast turned on the human chief and bit him in the leg and began to toss him around." He put another rib in his mouth and emulated how the razor beast rag-dolled the human. Dalen nearly shot soft drink out his nose. "Snuggle Bunny got up and grabbed the razor beast with both hands." He grabbed another rib and placed them at an angle with their ends touching. "One hand on top part of mouth and one hand on jaw." The Big Guy used the ribs to demonstrate the jaws of the razor beast's mouth, and he showed Dalen how he pried both hands into its mouth and struggled to pull the jaws apart. He pretended to pull as hard as he could.

"What happened?" Dalen asked.

Snuggle Bunny flexed with all of his might and bellowed louder and louder. As Snuggle Bunny's yell reached a crescendo, his arms went loose, and he pulled the ribs apart, yelping how to imitate the sound the razor beast made as his jaw snapped in half.

"Wow, Big Guy! So, you saved the chief?" Dalen hit his cup against Snuggle Bunny's mug again, splashing ale and soft drink all over them and the table once more.

"Human chief bleed with Snuggle Bunny, and both lost brothers that day." Another crash of cups. "Human chief say, he not just chief but king."

Dalen stopped him there, "Wait? You saved King Gavin

of Venger?"

The Fire Jinn raised her glass to Snuggle Bunny, "My man."

"Yes. Chief say he is King Gavin of Venger. He says that since I had no tribe and no family because the last of them died saving him and his men, that Snuggle Bunny and King Gavin were now brothers."

Dalen's jaw dropped. "Brothers?"

Snuggle Bunny smiled and nodded. "Gavin put his hand on his leg and covered it with blood. Then King Gavin took my hand and swore on his lifeblood that Snuggle Bunny and King Gavin were brothers. Snuggle Bunny now lives in the castle and protects the greatest treasure of Venger."

Dalen leaned in. "What is the greatest treasure of Venger?"

With great pride, he said, "Venger's future, Princess Joanna."

Dalen was amazed by the entire story. He congratulated Snuggle Bunny and then toasted a couple more times. They talked through a couple more platters of food and each time offered different choices, as what each of them wanted changed throughout the night. On one of the final rounds, they had a chicken-nugget-eating contest that three other patrons joined in on. Snuggle Bunny was gloriously victorious, and then he said farewell and headed for home.

Dalen went back to the tent only one more time and laughed at himself as he made a nice salad and brewed a cup of mint tea.

16

A DIVINE CONNECTION

The next morning, Dalen was sitting in the middle of his training circle, clearing his mind for the day's lesson, a practice that he had gained considerable skill in while at the Temple of Light. Brother Faith's words had been confusing at first, but once he learned how to unlearn, the monk's logic made sense: "The greatest student is the one that can bring a clean piece of parchment to the lesson."

Some things can only be learned if you are willing to set aside what you already know. The world is a funny place, and even if what you know is right, it doesn't mean it is the only truth. Dalen remembered it was the first real lesson he learned when he got to the Temple of Light. It all came about on his second day there when he was thinking about wading in water.

Dalen was standing in a shallow pool at the temple. He'd allowed his mind to wander into imagination and magic, and he had rested his foot on the surface of the water, pretending to stand on it.

"What are you doing?" asked Brother Faith.

"I heard once that it was impossible to step on the same water twice," responded Dalen. He had heard it in an old film, and he always thought it sounded deep.

Brother Faith considered what Dalen said carefully before he responded. "From one point of view, I can see what you are saying, and I feel that there is a truth to it. The water continues to change its shape as anything disturbs it, so the water your foot touches will move when you do, and as you set your foot down again, the part of the water you are touching will be a different part of the water than you had been touching before." Dalen blew out his air in relief. He didn't want to sound dumb while quoting a movie. Brother Faith chuckled to himself, and then added, "From another point of view, all of the water in that pool is connected. One water, if you will, and any place you stand in that pool will be on the same piece of water. So, I would have to say the opposite is true as well." Brother Faith splashed some water at Dalen. "One is yes. The other is no. Both are truth, so I guess it just depends on which truth you wish to see."

The next day, in his other class, Master Ki had then asked him to explain how and why that was possible. It was one thing to be able to grasp it, but then to explain it in detail so that it could be understood was more difficult. He'd worked on clearly articulating it for two days, during which Master Ki gave him no other tasks until he could answer his question. Dalen would guess at an answer, and Master Ki would then ask questions that completely countermanded his whole understanding. It was frustrating and, to Dalen, Master Ki was not helping — he was just telling him he was wrong. He was irritable and wanted to quit a few times, but Master Ki sat him down and helped him with his anger. They worked on breathing, and Master Ki reminded him that he was here to learn, and if he were going to learn anything, he had to first learn to learn.

On the third day, the answer came to him while he was watching Master Truth and Master Love debating. The debate had to do with a single individual on two different points in their life, one being at the moment they reached their highest enlightenment, and the other at the moment where they hit rock bottom and began their climb upward. The question was, "Which one was more powerful?"

Master Love was a beautiful woman in her late thirties with sandy blond hair with a natural curl that cascaded down her back. She wore the black and white robes of a master and was the head healer at the Temple of Light. As a healer, her viewpoint was that, the healthier you are, the stronger you are, so she spoke for the individual at their peak. She believed that once they reached their highest understanding, they would be their most powerful. Her argument was based on the idea that, at that point, they would have cleared themselves of their traumas and let go of the negative traits that had kept them powerless in the first place. She suggested that the work they'd done to achieve their goals of enlightenment would've made them a stronger and more powerful person.

Master Truth listened and agreed with her points. Not once did the Air Jinn argue her points while she made them. Master Truth just took in everything she said as if it were the only truth in existence. When she had completed her thought, he sat back for a moment, considering what she said. Finally, he stated, "I see the truth in what you say."

Master Love bowed and thanked him, then she kneeled before the Air Jinn and entreated, "Teach me to see more."

Master Truth smiled and gestured for her to rise. When she stood, he looked at her with kind eyes and simply noted, "It is easy to be happy on a beautiful, sunny day."

Master Love teared up. She put her hand over her mouth and tried to compose herself; the whole time, her eyes darted back and forth as she visually put everything in a new order. It was learning on some sort of master level that Dalen couldn't completely grasp.

Master Truth noticed Dalen watching and gestured for him to join. "Brother Dalen is in training here and is trying to understand the nature of truth. Could you offer up what you can now see? It is a wonderful lesson for him because he is at the beginning and, besides, it would be good for you to speak this truth while it is fresh in your mind."

She smiled and wiped tears from her eyes. "It is true that

once we have let go of the things that made us powerless, including the belief that we are weak, we become more empowered. With the freedom of not being burdened by our negativity and traumas, we have the power to make the choices and take the actions that we choose. Yet it is in our hardest moment that we are the most powerful. It is easy to act when you are unencumbered, and it is easy to be powerful when you have power. Now, imagine how powerful you have to be to act when you are tied down by your own thoughts and feelings. To rise up from a deep depression. To take that impossible step when you are so broken you don't believe that you can." Tears rolled down her face. "To be able to believe when you believe that there is nothing left to believe in. To stand when you have no strength. To fight when there is nothing left of you. There is nothing more powerful than taking a step that you believe to be impossible." As she sobbed, she reached out for the Air Jinn. He waved his hand and was covered in a golden aura of light just as she hugged him. "Thank you, Master Truth. I had almost forgotten." She took a deep breath and looked Master Truth in his eyes and smiled. "It is easy to be happy on a sunny day."

The memories of Dalen's first day flooded his memory and, at that moment, what Brother Faith had said about honoring the broken and painful version of himself made sense. "I see why you changed your mind," he then stated.

Master Love let go of Master Truth and gave him a bow of respect. She turned to Dalen. "The only part of my mind I changed was to change it to a blank page to be written on."

She was still composing herself, and Dalen thought she

must have misunderstood. "No, I mean you changed your mind about your original truth."

She raised an eyebrow. "I still think it is true."

Dalen then thought that maybe it was he who didn't understand. "But now you think the other is true."

It was Master Truth that answered. "Understanding truth is not about changing one truth to fit another. It is about seeing both truths as a larger understanding."

"Masters Truth and Love, I am trying to understand." Dalen's frustration had reached his limit. "I have been working on this for a couple of days, and I just can't grasp how two opposing truths can both be right." He dropped to his knees. "Just help me understand."

The jinn reached out and plucked a coin out of nothing. "This is a Master's Coin." He held it up so he could see its face. "What can you tell me about it?"

Dalen looked at the coin and was surprised that he was able to answer the question. "It's made of gold and has a dragon on it." Dalen smiled and looked at them both. "It's a promissory note, guaranteeing an audience with the Gold Dragon of the East, the wisest being in the corporeal worlds."

Master Love was openly surprised. "That was impressive."

Master Truth nodded. "Is what you told me true?"

Dalen nodded. "To the best of my understanding, everything

I told you is true."

Master Truth smiled. "What you have said is absolutely true." He closed his hand and, when he opened it, there was a silver coin that had the same emblem that was at the center of Dalen's Training Circle. "This is an Initiate's Coin. What can you tell me about it?"

Dalen looked closely at the coin that was in the Air Jinn's hand. "It is made of silver and has a magical symbol of the seventh Element of Reality on it."

Master Truth nodded again. "Is what you told me true?"

Dalen nodded. "To the best of my knowledge, I am telling you the truth."

Master Truth closed his hand again. "The Master Coin is gold, and the Initiate Coin is silver. The Master Coin has a dragon on it, and the Initiate Coin has a magic symbol. They are different in every way. Like Yin and Yang. Two truths that are completely different from each other." The jinn took Dalen's hand and dropped a coin into it.

Dalen picked it up and immediately understood. He was holding a single coin that was made of gold on one side and silver on the other. "Like heads and tails of a single coin."

All of the sudden, it made complete sense. Master Truth's voice was calming as he put words to Dalen's thoughts: "You can look at either side of it and understand the truth about what you are looking at, and you can stop right there and say you know

348

the truth. You can flip it over and only look at the other side of something and understand a completely different truth. You can stop there and say that you now understand a new truth, and you would still be right. But it is when you can look at both sides and understand both truths that you begin to understand what the truth of it really is. A single coin. Only then can you begin to look at other truths. Truths like why both the Master Coin and the Initiate's Coin are the same coin."

Dalen laughed.

"Assuming that they were two different coins is why you couldn't see the truth at first," added Master Love. "The truths we create can sometimes make it impossible to see a larger truth, which is why when I try to understand something, I clear my mind of what I know, even if I know it to be true."

Dalen tried to give it back, but Master Truth held up his hand and gave him a small nod. "It is yours. You have learned your first lesson here at the Temple of Light, and you are now an Initiate." It was too large to fit in the small pouch around his neck, so he slipped it into the bindings at his forearm and kept it there the entire time he was at the temple. Often when he was learning something difficult, he would remember the coin, and it would help him focus and open himself to new possibilities.

Since that day, Dalen made it a point to practice setting aside what he felt and believed so that he could be open to new truths. As he sat in the Training Circle and prepared for the next lesson, he reached into his pocket and found the coin. "Today I need to be clear. A clean sheet of parchment." Dalen finished getting ready, and when he felt that his mind was truly open, he stood up and addressed the Fire Jinn, who'd been patiently waiting for him. "Okay," he declared, "I wish to learn the Soul Sphere."

The Fire Jinn pointed to the yellow glyph that was directly in front of him. "This is the Divine Element. To be able to access it, you will have to understand what it is. To do so, there is a strong chance you will have to set aside what you believe so that you can be open enough to understand what will be explained."

Dalen gave his traditional bow. "I am a clean piece of parchment."

The Fire Jinn raised an eyebrow at Dalen. "We shall see." She gestured toward the door. "What you seek lies on the other side of the door. All you need to do is walk through it."

Dalen thought to himself that he was going to have another adventure in Dorn's perhaps, and where the point of his tavern is to be what you need, there are some things best left to the experts in the field. Thus, as Dalen stepped through the door, he did not exit into the tavern but instead found himself stepping into a completely different arena.

Dalen was astonished at the sight of the room before him. He was in a large marble cathedral. The only thing that rivaled the sheer size of it was its beauty. Dalen marveled at it for a while, just taking it in. It had sweeping archways that met in the center of the cathedral in a stained-glass ceiling that poured sunlight through in waves of color. In the center of the floor directly below the window was a circle made of a brilliant, white metal that appeared to produce or reflect its own light, and it was surrounded by pews in multiple directions, much like a theater in the round.

"Where are we?" Dalen breathed, filled with awe.

"We are in the Temple of All Faith," the Fire Jinn replied. She led him toward the circle in the middle of the room. "There is someone I want you to meet."

At one of the last pews closest to the circle was a man, still young-looking but probably in his thirties. What caught Dalen's attention first was that he looked almost exactly like Mathias. They could very easily have been twins, but this man didn't have the withered look of a hard life like Mathias. His face was fuller and bright, and he had short hair and a beard but no mustache. His clothes instantly let Dalen know he was some kind of a priest. He was dressed in all black except for his white collar, yet he also wore a white robe that only a priest of the Brotherhood of Light would wear. He was sitting long ways in the pew with his legs up, and Dalen noted that he was barefoot. He was conducting with his toe while he hummed a tune to himself.

He stopped humming as they approached and, without turning around to see who was there, he inquired, "What can I do for the both of you?"

"You knew there were two of us?" Dalen asked.

"I can perceive all Divine Beings." He smiled and looked up at Dalen with a wink. He swung his feet over and stood up with a stretch and a crack. "Welcome to the Temple of All Faith. I am

Diem. How can I be of service?"

"Diem?" asked Dalen. "As in Carpe Diem?"

Diem let out a chuckle through his nose and nodded. "Yeah. That was the favorite game of the kids at school." He crossed his eyes and stuck out his tongue. "No, but really, Carpe Diem is a phrase that means 'seize the day.' I am the day that can be seized." He smiled and bowed. "How can I be of service to you?"

Dalen was at a loss for words for the moment — he had practically forgotten what he was doing or why he was there. While his mind scrambled for solid ground, he threw out a question that he hoped would buy him some time. "Temple of All Faith. How does that work?"

"Amazingly well, actually." He smiled and just stared playfully, waiting for Dalen to say something else.

Dalen couldn't help but like this priest. There was a light within him, and Dalen felt drawn toward it. He reminded Dalen of Master Truth in a way and felt that they were going to become friends. He knew that he was there to learn, so he redirected the question. "I meant, how can you have a temple for every faith? I ask because, where I come from, many religions can't get along with each other and the idea of having one place that covers every religion is hard to comprehend." He got down on his knees the way that he saw Master Love do years ago at the Temple of Light. "Help me see more."

Diem smiled and glanced over to the Fire Jinn. "You

brought me someone ready to learn."

She tilted her head sideways toward Dalen, who was still kneeling. "Did you expect anything less from me?"

Diem frowned and nodded in agreement. "Good point." He turned his attention to Dalen. "Are you ready to relent to whatever it is I have to offer?" Dalen nodded. "Then, in this moment, you understand all you need to know."

Dalen smiled because it sounded exactly like something that Master Truth would have said. "Train me to learn what I understand, so that I can know it."

"Then you will be trained." Diem glanced back to the jinn. "I like him."

"Yeah," she smirked. "I am pretty fond of him, as well, and what he creates."

Diem smiled and raised an eyebrow. "Agreed. Speaking of which, you are hot."

The Fire Jinn cocked her head and replied with an almost bored tone, "Fire puns? That's what you got for me?"

Diem laughed, "Yeah. I thought it was fitting. Not only am I referencing the point that the very image of you is something that he is creating in itself, but I am also referring to the point that his conception of you is quite beautiful and that you are made of fire. It is a three-way pun with a compliment." He cocked his head and gave her the same look. "How many people work that hard for you?"

The Fire Jinn paused for a moment. After she made her decision about what Diem had said, she shrugged and nodded. "Fair enough."

"As for you, we need a place to start." Diem returned his attention to Dalen and the task at hand. "I love that you have cleared your thoughts so that you can learn, and you will need that skill, but it would be best to use the images that you do understand to help with this process. What do you know about the Divine Element as an Element?"

"I don't know anything, really," acknowledged Dalen. "That is why I am here."

Diem nodded. "This will be the first thing you have to let go of." Dalen was unsure but nodded. "Okay, first come and get up off the floor. The respect is noted and taken in. Thank you, but this is not how the Divine works, no matter what certain religions tell you." He sat back down on the pew and motioned for Dalen to take up the pew directly behind him. When Dalen sat down, Diem turned around and rested his forearms on the back of the pew with his chin resting on them. "Is this the first Element you have learned?"

"No." Dalen dropped into test mode. "I have learned the Natural Element and the Kinetic Element. I have learned the Quantum Element and the Element of Imagination and the Observer."

Diem smiled. "Good. They can seem to be vastly different, but what can you tell me about what they have in common?"

That sentence profoundly resonated with Dalen. He knew that the Fire Jinn had mentioned it once, but all of a sudden it made sense. He reached into his pocket and retrieved his Initiate Coin, flipped it over, and then laughed.

"They are the same thing." His eyes teared up as he began to understand. "All of the Elements are only aspects of a single thing. Each in their own right is different, but in the end, they are concepts of a single truth. The same way that I am Dalen Pax and Brother Truth. They are both me, but they are different aspects of myself." All his training up until now flowed through his mind so fast that he had to activate the Kinetic Field and slow things down to be able to see it all. "In both cases, there are two Elements that effectively create a sphere. The Body Sphere and the Mind Sphere are both a single Sphere of Reality seen from two different points of view."

It was now pouring from him so that he had to relent to the understanding flooding his being. "Both spheres are comprised of two Elements that are connected. An inward and outward breath. A field in which all things are one and the ability to act within that field."

Tears of understanding welled in his eyes, and he remembered Master Love as she learned, and he wondered to himself if this was what she had felt. "In the Body Sphere, the Natural Element creates an understanding that we are all one and allows us to connect to that oneness in a very physical way. The Kinetic allows us to move through the physical world and, with that connection, we can also move within ourselves and find the flow of perfect oneness."

Dalen took a couple of breaths, but the universe was not done with him, and he continued with his line of understanding. "In the Mind Sphere, the Element of the Quantum Field creates a superposition, during which all things are in every possible wave of existence all at once, effectively making everyone and everything everywhere one. This again creates this oneness, but instead of physical truth, it is a perceived truth that happens not during the physical reality that is being imagined by the Observer; instead, it takes place in the frames in between reality. As the Observer, we can move in and out of this field and manifest literal creation through the ability to affect the infinite waves of possibility in the Quantum Element. So, in fairness, there is no difference between them except for how they are being perceived and used." Dalen finished his thought, and the universe let go of its grip on his mind and soul. Dalen sat there, breathing and crying, as his mind went over what he'd just said as if it were the first time that he'd ever heard it.

"Beautifully put." Diem sat there for a long while, watching as Dalen processed everything he'd shared. His patience was unwavering. He never pressed Dalen to finish. He simply sat back and returned to the tune he was humming when they first arrived.

The jinn was slowly flying and dancing around the large circle on the floor to the tune that Diem was humming. Neither of them seemed to be in a hurry and relented to however much time Dalen needed. When he finally was ready, he took a deep breath and nodded.

The Fire Jinn kept dancing but began to flare. "The second wave is bigger. But you can do it."

Dalen cleared his mind the best he could, and asked, "What second wave?"

Diem had waited for him to ask and responded with his original question. "What can you tell me about the Soul Sphere?"

Dalen gripped his seat as he felt his mind open again, and he watched as the pieces fell into place. The world stopped moving, and in the frames between the moments, Dalen understood.

The Fire Jinn erupted as if Dalen's understanding directly affected her. She expanded in size and a beautiful line of pure light sprung from her solar plexus and connected to Dalen in the same location. As it did, a line from Diem appeared as well, and it attached itself not only to Dalen but also to the Fire Jinn, as every third bead in the set of seven on the Beads of Fire lit up.

"There is no difference between the Soul Sphere and the other two. Like the other two, it is only an aspect of a single thing. The Soul Sphere is made up of two Elements. One Element is somehow connected to a oneness that connects all things, and the other Element is dedicated to the ability to move within it and to interact with that field." As he finished, Dalen found himself lying in the pew. Tears coursed down his cheeks, pooling in his ears. It was that sensation that grabbed his attention, and so he sat back up and looked over to Diem.

"You do your teacher honor today, son." Diem smiled at

the Fire Jinn as she slowly returned to normal size. "Now comes the hard part. Now we have to cover what is different."

The lines were still there, and they flowed like smoke made of light, but somehow, they still held their physical properties. Dalen had always connected to the Fire Jinn and was unsure why Diem was also connected now. "Through my training in the Body Sphere, I have learned that the glowing stones in her were chakra points. I've figured out the Beads of Fire were seven sets of seven, and that each bead in that seven was directly connected to one of these points." Diem nodded with understanding but didn't interrupt Dalen's thought. "I have also come to understand that when I am connecting to an Element, I can literally see the connection I have to her through the beads in that Element because the Beads of Fire light up as she does. That has something to do with how the beads work in connecting me to her so that I can see her because she is actually just an image in my mind. She is too big for my mind to really see her here."

"I am with you so far, and so far, so good," Diem agreed with a very casual tone as if Dalen had been explaining the use of a toothbrush.

"Then why am I connected to you as well?" asked Dalen.

Diem smiled. "Good question. That question has many answers that in fact is only one answer, but it can be meant in many ways, even if the same words are used to answer it in many forms."

Dalen blinked a few times. "What?"

"You are connecting to the Divine Element. Just like the other two Spheres, there is a oneness. You and I are one. You see our connection through this line because you are connecting into the Divine Element, and I am a Divine being."

Dalen was surprised by the answer and what it suggested. "You mean you are -"

"Yes," Diem interrupted. "But that is only one of the things that I mean."

"So, you are saying that you are God? Like capital 'G' God?" Dalen's tone was filled with skepticism.

"God is a title, not a name," Diem explained. "It would be like calling a king, King." He laughed and then had an impromptu conversation with an imaginary king. "Hello, King. How are you today? Pardon me, King, can you pass the salt?" He shook his head. "Who is your God?" He stood up and walked over to the circle and gestured to it. "Place your deity here."

Dalen stood up and walked over, but with every step, he felt a sense of dread welling up within him. He'd never really thought about it. He'd been forced to go to church in a couple of the houses that he'd been put into, but he'd never really paid attention. He always had considered it 'their God' and had never been able to connect to it.

"I don't have a single religion that I am connected to. I don't know the names of those Gods anyway, and they are really different from one another," Dalen sighed, feeling defeated. "So, I guess I have a few? But each religion I have heard of says that their version is the true and only God, and so I don't know which one is right."

"Many people face that question all the time." Diem gave him a big hug in the same way that a parent would embrace their child. "That is why you are here. The very first thing you need to know about the Element of the Divine is that it relents. The same way I have relented to you and all that you have needed from me. As Divine Beings, both the Fire Jinn and I have demonstrated this the entire time you have been here."

Diem let him go and took his seat back at the pew. He waved Dalen over, but this time he patted space on the pew right next to him. Dalen came and sat down. "Give me a second," Dalen requested. "I need to still my mind." When he was ready, Diem got up and faced him.

The Fire Jinn flared a little. "I feel some learnin' coming on."

Diem smirked at her and began, "I first want you to revisit your understanding of how the Spheres work. Let's look at the Element of Quantum. What is its natural state?" he smiled. "And yes, there is a pun there"

"The Element exists in a state of oneness, where all possible versions of the reality of it exist all at once," Dalen stated. "I'm not sure where this is going."

"What happens to it if you observe it?" asked Diem.

"It snaps into a singularity, called reality, where it becomes only one thing."

"Is it only that?"

Dalen answered instinctively, "Only while it is being observed, but that is not a constant. If you consider the frames between the frames that you perceive, you are looking at it less than one percent of the time. The rest of the time it remains in its state of being everything."

Diem raised an eyebrow at Dalen. "Between the frames, what happens if your perception changes?"

"I was able to have something move to another location by perceiving it there." Dalen was still immensely proud of his achievement.

Diem stepped forward and high-fived him. "So, the field stays in a state of being everything. If you observe it directly, it snaps into a single image, but with perception, it will change its reality. It can do this because it is every possible thing all at once?"

"Yes."

"Now, is what you just explained also how you could explain the Divine Element, since they are, in truth, one?" Diem said with a glint of inspiration in his eyes.

Dalen set aside all he thought he knew about God and what that meant. He did his best to clear his page and leave only the diagram of a Sphere of Reality and how it functions.

"The Divine Element would have to be the field. The outward flow. It would be everything. I have heard of God being referred to as omnipresent — that God is all things and even everyone," Dalen suggested. "This would be the Infinite everything that is required."

"You are doing great!" Diem took no action to suppress how well he thought Dalen was doing. "What happens if you observe the field from a different perspective?"

Dalen tried to run some simulations in his head. He took the time to slow his heart and slide into the place between the frames. He opened his mind and relented to the idea, but he couldn't see it.

"This is a very hard thing I am asking of you." Diem took a breath. "Take a simple image of what people have thought God might be." Dalen pictured an old man with a white beard dressed all in white. "Okay. Very Zeus-like. Now put him in a room with Odin. Have both of them standing around and talking to Ra." Dalen pictured it as a large white room with nothing in it except for the Gods. "Now, imagine that each of them is a concept of something that is all of them, but you can see them all because the Divine Element is in superposition and they are waves of possibilities of what this one Element can be."

"I can see it. If I look at any one of them directly, they snap out of superposition and into a singularity that I would then recognize as God."

"And what happens when you change your perspective?"

"Since it is in superposition all of the time, whether or not it is specifically being observed by you, it would merely change the wave of possibility that you perceive."

"What happens if I look at one of them and you look at another?" Diem asked slowly, as if the sentence was delicate.

Dalen thought about it for a moment and looked at both perspectives in his mind. "One person would perceive one and the other would perceive the other."

Diem moved to Dalen and dropped to his knees right in front of him. "The Divine, by its nature, relents. It will be anything and everything you ask it to be."

The Fire Jinn added, "We, in turn, relent to it. When people pray, it is a request more often than not, and often the request is made with the understanding that there is a larger plan that they hope their request can fit into." She was on fire again as Dalen's old understandings burned away. This new change was creating new paths for him to grow.

"Now, if you can," continued Diem, "imagine every deity from every pantheon of every religion, from every world, in that room."

First, Dalen had to make the room bigger. He began to imagine every God and Goddess he had ever heard of, and then his mind kept going. He imagined Gods from different cultures from different worlds, unknown Gods from lost civilizations that have not existed for thousands of years from remote worlds that faded out long ago.

One of them turned and faced him, and it was Diem. "This is the Divine Field." As Dalen directly looked at him, his image of the room and all the Gods and Goddesses collapsed in and all of it focused on the one individual who was kneeling before him in real space. Time began to move once more, and Dalen found himself sitting in a pew, looking at Diem and the Fire Jinn, who was burning in beautiful tones of yellow fire tipped with white.

Dalen looked up at them with tears in his eyes. "They are all one." His emotions got the better of him, and he relented to the tears.

"Yes, Dalen," Diem's voice was sympathetic and a little sad. "It is all one. Every concept of a God or Goddess that has successfully connected an individual to the Divine Element is correct."

Dalen dropped knee to knee directly in front of Diem. His mind filled with memories of the world he came from and its history. The destruction of people's lives. The witch hunts. The Crusades. Battle upon battle, fighting over whose God was right and whose God was real. Going back thousands of years. "But ..." Dalen's heart shattered into a million pieces, "All that war and death."

Together they wept.

The Fire Jinn finally spoke and brought them both back to where they were and what they were doing, "Humans have a tendency to connect to two concepts that have caused much of the destruction in many worlds." Dalen looked up at her. She had flared down and changed her flames to blue crested in white. "Anything different than what I think is wrong, and anything different must be lesser than I am." Her flames flared back up to her beautiful orange hues of light. "One of the true travesties about humans is that their own unique and beautiful images of the Divine Element separate them. With a perspective of the whole, humans would realize that they are so very much alike. It would give them something to stand together in. If they could only see that their amazing, beautiful, and perfect images of the Divine were absolute truths of an individual perspective of something that truly makes them all one."

"Why don't they?" Dalen pleaded.

"Free Will," Diem answered as he composed himself. "That, and the concepts the Fire Jinn spoke of. Many cling to these concepts of separation, even though many of their religions directly say we are all one. In many worlds, at one point, it was either fear-based or a means to convince folk that they had to come to religious meeting places and give money and sacrifices to the religions because those locations and the 'holy' men and women were the only way to reach the Divine Element. People were convinced that their perception of the Divine Element was the only true way to connect. It got butts in the seats every week and convinced people not to stray. This is what causes separation. This is what causes people to say that their religion is the only one that is real or even matters. That thinking is what causes wars and pain."

Diem took a deep breath and released it slowly. As he did,

he began to smile and the warmth in his face and eyes returned. "But! This has nothing to do with the Divine Element that we are connecting to. That is their thing and, with free will, they will do what they choose. Don't get me wrong. I still stand by the idea that every single individual image of the Divine that is created is perfect and beautiful. I love every one of them because I am a part of the Divine Element and, because of that, in a way, every connection to the Divine is connected to the thing that I am a part of. I send every one of them my love and respect. It is not the connection that is to blame. It is an anomaly within people that creates prejudices, fear, and hatred of anything different. It is the very same anomaly that forced magic to flee the world where you have been living."

Diem rose from the ground and then helped Dalen up while he continued, "This understanding of the Divine Element is all-encompassing. No one is left out. The only ones who do not connect are those who choose not to and, in those cases, the Divine Element relents to them as well."

Dalen wiped his face and nodded. "Okay. What's the next step?"

"The one you take to get to the next one." Diem quickly flicked his eyebrows up and smiled at Dalen.

Dalen began to laugh mockingly, then abruptly stopped with a serious look on his face. "Funny."

"Yeah?" asked Diem. "Well, you needed it."

Dalen thought about it for a second and then nodded with

a shrug. "Fair enough." Then he laughed for real. "I guess giving me what I need, whether or not I know I need it, is kind of your thing."

Diem laughed with him, "Indeed. It is." He bowed to him in the style of the Brotherhood of Light.

Dalen paused. "Question."

Diem smiled. "Answer."

"What is the garb you wear? I recognize most of it, but it comes from different beliefs from two different worlds." Dalen tried to be as brave as he could. "What are you?"

Diem smiled. "Damn good question." Diem went over to the circle. "This circle is infused with every form of magic possible. The metal itself is called celestium and, for lack of a better term, it is a holy metal. Angels make their swords and armor with it." Diem then pointed to the stained-glass window in the ceiling. "The light coming in is pure Divine Light. It's the raw essence of the Divine Element that you are now aware you are connected to. The glass itself is enchanted to reflect the perception of someone who stands in the circle. Do you understand?"

"Partly," Dalen replied. "It physically changes?"

"Yes," answered Diem. "The glass changes, and thus how the light projects through it is changed."

Dalen chuckled. "Just like when someone perceives the Divine Element, it projects the understanding that they create." Dalen face-palmed himself with a loud smack. He looked to the Fire

Jinn, who smiled and landed next to him. "I get it. I see you like this because you are also a being from the Divine Element." She nodded. "You are taking the form that my mind is creating because you are relenting to the image I create."

"Yes," Diem confirmed, "exactly like that."

The Fire Jinn took Dalen by the shoulders and put her forehead to his. "I am what you see through the filter of your perception."

"As am I," added Diem. "You asked me about my clothes. They are reflections of beliefs you have had. Your mind recognized me as part of the Divine Element, so you see me in clothes that would fit someone in that field. It combined a couple of religions because your mind and imagery are pulled from more than one source."

Dalen closed his eyes and tried to block out all distractions. The Fire Jinn and Diem were still in his sight. "So, you are just a construct of my perception?"

The Fire Jinn responded, "Everything you see is a construct of your perception."

Before Dalen could respond, Diem added, "I am also incorporeal, and thus your mind must create an image that it can understand. To do so, it takes concepts and images that you use as references in your mind, like dreaming, to create a cohesive and instantly understandable being." He waited for Dalen to process this and then went on, this time with humor. "Would you have preferred just a black silhouette of a being with white lettering in the middle of it that reads 'place deity here'?"

"So, you are God?" Dalen felt a mix of elation and fear and awe, all at the same time.

Diem face-palmed this time. "With the capital 'G' again. I think for this understanding, you will have to curb the 'G' word. It is not helping you at all and, in the end, it is causing confusion."

Dalen was worried that he had offended Diem, but the Fire Jinn responded to his thoughts before he could react. "This is not a man in front of you. What stands before you is an aspect of the Divine Element in the only form you can understand right now. Nothing more."

Dalen began to feel more afraid than anything else as he turned back to Diem. "I don't know what you are then, and I don't want to offend you."

"Hi. I am Diem. I am the day that you seize. I am the light that shines on you. I am the light in your heart when things are dark. You could never offend me." The light in Diem grew, and a pulse of luminescence moved down the line that had been connecting them. When it reached Dalen, his chakra began to glow. "You know the piece of Divine that dwells within and connects you to the Divine Element?"

"You mean my soul?" Dalen asked.

Diem looked to the Fire Jinn who smiled and took a sip of her cup, and then back to Dalen and nodded. "It is in that connection that I exist, but what you see is unique to you. Another would see someone else. I am not the important thing. What is important here is the Divine Element." Dalen nodded in acceptance, so Diem continued. "The Body Sphere is the motion and actions you take in the physical world to create magic, and the Mind Sphere is how you can manifest the magic into the movements through thought. It is the Soul Sphere that dictates the connection to the energy that creates magic in the first place. Action and thought can be meaningless without connection. Connection and thought are useless without action, and action with connection can be reckless without thought. It is only when you connect all three that they create magic properly."

Dalen took it in. What Diem had said touched the core of his being and, not only did he understand the concept, but he felt the meaning of them from within. "I see the wisdom in that. I believe I grasp the Divine Element. What is next?"

Diem smiled. "Another excellent question. You are just filled with them today. Allow me to respond with a rewording of your same question. If you use the other two Spheres as a road map, what's next?"

Dalen thought about his years in the Brotherhood of Light. "Now that I know what the field is, I would now have to learn to tap into it on purpose and be able to use that connection to channel and then manifest it into the desired energy — or magic — I required."

Diem gave a small bow and smiled. "Welcome to the Element of the Arcane: the act of connecting to the Divine Source of all things, and then wielding it into specific fields of intent called Rites, Rituals, and Spells."

"The Arcane Element?" Dalen was beyond excited. "How do I learn it?"

Diem smiled and shrugged. "How did you learn the Body Sphere?"

Dalen, with pride, declared, "It took years of dedication, work, and practice."

Diem agreed and headed back toward his favorite pew. He pointed to a door along the wall to his right. "Kitchen and rectory are over there." He pointed to the door that was on the wall to his left. "The bunk area is over there."

Dalen laughed to himself. "I should have seen that coming." He looked over to the Fire Jinn. "At least you are still with me this time."

She smiled and nodded, "I never left."

17

THE DAY
YOU SEIZE

Dalen spent many years working side by side with Diem.
Together they helped anyone who came to the Temple of All Faith.
During that time, he became familiar with an entire pantheon of
Gods and Goddesses from the world that he had been brought to.
Each one was a God or Goddess that he'd never heard of before, so
he was able to see it with new eyes as he learned the rituals and
prayers of each without preconceived ideas and notions.

During the first year, Diem taught Dalen how to perform all
the ceremonies, sometimes only hours before he'd have to perform
them, and then he would give counsel to any who sought it. Often
Diem or the Fire Jinn would stand right next to Dalen and speak the
words with him so he wouldn't forget a part, but Dalen performed

all possible rites. He also stood as Guardian over the circle during certain ceremonies that required only women to be within the sacred space.

Dalen learned that there were two Temples of All Faith that functioned the way this one did. This one held space for anyone who worshiped either a good or neutral deity or belief. The other was on the other side of the world, and it catered specifically to all those who followed a neutral or evil deity, and it had something different but equal to the sacred circle at its temple.

The circle truly was sacred. Besides being made of celestium, it was infused with every possible form of magic. The reason why was that people from many beliefs and differing regions came here to perform their rituals. The Divine Light was eternal and always shined into the circle and welcomed all who sought it out. As someone would step into it, the stained-glass ceiling of the temple would change, molding the light that passed through it. With each ritual or ceremony, the light projected through created all of the glyphs and symbols required for that event onto the floor. The circle would then fill with a magic resonance on the floor to create a glyph that would not be lost by people standing on them while in the circle. Over the years, almost every ritual that could be imagined had been performed there. Live births to funeral rites and all rituals in between — including religious weddings and old mystical arts that involved crones and cauldrons — blessed this circle. In each, the circle was bestowed with the Divine Light that was projected into the necessary field of intent.

Learning about the circle in the floor and the stained-glass window in the ceiling sparked new avenues of learning. Dalen learned about imbuing an object with Divine Energy. Even something like a magic ring that can turn its wearer invisible, which is recognized as Arcane magic, was initially imbued with its Arcane energy from a Divine Source. Sometimes Diem was asked to recharge a magic object or help repair one. Often it was just a matter of standing in the circle and thinking about what was needed, and the ceiling would relent and recharge the artifact or sometimes remove negative connections that the object had picked up. At one point, Diem asked Dalen to help bless Rune Stones. It was then that Dalen learned the difference between a Rune Stone and a rock with a mark scratched into it by imbuing a field of intent into them while being powered by the Divine Element. He even studied the glyphs that he himself was learning, and he discovered the meaning of the other glyphs that were around each Element. The smaller glyphs around the Elemental Glyphs were the Connection, Perception, Use, Frequency, and Creation of each Element.

Dalen spent years learning about them all, but since his first day, he'd never found the religion or deity that resonated with him. All of his free time was devoted to meditation in the circle, sometimes seated and sometimes standing, yet when it was only him the results were always the same: the window would turn clear, and nothing would be projected into the circle but direct light. He wondered if it was because he had to pick one from the world that he had come from, but Diem assured him that it had to do with his understanding of the Divine Element. Then he would encourage Dalen to continue to seek what he was looking for.

"You know what is funny about the Divine Element?" Diem

mused. "It's always directly in front of you, being as loud and as obvious as it can be. Just like the Divine Light that continuously shines in the circle. It's up to the individual to see it."

So Dalen passed days and days in the circle, trying to see what the light wished to tell him. Over time, it became normal for travelers who had come to the Temple of All Faith to find him standing in the circle, illuminated by the light, praying. Because of this, people began to refer to him as Father Light. Time passed, and Father Light became renowned as the Priest of the Light, and more and more people came from all over, specifically asking for him. After a while, he was performing all of the rituals and rites with such frequency that it reminded him of the continuous repetition that he'd previously needed to master the styles and movements in his training in the Body Sphere.

Sometimes when the temple was quiet, he sat with Diem and the Fire Jinn in the dark, with only the beam of light from the ceiling to see by, and they'd talk about the day and the ceremonies that were performed. Often, the conversation was about how remarkably similar the rituals were.

"Truth is truth, no matter how it is said," Diem mused one night while things were quiet.

"Master Truth used to say that when I trained at the Temple of Light," noted Father Light.

Diem smiled at him and tugged on his white robe. "That's where I learned it."

"The Brotherhood has come here to perform a ceremony?" asked Father Light. "It must have been before my time."

Diem smiled and rolled his eyes, which eventually landed on the Fire Jinn, and both of them shrugged at each other. "Unfortunately, no. But it would be amazing. The circle has never had a ceremony done by one of the Brotherhood of Light."

"I am a member," Father Light said. "Or at least I used to be."

Diem looked over to the Fire Jinn, who nodded, and then back to Father Light. "I don't believe it is something you *were*. I believe it is something you either are or aren't." Diem leaned in. "So, which is it? Does Brother Truth still exist?"

After years with Diem, Father Light had grown very accustomed to the man knowing everything about him, so Diem's knowledge of the name 'Brother Truth' wasn't a shock, but hearing it was. It was a name Father Light had almost forgotten. "I would have to find him again, but I am sure he still lives within me."

"Good!" Diem cheered. "Then tomorrow I have a request."

Father Light gave Diem a nod, "Anything that is within my ability I will do."

Diem nodded back. "After the morning's blessings, I would like for you to perform a ritual from the Brotherhood of Light."

"Absolutely, my friend. Which one?"

"A Leap of Faith."

376

The Fire Jinn looked to Father Light. "Are you ready?"

Father Light smiled and gave Diem a small bow. "As you wish."

. . .

The next morning, Father Light awoke and sensed that he was alone in the temple. He dressed and reactivated the Beads of Fire.

"Good morning," the Fire Jinn said and stretched her back. As she did, her fire brightened. "How are you this morning?"

"I am well, thank you." This had become routine for them. "I would ask you how you are, but I already know the answer."

"You do?" she inquired.

"Yes, of course I do." He smiled at her. "You are an incorporeal being. You are not affected by time, so the answer is 'the same as always.'"

She gave him an overly dramatic slow hand clap. "Look at you starting to understand and whatnot." She flew along next to him in a position resting on one side, with her head in one hand, as if she were lounging in the air as she flew. "But, in the moments in which you perceive me, I also have a perspective and thoughts and feelings."

Father Light stopped dead in his tracks and looked at her. She smiled and shrugged. "Fair enough," he admitted. "What are you feeling right now?"

"I am feeling like asking you what you are doing," she quipped. "What are you doing?"

"I am looking for Diem," he stated and then continued his search.

The Fire Jinn caught up to him. "I am sure he is in the temple somewhere. Oh, I know! Is he supposed to be doing morning blessings?"

"No, I am."

"Well, they start any minute," she replied with a smirk. "You better hurry."

She was right, and so Father Light hastened to the main chamber and stood in the Circle, deciding to continue his search after the morning blessings.

This was one of the ceremonies that the Temple of All Faith provided for any who wished to come. That morning, there were only three present: an old woman who had been coming to the morning blessing for years and a young couple who had been married the day before and wanted to receive one more blessing before heading off into their new life. All three of them stepped into the circle and different symbols and images of their faith appeared around them while the center where Father Light stood remained clear. He then allowed the light to slowly engulf everyone, and all their symbols lit up brightly. Father Light spoke a few words to each of them, offering blessings from the pure Divine Element.

Afterward, the young couple approached him. "Thank you

so much," they said. "It means so much to us that you could offer us blessings into our future. It is truly special that it was you who performed our blessing."

"Absolutely. May the Light shine on you," Father Light smiled, happy to bring them such joy. They were both extremely excited and smiled at him with wide eyes. Both of them gave Father Light an awkward, nervous bow. Father Light reached out reassuringly. "You don't need to do that." They both stood up, confusion clouding their faces. "I don't want your admiration; I want your friendship."

Tears glimmered in their eyes, and then they both hugged him. "Thank you, Diem."

"Diem?" asked Father Light, then he realized why they'd been acting so strangely: they thought that he was Diem. "I am Father Light."

"Yes, of course," they replied. "The Light of Day. The Light We Seize." They smiled and thanked him again, and then the couple left the temple.

Father Light turned to the old woman. "You have been coming here for a long time." She nodded. "You know the difference between me and the other guy here at the temple, right?"

She looked perplexed. "I've been coming here for twenty years," she affirmed before continuing. "You are the only person I've ever seen here, Diem."

Dalen felt like gravity was failing him. "You don't know me

as Father Light?"

She smiled fondly. "Oh yes, of course I do. I've been coming here for many years, as I said." She began to count on her fingers: "Father Light. The Light of Day. Father Day. Diem. I know you by many names." Father Light smiled weakly and did his best to hide his confusion. "Thank you for the blessings all of these years. You have been a godsend. My daughter is moving me into her home today, and she lives far off in the capital city of Venger. Maybe someday I will see you there. Goodbye for now, dear soul."

Father Light was stunned and was unable to respond until long after the woman had left. Instead, he turned to the Fire Jinn: "Why do people think that I am Diem?"

She looked at him and echoed the same words said to him on the day he first arrived. "Diem is an aspect of the Divine Element in the only form you could understand at the time, nothing more."

"Where is Diem?" Father Light was filled with uneasiness.

"You'll find what you are looking for in Diem's private chamber." She gestured toward the sleeping quarters.

Father Light had never been inside Diem's personal chambers. He'd wondered what was in there many times but wasn't the type to go snooping. Now that the Fire Jinn had said Diem was there, he was excited to finally find out what was behind that door. When he got to the door, he knocked gently. He waited for a few moments before the Fire Jinn suggested that he was going to have to go in on his own. Father Light took a deep breath, opened the door, and stood frozen in disbelieving silence.

The room was empty save one thing: a large mirror stood in the middle of the room, facing the door. Dalen had not seen a mirror since the day he'd arrived. He began to ask Diem what was going on but quickly realized that he was looking at his own reflection.

Unnerved to his core, he was unable to process what he was looking at. He knew the reflection was of himself, but he couldn't believe how much time had passed — close to twenty years, by his guess. That was shocking in itself. But in the slow passage of time, he hadn't realized that the image of Diem had been himself in his thirties, but there he was, as plain as day.

"I don't understand," he stammered shakily. "How am I Diem?"

"The same way you were Brother Truth," the Fire Jinn said simply.

"But he trained me."

"You trained with an echo in time of who you would become. You needed a way to connect with the Divine Element. Diem was a way for you to do so. The day I first brought you to the Temple of All Faith, it was just you here."

"But he was here — I remember him!" He was now more confused than ever.

"You reached out and touched the Divine Element," she

explained. "When that happened, it relented to you and created something you could understand. Because you've never had an image of the Divine through any religion, your mind created a 'Holy Man' instead."

"But I wasn't a holy man."

"No," she acknowledged. "Not at seventeen, but you are one now."

"Yeah," he muttered. "Okay." But things still weren't okay.

"The Divine Element is no more corporeal than I," she reminded him. "Time doesn't matter. The image that was created was the one that was closest to the Divine Element but in a form you could understand..."

"So right now, I am closest to the Divine Element that I will ever be?" Father Light asked.

"Well, actually a few minutes from now is the marker, but no," teased the Fire Jinn with a hint of joy. "You will continue to grow and one day will be as much of the Divine as I am."

"Then why did I not see that version of myself?"

"Because you would not have comprehended what that meant," she instructed. "When you first met Diem, what were your first thoughts?"

Father Day answered quickly, "I thought he was a priest."

"Exactly." She posed in front of him. "I am a being that is Celestial in nature. I am kin to angels and demons. By my very makeup, I am a Divine Being, but did you read 'Divine' from me when you met me?"

"No, actually," Father Light admitted, fascinated. Jinn officially were neutral angels — or neutral demons, for that matter. Or maybe both. Maybe neither, but no matter which way he looked at it, she didn't seem to be a Divine Being. The Fire Jinn was something else to him completely.

"So, simply being the strongest connection to the Divine Element would not give the best understanding."

"But who have I been talking to?" Father Light had to take a breath and regain his composure. "I know I didn't teach myself all of those rituals."

"You have spent this time conversing with the Divine Element directly." She touched her solar plexus, and it flared yellow as the line that connected them at that location appeared as if from mist.

"How?"

She smiled and left the room, knowing that he would follow. "Every being that can claim to exist has a spark of the Divine within them. Some call it a soul. Some call it the superego, and some choose to call it their Higher Self." She left the bunk area and entered the main chamber. "This Higher Self is the part that connects each of us to the Divine. It powers the machine you call your body. Without this spark of the Divine, the body dies."

Dalen set down the mantle of Father Light for a moment and tried to simply be a student listening to his teacher. "Okay," nodded Dalen, following her. "I can grasp that."

"That is who Diem has been to you: a way for you to see yourself as a Divine Being," she stated it so matter-of-factly that Dalen had no time to doubt.

She turned at the edge of the circle and faced Dalen. "After years of practice and learning, it is who your Self is as well. He has become a part of you, and you a part of him." She gestured toward the circle. "And now it is time for you to be more than you have ever been before."

"Yeah?" asked Dalen. "And what's that?"

She smiled, "Being greater than the sum of your parts."

Dalen laughed, "No pressure."

The jinn drew nose-to-nose with Dalen. "Nothing could be easier." She made a face and then flew back, tracing the edge of the circle as she went up and around. The stone at her throat began to glow blue. Moments later, her flame turned yellow and then to a white that licked up in beautiful sapphire blue peaks. "Speak your truth, Dalen."

Dalen took a deep breath and stood in the center of the circle. The ceiling changed and all the color faded, and Dalen stood in pure white light. He looked up into the luminescence, and even though it was bright it did not hurt his eyes. He waited for something to happen.

"I relent to you," he declared out loud. "For years I have stood in this light, waiting for understanding. I have been waiting for you to show yourself so that I could dedicate myself to you. I have waited to feel you in the warmth of the light of a Sun God. I have looked for you in the Goddess and her phases of the moon. I have sought you in the Hunt. The Heart. The Home. I have reached for your strength as we created together in the Forge. I have sung your songs and spoken your words in all the faces of Gods and Goddesses ... and here is my truth:

"I have found you in them all. I fly in your wind, and I swim in your sea. I have climbed the mountains and found you, not only at the summit but in every step of the way. I have stood in the fires that have forged me and always you have been with me, for you are a part of me, as I am you, and together we are one." Dalen inhaled deeply. "I stand before you whole, as I truly am."

From the light came a voice that spoke to Dalen as if it were his own thoughts. "And who is that?" As the voice spoke, the ceiling changed and all around him, his Training Circle was projected into the circle.

"I am all that I have ever been." Dalen watched as the frames slowed down, and the Fire Jinn turned from white to ultraviolet. Time finally became so slow that Dalen could see the spaces between the frames that he perceived like a strobe light. As the distance between the frames continued to expand, Dalen moved into superposition, and as he did he moved from being only in the center to also being in the Glyphs of Imagination and of the Observer. He didn't walk or jump, but he was nonetheless there during the flashes between the frames. The last two beads in the set of seven flared and two silver lines from the top of his head and from his third eye reached across the circle and connected the two versions of himself.

"I am Brother Truth." The Natural and Kinetic Elements lit up on the Beads of Fire, and the Fire Jinn exploded into red and orange flames. Dalen watched himself step away from the center circle as Brother Truth, yet he was still standing in the center even as he moved across the circle to the Kinetic position and began to build Ki through his movements. Silver lines connected Brother Truth to Dalen, and he could feel his Ki growing, not only as Brother Truth but as Dalen as well.

The Fire Jinn's color moved through the spectrum of visible light. She was now white with tips of sapphire. She smiled at him and bade him continue. She moved into the light from the ceiling and was no longer able to be perceived as anything other than the light itself.

"I am the Day I seize and the Light I seek." The light intensified as it had done when imbuing an object with Divine Energy. It engulfed him, saturating him from different angles and different perceptions. Dalen saw it all happening from his position at the Imagination Element and, at the same time, he felt the energy build from behind him, as Brother Truth watched the Divine Element ignite and he channeled its power directly.

"Use it," Brother Truth called out. "It is pure energy. Flow with it, Brother." Dalen watched from the Observer as he stood in the center. That version of himself pulled with his Ki and channeled it through him. The Divine Element relented and flowed through him again while Father Light stood on the Arcane Glyph. It lit up, and silver lines of magic sprang from him and connected to Dalen at the solar plexus and throat.

"Dalen," said Father Light. "You are more powerful than you can possibly imagine from here. I am so proud of you, and you have come a long, long way, but you need to take one more step." Dalen processed this from four different perspectives simultaneously, and his body, mind, and soul felt like they were fracturing. "You are greater than just your parts. You are the thing that is all of us."

The pressure built, and Dalen watched from the other three perspectives as he fell to his knees. They held their Spheres as they experienced all of Dalen's life come into clarity. The world stopped moving between the frames, and all that was there was Dalen. The world was quiet and dark.

The only thing Dalen could see was his Training Circle. All the glyphs were lit except for the center where he stood. He was seventeen again, but he remembered every second of his time in the Temple of All Faith.

From the Darkness, another seventeen-year-old image of Dalen wandered out and stood on the Imagination Element. "Who are you?"

A moment later, Brother Truth also emerged from the Darkness and walked into the circle. He stepped onto the Kinetic

Element, beaming with great joy. "Who are you?" he asked.

Father Light then appeared, standing on the Arcane Glyph. He put his hands together and light poured from them. When he opened his hands, a small item glinted in his palm. As he threw it to Dalen, he asked, "This is your Leap of Faith." He smiled and gave him a nod. "Who are you?"

The small object flew through the air and Dalen caught it instinctively. When he looked to see what it was, he held his silver figure in his hands. He closed his eyes and gave it a blessing. When he opened his eyes again, the figure was glowing.

Dalen laughed and looked at the three of them. Tears filled his eyes. "I am the being that is you." He let the tears roll down his face. "The true being that each of you is an Element of." Dalen looked to each of them, smiling. They faded from his sight, but he knew that they were not gone. The final Glyph in the center ignited. "I am Dalen Pax, the Reality Bender."

18

BECOMING
THE DREAM

Dalen's Leap of Faith that he had taken in the Temple
of All Faith left him spent. For two days, he rested. Except for
his bodily needs, he slept. His dreams were filled with flashes of
memories from all of his trials as his mind worked to piece together
a coherent acceptance of who he was now, as a whole. From time to
time, the Fire Jinn would be with him in his dreams, and she helped
him. As she did, she reminded him that there was more to come —
that being able to wield magic and controlling it were two different
things. At other times, Dalen and Brother Truth went through
his lessons, practicing control and clarity. They sparred for what
seemed forever in the dream; the entire time, Brother Truth coached

him through every strike and defense while also serving as Dalen's opponent, and Master Ki watched from the side of the courtyard of the Temple of Light.

Dreams can be fickle things and tend to change without notice. Dalen would be training with Brother Truth in the Elemental Circle in the Courtyard of the Temple of Light, but then the world would shift, and he'd find himself standing in the circle at the Temple of All Faith, while Diem told him to think of a specific ceremony of a particular Goddess. As he did, the stained-glass window would change, altering the glyphs and symbols on the ground. Then, Diem would instruct him to not just think, and this was key: he had to *be* another ceremony from a completely different God, and Dalen would alter his connection to the Divine and the stained glass would match him. Again and again, they would go through it, altering the perception to change the patterns, to create the desired effect, until Dalen could do any of them as a reflex.

Eventually, from another perspective while he slept, time slowed down and he slipped into the frames to see it as a whole. He stood in the circle, but it was in the courtyard of the Temple of Light. Father Light and Brother Truth had fused into a single being. They wore the same robes that Dalen wore when he first made the jump, but now there was an extra prayer cloth draped over his left shoulder, hanging about to his knee on both sides and cinched with his belt. When Dalen saw it the first time, he could only perceive parts of it, but now looking at them together, it made sense. The Monk and the Warrior. The Priest and the Mage. Then both of them together as a whole.

Master Truth watched from the seat that he always took. He reached over and, for the first time, took his cup. He raised it as a toast to Dalen and drank deeply. "Drink with me," he said. "I have your favorite, but you are not going to be able to enjoy it unless you are whole." And he gestured to Brother Light.

Dalen could see from his own perspective or from that of the being that was both Brother Truth and Father Light. He took out his coin and looked at one side and then the other. He understood that to see more, he would have to see both sides as one, so he moved his perception between the frames again and chose to have his perception be theirs, and then the three of them were one. Dalen walked over to the old Air Jinn, took his own cup, raised it in respect to his teacher, and then took a sip.

"You would ask me how I am but, since you know I am incorporeal, you know the answer," Master Truth grinned at his little joke and continued. "I am sure you have other questions you wish to ask me."

Dalen sat down and took a breath to enjoy this moment in time. "It's been twenty years since I have been right here. I am glad that I get to talk to you again."

"Dalen, if you truly need me, this is where I will be." Master Truth took a sip of his tea. It distracted Dalen as he responded, "At the Temple of Light?"

"There, too." Dalen looked up with one eyebrow raised but decided not to question the Air Jinn's response once he remembered that he was dreaming. "What other questions do you have for me, Dalen?"

"Why hadn't anyone warned me that Mathias is somehow me from the future?" The world held still for a moment and thunder rolled across the sky.

"Because, when you started the journey, you were in no place to understand that." He took a sip of his cup and added, "And I was aware of this moment since the moment I met you. I knew you would reach this understanding and, when you did, you would be the man you are today and have the facilities to handle it." When he finished, he drank the last bit from his cup and set it down, just in time for Dalen to drop to his knees so they were at the same height to physically hug the jinn.

"Thank you," Dalen said with tears in his eyes. "Thank you for your protection, your guidance, and your faith in me." Dalen looked Master Truth in his eyes. They resembled a storm trapped in glass and, for a moment, Dalen almost got lost in them. "I am still trying to completely understand this incorporeal thing." They both laughed at the running gag and Dalen stood back up. "Hey, are there things you are still not telling me for the same reasons?"

The Air Jinn's eyes flashed with lightning, and he gave Dalen a mischievous smile. "Absolutely."

"Why?"

"Because you are nowhere near the end of your journey, and you still have a lot to learn. Until you do, you are not there. Once you are at that point, you will know. The good news is that you are here today, and I will answer your questions on the subject you asked." Master Truth walked Dalen over to the circle.

It made sense in a way. Dalen was no longer a seventeen-year-old boy. He may look it, but he was so much more now, and he had the capacity to understand and deal with harder truths. It made sense that one day in his future he would understand better and, hopefully, not at the cost of becoming Mathias in the first place.

"Is becoming Mathias something I have to do?" It was Dalen's true fear at the moment. He remembered the last time he'd seen the magician outside of the museum. He'd been filled with such desperation, and what Dalen could infer from that conversation suggested that Mathias's life did not go well.

"No," Master Truth replied, to Dalen's great relief. "It is my greatest wish that you never walk the path that he chose."

"Can you tell me what happened to him, so that I can make sure I don't repeat his mistakes?" Dalen asked, and then he closed his eyes and cleared his mind so that he could take on this new understanding.

"No corporeal being should know too much about their direct future, but since time has been altered, I will tell you what you need to understand for now. Agreed?"

"Time has been altered?"

"Yes. At great cost."

"What was the cost?"

"The very existence of the one who altered it."

Dalen was surprised by this. "What do you mean?"

"You have learned about the Element of Fire. And, in this learning, you understand that fire changes by wiping out what was there to clear the area for new growth."

"Yes," Dalen responded.

"When time was changed, events changed, and the beings who lived it stopped existing because they were an eventuality of a timeline that now never existed. Existence itself was wiped out and a new timeline replaced the old one as events unfolded differently. Mathias is an echo, still trying to fight for his existence."

Dalen took that in. What could be so bad a person would be willing to wipe everything from existence just to be able to change it? Then a scarier thought struck Dalen: "Who changed the timeline?"

Master Truth stopped at the very edge of the circle, and with sad eyes confirmed, "You did."

It was what Dalen feared. "Why?"

Master Truth arched his back and raised his chin, and then his voice filled with pride, "To guarantee that Mathias and his master, a genie by the name of DeSalvo, never came to be."

Dalen was now confused. "But Mathias does. I met him. Meeting Mathias is how I got involved with all of this in the first place.

"Indeed," nodded Master Truth. "He set you up. DeSalvo had been pushing your anger all that day. You even noticed him in the principal's office for a moment, but then you were distracted by people coming into the room and you forgot, just like the spell Mathias put on you in the museum."

"How do you know all of this?" Dalen asked, as the memories of his former life flooded back in.

With a bemused look on his face, the Air Jinn responded, "I am Master Truth. I know all." And then he chuckled. "Mathias used his magic to rile up Ben and his friends into a frenzy and then sicced them on you so that he could save you. Then they sent Ben into a loop, ensuring that Mathias could 'help' you once more and that you would feel beholden to him sufficiently to fetch the Beads of Fire for him." Master Truth seemed sad. "It was a terrible cycle. You gave the Beads to Mathias, and he granted you the ability to wield magic but with none of the training that you've now received. Just raw, unadulterated power. Mistakes were made in the absence of knowledge, and you grew up living with those mistakes. Eventually, you recognized the guy in the mirror as the person who took the Beads of Fire. Somewhere in there, you met DeSalvo, and he helped you figure out how to slip between the frames of time, believing that, if you could get a hold of the Beads of Fire once more, you could fix the problem — and time had already shown you where and when you could claim them."

Dalen closed his eyes while listening to Master Truth's words, taking them in as a new truth. "Why did I have to trick myself?"

"The person who taught you to move in time was DeSalvo. You found him while trying to locate the guy who'd taken the Beads of Fire before you realized it was you. He helped you to that conclusion and then taught you to move through time. But he warned you over and over again not to change the timeline. That's one of the reasons why you used the name Mathias. The younger version of you put him in a corner and said he wouldn't help without a name, and Mathias was the name that DeSalvo had given him. The second was because that is what had been said when he met himself as you. Without the ability to change the timeline, you continued to take the exact same actions. It's why you were always so vague with the younger version. You dared not change how things went down, even to the length of making them happen."

Dalen started to see why a change was needed. "What happened once he ... I mean, *I* got them?"

"At first it seemed like a victory, for both yourself and the master who controlled you."

"Master?"

"Yes, the Mad Genie DeSalvo, who then took over that version of Dalen and never let him go until the end. Through him, DeSalvo wielded magic from dark places, and it was the world that paid the price."

Dalen felt sick but had to know the fate this version of himself faced and what convinced him to change time. "What happened next?"

Master Truth gestured for Dalen to stand in the circle and, while Dalen got into position, he finished his tale. "DeSalvo had been tricked and then trapped into being a genie instead of a free jinn, and he believed with the Beads of Fire he could ..." Master Truth struggled with the right words, "trade places?" Dalen could see he wasn't happy with the words but had nothing better. Dalen didn't like the sound of his fiery friend being enslaved as a genie. "Once he had the Beads, he took them to a very sacred and dangerous place." He inhaled deeply. "There is a cave where the essence of time has solidified into existence as a pillar of pure magic. Once you touch it, you can access and change a single moment in time. It is guarded by many dragons, and it needs to be. Countless people want to go back and change just one thing, but what is often not understood is that once you do, the timeline you came from no longer exists. DeSalvo was counting on this principle — that it would change an entire timeline so that he was never enslaved. There was a moment, a 'True Perfect Moment,' and you made a wish that changed one moment in time ... and in doing so ended that world."

Struggling to grasp what would have driven him to take such an action, Dalen hazarded a guess. "I did it to save the Fire Jinn?"

"You did it to save everyone. It is why you were granted a Perfect Moment from the universe." Master Truth nodded in assurance.

"What did I change?"

"You moved yourself forward in time just six hours that

night in the museum."

"I remember that," Dalen recalled. "When I first saw the Beads of Fire, I thought that I was in a trance because of the Beads."

"You lost no time. You were just moved to a different location in it."

"How would that change everything?"

"You're here, aren't you?"

Dalen's mind raced. Flashes of understanding. He lost time in the museum, making him be there as they were packing. If he had just gotten the Beads of Fire, he would've walked out to Mathias and handed them to him. Because of those 'lost hours,' people were arriving when he fetched them and he'd put on the beads to try to conceal them... thus connecting him to the Fire Jinn, who then took him in a completely different direction. Instead of being infused with magic but lacking knowledge, he'd learned it correctly, creating a completely different timeline in which Mathias never existed. "What about the Mathias that I saw outside of the museum?"

Another wave of sadness washed over Master Truth. "His timeline ceased to exist. He can never go home. As a matter of fact, if he tries to slip between the frames for time travel, teleportation, and any of the other useful tools that can happen there, he will just stop existing. He was still corporeally there when time changed, but it is the older version of himself — the one that was disjointed from time. The one you saw outside the museum is a ghost of a timeline that has been replaced by this one."

Dalen saw something coming, but he couldn't make out what it was yet. "That's a good thing. Right?"

"It depends on how you look at it." Master Truth started so many conversations this way that it had become habit for Dalen to expect it.

Dalen reached into a pocket and produced his coin. "It always does, Master. Help me understand."

Master Truth nodded and smiled. "You do the Temple proud." Master Truth gave him a proper bow. "The good and the bad stand hand in hand. You made an amazing choice when the world gave you the chance. That is good. You will never have to make that choice. That is your new fate. This is something to be celebrated ... but because you are now the new version, it falls upon you to remove the final shadow. This is also your fate."

"I have to face Mathias. If what you say is true, then he has many more years of direct practice with magic than I have. Oh, sure, I can activate the Reality Sphere, but I don't know how to wield it. There is no way I can beat him, Master Truth."

"It is your fate," Master Truth imparted with certainty.

"Why is it my fate?" Filled with fear and frustration, Dalen realized he'd yelled at Master Truth and immediately apologized.

Master Truth showed no sign of anger. He relented to Dalen and allowed him to feel his frustration and, when Dalen had calmed himself, he answered. "When you trained in the Divine Element, you learned that there is a part of you that is directly a piece of the Divine Field."

Dalen nodded, "My soul, my Higher Self."

Master Truth flew over to Dalen. With one hand, he touched the stone on his throat, and with the other, he touched Dalen's third eye. As he spoke the words, Dalen understood. "That part of you is incorporeal. It has been every version of you that you have ever been or will ever be. It is that part of you that made the wish at the Pillar of Time, and it is the part of you that now must fulfill that wish."

Dalen stood there blinking, taking it all in. Master Truth moved outside of the circle and waited for what seemed like hours in the dream. "So, how am I supposed to defeat Mathias?"

"It is the responsibility of any and all who choose to walk this path to face one's self. You are going to have to face it in a very real manner." The jinn moved a few feet further from the circle. "You will face him."

"You see it directly?"

"I know it as well as I know this moment."

"How do I beat myself, when the darker version of me has already learned so much?"

"And you have not?" Dalen felt a shift as the part of him who was Brother Truth felt Master Truth build up his Ki through the

400

Natural Field and begin to charge it as well. At the same moment, he felt the part of him that was Father Light directly connect to the Divine Field and then imbue it into his Ki, creating a magical resonance. His mind slowed down, and he watched as Master Truth released a ball of magical fire from his hands. He remembered the moment when Mathias healed him. He pictured it in his mind, how the magic manifested from his Ki. He changed his own energy and brought it to his center, and then he spread it like a wall in front of him. As he did, he watched as the Arcane Energy relented to his will, creating a screen in front of him and blocking the oncoming attack.

It was brilliant and simple. All he had to do was to take each action in balance with the three Spheres of Reality. "This is the true nature of magic," said Master Truth. "Magic is not one or the other. It is the Element that is in the center of the wheel. The Element that is all forms of magic as a whole. The very spirit of ether."

They trained for as long as was needed. Dalen learned that he could change the magic the same way he changed the stained-glass ceiling, and he wielded it the same way that he moved his energy and Ki. With the ability to manifest it into reality and move between the frames, Dalen could now cast any spell he could imagine, feel, and act upon.

...

When he felt he was ready, he said goodbye to his friend and Master and chose to wake up. When he did, he found Dorn and myself sitting in his room with him. Dorn had asked me to stay after the Dinner Dash Delirium to help out his friend. I had been running him through his trials and dreams for almost three days straight. His experiences and I had merged into a single understanding, and it was as if I too had gone through all that he had. I was exhausted and leaned my head against the wall. "You are an amazing dude." I laughed a little as tears ran down my cheeks.

Dorn handed me some water. "Take five, Will of Grey. You earned it."

Dalen rubbed his eyes. "Good morning, guys."
Dorn said good morning in return. I just waved and said, "Hey."

Although he had not expected company and it was definitely a surprise, he spoke with kindness. "Why are you guys in my room, and why does he look like he just ran a hundred miles?"

"This here is the Grey Bard, Will of Grey," Dorn patted me on my shoulder. "I asked him to help you work things out. One of his abilities is to clarify dreams and help the dreamer understand them better. And full disclosure: I also had Silver come in a couple of times to help your dream transitions go smoothly."

"So, it was him who created my dreams?" Dalen asked.

"Not a bit of it, dude," I interjected before Dorn could respond. I gave Dalen a hand gesture of holding down my index and middle finger, with my palm facing myself. In my culture, it was a positive sign, much like a thumbs up. "That was all you." I laughed as another tear rolled down my cheek. "All you. All over the place, dude."

"However, he has been helping you see your own visions clearly and with lucidity for almost three days straight," remarked Dorn. "Truly impressive."

"Dude," I said with a smile. "It's all good, dude. Totally worth it. If it means anything, I think you made the right choice."

"What choice are you talking about?" Dalen asked.

"All of it. Just like the Elements of Magic, there are many elements to your choice, but if it were brought all together and then made into a single concept, the choice you made was to become the Reality Bender, Dalen Pax." I was exhausted and could barely move, but I smiled. "Outstanding."

Dorn was helping me to my feet when Dalen stopped us. "Thank you." I could see his heart as he spoke. "I can tell that helping me took a lot out of you. If you will allow me, I can help." At my nod, he took my hand and closed his eyes. He ignited all three Spheres at once and channeled energy through himself. As he did, he envisioned the intent of the magic, and then he moved it through his body and into his palms. As the light flowed through his hands and fingertips, it flowed into me in pulses. After only a few such pulses, the light dimmed out and Dalen let go of my hand.

He had healed my exhaustion. I had watched him connect to the true source of everything and convert it into healing magic. I took a deep breath in and let it out. I decided to give him a little magic of my own. I connected to him, and in Grey Speak I said, *Dude.*

Dalen's mind opened in a new way than it ever had before. All three of the Spheres were open, but this was different. Dalen's mind could sense my relief and the new energy that I felt. He knew my gratitude and understood that the one word held all of the meaning, both telepathically and empathically, as well.

Instinctively, Dalen tried to maintain the Spheres the way they were and to collectively think that it was cool that I could speak like that and that he completely understood. He also felt with his heart that he was glad to help, and then he spoke back. *Dude.* I had never seen anyone but one other pick up Grey Speak so fast.

Dorn smiled. "Not to interrupt this riveting conversation, but Dalen has things he has to do, and we should go."

I smiled and said *Dude* again, and then got myself moving toward the door. I was stalling because I wanted to see where this went.

Dalen immediately put on the Beads of Fire. The Fire Jinn was waiting for him, of course. "I am ready to go." He knew there was no turning back, and he believed he was prepared for whatever might await him.

She was hovering in the middle of the room with her arms folded. "Hey, it's this guy!" She flew over and hugged me.

Dalen was a little surprised that I could see her, but he was even more intrigued that I could touch her. "You know each other?"

The Fire Jinn spun around and pointed over her shoulder

toward me with her thumb. "This is the guy I keep talking to." Dalen blinked at her blankly. "Never mind. Yes. I know him. I have ... uhh ... worked with him before." She floated back over to Dalen. "Speaking of which, do you want to say goodbye to everyone?"

Dalen made a choice right there that if he was going to win, there was no reason to act like he wasn't coming back. "Nope, I'll see them tonight," and gave me a wink as I stood by the door.

The jinn smiled and flared a little with joy. "Now that sounds like someone who plans on winning."

"Do I?" Dalen was hoping for good news.

"That will depend on a couple of things, and not all of them are in your hands." She did look concerned. "Promise me something, as both of our existences depend on it."

Dalen tried to bring humor to a tense situation. "Well, if you put it that way, then sure."

"No matter what happens. No matter the cost ..." She looked him dead in the eyes. Dalen saw the fires of her soul burning through them as she made her plea. "Do not let DeSalvo get his hands on the Beads of Fire or this will just loop from here. It has to end."

Dalen understood what was in front of him and what was on the line. "I swear to you, I won't."

The Fire Jinn then continued, "There are at least two wishes you will have to grant, and I want you to fulfill them both.

You were taught in the style of the jinn. Jinn magic is at its strongest when it is granting the wishes of others."

"Why is that?" Dalen wondered.

"In the legends, genies could only grant the wishes of the person who carried the object that they were tied to. The key was the link to the object. The truth is that genies often possessed their 'master' and then never let them go, and the only wishes they ever granted were their own. The jinn, on the other hand, are different, and the purpose of connecting through an object is different as well." She looked up as if staring into the heavens. "Jinn are neutral, true, but we are still Divine Beings, and we are at our greatest power when we relent to the needs of others."

"That's beautiful." Dalen's eyes welled up with tears. "You keep giving me reason to respect you more and more." She smiled and took a small bow. "Alright, whose wishes will I be granting?"

"David's."

"David will wish for something?"

"Indeed, he will."

"And the second person? Whose wish will I grant?"

"Mine, but I will not tell you what it is right now. I will only tell you when it's time."

"I will not let you down."

"I am proof of your chance of victory." She smiled

and took him by the hands. "Are you ready to go back and save your friends?"

Dalen Pax then made the choice that his entire life had funneled down to — a single choice that would direct the rest of his life and help sculpt the face of our world.

"I can do this." He took a deep breath. "I am ready."

He closed his eyes and thought of the dance where he was going to meet his friends. He felt the frames shift, and he recognized the moment when he was once again in the world that he came from.

19

THE DANCE

"So glad you chose to join us." Mathias greeted him with a tone that sent a chill down Dalen's spine, and he opened his eyes to see that all of the people who were at the dance were frozen in time except his friends, who had their hands tied in front of them and were on their knees. "We were beginning to wonder if you were ever going to show up." He gestured at the students, frozen mid-dance. "It seems that time itself hangs in the balance, and this moment will last forever until this is decided."

"I know who you are. It is already too late." Dalen moved towards Mathias but as he did, Mathias put a knife to David's throat.

"Stop right there or, so help me ... I will kill him."

He pressed the blade against David's throat. "I don't want to, but this reality doesn't matter. I will kill all of them to get the Beads of Fire and, once I have them, I can fix all of this."

"Not going to happen. Just let them go." Dalen took another step forward.

"Dalen," said David. Mathias screamed at him to shut up and pressed the knife harder against his neck. David sucked in a sharp breath as the blade nicked his skin and blood began to trickle down his throat.

"Just give him the beads, Dalen!" cried Travis.

"Don't give him crap, Dalen!" Even in the face of imminent danger, Adam showed no signs of fear.

"Shut up, Adam!" Travis muttered under his breath.

"Shut up, everyone!" Mathias screamed, losing all sense of decorum. "Dalen, I want you to hear me and believe me. Give me the Beads of Fire right now or I'll kill all of your friends!"

"Dalen!" begged Travis. "Give him the damn beads!"

Dalen looked at his friends. Travis's eyes pleaded with Dalen to do the rational thing. Then he looked to Becky, who had been waiting for Dalen to look at her, and she mouthed the words, "You got this."

Dalen looked over to Ben, who had worked his hands free. He doubled up his fists and indicated that he was ready to strike Mathias at Dalen's signal.

"Dalen," David met his gaze. Time held still for a moment as David's words echoed into the air. "Dalen, I wish you the ability to win."

Mathias closed his eyes in disappointment and frustration and, without a single word, slit David's throat, pushing him roughly to the ground. The kids' horrified, helpless screams echoed through the gym, and some covered their eyes as their friend lay bleeding out on the ground in front of them.

Dalen slowly looked up from David's crumpled body and met Mathias's eyes with an expression that gave Mathias pause, as he answered David's request: "As you wish."

Mathias maintained eye contact with Dalen. To drive the message home, he intended to make his way down the line, slashing their throats one-by-one until Dalen relinquished the Beads of Fire. After all, he knew what he was doing and that it had to be done. Besides, the knife he was using had been given to him by the Genie DeSalvo; he'd been told that it was a magical knife that, if used to mortally wound someone, would not end them but put them into a state of suspended animation. Still looking at Dalen, Mathias reached over to grab the back of Ben's head.

Dalen nodded, and Ben shot straight up into a standing position. He had shifted his weight to his right and brought his shoulder into Mathias's jaw with all his strength, sending him reeling backward. As Mathias caught his balance and turned back to face his line of captives, it was just in time to watch Ben say, "Hi!" and punch him in the face. Mathias responded with a blast of energy that blasted Ben back into the others.

At that moment, Dalen slid between the frames, shifting the flow of energy here, altering it there, changing it so that, as he did, the bindings that had held his friends loosened. As the moment passed and Ben crashed into the others, they were able to wriggle free.

Becky scrambled to her knees, crawling to where Ben was sprawled. Her fingers fumbled along the side of his neck in disbelief, but there was no pulse. "No, no, no, no, no, no, no," she cried. She rolled him on his back, lifted his chin, and felt for breath. "He's not breathing!" Rushing over, Travis recalled his first aid training in Boy Scouts and began CPR. Kneeling by Ben's chest, Travis started compressions and indicated that Becky should do short breaths. They quickly fell into a rhythm, determined to save their friend.

Right then, Adam cried out with great fury, "These are the moments we live for!" At the same time, Dalen pooled his energy and brought it all in, becoming the center of the charge. Mathias's eyes shifted from what was going on around him and locked onto what Dalen was doing. "You think you are strong enough to defeat me? I don't care what David wished. You will never beat me. Never!"

With that, Adam blindsided him, knocking him from his feet. As he straddled Mathias, Adam growled, "Not alone." Using one hand, he gripped Mathias's throat; the other he balled into a fist and, like a piston, began pounding Mathias's face.

Adam got about six good hits in before Mathias telekinetically lifted Adam off him and threw the teen against the wall. "I warned you, Dalen." Mathias slid his hand down over his face for a moment, and then pulled his hand down the rest of the way. As he did, the wounds from Adam's attack closed, healing instantly and completely. "Do you not understand? I will kill every one of them." He threw his knife at Adam, who tried to bring up his arms to protect himself.

Time slowed and, as Dalen moved through the frames while everything was in superposition, he perceived all the possible places the knife could be. In all the possibilities, he saw his hand holding the knife and forced reality to collapse on that truth. The knife aimed at Adam never arrived. Instead, the knife rested in Dalen's hand, and he immediately recognized it as the knife from the museum.

Hovering near, the Fire Jinn explained, "It is called 'Soul Freezer,' and it puts the victim in a state of suspended animation. This means that David is still alive. When this is over, take him to the Brotherhood of Light. They will know how to bring him back." A sense of relief coursed through Dalen that hope for his friend was not lost. However, Mathias was still a powerful magician and as desperate as a wounded animal, and Dalen knew if it came down to it, Mathias would kill them to get the Beads of Fire.

As time returned to its usual speed, Ben coughed and sputtered, trying to sit up. Becky let out a soft cry of relief as Travis hurriedly checked Ben's vitals. Somewhat reassured by what he found, the three of them huddled on the ground, trying to protect themselves and each other.

As Mathias advanced toward them, Becky surged to her feet, standing between the magician and Travis and Ben. Travis was still holding Ben, trying to get his breathing under control. "You will not hurt him! I love him, and I am not afraid to admit it." Tears ran down her cheeks. "It took me a bit, but I recognize you, Dalen." She stepped toward Mathias defiantly. "Are you going to kill me?" She was filled with rage and spoke with a voice of strength that Dalen had never heard from her. "Well, then do it." She took another step forward, and her tears transformed into strength. "Do it!" she screamed, voice cracking not from fear but from determination. "I'm right here. Destroy me!" Becky's eyes changed, and she stared down Mathias in defiance as she whispered, "I dare you."

"I am doing all of this to save you!" Mathias shrieked. "You got lost in time, and I can't save you without the Beads of Fire! Don't you understand? I am doing all of this for you." He swung around and caught Adam mid-charge. Telekinetically, he kept his momentum, sending Adam careening into the rest of his friends.

"Fool me twice, shame on me," he shook his head disapprovingly and then looked over to Dalen, his eyes vacant of reason. "You know that I consider all these people expendable. I don't want to have the memory of killing them, but with the Beads of Fire, I can change time, and then none of this will ever happen — all of these people are ghosts of a timeline that will end. They don't matter."

Dalen could tell that Mathias was psyching himself up to believe his own words so he could do what he thought was needed. "Okay. Okay. You can have the Beads. My friends may be gone for you, but I don't want to watch them die. You can have the Beads."

"No tricks." Mathias was unhinged and barely holding

himself together. "You and I both know I can't take them from you."
He put out his hand. "Take them off and hand them to me, and I will
leave you to your fate. If you make me wait even one more moment,
I will hurt them in ways that will make you beg me to kill them."

The world came to a halt, but it wasn't Dalen who did
it this time. The Fire Jinn flew over to stand directly in front of
Dalen. "It's time. I need you to grant my wish."

"If this is the moment, then this is the moment." Dalen
took a deep breath and looked her in her eyes. "What must I do?"

"I wish for you to tell me goodbye."

Dalen's heart sank. "What do you mean? How can you
leave me now?"

"Mathias will kill them right now to get the Beads of Fire.
He would kill them — everyone here — and you, if it meant getting
his hands on them. The Genie DeSalvo is pushing him, and his will
has broken. You have to act now, or all is lost."

Dalen nodded. "What must I do?"

The Fire Jinn wiped away one fiery tear. "You have to
destroy the Beads of Fire. With them gone, the genie in him will
abandon his pursuit and leave him."

Dalen saw the logic but was hesitant. "I can't do this
without you."

"You will never be without me. The Beads of Fire were
created so that you could make contact and undergo the first of

414

many changes. You have done so much since then, and I bet if you tried really hard, you could find me again without them."

Dalen closed his eyes and took a breath to refocus his mind and heart. "So, I will see you again?"

"When you drink from the Fountain of Truth, you will see me again." She winked at him. "Now go kick your own butt."

Time snapped back in with a kick, and Dalen knew he had to separate Mathias from his friends, so he taunted Mathias to follow him outside. He looked over to the Fire Jinn, said goodbye, and took off the Beads of Fire. "Come on, DeSalvo. You want the Beads of Fire? Come and get them!"

Dalen made it outside and turned to wait for him and Mathias did not disappoint. The doors to the gym flew off their hinges and, if it weren't for Dalen's reflexes, would have hit him. "Hand the Beads to me now."

Dalen glared at him in defiance. "I said, come get them."

The ground shot up all around him, but it wasn't Mathias that had done it. Dalen saw the old man too late to respond to him, and the ground swelled up and swallowed Dalen alive except for his face and his hands. The man was dressed all in black save for the banner made of moving fire draped over his left shoulder; so similar was it to Mathias's that Dalen knew immediately it had to be DeSalvo.

"Gladly," the old man sneered. "You should never have taken them off." He laughed softly and clapped his hands together.

As he did, the ground began to constrict, crushing in on Dalen. "Powerful things, words." The old man tapped a stone that was black as onyx that he wore at his throat. "Powerful things." He walked slowly over to Dalen, who was losing the ability to breathe. "I believe you said, 'Come on, DeSalvo." He pointed to himself. "You want the Beads of Fire? Come and get them!'" He let out one blurt of laughter. "That would be a magically-binding contract. Thank you. I believe I will ... Come get them."

Dalen tried to move but was trapped and the ground was still constricting. Dalen's mind tried to focus, but as he did, the old man touched the stone at his throat, and simply whispered, "Fear." For a moment, just as it hit, Dalen saw the old man and the darkness behind him through time. It was the anomaly. It had been there all along, driving him slowly insane with fear and anger. It was the darkness behind the fear, behind the rage, and for a thousand years it had been creating it and feeding on it, and the world had made the darkness immensely powerful indeed.

Dalen stood at the fork in the road once more, but this time Dalen's fear didn't stay on its road. It came at him, stumbling like a walking corpse. "He is a full genie. You may have had a chance against yourself, but that is not just a magician, that is a full-fledged genie." It jumped on him. "He is magic itself."

Dalen couldn't hear Dorn as he called to him from the crux of the fork. His fear was upon him and screaming in his mind. "Get off me!" he cried, but his fear was stronger than ever.

"You can't defeat him. Give in!" it demanded.

416

Dalen tried to fight it off, but it grabbed at him, fell on him, and made Dalen carry his weight. Dalen looked to the other road and found only darkness.

Dalen could hear the old man's laughter echoing from all around him. "Yes," he whispered. "Sink into the fear."

Again, Dalen looked to the other road. "I know you are there!" he pleaded. "Give me the strength to do what I need."

His fear grabbed him by his face and screamed, "No one is there! No one is coming to help you! You are alone!"

Dalen reached out with his very being into the nothing and it was there, in the rock bottom of oblivion. He found what he was looking for. "I am not alone. I can feel him."

The fear pulled Dalen to the ground, and again it looked over to the other side of the fork and found it to be empty. "There is nothing there. We are alone, and there is no hope!"

But there was someone there, and hope was not completely lost.

Since the beginning, Dalen had not been alone. Someone stood with him as he talked his way out of the fight. He was not alone when he faced his foes. He was not alone as he walked through the park and hid in the shadows of the trees. Someone was with him as he moved through the corridors of the museum. Dalen was not alone as he made his first leap, nor was he alone as he took his last. They were with him as he learned about magic. They felt his pain at the loss of David and laughed with him as he had dinner with orc-kin, and even now they were with him in the moments when all seemed lost.

Dalen's mind couldn't see it at first because he didn't understand what he was looking at. His mind began to take images and put them together to explain what he was perceiving.

A being that took the image of Dalen as a jinn stood before him. He had beautiful stones at each of his chakras that looked as if they were made of silvery celestium. He radiated light and Divine Energy from his very being and was almost too bright to look at directly.

You are the one who holds the Beads of Fire now. It is your power, and only your power that can save you, but you must choose it. Free will is funny that way.

Dalen's mind cried out. He didn't know what choice he had to make.

The jinn filled his mind with his presence until there was no room for fear. *The choice is simple. Are you trapped here in a moment in time when you are helpless to do anything? Or are you more powerful than that?*

Dalen's heart harmonized with the jinn, and all at once, Dalen knew what he had to do.

Make the choice. You need to. Decide right now that you are powerful enough to make a difference. You have the power to save this world. I brought you to this moment so you could be right here. Right now. Knowing what you now know.

This was it. Everything that he had been trained for up until now was to prepare him for this moment. Dalen knew it in his heart.

Connect to me through the Natural Element and find the place where, like all things, you and I are one.

Dalen's mind opened like an iris, and he instantly was connected to the Body Sphere. He reached through the infinite tendrils of perfect connections that all things that are real have with each other and found the jinn. He was more powerful than anything Dalen could have imagined, and he carried with him a sense of the Divine. Dalen still could not tell who this jinn was, but he was more powerful than Master Truth, Master Ki, and the Fire Jinn combined. As Dalen felt the jinn's connection, there was a sense of home and Dalen knew in his soul that he could trust him.

Imagine all of the different ways that this can go and find one where you defeat this foe.

Dalen did as the jinn suggested and searched the Quantum Field for a potential reality in which he could defeat DeSalvo.

The jinn took a deep breath and then looked into Dalen's eyes, staring through him to his very soul. With words that held strength but were supportive and encouraging, he commanded, *Now ... make it real and act on it.*

Dalen's mind refocused. A surge of power was at his command as he gathered his Ki and his strength was restored.

The frames slowed down to where there was space between

them. DeSalvo was unaffected and moved with him in time. "Oh no, you don't!" he cried and reached for the Beads, but it was too late.

Dalen concentrated, and time froze between the frames of reality. Between the frames, he was able to split into superposition. He saw himself in his greatest form, the version of himself from his dream that he had become when combining all that he had been. He allowed one frame to pass, and then he moved his consciousness from the version of himself that was trapped in the rock to the other. He then allowed time to begin. One moment he was looking at himself, strong and prepared, and in the next moment, he was that person and was looking at the version of himself trapped in the ground. DeSalvo tried to grasp for the Beads of Fire, but they were no longer in the hand of the one who was trapped. They moved with Dalen and, one moment later, the version of him that was trapped vanished as reality and time began to move again. The genie roared with frustration.

DeSalvo looked over to the version of Mathias that he controlled and shrieked for him to get Dalen. Dalen charged his Ki and blasted Mathias back through the opening in the wall where the doors had been as though it was nothing.

"DeSalvo. We haven't formally been introduced." Dalen gave DeSalvo a short bow as he walked up and stood toe-to-toe with the old genie.

"I know you better than you might think." DeSalvo grabbed Dalen by the elbow of his right arm and tried to hit him with a pulse of negative energy.

At the same moment, Dalen reached out with his left hand and grabbed DeSalvo's forearm just below the elbow, even as he stretched across with his right hand and touched his left arm, creating a circuit. Dalen channeled the energy through the circuit and into his left hand, and the curse DeSalvo tried to hit him with was directed back into him, plus whatever Dalen added to it. It knocked DeSalvo back about five feet. "Have you met Brother Truth?"

DeSalvo was recovering quickly from the hit he took. He looked up at Dalen, glaring at him with hatred. "Never heard of him." DeSalvo fired off three blasts of magical energy, and Dalen slowed down time so that he could not only dodge each blast but have an opportunity to study exactly how DeSalvo was casting his attack.

Dalen ducked under the first one and then moved like water as he dodged his torso to the right to avoid the second. Then he planted his right hand on the ground and pushed up and forward to build momentum while jumping with all of his might to leap over the third. He used the Element of Air to help him get height and distance and, with a combination of Earth and Fire, came down on DeSalvo's face with a hit that felt like a burning stone. "Perhaps you know Father Day." Dalen connected to the Divine Source of all things and charged his Ki into the same attack spell that DeSalvo had just used, knocking him back with a couple of blasts.

Dalen had hit him with only a fraction of the power that the mysterious jinn had helped him tap into. It was the strongest power he had ever channeled, and he decided to use it. Instead of

using it outward as an attack, he inverted the flow and brought
all of it inward to the center of his being, and his Heart Chakra
began to glow from within. The universe relented, and Dalen's circle
appeared around him on the ground.

"What is this?" the genie insisted. "How could you know
this magic?" he demanded. "It's impossible for you to conjure this
circle unless you ..." DeSalvo stopped and the stones on his body,
in the same places as the jinn's, began to radiate with black clouds
of energy.

Element by Element, Dalen activated the Spheres of
Reality, and as he did, he lit up the Beads of Fire. They flashed
with power and light.

"This is not possible! You can't!" DeSalvo focused all his
energy, "You can't be!" he screamed and blasted everything he had
at Dalen in the form of a beam of pure Dark Magic.

Just then, Dalen ignited the center Element and became
one with the magic. The genie's magic hit Dalen with all the force
and ability that the genie possessed, but as it did, Dalen changed
his perception like the stained-glass window, and with it, the magic
changed as well.

The only thing the genie had successfully done was charge
Dalen for a massive blast that Dalen redirected at DeSalvo, and it
hit him as a physical beam of pure light.

DeSalvo screamed in pain and anguish as the light engulfed
him. Dalen allowed himself to be the conduit as all of DeSalvo's

power and all of his own poured from his being.

When it stopped, DeSalvo was kneeling on the ground, sizzling with smoke. "How? How can you beat me? You are still a corporeal being. How do you have so much power?"

Dalen knelt at DeSalvo's side. "You are as powerful as the magic you were given." The genie reached into his pocket and pulled out what seemed to be a small black piece of metal, looking at it with heartbreak. Dalen understood that it was the genie's version of his silver figure. "You are held to it. Trapped by it. Because of this, you will never hold the power I do."

The genie was grievously wounded and knew he had lost, yet still he angled to get something for his loss. "Why is that?"

"Because I follow the first rule of magic."

The genie laughed for a moment, but it hurt too much to continue. "There are no rules to magic."

"Rule one: you are only as powerful as you believe you are. And you know what?"

The genie snarled at Dalen. "What?"

"I no longer need these." Dalen charged his hand that held the beads as the world slowed all the way down.

"No! Don't do it! They will be lost for all time." The genie panicked, but he couldn't stop Dalen. In one frame, Dalen had them and, between the next frame and nothing, he let them go into infinity. As the next frame materialized, they were gone. "I will make you pay for this — I swear it."

With that, the genie dissolved into smoke the color of night, the piece of black metal clanking discordantly on the ground as it passed through his body.

"Come and see me anytime, DeSalvo." He waited there until the black fog dissipated, wafting away into the night. Once it was gone, Dalen raised his hand and magically returned the door to its original state and position and then walked back into the gymnasium to find his friends. They had gathered around Mathias, who lay dying. Time had caught up to him, and without the magic of the genie, he was fading from existence.

"I'm sorry." Tears ran in tracks down Mathias's cheeks and, for the first time, Dalen could feel something real from him. "I had to save my friends. They are all gone, and I had no other choice."

Dalen knelt beside Mathias. "It's ok."

"No. It's not. They are all still gone forever."

Dalen took one of his hands and held it tight. "Your timeline is gone and now this new one has taken its place. Don't you see you have won? You wanted to bring them all back and look: here they are."

The others began to argue that Mathias killed David and got what he deserved, but Dalen explained. "Mathias is me, from a future that no longer exists. He did all of this because he believed that he could save all his friends. All of you." Dalen let that sink in for a moment. "How far would you go to save any of us?"

Adam argued, "But he killed David."

"David's not dead." They all erupted with questions. Dalen produced the knife that he'd taken during the fight. "This knife freezes the soul of someone mortally wounded by it. He isn't dead; he's in a magical sleep."

Travis asked, "Can you revive him?"

Dalen smiled. "If you wish it."

Mathias was almost gone. "You can bring him back?"

"I know someone who can." Dalen patted his hand. "It's okay now. All of your friends are okay, and we are here. You see? You have won."

Becky held Mathias's other hand. "Yeah, look. We are right here."

Mathias smiled and closed his eyes, and then he faded from sight.

Time made its conclusion about which timeline was going to exist, and so the world began to move once more. Abruptly, music blasted around them, and teens danced and milled as though nothing had happened.

Dalen used his magic to move David's body into the boys' locker room so that it wouldn't be seen and then suggested that they step outside.

"Hey, a little help?" asked Adam. He had gotten somewhat

injured by being flung around.

Dalen reached out with his hand and put it to Adam's chest. He closed his eyes, activated his magic, and converted it to a healing spell.

"Thanks," Adam said. "I wish I were better at fighting."

"I wish I was too," added Becky.

Dalen smiled. "Travis has also wished for me to take David to some people who I was told could heal him." He raised an eyebrow. "I only know one place where I can grant all of those wishes. You want to go?"

They all agreed. But then Ben put up a finger. They all looked at him and gave him the floor. "I have a wish that I want to ask for before we go."

Dalen raised an eyebrow on one side. "What do you wish, my friend?"

Ben smiled, then sheepishly checked with Dalen that David was truly going to be ok and that they had a moment to spare. Dalen laughed and nodded. "Then, in that case, I do have a wish, and only Dalen can make it come true."

"What's that, Ben?"

"I wish to see Dalen go into that dance," Ben said with a grin. "Go, find Kim and dance with her. I talked to her, and she is waiting for you inside."

Becky rolled her eyes. "After all that, you still want to go to the dance?"

"Yes. I have done so many things I am not proud of, but today I killed Toad once and for all, and I got Dalen a date with the girl he likes. It would be a shame if I don't get to see him dance with her at least once. It means something to me." Ben smiled and then directed his attention to Travis. "Thank you both for saving my life back there. But what's the point of living if you don't dance with the girl?" He nodded toward Becky, who blushed. Ben grinned mischievously at Becky. "I know you weren't talking about me when you were confessing your love."

"That's different!" she snapped. "I thought we were all going to die."

"I knew," said Travis, and Becky's eyes widened with embarrassment. "I have always known." He nodded to Ben. "He's right. What's the point of surviving if you don't get to dance with the girl?" Travis took Becky's hand, who blushed some more, and they went back inside.

Ben slapped Adam on the back. "Hey, my man ... Kim has a friend."

"She does?" Adam's mood changed drastically and, with a comically suave voice, he said, "Let's go."

"Yeah," Ben pushed Adam towards the door. "I wouldn't leave you hanging." Ben got to the door and looked back at Dalen. "Come on, D. Don't keep her waiting."

Dalen shrugged, "Carpe Diem."

Adam laughed. "Carpe D.M.? Seize the Dungeon Master?" He shook his head and went inside.

"Not exactly," Dalen smirked and shook his head as he joined his friends inside.

...

After the dance, they met outside once more. They decided to leave together, with the plan that after their adventure they would return to this moment, and their friends and families would not even notice that they'd been gone. They knew that there might be risks and even a small chance that they might not get back, but they decided together that they were not going to abandon David. As Adam put it so perfectly, "These are the moments that we live for."

Dalen opened the frames of reality and brought his friends into the Quantum realm for only a moment, and then brought them back in at a new location.

Together, the six of them including David arrived in the stone courtyard of the Brotherhood of Light.

"How did we get here?" asked Becky.

It was Master Truth who answered her.

"With a Leap of Faith."

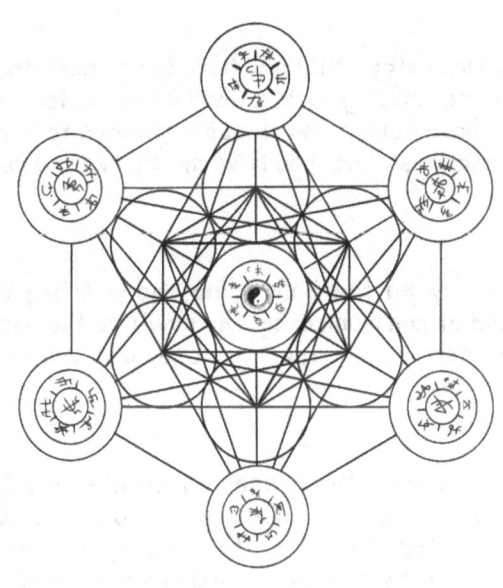

KEEP AN EYE OUT
FOR BOOK 2

THE CHRONICLES OF TIME SERIES
DALEN PAX AND THE HEART OF STONE

Acknowledgments

Tannya Derby
Thank you for the countless steps that you have been there for. You have been a guide, a teacher, and the amazing wizard behind the curtain. I am completely aware of how much you have helped and the cost you had to pay to walk a newbie like me across the finish line. You have my thanks and respect.

Kim Edwards
You were the one who really got this ball rolling, and your help with creating a comprehensive method of communicating the magic to the page was instrumental. Thank you for your time, effort, and collaboration.

Melody Noceti
Almost thirty years ago you were there when my world started, and it wouldn't feel right for you not to be here now. You have been a friend over the years, and I could not have asked for a better editor. You know me so well that you can edit in my voice. This has been a magical experience. Thank you.

David Noceti
Working with you was an absolute joy. You helped create my dream, and I look forward to working with you for many more covers to come. Thank you for your patience and for working with me to create something that I am truly proud to have on the cover of my first book.

The Teafaerie
Thank you for being there every step of the way. Writing this series has brought us closer as brother and sister. I will always be thankful for the time we spent reading chapter by chapter, and thank you for your input. You helped me answer the questions I never thought to ask.

Billie, Erica, Misti, Lou, and Kim
Elementals. I look back in time and see that this book would not have been written if it weren't for you ladies. I may have written it one day, but it would not have been this. It would not have been as powerful. It would not have been true.

Ollie
Thank you for being my inspiration in this world.

What is Dyslexie Font?

Each letter is given its own identity making it easier for people with dyslexia
to be more successful at reading.

The Dyslexie font:
1 Makes letters easier to distinguish
2 Offers more ease, regularity and joy in reading
3 Enables you to read with less effort
4 Gives your self-esteem a boost
5 Can be used anywhere, anytime and on (almost) every device
6 Does not require additional software or programs
7 Offers the simplest and most effective reading support

The Dyslexie font is specially designed for people with dyslexia, in order
to make reading easier - and more fun. During the design process, all
basic typography rules and standards were ignored. Readability and
specific characteristics of dyslexia are used as guidelines for the design.

Graphic designer Christian Boer created a dyslexic-friendly font to make reading easier for people
with dyslexia, like himself.

"Traditional fonts are designed solely from an aesthetic point of view," Boer writes on his website,
*"which means they often have characteristics that make characters difficult to recognize for people
with dyslexia. Oftentimes, the letters of a word are confused, turned around or jumbled up because
they look too similar."*

Designed to make reading clearer and more enjoyable for people with dyslexia, Dyslexie uses heavy
base lines, alternating stick and tail lengths, larger openings, and semicursive slants to ensure that
each character has a unique and more easily recognizable form.

Our books are not just for children to enjoy, they are also for adults
who have dyslexia who want the experience of reading
to the children in their lives.

Learn more and get the font for your digital devices at
www.dyslexiefont.com